BE

BY TRACY FONTAINE

Published by Starry Night Publishing.Com
Rochester, New York

Copyright 2013 Tracy Fontaine

For June! 1
Enjoy Lilly and friends!
Tracy Fontaine

Tracy Fontaine

<u>Disclaimer:</u>

This book is fiction. Some of the locations and events depicted do exist, but they have been dramatized for entertainment purposes. All characters are fictional. Any resemblance to anyone living or dead…or living again, is coincidental.

Contents

Tracy Fontaine

<u>Dedication:</u>

This book is dedicated to my loving husband, Eric, for his support and inspiration, and also to my sister, Kelly, for her enthusiasm and support ever since she devoured my first draft.

Tracy Fontaine

<u>Acknowledgements:</u>

I wish to thank the following people for their support and encouragement: my husband (Eric), my parents (Lucy and Dennis), brother (Scot), and sister (Kelly F.)., as well as the friends and family who never stopped asking about my progress on this book, especially Joe, Peggy, Lori, Kelly, and Teresa, for their thoughtful contributions.

Special thanks go to my two editors: Rodine Dobeck, who helped me find Sam's voice and enrich Lilla's story, and Casey Sullivan, who took me through the final stages of tightening the story while checking for logic, consistency, and grammar.

I would like to express appreciation for the workshops offered at Rochester's Writers and Books. Also, deep admiration goes to the city of Rochester and to Mount Hope Cemetery for their rich histories and inspiring beauty.

Tracy Fontaine

Chapter One: A New Beginning

Sam went to heaven. My parents went to heaven. Aunt Doris went to heaven. At least I think they did. I wouldn't know from experience. Apparently, not everyone goes to heaven or hell when they die. I found out first-hand. Many spirits like me are stuck here among the living. One of them could be reading this over your shoulder right now. Don't worry - you're safe from me. When you read my story, you'll see I have more important things to worry about than haunting you.

****

There was nothing special about the night I died. I performed the same rituals I did every night for the past three years since arriving at Winfield Acres. I hit the bathroom and dropped my teeth into a cup before shuffling over to bed and leaning my cane against the nightstand. My sore hip had plagued me all day and I couldn't wait to lie down. Nights were growing chilly so I tugged an extra blanket over the comforter. Crawling under the covers I drifted into a cozy sleep, and that was that.

The next morning was no more remarkable than the night before. Always an early riser, I eased myself out of bed before daylight. The pain in my hip had disappeared after a good night's rest. Mornings were always better. I made my way to the chair by the window without needing my cane, and put my feet up to watch the sun rise. The skyline was unusually bright for so early on a September morning. Crimson trees glowed at the edge of the property. How I loved watching the leaves change. Fifteen years, and I still wish Sam could be here to see this with me.

Right on schedule, my aide, Peggy, appeared through the doorway.

"Hee-eey, Miss Lilla," she sang. "How're you doing this fine morning?" she asked, breezing past my chair and heading straight toward my bed. Funny, she hadn't seen me sitting right in front of her. From behind my chair, Peggy sniffled and remarked "Oh, no. Oh, my dear sweet Jesus." Abruptly she left my room.

I looked in her direction to see what she was going on about. I was kind of smiling until I turned around. "What the hell?!" I shouted. Was that me…still in bed? "No, I can't be there…I'm here by the window…"

Apparently, the morning sun had risen but I had not. My little body was still under all those blankets where I'd left it. I jumped out of my chair and rushed to the bed. "What—what's happening?" I asked aloud. Reaching up I gently patted down the part of me that stood by the bed. My form appeared solid enough, but my hands went right through my face, and through the rest of my body, too.

At that moment I knew. I knew I was dead but could not believe this was the end of the little old lady that I used to be. I couldn't stop staring down at that body as if it was a stranger. Was she cold yet? Were her wrinkles still mushy? Had her skin become rubbery? I moved my hands toward the part of me that remained in bed. About an inch before touching that face on the pillow, my hands trembled. I jerked them away from the bed. I couldn't bear the ghoulish thought of touching my own dead flesh.

Peggy returned with Janet, the charge nurse. After the two of them checked in vain for signs of life, they stood over my bed sniffling and dabbing tears from the corners of their eyes. Although I stood on the other side of the bed, they could only see the body under the covers.

They didn't know I was standing right there!

I whispered loudly, waving my hands in front of their faces. "Peggy? Janet? Hello? Hi!" They couldn't hear my voice or see me waving!

Peggy clicked her tongue and sighed. "Mercy, it won't be the same without our little Lilac Lady. I hope I'm as 'with it' when I'm seventy-eight," she said quietly, shaking her head slowly.

Janet squeezed Peggy's hand. "Yeah. Lilla kept things hopping around here. We'll miss her, all right. You know she was eighty-eight, right? Not seventy-eight. Even harder to believe, huh?"

Peggy put a hand on her hip and leaned to one side. "Eighty-eight? For real? You kiddin' me?"

"No," Janet replied. "She was born in 1940, and it's 2028 now. That makes her eighty-eight by my books."

Peggy looked down at my body still shaking her head. "Wow. That little jokester. She told me she was seventy-eight. Can you believe that? Lyin' about her age…at this age! You were really something, all right," Peggy said to my body. Reaching down she gently patted my arm.

Janet, putting her hand on Peggy's shoulder, spoke softly, "At least she's with her husband, now. The way she talked about him all the time…you could tell how much she still missed him."

"Mmm, hmm. That's for sure. But you know what?" Peggy said through a teary smile. "Her and Sam? They're walking in the gardens together, now."

"That's such a sweet thought! I can see her stopping to sniff every lilac on the way."

"Mmm, hmm." Peggy gave a quick look skyward. She nudged Janet gently with her elbow. "I only hope someone up there remembered to do the weedin'."

"Peggy!" Janet feigned shock.

Neither Janet nor I were truly put out. Only Peggy could get away with saying something like that about a person who died only a few hours ago. She told it like it was. It was no secret how I pestered the groundskeepers here at Winfield Acres about trimming the brush so the flowers could get more sun.

Janet smiled slightly as she composed herself. She dabbed her tears and cleared her throat. "Well, I guess I'll go break it to everyone and get started on the paperwork."

Peggy and Janet gently crossed my hands over my chest and pulled the blanket over my face. They walked slowly out the door, closing it quietly behind them.

I looked sharply around the corners of my room. Peggy's words about me being together with my husband Sam haunted me. I wasn't with him. I was still here. Wasn't I supposed to go down some sort of tunnel with a light at the end? Shouldn't I hear the calls of family members who'd gone before me? People with near death experiences are always talking about that stuff. Shouldn't I experience that and more if I'm really dead?

"Sam," I whispered. "Sam! Sam!" I whispered louder. Then I began shouting. "Sam, c'mon! Where are you?!" I yelled to thin air. I paced across my room, waving my arms in front of me, feeling for an invisible doorway to lead me away from this earth. Nothing. I stopped near my window and whimpered quietly. "Oh, Sam. We were together for over fifty years. Please come get me. Somebody please help me!" I sobbed.

Sam had been dead since 2013. For the past 15 years, there had been no question in my mind. I would be with him again when my turn came. I had to be with him! We had shared such wonderful lives! After all of the strange situations that brought us together, I refused to accept that I was left behind.

****

Sam and I met in college, which in itself was a miracle of sorts. I grew up in a tiny town in northern New Hampshire. Sam was from right here in Rochester, New York, but we met in North Carolina. We never would have discovered each other if we both hadn't attended Watson University, hundreds of miles away from each of our hometowns.

Financially speaking, we both made it there by the skin of our teeth. As for our social graces, neither one of us felt like we really fit in with our suave southern classmates. So when the two poor kids from The North found each other, we bonded instantly. We shared so much, from our dry sense of humor to our similar childhoods.

Both our families had small wallets but big hearts. Sam couldn't afford to take me on expensive dates during college, but he always found romantic ways to let me know I was his girl. During class, I'd find little love letters tucked into my notebooks. Sometimes he'd surprise me with a picnic lunch under the oak trees.

The first time he brought me a flower, he was walking me to English class. He handed me a huge red chrysanthemum. I smiled at the sweet gesture. Then I realized I had to walk into class holding this gargantuan flower that Sam had no doubt lifted from the greenhouse. Oh well. There wasn't anybody from our gardening classes in my English class, so nobody would rat on us. I spent the whole class admiring my flower and daydreaming of Sam.

He brought me flowers almost every week but he was careful to bring me only a couple at a time so the "greenhouse police" wouldn't notice anything had been trimmed from the class projects.

Sam and I both studied horticulture and landscaping at Watson University. We'd lay under the oak trees and talk of the day when we'd run our own greenhouse and we could pick as many flowers as we wanted. Our shared passion for gardening took us farther than we ever dared to dream.

Eventually we did start our own business in Rochester, and that was only the beginning. Over the years we planted all kinds of gardens for the city. We hosted radio and television shows. We even wrote gardening books that sold all over the Northeast. Our love for each other and our appreciation for each other's talents grew stronger each year. If that wasn't destiny, I don't know what is.

****

We were always so happy together. What the heck could be keeping us apart now? I shouldn't still be standing here next to my dead body!

Tilting my head I looked up even though I knew I wasn't going to find any answers on the spackled ceiling of the nursing home. I leaned on one foot, hands on my hips. I finally got enough nerve to reach over and pat my sheet draped body. My hand approached the surface of the sheet, but it didn't stop there; it passed through the sheet and into my body!

Oh, God! Oh, God! Gross! I jerked my hand away and jumped back so far I went through the wall into the next room. That really freaked me out! Looking around frantically, I wondered if anyone could see me. I was in Cora and Heather's room, but they were still asleep. I reached toward the wall and tried to feel it, but my shaking hand went right into it. I couldn't feel anything. I put my arm and leg into the wall, too. I forced my head and the rest of my body through the wall until I was back in my own room.

I had closed my eyes and held my breath through the whole thing, which seems silly when I look back on it. Dead people don't have any breath to hold. As for closing my eyes, it's not like I needed to worry about getting dust in my face. It took a while to let go of reflexes like those. They're just normal things we learn from our living bodies.

The door to my room opened slowly. Janet and Peggy stood close together, silhouetted against the light from the hallway. Their long shadows stretching across the floor indicated the room must still have been pretty dark. They entered quietly and stood next to my bed in the swath of light from the doorway.

"It's still early. Nobody's up yet," said Janet. "We'll move her to the Tobias Room until the funeral home picks her up. I called her niece, Helen. Remember her? She's making the funeral arrangements. She's driving up from Pennsylvania and should be in town later today."

Peggy responded through choked sobs. "Okay, they're bringing the cart up right now." She reached over and touched Janet's arm. "I am so sorry I'm such a mess, Janet. She was a really nice lady. I know she used to be the Lilac Lady to other people, but she was my 'Wisecracker', 'specially after she lied to me about her age. I still can't believe she got away with that one," Peggy winked. "We'll miss her around here."

"I know," said Janet. She put her arm around Peggy's shoulder. "But at least she didn't suffer for months before it happened. And she was sharp right up to the end. Why don't you get some coffee? When Cora gets up, spend a little time with her. I'm going to my office to finish up the paperwork."

They left just as two men arrived to move my body. It was amazing how easily they lifted me onto the transport cart. I was so small! I never realized until I looked at my body from across the room. I'm sure having two workers was just a formality. Either one of them could have hoisted me with one arm.

They wheeled my body down the hall to the Tobias Room, a small room near the service elevator, where the stiffs wait for their first ride in the back of a hearse. They try to be discreet but everyone knows what's going on. A somber mood grips the floor for a while every time. On this floor we all had most of our minds, but our bodies were old. None of us could help thinking about who might be next and how much time each of us has left.

Just then, my best friend, Cora, stopped outside my doorway. Leaning on her walker she peaked in to my room to see if the cart they wheeled out was what she thought it was.

Jesus, Cora! Of all the days to get up early!

Seeing my empty bed, she stepped back. I thought for sure she was going to fall, but her white knuckles held fast to her walker. She looked sharply around her, mouth agape, realizing it was true. She started shuffling toward the Tobias Room, her long thin gray braid swinging from one side of her back to the other.

An aide at the nurses' station called out to her. "Cora? Cora, honey, why don't you come back here and relax? It's almost time for breakfast."

Cora paused, raised her arm slowly and flipped the attendant the bird. That aide hadn't been there long. She'd learn if anybody calls Cora "honey," he better be a six foot tall biker handing her a shot of tequila.

Peggy spoke quietly to the woman at the desk. "It's all right. She needs some time before the funeral parlor arrives."

Cora kept walking. I came out of my room, apparently unseen, and followed her down the hall. I was still moving my legs, trying to walk, but it was a useless gesture. My feet weren't even touching the ground. I hovered down the hallway behind Cora. Turning the doorknob she entered the Tobias Room. Wouldn't you know the door wasn't locked? I was pretty sure it was supposed to be locked while a body was in there.

I still wonder about the name of this room. Did the Tobias family donate lots of money to the retirement home, only to be thanked by having their name put on the room where they kept the dead bodies? I'm sure they would've been honored. Leaning against the door frame, Cora appeared much more tired and older than I remembered. Maybe it was me, seeing things more clearly now than with my own old tired eyes of yesterday.

Cora was usually a tough cookie, but at the sight of her best friend's body, her shoulders drooped, her head dropped forward, even her tattoos sagged in sadness. Once upon a time her skin may have been a living work of art, but today her wrinkles resembled a faded disheveled blanket.

I'd never seen her cry, but tears welled up in her eyes. She stared upwards, trying to blink them away. Believe it or not, it bothered me more to see her like this than it did to see my sheet-draped body on the cart beyond her. "Goddammit," was all she said before Peggy stood with her.

"Hey, Core. This stinks, alright," said Peggy. She glanced over Cora's shoulder, and sighed. "You two were quite a pair. Yup, we're sure going to miss her. It's time you got dressed and ate some breakfast. I can smell the French toast from here. Around ten o'clock the floor will get together to share our memories and say goodbye." Peggy put her arm around Cora and they went to join the rest of the ladies in the Common Area.

Meanwhile, my cadaver was getting colder by the minute, all alone in that room. Now that my spirit was separated from my body, neither part belonged to this world. What would become of my spirit once my body was buried? I needed to get out of there, out of that room, away from that body.

I don't know how it happened, but suddenly I went from standing next to my body to standing beside Sam's grave, soon to be mine as well. I gasped at the sudden change in my surroundings. Less than a second ago I stood in a tiny room at Winfield Acres, and now I was inside Mount Hope Cemetery.

I had no idea how I arrived here from somewhere else. In my panic I didn't pay attention to details. I knelt near Sam's headstone and lifted my hand to trace the outline of the engraving. "Samuel Woodworth. My Beloved. Until we meet again."

"That's odd," I mused aloud, touching Sam's headstone. My hand actually rested against the marble and wouldn't pass through it like the walls of the nursing home. I didn't understand, but I embraced the support offered by this solid surface. I leaned my whole body against the stone, hugging it and longing to find a way to be with Sam again.

I wasn't fatigued, and my eyes couldn't create real tears any longer, but I took my spirit through the motions of despair anyway. My shoulders shook. Pounding my fists against Sam's headstone, I wailed openly, "Sam, where are you? Please come for me. I can't stay here! I don't belong here any more!"

From behind me, someone gasped and exclaimed, "Oh, my god!"

I turned quickly to see a woman backing away from the edge of the grass near Sam's gravesite. She looked right at me. She could see me! What did I look like to her - an old lady? An angel? Hey, it's a stretch, but you never know.

18

Oh, please, talk to me!

She was the first person to see me in my new form. I was thrilled to still exist to someone. Maybe she could help me feel less alone. I rose to a standing position and extended my arm to greet her. I tried to look as friendly as possible but she didn't respond as I had hoped. Her eyes grew wide, and her knuckles turned white as she put a death grip on her keys. She took off running toward her car, glancing over her shoulder to make sure I wasn't following her.

She saw me all right, but she was scared out of her wits. Was I now a ghost in a cemetery? The kind people talk about around campfires? Was I going to haunt living people? This was worse than I could have imagined. It was bad enough I didn't get whisked away to Sam, but now I scared somebody. I felt like a freak. Would that lady tell others about me?

Fortunately, I didn't think anyone else had seen me. I needed privacy to figure out what was happening, so I thought I better hide myself until nightfall. I decided to wait it out in the little Sisters of Mary Chapel right next to our gravesite. It was dedicated, back in the 1800s, to the female saints of the Bible. It was open to the public only on special occasions. I knew I'd be safe in there for at least one night. I had gone through my bedroom wall, so I might as well go through the chapel wall, too. Why use doors anymore, right?

Charging into the stone wall of the chapel I bounced right off. My body slam sent me reeling backward through midair. "Ow!" I cried, recoiling in pain. Then I realized that, although the jarring thump surprised me, I hadn't felt a thing. That was bizarre to say the least. After a hit like that, I should've busted my face in three places.

I checked for injuries but, just like in the nursing home, my hands passed through what used to be a body. I didn't have any flesh to bruise or bones to break anymore. Great, I was always clumsy in life. I couldn't get through a day without stubbing my toe or bumping my head. Would I now spend eternity tripping through the cemetery? Some afterlife.

When I touched the wall of the chapel the stone remained firm against my hand. I couldn't feel its roughness, nor if it had been warmed by the sun, but there was a resistance through which my hand could not pass.

I felt along the outside of the wall, looking for a spot that would allow me to squeeze in, but I couldn't find a way through the stone.

Does this mean I really can't pass through things like I thought I could? Maybe the wall is just too thick.

I didn't want to wait until someone opened the doors. That might not be for weeks, and I didn't want to risk being seen again. My first thought was to try the stained glass windows even though they were about seven feet above the ground. Jumping as high as I could to grab the window ledge, I shot into the air like a circus clown out of a cannon. I seriously underestimated how far that leap would take me, now that my spirit didn't have a body to drag around. I ended up near the edge of the roof and needed to descend about ten feet.

Just in case the window was as solid as the wall, I tested it. My hand slipped through with no problem. I eased myself gently through the glass into the chapel. Once again I scrunched my eyes and held my breath. "Living" habits are hard to break. I waited to hear if somebody might have seen my acrobatics and headed for the chapel to investigate, but it was silent outside except for a lawnmower in the distance.

The stained glass window through which I had entered the chapel glowed beautifully, lit from behind by the morning sun. But its depiction of the Blessed Mother's bodily ascent into heaven mocked how I felt about my own earthbound soul.

I hadn't been inside this chapel in ages. I had almost forgotten how plainly it was furnished, with only a tiny lectern and eight rows of pews. The saints dancing across the glass windows provided the only color in the whole place. The chapel used to be open all of the time. Back then there were always at least two or three old ladies praying, shawls draped over their heads.

On sweltering days I used to duck in here when I needed a break from working in the cemetery flower beds. I'd sidle in and lean against the stone walls. There was something sensuous about the cool rough surface against my sweaty back. I often fantasized about Sam making love to me right against that wall, sandwiching me between his warm smooth body and the cold jagged stones. The thought of that contrast had been an incredible turn on.

I used to wonder what the devout little old ladies would do if they knew I entertained such carnal thoughts while they said their rosaries.

Over the years, those old ladies from another more pious generation died off. They were replaced by truant teenagers looking for hidden sanctuaries to get high and have the kind of sex I used to imagine. Only it seemed dirty when they actually did it instead of me merely fantasizing about it. So the chapel doors were locked to protect the inner sanctum from vandals and horny teenagers. Sadly, the chapel was only opened for special occasions now.

I returned to my old spot near the doors at the back of the tiny room. Leaning against the wall I realized I couldn't feel the cool dampness I used to relish on those hot summer days. Just like I couldn't feel the warmth of the sun on the outer walls. The only thing I felt were the jagged edges of the stones themselves. They reminded me of Sam's gravestone, the only things that felt tangible and real since leaving my body.

I needed to surround myself with something real, because I wanted to believe that I was still real. Sitting on the stone floor, I pulled my knees to my chest. I leaned into the corner, the walls pressing firmly against either side of me. It was a pathetic hug from lifeless stone but its solid support comforted me. I had never felt so alone.

Crouching in my corner, I watched the illuminations from the stained glass windows change as the sun traveled across the sky. Lengthening shadows announced evening's approach, then nightfall's descent. Finally, the chapel walls and windows were bathed in a bizarre light, a hue like I'd never seen before. Nightfall must have come. It should be dark by now but I could still see everything as plainly as if it was midday.

Nighttime cloaked the chapel and the sky outside in a strange palette of ambers and grays, yet everything was so crisp. I clearly saw every piece of glass in the windows and every detail of the leaded panes. Every branch on the maple tree just outside the Joan of Arc window was visible as plain as day. This was a huge relief. I had been dreading the dark of night while staying alone in the chapel in the cemetery. I didn't know what to expect, but at least I could see it coming.

Of course the only thing I wanted to see coming at me in the cemetery was Sam. If he's going to find me, this will be the spot. We spent much of our lives building gardens right here in the cemetery and down the street in Highland Park. The surrounding landscape was a testament to our devotion to each other and to our passion for gardening. We couldn't have achieved any of this without each other.

I wanted to return to Sam's grave, but I didn't know if I was ready to leave the embrace of my corner. Lights flashed outside of the windows every now and then. As the night wore on, those lights became busier and busier. I figured a thunderstorm must be brewing. It reminded me of too many scary movies I'd watched.

I didn't want to be outside in the cemetery when the storm hit, so I stayed where I was. The rain and thunder never came, but the flashes continued all night. I could even see them when I closed my eyes. The only way to block them out was to turn my face into the corner where the stones protected me from the world.

I cowered on that floor until morning. At least I was pretty sure it was morning. Human nature judges the passage of time based on nightfall and daybreak, but that distinction had disappeared since my death. Another thought occurred to me: I had been sitting in the corner for a full day and hadn't felt any of the usual bodily demands. I didn't sleep because I hadn't gotten tired. I hadn't felt hungry. I didn't need to use the bathroom. I'd been in the same position on a stone floor all night and didn't feel sore or cold.

What a strange concept, not having to punctuate my day with lunchtime, bedtime, or stretching exercises. I didn't miss any of it, really. I didn't know exactly what I was going to do with myself, but I have to be honest. At eighty-eight years old, all of those trips to the bathroom were a real pain in the ass. Whatever new journeys lay ahead wouldn't have to revolve around my bladder's schedule.

I had a hard time believing I was dead. Although autumn marked the end of a life cycle for flowers and the leaves on the trees, it had the opposite effect on me. My energy used to soar in the fall. Just two days ago at The Acres, I'd been begging for someone to take me for a walk down the little trail behind the complex. Lying down and dying was the last thing I expected at this beautiful time of year.

I wasn't ready to start investigating the world around me just yet so I spent the day inside the chapel, pondering how to move about without scaring people. I looked out all of the windows and watched people pass by with their strollers and dogs. What a refreshing sight after being in the nursing home. It was pleasant to see young active people, so full of life.

Actually, I felt closer to these living people than that old frail body I left back at The Home. New energy flooded through my soul. The antics of the squirrels enthralled me. The trees blew in the wind beckoning me to fly through the swaying branches.

Oh God! What am I thinking?

Sure, painless freedom and new life called to me, but I needed to focus on whatever direction would help me find Sam. I felt guilty about letting my thoughts wander away from my reunion with my wonderful husband. Pulling myself away from the window I curled up in my stark little corner again.

It must have been two or three days before I finally left the chapel. I don't know exactly. Time was already becoming a distant concept to me. Every time nightfall came, that strange light flickered outside. I decided it couldn't have been lightening all that time, but I was still wary about exposing myself to it. Finally I reasoned nothing could happen to me that could make things any worse than being dead.

One night I cautiously ventured out of the chapel. This time I tenderly approached the wooden front doors. Much to my relief I easily slipped through. Under beautiful moonlight, headstones and monuments cast long shadows over the ground. Musical sounds of crickets and other nighttime creatures hummed through the air. The crazy flashing lights had stopped for the moment, for which I was grateful.

Sitting on the ground I leaned against Sam's headstone, reminiscing about our time together. If I couldn't go to him, maybe he would come to me on these grounds. Maybe I should just calm down and wait for him right here.

I was amazed how well I could see everything despite the darkness. The graveyard emanated an enticing stillness. As morbid as it sounds I always enjoyed the history and beauty of cemeteries.

This one in particular, Mount Hope Cemetery, in the heart of Rochester, evoked a special fondness for me and Sam. We spent a lot of time on its restoration. We were hired to work on the large projects, but we spent countless hours as volunteers tending to the smaller areas, too. There was never a shortage of work around here.

The oldest sections of Mount Hope date back to 1836. Back then this uneven piece of land was useless for farming, so the city decided to use it for gravesites. At that time the unsanitary burial plots scattered throughout the city threatened to contaminate drinking water. The townspeople moved the bodies from dozens of tiny crowded cemeteries and reburied them here in what used to be the outskirts.

By the late 1800s Mount Hope turned into a beautiful Victorian cemetery. Cobblestone roads curved through basins carved by glaciers. Huge trees lined the walkways, and fancy benches dotted the river's edge. Its shadowy gullies were beautiful anomalies amid the flat expanses of Rochester. I'll never know how they ever managed to bury people on the sides of some of the steep banks, especially in the days of horse drawn hearses. Over the years I half expected to see bones popping out of the hillside, as the earth absorbed their old wooden coffins.

When Sam and I came to Rochester after we graduated from college, we fell in love with the amazing blend of history and dramatic landscape. We immediately adopted it as one of our special projects. I guess if he wanted to find me, this would be as good a place as any to wait for him. Pretty soon I would be lying next to him, six feet under the ground, which struck me as oddly funny. We used to joke how we spent most of our lives together covered in dirt.

Sam spearheaded the effort to turn this cemetery into an inviting piece of history. We restored it as an artistic tribute to the past. Visitors strolled among the fountains, much like the Victorian crowd did in the olden days. Mount Hope Cemetery became as popular as any of the local parks.

When Rochester revived the Lilac Festival, Sam and I jumped in with both feet to help wherever we could. People already knew me as The Lilac Lady from back in our radio days. They honored me as the Grand Marshall of six Lilac Festival parades. Sam had five Grand Marshall banners of his own in his closet when he died.

The city council thanked us for our efforts by giving us a small corner of the cemetery, where Sam and I would be buried next to each other. I planted several lilac bushes to shade our little spot. When Sam died, I added a bench and a birdbath, so the birds and I could keep each other company when we visited Sam's grave.

Sometimes, as I sat on the bench, reminiscing, one of the cemetery walking tours would stop by. The tour guides got a kick out of presenting the Lilac Lady in person. I was more than glad to answer questions. It was flattering to be remembered. After I'm buried I'll probably still be included in the tour, but for a different reason. I will officially be the last person to be buried in Mount Hope.

This cemetery has been full for over ten years, since about 2015. And I mean full! They tucked bodies into every square inch of this place. When the grassy knolls filled up they crammed urns into mausoleums. When available space was nearly gone, people rushed to scoop up the last plots. The running joke was that people hurried their own deaths just so they could rest in eternal peace alongside Susan B. Anthony and Frederick Douglass.

The graves in this cemetery span almost two hundred years. The first body and the last body are always popular with the tour groups. They love that stuff.

Tracy Fontaine

Chapter Two: Amelia and Jodi

As I ventured out of the chapel into the cemetery, I felt like a tourist. Even though Sam and I spent countless hours on these grounds, this was the first time I ever walked through here in the middle of the night. Pine trees swayed eerily over the gravestones. I listened to the wind in their branches and reminisced about the day Sam and I planted those trees over fifty years ago.

The wind died down long enough for me to hear voices from behind some bushes. I ducked into the shadows near the edge of the chapel. Three drunken guys staggered up the side of the hill and plopped down on my bench.

Some things never change. I used to pick weeds and beer bottles out of the flowerbeds almost every week.

The boys pulled beers out of their pockets, as if they needed more. They weren't the first kids to get drunk in a cemetery, and they certainly won't be the last. I planned to ignore them until they either got bored or threw up and decided to leave on their own. That is until one of them smashed a bottle on Sam's headstone. That burned me up.

Before I realized what I was doing, I swooped out of the shadows, and yelled, "What the hell was that?!"

Needless to say, I scared the crap out of them. I didn't mean to threaten them. I just wanted them to straighten up. But I'd forgotten I'm not a little old lady wagging a finger anymore. I was a ghost hanging in midair. I might as well have been swinging a machete.

I'd never seen anyone sober up so quickly. They ran so fast, they didn't even stagger! I couldn't believe little old me actually did that. Two of them were gone in three seconds flat. The third one fell off the back of the bench, repeating "Oh, shit! Oh, shit! Oh, shit!" while he ran backward in a straight line. Impressive, since he was the worst off of the three.

Even though they freaked out when they saw me, and even though they left broken bottles all over the place, it was worth the laugh. If you could have seen the looks on their faces! I hadn't seen anything that funny in my entire time at The Acres. I laughed all night at the thought of myself as the reluctant frightener I'd become.

That comic relief came just in time. I was getting a little uncomfortable about the nighttime cemetery thing. I hated to admit it because I love Mount Hope Cemetery so much. It was probably because I felt so alone. It was creeping me out until I thought about it some more. What was I afraid of – ghosts? Well, guess what – I had crossed over to become one myself. Of that I was pretty sure. I started thinking about what I would do with myself next. Where would I go? What should I do to find Sam?

Just then, I saw something near the edge of a tree. I peeked around the side of a crypt to see if those kids came back, but they were long gone. Instead, I saw the image of a dress, a glowing form of a woman, actually that of a teenage girl. A flickering aura surrounded her as she hovered nearby.

She must be dead like me. Do I glow, too?

I approached her on her right side. She glanced at me and moved away. I moved closer, but she fled quickly toward the deepest part of the cemetery.

I had to find some answers from the only other spirit I'd seen. I chased after her, but I couldn't keep up. It was difficult controlling my new floating mobility. The girl flitted around the gravestones and through trees like a magical firefly – so quick and sure of her motions. I, on the other hand, was still going needlessly around the trees. My legs bumped painlessly along the impenetrable marble gravestones. I overcorrected when I wanted to change directions. I swerved uncontrollably among the mausoleums. I must have looked drunker than the teenagers. The harder I tried, the faster the other spirit flew.

I stopped when I realized how ridiculous I must look. I figured she had all but disappeared anyway, but then I heard her laughing. She emerged from behind a tree, and I could just make out a girlish human shape. She was more of a hazy aura than a solid physical form. She was very cute and quite amused with herself.

As she appeared in full, however, I became frightened. The left side of her face and body were horribly grotesque. She looked like she'd been crushed, or maybe burned. It was too difficult to tell without the presence of actual flesh. Her left arm and shoulder were misshapen and hung lower than her right side. The left side of her head looked compressed, with her cheek pushed up into her temple.

Her left eye was almost lost in the twisted remnants of that side of her face. Had she been disfigured and killed in a horrible accident? I took a noticeable step back and put my hand over my mouth to stifle my gasp.

Her amused expression quickly faded and she retreated into the night.

Oh, what have I done? I almost connected with someone who could help me and I scared her away!

What did I think I would find in the cemetery? After all, I was among other spirits of the dead. I was sure I would see even more grotesque things. If that was my new existence, I'd better toughen up. I had no idea how I appeared to her, perhaps I looked even spookier. Maybe I looked like a mean old hag who scared her more than she scared me.

While pondering what else might be out there, I realized another form was hovering less than two feet away from me - another female figure. Surprised, I held my ground. For all I knew, the other one could have sent this one back to avenge her for my insulting behavior. I looked around for escape routes, just in case. She must have sensed my fear as she slowly raised her hand to greet me. I decided I needed to trust her. She looked cultured and refined, in her long lacy dress. So far, I had scared four living people and one dead one. My communication skills stunk, so I figured I better let her take the lead.

"We were wondering if you'd ever come out of the chapel. We've been waiting for you to join us. It's okay. I won't hurt you," she said as she approached me.

Although I heard her voice, her lips did not move when she spoke. Somehow, she communicated her thoughts to me. I got the feeling she could understand my thoughts, too. The flashes I had seen from the chapel the night before must have been these wispy creatures. Ghosts? People? I really didn't know what to call them – or myself.

She took my left hand in hers and placed her right hand on my left forearm. At first it seemed like a welcoming handshake. Then a shock jolted through my hand. I jumped slightly, but I didn't break the contact between us.

Energy pulsed through my arm and images flooded my mind. Fast moving pictures of a life - her life. She was sharing her past with me, allowing me into her memory and to visualize her in the days when she had walked the earth in life.

There was a little girl skipping about, and as more images flashed by, I could tell it was this woman as a child. I saw her life unfold before me: she grew from a child playing in a barn, into a girl walking along a dirt road, then into a teenager riding a horse-drawn wagon into some little town. There she was again, very young, but getting married and moving into a house I recognized, not far from the cemetery where we stood. It reminded me of those old movies I used to watch on Sunday afternoons. I had to remind myself I wasn't watching a television show. These had been real people!

Born Amelia Remington in 1880 to a farming family, she seemed content. She spent most of her days strolling around their farm and surrounding woods writing poetry and stories. Of course, it wasn't practical to a farm family. Her family accused her of being "preoccupied with nonsense," but Amelia paid no heed. While the rest of the family finished all their chores and hers before sundown, she'd follow behind them reading her stories, asking "Isn't that Johnny clever? Don't you think his adventures are clever?"

Amelia often accompanied her father to deliver his produce to nearby towns. During one such trip she caught the eye of a successful Rochester businessman, Joseph Stewart. After a short courtship Amelia's parents gladly approved of the marriage.

From what I saw in Amelia's memory it was more of an arrangement than a marriage. Joseph would have a new bride who might be better suited to household domestic chores than tending crops. In turn, Amelia's family expanded their farm onto some neighboring property owned by Joseph. They even hired some local boys to work the new fields.

Joseph brought Amelia to live with him on Mount Hope, twenty miles away from her family farm and right next door to the cemetery. Horrified at first, she wondered how her new husband expected her to sleep at night with those spooky graves right outside her window. However, before long, she embraced the cemetery because it was so peaceful. She appreciated its solitude as much as that of the forests near her farm.

She spent more and more time in the cemetery, and continued to write her stories, often while leaning against a headstone as it inspired her.

Oh, the stories these departed souls could have shared! In fact, she began using names from the headstones for characters in her stories. She selected children's names, her way of immortalizing those tiny ones taken too soon. As she became more engrossed in her stories, she lost all track of time. One afternoon, she penned a fantastic tale of little Luther's family moving out West. Somewhere in the distance a clock chimed. She absentmindedly counted its strokes.

"…Three…Four…Five. Five?! Five O'clock?! Oh my, not again!" Amelia exclaimed as she jumped up. "Supper! He'll be home any minute." Clasping her journal, she ran all the way home.

She was completely breathless by the time she stormed into her neglected kitchen. Haphazardly she rummaged through her cupboards. She pulled boxes and bags from the shelves, smelling each one and shrugging as she threw handfuls of this and that into a pot on the stove. The ingredients melded into a gray mess.

A horrible smell invaded my nostrils. At first I thought it was the stench of some dead thing in the cemetery but then I realized it was Amelia's attempt at dinner.

"Oh…eeew!" I turned my head to try to shake off that stench. Instinctively, I wanted to gag and cover my nose, but I didn't want to break our connection.

It occurred to me I hadn't smelled anything since I died. Maybe I would only be able to "smell" things through other spirits' memories. It figured the first thing I smelled in days reeked to high heaven.

I could imagine how shocking the house would smell to an unsuspecting Joseph when he came home from work. Strolling up the walkway in his business suit he was quite handsome. It was hard to believe he was almost as old as Amelia's father. His genteel lifestyle had preserved his youthful charm. But his chiseled features turned mean when he was angry.

"What in God's name!" Joseph exclaimed when he opened the front door. Amelia braced herself as Joseph stormed into the smoky kitchen so quickly he forgot to remove his hat.

"Amelia, what happened in here?"

"Why, nothing, dear. I'm just fixing supper." Amelia forced a smile. "I've been working on it all day!" Amelia wouldn't look him in the eyes and her voice quavered when she spoke.

She paused, then blurted, "I really think I got some bad potatoes. Yes. That's it. They ruined my supper I was going to surprise you with. That darn Mr. Peterson and his old potatoes…"

Joseph walked toward Amelia, raising his hand he touched her on the arm and gently turned her around to get a better look at the grass stains on the bustle of her dress. Then he picked a leaf out of her disheveled hair.

I know what many husbands would have thought, but Joseph knew his wife better than that. He turned Amelia back around to face him.

"Okay, where is it?" he asked.

"Oh, supper? It will –"

"No," Joseph interrupted. "You know what I'm talking about."

Amelia's eyes darted downward for a split second, which was all Joseph needed. He went straight to the wood bucket and found her journal hidden underneath some kindling. He thumbed through the vignettes Amelia had penned less than an hour ago. The ink was barely dry. He rolled up the pages and tapped them on the table. He shook his head and sighed.

"I knew it!" he exclaimed. "Well, since you didn't make any bread for supper, you won't mind me using the empty oven for this!" He took a step toward the stove but stopped short. He threw the journal across the room. The pages flew in every direction. Amelia frantically collected them. She held them tightly to her bosom and stood far away from the stove.

Joseph raised his hands over his head in exasperation and shouted. "Supper's always late and barely edible, if you remember to make it at all! And this house! Look at it! It's never clean!" Joseph walked to the window. He parted the curtain slightly to peek at the new houses that had sprung up within the past year. As Rochester expanded, their country house had become engulfed by a burgeoning neighborhood. For better or worse they and their new neighbors could keep an eye on each other.

Still holding the curtain, Joseph turned back toward Amelia. "You know," he paused with his mouth open. He must have been debating whether or not to continue, but the words came spilling out. "Some of the folks around town have been talking about your behavior. They say you're strange…among other things I won't repeat. I can't have that. It's bad for business, and it's just not right. No normal person spends that much time alone in a cemetery!"

"Oh, Joseph! I'm trying! Really, I am!" Amelia pleaded from across the room.

"Not hard enough," Joseph chortled. "Otherwise you'd have supper on the table instead of wasting your time writing that nonsense." He pointed at the papers clutched in Amelia's white knuckles.

"Last night's chicken was the last straw. It wasn't even cooked…blood all over my plate…Good heavens, Woman! Any more dinners like that and we'll find ourselves buried next door within the week." As Joseph spoke those last words he nodded toward the cemetery.

"No. No more. I forbid you to waste any more time writing this drivel. In fact, if I ever see one piece of those papers again, I'll burn the whole lot of them!

"As for the house…" Joseph grimaced as he gazed across the kitchen and into the dining room. "I've hired some help, but don't think you'll have extra time to sit in the cemetery. Oh, no. It's time you learn to socialize with the living, not the dead.

"I've arranged for you to spend time with the wives of some of my clients, from some of the finest families in Rochester. They attended the best schools. You would do well to watch their every move to…refine your social graces."

"But Joseph…I don't…I can't…"

"No, dear. You mustn't argue. I've come to realize you're unable to manage the house. I'll let the servants see to those affairs. However I insist you attend social functions, starting with tea at Mrs. Anderson's house on Wednesday. A buggy will arrive here for you at two o'clock that afternoon."

Joseph began walking out of the kitchen before stopping suddenly. "Oh, I almost forgot to tell you. The first servant arrives tomorrow morning at seven to serve breakfast. I thought it best she start as soon as possible lest we go hungry one more day. A second servant will arrive later this week. From now on, they'll manage your household duties and they'll report to me."

Amelia's face drooped. "But Joseph, what am I to do with myself?" She raised her delicate hands to her mouth and looked around the kitchen. Not that she'd actually miss that room. "Am I to sit in the living room every day until you to return from work?"

"Don't worry, dear. Mrs. Anderson and her friends will teach you constructive ways to spend your time. I've suggested piano lessons. Perhaps you'll learn some needlework as well. You know, to make some bric-a-brac or the like for our home.

"You may do anything you wish…except write any more of those horrible notes of yours. I never want to see those papers again." Joseph nodded stiffly toward Amelia before he strode out of the kitchen. Amelia did not argue any further.

The light in the kitchen faded. The whole scene shifted to Amelia placing her stories in her hope chest. She never looked at them again during her lifetime. As per Joseph's orders, Amelia took her place among Rochester's socialites. Refined ladies guided Amelia through the maze of Victorian etiquette. She was groomed to take her place in society and she closed the cemetery chapter of her life.

She began absorbing the daily social rituals of her new acquaintances: how to dress, how to laugh, and how to obey her husband. Unfortunately her lessons came to an early and unexpected end. Joseph expended great efforts to keep her out of the cemetery when she was alive. He never dreamed he'd have to return her so soon for her own burial in 1902.

When the smallpox epidemic raced through Rochester at the turn of the century it claimed Amelia among its earliest victims. She succumbed quickly. I gasped when I saw her on her deathbed. Her body was covered with festering sores, her face completely unrecognizable. Too distraught by that last image, I couldn't bear to watch any longer.

Everything she showed me flickered by so quickly. My head throbbed fiercely and I began to feel dizzy. I had to pull my arm away. I swayed before her, in a bit of a stupor after that barrage of images.

She spoke to me again without moving her mouth. "Oh, dear. I'm ever so sorry. I'm afraid it was too soon to share so much at one time. You poor thing; your life ended not three days ago. You're not yet strong enough to wander through another body's whole life.

"It was my way to welcome you – to share our pasts. You'll be able to accept more in time. You'll get much stronger and you'll have more energy than you ever knew when you were alive."

She continued, using her mind to speak. She filled me in on what happened after she died. My lightheadedness diminished, but I was glad she was telling me her story rather than dragging my brain through her memory bank again.

She leaned against a gravestone and sighed. She held her hands so her palms faced upwards and shrugged her shoulders. "I really don't know why I didn't go to heaven."

Darn! I hoped she could help me, but I guess not.

"I'm sorry about that," she replied to my unspoken feelings.

In astonishment my mouth gaped when she responded. How stupid of me – if I could understand her thoughts of course she could read mine! "I'm sorry!" I apologized. "I figured any one of you would be able to help me figure this out."

Amelia's smile emanated pity. "Really, it's okay. That's why I told you right away. It doesn't make sense for me to go on until I answer the one thing you really want to know.

"After I died I felt the same way you do. I was sad I didn't go to heaven, but that didn't last long. You saw how Joseph forbade me from coming here. After I died I was actually happy I could come back. Nobody made me cook dinner in that hot, horrid kitchen. I burned my arm three times on that stove!" Amelia's face soured as she recalled unpleasant domestic duties.

Her expression suddenly brightened. "Here. Here!" She swept her arms out to her sides. "This is where I wanted to be, with all of the little tykes from my stories. Because of Joseph I neglected the poor dears for so long. Nobody ever got to read about them.

When I came back here in this form, I read all of the names on their graves again. And you know what happened? They came to me! My little friends were real and they were just like me! They were here the whole time!"

Amelia gazed over my shoulder. I turned to see a bunch of childlike spirits flitting around the trees. Every now and then one of them swooped over to Amelia for a hug.

"After I died they said I should stay here with them. How could I refuse? They're always so sweet to me. They never call me strange. They're much nicer than the living people I knew."

As she spoke those last words Amelia looked in the direction of her old house. It still towered over the North Wall of the cemetery. Like most of the large Victorians around the nearby university, the house had been partitioned some years ago. Now there was a flower shop on the first floor and apartments upstairs.

From where we stood, I could see the cupola peeking through the tree tops. "Do you spend much time in your old house?" I asked.

"Mercy, no!" She replied with wide eyes and unmoving lips. "I stroll around the yard sometimes, but only late at night. It's been many years since I've passed through those doors."

"Hmm. Aren't you curious about who lives there?"

"Naturally. But the last time I went inside I think someone may have seen me. I don't want to be 'the ghost lady in the haunted house.'"

"I suppose you're right, but I don't think I could help myself. I'd want to see everything they're doing in my old house. I'd look at their furniture and in their closets. I'm really bad…I'd probably even peek at their leftovers in the fridge…it would be fun if I knew nobody could see me!"

"Oh, believe me, temptation abounds," Amelia sighed, "but if they see me they would shout at me to leave. And…well, the very idea of being pushed out of my own home hurts my feelings!"

"Mmm, I guess I can see that," I agreed. "Like when those kids ran away from me? It was funny for a few minutes…but then it sunk in. I actually scared someone! I felt kind of freakish. I've always been so normal."

Amelia knew things that never occurred to me. Just because I was dead didn't mean I could do whatever I wanted. My little scene in front of those boys proved I didn't know what the hell I was doing.

I vowed to stick close to Amelia until I learned how to control myself better. Even though she frightened me when she sent her energy surging through my head when we first met, I felt fortunate having her in the cemetery with me. My arm still tingled from that sharing session. I checked my hand to see if she had left any marks, but everything looked just as transparent as before. Wait…my hand looked too perfect.

Where's my scar?

"Oh, it's gone. Just like my pox marks," Amelia responded to my thoughts again.

"What? How do you know what I'm looking for?"

"Aren't you looking for the cut on your hand? When you fell off your bicycle and landed on that broken bottle?"

"Yeah…how did you know about that?"

"Well, while I showed my life to you, I watched your life at the same time."

"Oh…Really?" I asked with raised eyebrows. "That's so weird. I didn't realize it worked both ways. How far back did you go? I was only eight when I cut my hand."

"I saw almost everything. Let's see…you grew up back east and met your husband at that college down south. I saw how happy you both were when you bought your house, and how sad you were when you lost him. At the end I even saw your death, just before you came here."

Amelia waved her hand in my direction. She was quiet for a couple of minutes. I could tell she wanted to say something but I couldn't quite read her thoughts.

"Actually, I already saw some of those things you just shared with me from your memory, only I saw them in real life," she began again. "I was right here when you and your husband were both alive. I used to think you didn't do anything but work in the cemetery. But when I saw your memories just now I saw how much fun you had at your home! After watching your married life, I understand even more why you miss your husband so much. Did he…?"

Amelia's voice trailed off before she finished her question. "What? What would you like to know?" I inquired. I wished I was strong enough to answer her question before she had to ask.

"Well...Did he really make breakfast for you every day? And did he always go to the market with you? And the two of you even went to vote together?"

"Oh, Sam? Cook? That was only on a couple of my birthdays," I replied nonchalantly. I waved my hand to dismiss Amelia's crazy notion about Sam making breakfast every day.

Only it wasn't crazy. It was true. Not only did Sam do most of our cooking, he always set a marvelous table with fresh flowers to boot. I kept it to myself because it didn't seem right to brag about it after watching Amelia's kitchen disasters. At the time I didn't realize how easily she could read my thoughts. Looking back, I'm sure she knew the truth, but she politely let it go.

My mind started racing with new questions for Amelia.

Maybe she saw something in my own memory that might help me find Sam.

"Jeepers! I told her I don't know anything about that!" Amelia snapped.

I gasped. "Oh my God! I'm sorry! I was just thinking! I wasn't really asking you a question. You weren't supposed to hear that!"

Amelia sucked in her breath, just as surprised as me. "You weren't supposed to hear me, either!"

After staring at each other for a few seconds we started to laugh.

Amelia peered at me. "See? You're stronger than you know. I'm going to have to think more carefully around you!"

"Same here," I replied. "I can't stop wondering why I'm here and how to fix it. I'll try not to bug you. Just ignore my questions. Unless you know something...then you have to tell me!"

Amelia sighed. "Okay. I really wish I had an answer for all of the new spirits who ask the same thing. None of us really knows why we're stuck here. Most of us have come to accept it."

She continued, "When I first returned to this cemetery after my death, I was terrified. Believe me, I know what it's like to think you're alone and to not know what's happening. Then it's almost more frightening when you see others like yourself.

You realize other spirits have remained on earth, and their fate has become yours as well. You'll meet lots of others. If both you and another spirit are willing you can exchange life stories like the way you and I just did."

Amelia looked toward the back of the cemetery. "This is our world now. Me, Jodi, those children…and lots of others. The children can be very shy. They don't trust adult spirits because sometimes it's hard to tell good souls from bad ones. You've seen Jodi already. I saw you trying to follow her."

Amelia laughed. "Jodi loves a good chase. Don't worry. You'll be as quick as her pretty soon. Just pick your feet up and try not to run into any stones."

Pity Amelia for being the first soul unfortunate enough to be cornered by me. Now she was stuck answering all of my questions whether I meant to ask them or not!

"Oh, I should tell you one more thing to save you the trouble of asking. No, I don't know how to get through a stone wall. Don't bother trying. Dirt, water, wooden doors – those are easy. For some reason solid stone is impossible to pass through. Maybe our energy is too much," Amelia shrugged.

She scrunched her face to whisper an ugly vision. "I've seen some spirits try to force their way through, but they become trapped in the stone, like a prison. It's quite gruesome, really. Nobody can help them after that." Amelia shuddered as if to shake such images from her mind.

Jodi had been listening quietly from a nearby gravestone, but she must have gotten bored. She looked at Amelia and then drifted down a nearby path. She didn't go too far though. Picking up a stick she drew pictures in the dirt, but I could tell she was still listening.

"Hey!" Jodi suddenly perked up and spoke to me, "Do you like to play tic-tac-toe?" She drew a grid in the dirt.

Wow, that's a switch! That is so sweet that she wants to play a game with me!

"You go first!" Jodi sidled over to hand me the stick with her good arm. She stood sideways, keeping her twisted left side noticeably out of my line of sight.

I reached out to take the stick but it fell from my grasp. "Oops!" I said. I reached down to retrieve it from the ground. As I wrapped my fingers around the stick, I looked over at the grid lines in the dirt to plan my strategy. I extended my arm to scratch my "X" in the center but when I reached toward the square I realized the stick was no longer in my hand. When I saw the stick still lying exactly where it had fallen I realized I had failed to pick it up in the first place.

I looked at Jodi, and she smiled broadly at me while she waited for me to retrieve the stick. I smiled back and reached for the stick again. When I tried to lift it a second time my hand passed right through it. And so it went for my third, fourth, and fifth attempts. When Jodi burst out laughing I knew I'd been had.

All right, what the heck did she do to this stick?

Amelia laughed, too, but at least she helped me out a little. "There isn't anything wrong with the stick. It's the way you're trying to lift it."

Why should it be so hard to pick up a stupid stick?

"Well," Amelia answered, "for one thing you don't have anything to hold onto it with. Your hand isn't a real hand anymore. You can't lift something with nothing. It's done more with your mind than with your hands. We just use the energy from our thoughts."

I smiled wryly at Amelia. "Really? Is that true?"

"Go ahead, then. Try it for yourself." Jodi said. She shrugged casually. I guess we were finally on speaking terms and on our way to patching things up. That is, until the little brat raised the stick over her head and hurled it at me as hard as she could.

Instinctively I held my arms in front of my face to protect myself, but of course the stick just kept going, right through my hands and head. It landed on the ground behind me. I wasn't sure she had actually thrown the stick until I looked down to see it lying on the ground. I lowered my arms ever so slowly, making sure she wasn't about to lob another one at me. Jodi's voice echoed all around me, the gentlest most angelic child's laughter I'd ever heard. How could such a sweet sound come from such a mean little creature?

In anger, I grabbed the stick and thought I hurled it right back at her. She didn't even flinch because I had thrown nothing but a dirty look. I heard Jodi laughing although I couldn't see her. She was hiding from me again, probably a smart thing to do right about then.

Amelia giggled. "If you really need to throw something, try a rock. It usually works for beginners. It will help you learn to use your energy to move pretty much anything."

So I picked up a small stone, clutched it firmly, and set it back on the ground. It was solid, like the chapel walls. I resisted the temptation to throw it at Jodi.

"See?" said Amelia. "Now try this." She lightly laid her hand over the stick and lifted it. Her hand was gently wrapped around it, but not really gripping it. She moved the stick back and forth, and then laid it on the ground. "The energy comes from inside of you."

I gathered all of the energy I could force into my mind at one time, and stared at the stick, challenging it to move without any contact whatsoever. Then I wrapped my hand around it and lifted. The stick trembled, but it rose with my hand. I had it! I swung it as gently as though it were made of glass. One small step…but I was mighty proud. Stick in hand, I bowed to Amelia's and Jodi's cheers.

Jodi reappeared, clasping her hands in front of her, doubled over in laughter at the sight of all this. She was cute in a comically grotesque sort of way. I looked at the marks on her face and body and wondered if Cora's tattoos would show when she died and became a spirit.

Even though I was irritated with Jodi for mocking me, I can't say I didn't deserve it for hurting her feelings the first time I saw her. I hoped the awkwardness of our first meeting had been forgotten. I guess I didn't have to worry about saying anything. Jodi saved me the trouble of an apology by reading my thoughts.

"Ah, don't worry about it. I'm sorry I threw that stick at you. Christ! I didn't know you'd get your underwear in such a bunch about it. I can be such a shit sometimes."

I looked at her for a minute with wide eyes. Her dirty slang belied her childish appearance. She had apologized, sort of, and we were on speaking terms, so I didn't care what came out of her mouth.

"Don't worry about it. I'm fine," I reassured Jodi. "I probably deserve it for scaring those teenagers and laughing at them when they ran away from me."

Amelia was laughing with her hands held together just like Jodi. Holding their arms at shoulder height, with their hands clasped around their wrists, they looked like genies about to grant a wish. I stood there, smiling to go along with them, but I really didn't understand what was going on. My curiosity finally got the better of me.

"What's this, anyway? Some sort of secret club handshake?" I asked as I shook my hands in front of me to mock them.

They both started laughing again. I waited for them to calm down. "Oh my," Amelia said as she composed herself. "Oh, Lilla, you should learn about this if you don't want people chasing you all over the cemetery. This is how we protect ourselves so they won't see us."

"So who won't see us?"

"Them." She nodded toward the street. The living. If you had done this earlier, you might not have frightened those people."

I was still trying to get used to Amelia and Jodi communicating without moving their lips. Amelia used a lot of facial expressions as her thoughts conveyed her message. She was extraordinarily animated when she spoke.

"Normally they can't see us, but when we're really emotional I think we must release more energy. It becomes so strong they can see us. But if we clasp our arms together in front of us like this, we can keep it to ourselves. Believe me, I've scared lots of people worse than you did. That went on for years, until another spirit showed me how to do this."

Opening my mouth to ask a question that had been forming in my mind, I forgot my thoughts materialized more quickly than my mouth could form the words. I heard what I was saying to Amelia, but my mouth was moving about two seconds behind the words. It probably looked like a badly dubbed movie. My thoughts were lighter and faster than ever, even before old age had slowed me down. "How…How…How come nobody saw me at Winfield Acres?" I had been wondering and finally figured out how to ask using my thoughts on purpose.

Amelia thought for a minute. Then she replied, "Maybe your energy isn't as strong when you first die. I've had some close calls when I thought someone saw me. We all have, right Jodi?"

Jodie nodded emphatically.

Amelia continued, "But I closed my hands quickly enough for people to convince themselves the light was playing tricks on them."

I started thinking about all of the time I'd spent in this cemetery during its renovations. "When I used to garden here, it felt like something was watching me, maybe ghosts. At the time, I figured I was letting my imagination run away with me. Sometimes I scared myself so badly I'd have to go home. Now I wonder if that was for real. I used to think I saw a little man in overalls once in a while, but only out of the corner of my eye. I thought it was somebody who must have lived around here, checking our work while he was out for a walk."

"I knew it," said Amelia. "That's Harvey. He did spend a lot of time watching you and the other workers all over the place in here. We tell him to be careful. He spends too much time right out in the open near so many people. He gets so worked up that he never even tries to hide himself. He doesn't believe it works. Truly, he doesn't care if people see him. He really wanted to keep an eye on you"

"Me? Why me? That's creepy!" I looked over my shoulder. "Is he here now? Should I be afraid of him?"

"No, he's harmless enough, just crotchety. He wanted to see what you were doing to the flower beds. You know, he took care of this place for over thirty years. I even knew him before I died. Then, when he died in 1930, everyone was so busy with the Depression they didn't have time to worry about this place. A few years later things started falling apart. You and your friends were the first ones who stayed for longer than just a funeral. Harvey never admitted it, but I really think he was happy that someone cared again."

"Phew! You scared me for a minute. I thought I was going to have to look out for him."

"Oh, he'll show up one of these days, but you needn't be afraid. I'm sure he'll want to talk with you now that you're here with us. He loved your rose garden next to the fountain over there," Amelia pointed to the North Side, "but he hated those marigolds you planted near the front gate."

I was surprised to hear anybody could not like my little marigolds! They were so cute against the dark stone gateway! "Well he must have loved it when the kids around here pulled them out and threw them in the road."

"Well…it wasn't always the kids," snickered Jodi. She'd been quiet for a while. I'd almost forgotten she was still listening in the background.

"What do you mean?" I asked. "No way. Are you telling me Harvey did that all those years?"

"Yes, he's not shy about letting someone know if he doesn't like something." Amelia mused, "Odd…he said he didn't like them because he remembered how wretched they smelled when he was alive." Then Amelia leaned over to me and whispered. "When he was alive, that man could kill an oak tree just by sitting under it for an hour. Swear on a stack of Bibles. He never took a bath. When I would sit to write my stories, I knew he was near me without even looking up. If you ask me, death couldn't have been too bad for him. He got to leave that smelly body behind."

"Well, when I see him I'm going to let him know I think it was rude to pull out the marigolds. After all of the things I did for this place, he could have left them alone, at least."

"Lilla!" Jodi shrieked. I turned around just in time to see a plastic flowerpot hurtling toward me. Instinctively, I reached up to grab it so it wouldn't hit me in the face. None of that mattered anymore, but it would take time for me to accept the fact that objects could pass as harmlessly through me as I could through them.

I was getting stronger and more in control by the minute. Not only did I catch the flower pot, I held it for a few seconds before it fell through my grip to the ground. It broke into two pieces when it hit the ground. I looked suspiciously at Jodi, questioning her intent. "Aw, c'mon! Again? Wasn't once enough?"

"See," said Jodi, "you're getting stronger. A lot stronger! Just believe you can move something and you'll kick butt in no time. It was just a test!" she teased.

"It was self-defense, you twerp! Thanks for the great scare. That was loads of fun," I replied sarcastically. I wasn't amused with her little jokes because I was still a little jumpy about my new situation.

However, I did feel a little stronger than when I came to the cemetery immediately after I died. I realized this transparent spirit was all I had left of myself, so I better figure out how to use it. Jodi's little gag did show me that I had capabilities I didn't understand yet. Hopefully I would figure them out before I really needed them.

Tracy Fontaine

Chapter Three: Marcie and Harvey

I marveled at spending my first night completely outdoors. It was weird not to wake up in the nursing home, or any other building for that matter. To the rest of the world I rested in eternal peace, but the truth was I would never sleep again. I no longer needed walls or ceilings surrounding me. In my new outdoor home, the birds chattered like crazy. Sounds were so much deeper than I ever heard during my lifetime! Maybe I was capturing birdsongs not just from nearby trees but from miles away, too.

A couple of sparrows flew into my gut and right out my back. Although startled, I resisted the urge to grab my stomach and feel for a gaping wound. I did peek down at myself, because it was still surreal to know I didn't have any substance to me.

It was not an unpleasant sensation, blending in with the morning fog, I felt somewhat wispy myself. Feeling so free of discomfort; the cold, damp night air hadn't bothered me at all. I could also see remarkably well, even in the blackest of night. Amelia had disappeared into another part of the cemetery. Jodi said she was going to Laverne's place. I wasn't sure if Laverne was living or dead, but Jodi took off before I could ask. Since they were both doing their own things, I decided to explore the cemetery like I never had before.

Flitting gingerly around the crypts, I managed to avoid thudding against any stone walls. I picked out distant tree branches and drifted up to touch them. Most of the time, I hit my mark. I only overshot a couple of times, but I stopped myself before I got too high up. Looking down at the ground far below, became less frightening as gravity lost its tug on me. Besides, I didn't have bones to break, anymore. Even if I couldn't feel it, I knew the wind must flow through my whole body.

Nor did I have that sinking sensation in the pit of my stomach when I rocketed from the treetops back down to ground level. This was incredible for the girl who used to get sick as a dog on Ferris wheels. Before I knew it, I was at the farthest corner from Sam's grave. I couldn't even see the chapel anymore.

I wondered how quickly I could float back there, so I rose above any stone structures that might give me grief. Strangely, before I thought I had even started, I was already back at the chapel.

It was so weird. I didn't pass anything to get from one place to the other. Maybe all I had to do to get from one location to another was to wish myself to a different place. That's probably why I didn't remember the trip from Winfield Acres to the cemetery. At the time, I thought I just wasn't paying attention because I was upset after discovering my body, but now I believe I simply popped from one place to the next. I wanted to do it again, to see if I could go somewhere on purpose.

Wherever I went would have to be somewhere without many of people around during this time of day. The last thing I needed was to pop into a supermarket and make some poor shopper drop her eggs. I didn't know if I could hide myself by holding my arms together, like Jodi and Amelia had shown me. I couldn't decide if I should believe everything they told me. In case that silly handshake thing was a joke, I wanted to remain as discreet as possible while experimenting. I didn't want them or anyone else to see me practicing.

I decided to go to one of Sam's and my old hangouts. Almost immediately, after I thought where I wanted to go, I was standing in that very building. Not bad, if I said so myself. Actually, I was impressed as hell – it was amazing!

Standing in Darkness, I was back at our favorite nightclub. You might have gathered from the name - this was not a glittery disco. This place was for the outsiders. In the '70s, it was punks in Dead Kennedy shirts; then in the '80s, it was black-clad Goths. Sam and I appeared more "normal" and slightly older than the other regulars, but at this place nobody cared.

As gardeners, Sam and I were surrounded by flowers and bright colors all day. Sometimes we needed a break from the chipper people in our horticulture world. Occasionally it was fun to tour the underground; Darkness drew us in to its dank building with black walls. I couldn't believe it still existed with the same name! I supposed misfits will always need a place to find each other.

Apparently, I wasn't the only one still drawn here. A man's spirit swayed on the quiet, oddly sunlit dance floor, to music only he could hear.

Actually, I thought I heard strains of "Under the Milky Way" by The Church wafting faintly through the air. That was a great song. I couldn't tell if the music was in his head or mine.

On the nights when the club was open, did the living patrons dance right through him? Could they sense him or vice versa? I would like to have pondered that longer, but I needed to get back to the cemetery before I lost my sense of direction. I didn't want to be stuck here like that guy.

Not to worry. Once I decided to get back to the cemetery, I found myself right between Sam's grave and a big yellow excavator. I looked quickly from the excavator to the piece of grass that had been marked with stakes. Was I alive only two days ago? It seemed much longer than that. I almost couldn't remember what it felt like to support the weight of a body.

I stood in the middle of my plot, wondering if maybe the forces of the afterlife just couldn't find me. "Here I am! C'mon, take me!" I called out to "whomever" and raised my arms, hoping they could lift me from this earth. Nothing. "How long will I be here?" I yelled. I'll never know who they are or if they heard me. In frustration, I threw my arms down and gave up. It was worth a try.

Someone had left a bucket near my headstone, so I wandered over and peeked inside to find weeds, dead flowers, and broken beer bottles. Gee, that could've been my bucket twelve years ago. Someone's tidying up for my burial.

The volunteer gardeners took wonderful care of Sam's gravesite when I couldn't handle it anymore. This one was still here, kneeling on an old blanket, pulling weeds. All I really saw was her rear end sticking out from behind one side of the bench and a tattered straw hat peeking over the middle of the bench.

Wait a minute…No way! I recognized that hat with flowered pins and a huge purple scarf. It had to be Marcie Robb. She stood up, revealing yellow sneakers, long black skirt, and flowered t-shirt. Definitely Marcie. I hadn't seen her in twenty years but I remembered her easily enough. She was a tad older and plumper, but still sporting those funky outfits.

I liked Marcie. She was a hell of a worker. Decades younger than Sam and me, she hoisted plants that had become a little too heavy for our aging bodies to lift.

No matter how dirty the job, Marcie was a trooper. When Sam and I installed the raised herb garden for the group home near the park, we ran out of supplies by the middle of the afternoon. By the time Sam returned with more timber, most of the volunteers had left for the day, except for Marcie. She stayed until after midnight, helping us tamp the last of the dirt.

Despite her dedication, the group always kept her on the fringe. Many of the women considered her strange, but I enjoyed the company of a few odd characters here and there because I was so straight-laced and mousy. They kept things interesting.

Marcie and I gardened alongside each other a few times in the cemetery. Her imagination amused me. Occasionally, she'd pause from digging and look around. "Oh! This place is so full of energy! It's flowing all around us," she'd say.

I would smile and laugh to myself. Then I'd encourage her by saying something like, "I don't know about you, Marcie. I think the only energy in a cemetery comes from us working so hard."

"Well, we're not the only ones here," Marcie would explain, squinting and looking around. "The spirits are all around us, really, but don't worry. They only want to see what we're doing in the dirt all day." Then Marcie would look around, smiling at her imaginary friends, before getting back to her work.

That crazy talk prompted the other volunteers to gradually stray toward other parts of the cemetery to get away from "Spooky Marcie." I was amused by her psychic senses, but I didn't believe in that stuff back then. Of course, now, it's a different story.

I'm sure Marcie noticed how the other women scattered within minutes after she arrived. They suddenly remembered a forgotten trowel in their car or they urgently had to empty their bucket of weeds. Instead of returning to work alongside Marcie, they'd find another distant garden to tend.

I always wanted to scare the others and tell them Marcie showed me some ghosts, but I was afraid they would get scared and wouldn't come back to help anymore. More importantly, I wouldn't want them turning Marcie into more of an outcast than they already had. Marcie's musings made my work days go faster, so I let her go on as long as she wanted.

I have to admit I was a little choked up seeing someone who had known both me and Sam so well. Marcie dropped some weeds into her bucket and stood up to stretch. Closing her eyes, she let out a big yawn. I hadn't thought to hide, until it was too late. When she finished stretching and opened her eyes, I was only a few feet away, right in front of her. That wiped the yawn right off her face. She jumped and squeaked out a little "Oh!" but she didn't run away.

That's a good sign, considering how the other lady took off the other day.

She stood very still, like she was watching a timid animal and didn't want to scare it away. Sizing each other up, we both wondered, "Okay, she sees me — now what?"

I didn't see the point of sticking around long enough for her to call others over to see me. However, I didn't want to merely float away either, lest her eyes followed me through the cemetery. Slowly, I folded my hands in front of me and wrapped them around my forearms. As I folded my hands and arms more tightly, I felt something pushing against the front of my body, as though I were holding a large object against myself.

I must have been corralling my energies. I hoped Jodi and Amelia had not been fooling with me, and that this was really a way to cloak my physical image from her. It seemed to take forever to work. Finally, I got the impression that Marcie no longer saw me. Her gaze softened and she blinked to moisten her eyes, dried out from staring no doubt. She took one large step forward, her neck straining and arms outstretched, feeling the air where she'd last seen me.

As she walked, she passed through me. I hadn't moved for fear of releasing energy. I could feel it churning within my grasp and pushing against my arms. I didn't know what would happen if it broke loose. Marcie kept walking very slowly, looking high and low. I turned slowly, keeping my arms firmly clasped. She was busy checking the other side of the excavator, so I moved away from her, ever so cautiously, until I was sure nobody would see me.

I had intended to wait a few more minutes before I released my hands, but I was jolted from behind by something hard against my back. My arms flew open with a flash of loosened energy.

I turned to see two young spirits, a boy and girl, holding a rock where my back had been.

"Holy cow! You scared the bejesus out of me!" I exclaimed.

Immediately they dropped the rock to the ground and flew away laughing. I supposed kids would be kids, whether they're alive or dead. The kids hadn't gone too far, and they ducked behind one of the family crypts. I knew they were watching me, so I used my latest trick to instantly move myself from where I was standing and reappear behind them. I swooped down in front of them, just clearing their heads. To show off, I did a couple of quick circles right around both of them.

I steered clear of the crypt walls. I was getting better at maneuvering. The kids just stood there watching me until I finished showing off. Even though they were children, I was younger than them in a way; I was a newborn in this spirit world. Once I knew I had their attention, I settled down next to them and laughed to let them know I wasn't angry or anything.

They stood very close to each other, looking up at me. The boy appeared to be about ten years old, and the girl about four. I offered my hand to them, but they backed away. "It's okay," I thought to them, "I'm Lilla. I just got here yesterday. So far, I've met Amelia and Jodi. What are your names?"

The little boy looked up at the name carved over the doorway of the Danforth crypt and then back at me. "Is that your name? Is this your family?" I asked. He nodded, and the little girl also gave a hesitant nod. She held onto the little boy's hand and moved closer toward his protective grasp.

"Are you brother and sister?"

"Yes, ma'am," his lips remained motionless as his thoughts spoke to me. "I'm Jimmy and this is Cathy. She's my sister. You're not going to hurt us are you?"

"Of course not! I wouldn't do that, even though you did scare me." I said. I laughed at the idea of them asking me if I was going to hurt them. They were already dead, for Christ sake! That's children's logic when they think they're in trouble.

We started moving along a cemetery walkway together. "Are there other spirits like you? Other kids?" I asked my new companions.

"Yes, ma'am," answered Jimmy. "We have lots of friends. There they are!" He pointed to his right. Four small glowing beings scampered around the fountain so quickly I could barely discern them as human forms. Jimmy and Cathy took off to play with their friends. There must have been horrible sadness when each of these kids died, but now they had company and seemed happy in this hidden world.

Several bicyclists passed the fountain, oblivious to our otherworldly activity. The children's spirits flew and darted about, playing tag and trying to outdo each other with midair acrobatics. My attention was so focused that I didn't flinch when a man and woman jogged right near me. Then an old man and his dog passed by. The dog walked right through me and I barely noticed. None of them seemed aware of my presence, for which I was relieved.

I must have been settling into my new situation, as troubling as it still was to me. At least I was controlling my emotions much better so I wouldn't scare people. I had enough to deal with, trying to figure out why I was still here and if I would find the true afterlife.

I wasn't sure what I wanted at that point, or if I would even have a choice in the matter. On one hand, I was happy nobody could see me, so I didn't scare people; on the other hand, being invisible to the living world became very lonely, nobody talking to me, or even nodding in my direction, as we passed on the street. Marcie's sighting of me must have been a fluke, but just to be safe, I decided to avoid those extra sensitive New Age types.

Quite a few living people roamed around the cemetery that day. It was nice to see so many people enjoying the grounds. I drifted back to my gravesite, meandering along the way, checking the flowerbeds near the North Wall. This little patch was about to burst into color. The autumn joy plants would turn bright red and really set off the purple of the sage plants behind them. Two hibiscus trees, bordering the other plants, were already displaying their large white blooms.

I remembered when this lush garden was just a sketch on a piece of scrap paper that barely survived the washer. Sam designed it for me as a surprise for our anniversary but he forgot his note in his pocket. It flew out when I shook his trousers to hang them on the clothesline.

When Sam returned from the store that afternoon he found the drawing on the kitchen table where I had carefully laid it to dry. "Aw! You weren't supposed to see that until the whole thing is finished!" he exclaimed to me.

"Why not? I love it!" I said as I walked over and hugged him. "And it's going to look great up near that wall."

"I know. That's why I put it there. Happy Anniversary!" he said, and kissed me.

I laughed. "Our anniversary was months ago!"

"Yeah, I know, but the only thing I got you was that rose bush for the front yard, and you planted it yourself! This time the work's on me."

"Really? I have to sit this one out? I don't know if I can do it, but I'll try."

"Yup. You point and I'll plant."

"Deal!"

True to his word, Sam didn't let me lift a finger except to point from the lawn chair he set up for me. Within two days, Sam turned that runny picture into one of the nicest gardens in the cemetery.

I was still waxing nostalgic about the garden when a man walked past me. He wore faded dungarees, an old t-shirt, and carried a large cup of coffee. He headed toward the excavator so I followed him. I stayed off to the side as he hopped into the seat and prepared to dig. Starting the machine he raised its arm as he drove closer to the gravesite. As the tip of the shovel took its first scoop of dirt out of the ground, I swore I felt nauseous, like there were butterflies in my stomach. I looked down to see if there really was anything flying through my body, but of course, nothing was there.

I can't believe that grave's for me. I can't believe I'm heading for that hole in the ground...

I wrapped my hands around my arms to make sure my emotions didn't get the best of me. I didn't want anybody to see me. Amelia's parlor trick worked earlier so I tried it again.

If this scene hadn't been so personal for me, I would have found it morbidly interesting. Of course, I'd been in the cemetery when they were digging graves, but I never paid much attention. It had been background noise while I gardened.

The excavator operator moved right along, and the hole and the mound of dirt next to it both grew larger.

Back in my gardening days, it would have been fun to operate that large equipment. I could have asked the groundskeepers if I could use the excavator to dig new gardens, but I never got around to it. I figured they weren't about to let me buzz around historic gravestones in a four ton tank with a giant shovel hanging off the front.

I eased into the excavator cab behind the driver. For the first time I watched everything up close. The operator's hands worked the levers without hesitation. A wave of melancholy came over me. The worker's strong arms and work clothes reminded me so much of Sam. For a second, I pretended we were starting a new flowerbed instead of digging my grave.

I looked down as the excavator pulled out the last few scoops of dirt. This morning I had been zipping among the treetops, a hundred feet above the ground, but from this excavator, that hole in the ground looked even deeper than that. It's all a matter of perspective.

The digging was finished, so the driver moved the excavator off to the side and stopped the engine. He finished his coffee and stepped onto the ground to check the hole. It must have passed inspection because he walked back in the direction from which he had come this morning. He whistled a happy tune for someone who'd just dug a grave, but I guess a job's a job. Finish it up and move on to the next one.

It was good to be some place new, so I remained in the cab of the excavator. Reading all of the instructions and warning messages posted inside the cab gave me something to focus on. The worker returned with a truck and a couple of buddies. Hiding myself behind a lilac tree, I watched them lower a large box into my grave. That must be the lining or something. I think it keeps the ground from sinking into the caskets. The funeral director probably went over it with me when I buried Sam, but at that time, I really didn't want to hear details about caskets imploding onto my husband's body. I had just paid the nice man for the standard "Grieving Widow Package."

I was impressed with the exact fit of the box in the hole and how quickly the workers finished setting it in place. Before I knew it, they released the ties from the truck and smoothed the sod at the edges of the grave. Then they laid a tarp over the hole and some beams over so nobody would fall in. When that was done, one of them said something about quitting time, so they jumped into the truck and the excavator and headed toward the maintenance garage. Everything was ready for my coffin. Great.

I sat on my stone bench, mesmerized by the pile of dirt that was to cover my body. Several hours had passed before I noticed the shadows lengthening along the ground. September dusk comes early. I always loved watching autumn shadows fade into night. I didn't know if I could appreciate it more now or before I died. When I was alive, I liked the mystery of darkness and wondered what might be out there that I couldn't see. Now that I was part of the spirit world, there were plenty of shadows, but the darkness held no secrets or surprises. I could see more now than I ever could before. There was no such thing as complete blackness. It was almost too much for me, a visual and auditory overload without any quiet dark places where I could retreat.

Would I find peace when my body was buried? I went over to the edge of the grave and decided to feel what would happen to my body. Maybe it would be nice and quiet down there. I went through the tarp and into the box that lined the hole. It was as easy to see as if it was the middle of the day. I didn't know what the box was made of, but I could put my hand through it.

If I extended my arm far enough would it go into Sam's grave and through his coffin? Yuck!

I didn't want to know. I pulled my arm back quickly. I didn't like being down in that hole. Burial might be good for my body but my soul wanted out.

I was about to leave the grave when a male spirit poked his head through one end of the tarp and bellowed, "So when's the big day?"

He spooked me, but thanks to Jodi and those kids, I had lost much of my edginess. If he had tried that yesterday, I would've been in the next county by now. I slipped out of the other side of the tarp so I could see the rest of him.

I looked him over for a couple of minutes, an older man in torn overalls and a ratty shirt. His face was kind of round and scrunched, and his lips were sunken in. I wondered if he'd had any teeth when he was alive. Fortunately, we communicated with our thoughts and he didn't have to flap his gums to speak.

"You're Harvey, aren't you?" I asked.

"None other," he replied with his thoughts. "Guess it's time we met face to face. Feels like I've known you for years. I used to see you and your hubby here all the time. It's time you got to see me, too."

"Well, actually I think I have seen you," I replied. "A couple of times when I was working in the gardens…I was busy, so I didn't really get a good look at you. I just thought you were someone passing by. But now that I see you, I think I remember your dungarees."

"I wondered if you might've seen me when I watched you put up those gardens. You know, I never liked how you set up some of them plants."

What a jerk.

"So I heard. Are you kidding?" I asked incredulously. "Look, I know you took care of this place for a long time but that doesn't give you the right to judge. Sam and I worked hard around here, too. Our college professors were some of the best landscape people around. Where did you study before you ran this place?"

"Herendeen's Shoe Store, you old prune!" he yelled back.

"What? A shoe store? Did you get tired of sniffing ladies shoes and decide to come here and smell bodies instead?" Harvey's eyes widened and his lips quivered.

It took me by surprise. I never believed such a gruff person could get so weepy. "I didn't think I was that mean, but you hurt my feelings, you know. I, umm, I'm sorry."

"Mm. Yeah, me too."

Both of us wondered what to say next.

Harvey shuffled from one leg to the other and broke the silence. "You know, it'd do you good to come down off o' that high horse of yours before someone pulls you off," he said as he pointed in my face.

"What?! I…ugh!"

I can't believe he said that!

"Aw, c'mon…the way you used to bark orders around here? I half expected them to find you buried under one of your stupid trees with a trowel stuck in your head," Harvey continued while I stood there with my mouth open. "There's lots you don't know about how I started workin' here. You think I'm a hobo. I could explain it to you, or let you see it for yourself. You done any of this yet?" He held his hands out to me, like Amelia had done when she and I shared our memories.

"Mm hmm, Amelia showed me how to do that. She showed me her whole life. It was pretty awful. My head felt like it was going to explode. I don't know if I'm ready to do it again."

"Well, it's up to you," said Harvey. "The first time is the hardest. It ain't like nothin' you done before. They say it feels like you're gonna die. That's just stupid 'cause you're already dead!"

I thought for a minute. It would be interesting to see what this old fart had done with his life besides tear up my marigolds. "Okay," I sighed, "I guess I could try it again." I wasn't overly enthusiastic. "But if I get even a little dizzy, it's over."

"Agreed." Harvey looked happy. He really wanted to show me something. He offered to take it easy on me and just try for the short version of his life. He took my left hand in his, and we each put our right hands on each other's left forearm. At once the familiar energy surged through my arm. My head swirled with flashing lights and images, but having become stronger, I didn't feel overwhelmed. I knew what to expect, and I relaxed and watched Harvey's life play out like a movie.

It started with him as a little boy, running in and out of Herendeen's Shoe Store. Looks like he often played at his father's store. However, as Harvey grew older, he spent less time at the store and more time in the streets. He didn't want to dress up for work and he didn't want to be stuck inside that store all day. Much to his father's disappointment, his only son wanted nothing to do with the family business.

When he looked to be about twelve years old, he quit school to run with a rough crowd. To his credit, no matter how tough things got, he never stole anything or hurt anybody.

For several years, Harvey barely survived on odd jobs when he felt like working. He did everything from mucking out horse stalls to playing a fiddle on the street corner.

Things changed when Harvey met Aggie. They fell in love, eloped, and shortly after marrying, learned Aggie was pregnant. Harvey was so tender toward Aggie. I could hardly believe that loving husband was the same crude gardener whose ghost held onto my arm.

To provide for his new family, Harvey returned to his father's shoe store as soon as he convinced his father he'd cleaned up his act and settled down. With tears of joy, his father gave him a big hug to welcome him back.

Harvey didn't come back to the shoe store to please his father, and it certainly had nothing to do with donning spiffy suits, which he hated most of all. He constantly tugged at the stiff collars on his shirts. But he put on those clothes and went to work every day for Aggie and their baby.

Harvey lacked book smarts but he knew how to work the customers. He was an average Joe like them. His hair was disheveled, his grammar coarse, but it worked for him.

One well-dressed man inquired whether a certain shoe was available in black. Harvey leaned against the shelves and answered, "Nope. Ain't seen it."

"Ahem." Harvey's father cleared his throat loudly from the next aisle.

Harvey stood at attention and tugged at his collar. "Uh. I mean, no sir, we don't have that shoe in black. Only brown. But I'm sure we can get it for you. Don't be goin' to that Saunder's store..."

A barely audible cough arose from the next aisle.

"Um. Before you try another store, let me check the catalogue to see if we can't get it for you. We order lots of stuff for folks. We order the best shoes and you won't pay a lower price, either."

"Why, thank you," the customer responded, still holding the brown shoe. "Yes, please check the catalogue and let me know if you can order it in black."

The man stood at the counter while Harvey checked the catalogue. "Here you go, Mr. Belleweather," Harvey pointed to a picture of the shoe. "I'll order these in black for you. We should have them in three weeks or so."

Harvey's father announced he had to step out for a minute. As soon as Harvey heard the bell on the door indicating his father had left, he leaned over to the man.

"That Saunder's store? Over on Winton? Don't tell anybody." Harvey looked around to make sure his father was really gone. "I hear Mr. Saunders takes shoes home to his wife and daughters. They wear 'em to church and maybe even dances. Then they bring 'em back and sell 'em! Sure as I'm standin' here right now."

The customer's eyes widened. "Hmm. You don't say. I wouldn't imagine anybody doing that."

"Yeah, well you can believe it. So if you want honest service and the best shoes in town, you keep comin' right here. And tell all your friends now, too."

"I will surely do that. It was hard to find just the right shoe until today. You've been very helpful. I'll tell my business partners about your store. Thank you, Mr. Herendeen. I'll be in for those shoes when they arrive. Have a nice day, now."

"Yup! You too!"

Before long, Harvey was practically running the store by himself. However, the best part of his days was coming home to the little house into which he and his family settled.

Aggie would greet Harvey by the door holding little Seth. "Well, looky who's home!" Harvey would say when he opened the front door.

"Oh, dearest! Welcome home. Can you play with Seth while I get dinner on the table?"

Harvey smiled as he kissed Aggie on the cheek and took Seth into his arms. "Well, come here to Pop, little fella." He'd sit in the kitchen, with Seth on his lap, while Aggie piled stew into their bowls. "Well, I know what you've been doin' today!" He poked Seth's belly. "Growin' faster than them weeds out front. I swear, Aggie, he's gettin' bigger every day. Good thing I sold seventeen pairs of shoes today!"

"Seventeen pairs just today…and how many yesterday?"

"Twenty one!" Harvey smiled. "And the first thing I'm gonna do is buy you one of those little wagons to take to the market. You know, the ones they carry over at Peterson's?"

Aggie smiled. "Oh, Harvey, that would be wonderful! Lord knows I've had a time carrying Seth on one arm, he's growing so fast. I've been wondering how I'll manage when this next one comes."

"That's for sure! You can put the two little ones in the wagon and still have room for packages."

"Thank you, Love! If you're not too tired from work today, will you play your fiddle after dinner?"

"You know I'm never too tired to fiddle!" Harvey laughed, revealing that he did indeed have teeth in his younger days.

Harvey played the fiddle that night and every night while Aggie sang and Seth danced. This looked like the best of times for Harvey. This must have been the life he wanted to show me, but the most important part was yet to come. Very sad times descended upon Harvey soon after the night he promised Aggie her wagon.

Without warning, their pretty little house appeared, engulfed in flames. A flash of Harvey's pain tore through my head. I wanted to release my hand from his arm, but I knew he hadn't shown me everything he wanted me to see. I forced myself to hold our connection.

In the next frame of his life, Harvey knelt beside the grave of his wife and son, just over the knoll from where we stood. He couldn't bear to leave them, so he provided for them the only way he could. He took immaculate care of their graves, planting flowers and pruning bushes, speaking to Aggie and their son the whole time. Over time, he maintained larger and larger areas, and began directing the work crews. He moved into the tool shed and became the official caretaker.

His befuddled father sold the shoe store to someone else because he could no longer operate it without his son, and Harvey didn't want to be anywhere but in the cemetery, near Aggie. He didn't care what he did, whether planting flowers or digging graves. For many years, he worked hard in the memory of his family. As he aged he seemed a little happier, because he knew he would see Aggie soon.

One night he went to sleep in his little shed, dreaming of that day. He never woke up. His wood stove had gone out and he froze to death during the night.

The last image Harvey shared with me showed his spirit hovering near his stiff body, grasping for something in the empty air around him. "No, no! Aggie!" The words echoed through my head until Harvey released my hand and arm and the vision ended. Now I understood. I felt like the jerk.

He was right about making a long story short. He breezed through his life story in what felt like seconds. My hand buzzed with extra energy. Actually, it felt like it was asleep, but that went away after a moment. I felt a little dizzy, but it was nothing like that first trip through Amelia's head. I was glad I held on until he was finished. It was important for him to show me how he pined to reunite with Aggie in death, but had been denied that lifelong hope.

Like Harvey, I also felt cheated out of spending my eternity with Sam, but I no longer felt so lonely. I was sorry about what I'd said about him working in the cemetery so he could smell the bodies. Could I possibly have been crueler? Feeling worse by the minute, I avoided his gaze as I struggled for the right words to apologize.

"Mmm. Oh...don't get worked up or nothin'." Harvey spared me by speaking first. I was thankful he found the words for me. I hadn't actually addressed him to express my feelings, but my thoughts were all out in the open. There would be no secrets around this place.

"Oh, Harvey, I'm so sorry things happened like that. I'm as upset that you lost Aggie as I am about me being stuck here without Sam. Why does it have to be like this?" I gazed over all of the graves that were our only company...possibly forever.

"There's nothin' we can do about it, for me anyways. I don't know about you. Maybe you can still find your hubby. I just had to show you my sweet Aggie. Wasn't she beautiful?"

"Yes, very. Can you forgive me for being so rude? I had no idea you lost so much. I'm touched you shared your family with me."

"Yup, they were all that was worth livin' for," Harvey's voice trembled. "Me...I see now why you miss Sam so much, too. You were a lot like me and Aggie – just kids when you fell in love."

"Yeah, we were so young. Now I feel guilty because you lost Aggie so soon. At least Sam and I had many years together. Did you really watch us working here?"

"Sometimes."

"Well, I was surprised by what you said earlier about me on a high horse. I mean...I...was just so shocked that you think of me that way!"

"Boy, you were something, sometimes. Not all the time, but sometimes...you'd rattle off something you read in one of your fancy books and then make those poor worker bees dig up a whole patch they just put in."

I sighed, "I couldn't help it. I'd get so caught up in it. I wanted everything to look as nice as it could. Actually, I took a few of my layouts from some of the older beds. They were overgrown but I thought they must have been something back in their day. They might've been your gardens!"

"Well, I'll take that as a compliment." Harvey smiled for the first time since I'd met him. Then he turned around and grumbled, "You know, not everyone needs to pay money to go to school to learn how to pull weeds. Anybody who's not afraid of a little dirt under their fingernails can do this garden stuff."

And so it went. We roamed through the cemetery all night. One minute we bonded through stories of our married lives and our disappointment when we realized our spirits would not join those of our spouses. The next minute we argued about a bed of mums. We ended each round by agreeing to disagree. Otherwise, we would have argued forever about the minutiae of every single plant!

Even though we both empathized with the other about missing our spouses, we wondered how long we could stand each other. Harvey was mad because I told him I wouldn't let him tear up anybody else's plants, not even marigolds, so he set off to haunt some other part of the cemetery. That was fine with me. He had my sympathy and empathy for all he'd been through, but I'd had enough of his grumbling for one day.

Tracy Fontaine

Chapter Four: Memories

Beyond the wall of Mount Hope Cemetery, my closest friends and family prepared to say goodbye to Lilla Woodworth and wish her well in heaven, or wherever they thought she had gone. I don't know about other spirits, but I wasn't going to miss my own funeral. Honestly, I wasn't sure if I could handle it, but if it bothered me too much I could leave any time without anyone seeing me. I drew strange comfort from thinking that if any living people realized I was sitting next to them at my own funeral, they'd be more upset than I was.

My niece Helen was taking care of everything, bless her heart. Before moving into Winfield Acres, I prepared the arrangements for my funeral. I set money aside in an account in Helen's name. Helen and I had always been close, and she had agreed to be the executor of my estate. Her mother, Marion, was Sam's sister, but most people thought Marion and I were sisters because we were the best of friends. Over the years, Sam and I spent a lot of time with her family.

Sam and I never had children, but Marion's children would help us around the house. They made sure we had everything we needed. After Sam died, they helped me sell my house and move to Winfield Acres. That was my choice. I wanted to move before I grew too feeble to take care of my house or go to the store for myself. If I had my own children, I would have felt like a weight asking them to bring me food and wash my clothes. I certainly didn't want to burden my niece and nephew with that stuff.

Helen was busy enough caring for Marion, who insisted on staying in her own house after my brother-in-law died. Marion couldn't bear to leave the memories of the house where she and Don had lived for over fifty years. It was understandable. I had a hard time leaving my own house for those same reasons, but I was able to bask in Sam's presence in other places, every time I passed our favorite gardens or thumbed through one of the books we wrote. Having kids makes a difference, too. Helen and Tom's visits to the house where Marion and Don raised them became even more precious when they started bringing the grandchildren around.

Marion still got around okay. She had a friend who lived with her and they watched out for each other. Helen came up from Pennsylvania to visit once or twice a month. She often brought Marion to see me and we would rehash old times. I wondered if Marion would make it to my funeral. I wouldn't want to, if I were in her shoes. She was the last one in that family from our generation. No one wants to be the first to go but it's even worse to be the last. Who could blame Marion if she wasn't up for a funeral?

I wanted to see her, especially if she couldn't come to my funeral, so I went to her house. I figured Helen and her husband were probably staying there, so they might be discussing how the plans were coming along. Hopefully, Helen wasn't having any problems with the arrangements.

As soon as I wished it, I found myself in Marion's living room, where family memories warmed my heart. Sam and I spent hours roughhousing with the kids on this floor, actually, on this exact threadbare carpet. With my ghostly improved vision, I realized how worn the house looked. Old, like me and Marion. Dated wallpaper and faded furniture trapped the house in the past. Everything looked clean, but there's only so much one can do with a vacuum cleaner and furniture polish.

That's how it must have looked to an outsider. I'm sure Marion saw things differently. She probably looked at the horrid sofa and superimposed a forty-year-old image of her, Don, and the kids watching television. I would do that with my house and old furniture after Sam died. Memories are so powerful. I wanted to hang onto the good ones any way I could.

As I moved around the downstairs rooms, almost every piece of furniture triggered a memory. I didn't see anybody around. They must have been at the funeral parlor. I checked upstairs in case Marion might be home but found her bedroom empty. I heard a noise from Helen's old room across the hall, where Helen always stayed when she was in town.

Entering Helen's room, I discovered a fat, dumpy, old woman with Coke bottle glasses, and short, frizzy, black hair pawing through Helen's suitcase. She carefully removed each item from the suitcase and unfolded it to search through the pockets. Then she refolded everything and replaced them just as she'd found them.

66

She checked the pockets of the suitcase, too, and set her prizes on the bed: a few coins, a pair of earrings, and a tube of lipstick. She moved the suitcase to the floor near the window, where she must have found it.

What a little sneak! This must be that roommate. I can't believe Marion even knows somebody like this! I wonder what else she helps herself to around here.

She picked through another suitcase that must have belonged to Helen's husband, Bill. She found a stack of money in the side compartment. She only took a couple of twenties and put the rest back.

This was horrible! I wondered how many other times she had taken stuff from Helen. She took just enough to confuse someone, but not enough for them to realize they'd been robbed. Gathered her treasures she waddled down the hall to her room. Of course, I followed her. Fumbling in her top dresser drawer, she reached behind her underwear and pulled out a bag of chocolate covered peanuts. When she opened the bag, it was full of tens and twenties instead of candy.

She worked hard to cram the new money into the overstuffed bag. Folding the end of the bag she wrapped a rubber band around the whole thing. She hid it carefully behind her underwear and closed the drawer. The money would be safe there, as you'd be hard pressed to find anybody willing to rifle through her underwear.

The lipstick and earrings had their own separate hiding place, deep in the back of her closet, behind the shoe rack in an orthopedic loafer. I swear, some people work harder sneaking around than if they went out and worked a real job. By the time she finished digging through that luggage and hiding everything she stole, sweat beaded on her brow. Her face was practically crimson. I knew it was wicked to wish she'd have a heart attack…but I confess the thought crossed my mind. She was breathing heavily and lay down to rest. After putting her glasses on the nightstand, she pulled the covers over herself.

She was snoring in less than five minutes. It was only seven o'clock. Was she napping or did she go to bed for the night? Who cares? At least she wasn't causing any more trouble. I made faces at her from the foot of her bed while she slept.

It was getting dark and she wouldn't have been able to see me even if I had my fleshy body. It felt good to show her how I felt, even if it was in secret, although this is one person I would love to have frightened. I stopped short of kicking the bed. Another time I would look around her room and see what else she had stolen, but first I wanted to see Helen and Marion.

Before I took off to see if everybody was at the funeral parlor, I needed to do one thing, though. The earrings in the loafer, I wanted to return them to Helen, but I didn't know if I could move them. I hadn't tried to lift anything since I caught the flowerpot Jodi threw at me. I went over to the closet and reached into the side of the loafer. Wrapping my hand around the earrings, I focused my energy.

"Move with my mind, not my hand," I repeated to myself. I started pulling my hand out of the loafer, confident the earrings would come right out. My hand became stuck and the whole shoe lifted off the ground with my hand still inside. Great.

Yesterday I would have been impressed to lift that shoe, but right now I just wanted the little things inside. After some gentle finagling, I finally pulled the earrings out and left the shoe behind. Not only did I lift the earrings, I moved them through the air all the way back to Helen and Bill's room. I set them on the nightstand behind the clock. Helen would spot them when she got into bed, but that roommate wouldn't be able to see them from the doorway.

I just moved things through midair! Just like the haunted houses in the movies. Neat!

Taking one last peek at Sleeping Beauty I headed to the funeral parlor. Helen and I arranged everything with Baker's Funeral Home several years ago, and that's where I found everyone. I clenched my hands around my arms so nobody would see me if I got emotional.

I never liked calling hours at funeral homes. I thought about skipping them altogether when I made my arrangements, but Helen said people in the community would want to express their condolences. I reminded her those days were long gone. Nobody would remember me except some of my old gardening buddies, if they were still around. After a lengthy discussion, I finally agreed to have short calling hours for the ten or twenty people who might want to come.

When I arrived, I was stunned to see flowers arrangements spilling out into the hallway. A little plaque reading "Our Lilac Lady" marked the entrance of the viewing room. Potted lilacs bloomed on each side of my casket. In September? Lilac season was months ago! They must've been from a greenhouse.

When I remembered I couldn't smell anything anymore, my heart broke. I sniffed a few lilac branches, gently at first, and then took a huge snort. Nothing. Well, at any rate, they looked beautiful even if I couldn't smell them.

 I groaned when I noticed someone had placed me in a dress nearly the same color as the lilacs. Did they have to get so literal with the whole Lilac Lady thing?

Everyone probably thought I insisted on being buried in purple, when really I hadn't. I preferred my peach or burgundy dress. My irritation about the purple dress actually helped me out a little. It distracted me from other emotions. When I first arrived I didn't want to see my face, but the dress was a good segue to look at the rest of me.

I haven't appeared that good in years!

I looked so young, even if it was an illusion. Lying on my back in that casket had smoothed my wrinkles. I barely recognized the body in the casket as myself. It could have been a younger cousin who bore a faint resemblance to me. That's probably why I wasn't as upset as I thought I'd be.

Although, maybe it didn't bother me because I felt so good. That fleshy part of me in the casket had its share of frailties. The spirit part of me that stood next to it had so much energy and felt so light. I didn't even remember what pain or cold felt like.

I wished Sam could be here to share my new feelings. I wondered if he could see all of this fuss, wherever he was. Would he be as impressed as I was to see the crowd, including two former mayors, streaming in and out of the viewing room?

There were many faces I hadn't seen in such a long time! I recognized friends from the garden clubs and T.V. shows, and even some of the aides from Winfield Acres. The best part was seeing so many relatives from the younger generations.

Since they're spread out and everyone's so busy, they don't get to see each other very often. Nowadays it takes either a wedding or a funeral to get them together.

Conversations buzzed across the room as everyone filled each other in on what they had been doing since they last saw each other. It was the usual stuff heard at family reunions in any part of the country at any given time, but it's special when it's your own family. My nephew, Alex, and his wife plan to move to South Carolina when he retires next year. My grandniece, Sharon, is adding a sun porch to her house, and is helping her daughter fill out college applications. She hopes Casey gets that engineering scholarship to Syracuse University. She's also excited about her son, Michael's, wedding next April.

Most of the relatives were from Sam's side. My extended family is spread all over New England. The trip would have been difficult for any of my remaining cousins, who were well into their eighties. Their children and grandchildren were busy with their own lives. I wouldn't have expected any of them to make the trip, but they had sent several arrangements. They must have remembered how much I loved pink and purple because there was a gorgeous heart of pink carnations for "Cousin Lilla." Once again, I wished I could smell those great flowers.

A few of my closest relatives made it to the funeral parlor, though. My brother didn't come, but his three sons came with their families. I'm sure their teenagers had better places to go than to a funeral for a great aunt they had seen ten times in their whole lives. Regardless of whatever coaxing got them there, it was nice to see them. My brother's sons were Matt, Phillip, and Kenny, but I couldn't remember all of their kids' names. The last I knew, Matt and Phillip lived in New Hampshire, but and Kenny was in Massachusetts. Actually, he's been going by "Ken" for about thirty years, but he'll always be my "Kenny."

The two families mingled and chatted about how long it's been since they've seen each other. For many of them, it had been fifteen years ago, at Sam's funeral. Helen and Matt were talking about how sad it was that it was almost the end of a generation. There was only Helen's mom, Marion, on Sam's side; and Matt's parents, my brother and his wife, on my side.

I sidled up to Matt and Helen just in time to hear Matt tell Helen my brother had a stroke about eight months ago.

"Oh, no!" Helen gasped and raised her hand in front of her mouth at that news. Her brows furrowed and she placed her other hand on Matt's arm. "Oh, Matt, I am so sorry! I…didn't realize you had that going on. Aunt Lilla never mentioned it."

Holy cow! I never mentioned my brother's stroke because I didn't know anything about it! Oh, my poor brother!

I made sure my hands remained clasped around my arms. I needed to hear more about my brother, so I hovered close to Helen and Matt as they spoke. Helen and I both wanted to know how my brother, Albert, was doing.

"Thanks," Matt replied to Helen with an appreciative nod. "We didn't tell Aunt Lilla because we didn't want to upset her. He lost some function in his left arm and left side of his face, but he's been in therapy and he's doing so much better. He's got some movement back in his arm. He still has some trouble speaking, but he's a heck of a lot better now than he was three months ago.

"I usually try to call Aunt Lilla every couple of weeks to see how she's doing. I thought about telling her the next time I called. She wouldn't have been able to do anything about it. I figured I'd wait until Dad was in better shape. I didn't want to upset her when she's so far away."

Okay, I'll buy that.

He was right. I couldn't have done anything to help Albert from my nursing home. I might have worried myself to death months ago. I kept listening while Matt went on.

"It was hard enough with Mom so afraid she'd lose him. At first, we thought he'd have to go to a home. Mom got all worked up. She didn't know if she would stay in their house or move in with us. But, for now anyway, he's doing well enough for both of them to stay at home. Visiting nurses check on them, which really helps, and we check on them after work and stay overnight sometimes.

"At some point we'll have to move them. You know how it is." Matt tilted his head with a slight shrug. Then he straightened up and switched to a more cheerful voice. "Hey, how's your mom? Does she still live in her house?" he asked Helen.

Matt motioned toward the row of chairs nearest my casket. Marion was visiting with my nephew, Phillip, and his wife, Carol. They were showing her pictures of their identical twin daughters at their soccer game. Marion always wanted to see any of the girls' pictures that Phil sent me.

"Don't tell me. Don't tell me!" Marion said to Carol. "Uh. Oh…that…one…is…Shelly, right? Number three?"

"Right! I'm impressed!" Carol answered. "Most people think that's Kelly, because her hair was longer this summer. Then she got it cut for school and now Shelly's hair is longer."

"Oh, I can tell their faces apart," Marion pointed proudly at herself. Then she pointed her finger in the air. "I know, she said, pointing back to the photos. Shelly always had those dimples. Every time Lilla showed me their pictures I figured out which is which. I haven't seen them in a while," Marion said. She looked around the room for signs of the twins.

Carol chuckled. "Oh, they're hiding outside somewhere," she replied. Then she leaned over and whispered to Marion, "You know that age." Carol glanced up to make sure the girl's weren't nearby. "They're so self-conscious these days." Then Carol lowered her voice to a whisper and patted Marion on the leg. "They don't know if people are looking at them because they're twins or because they have boobs."

"Oh, is that all?" Marion laughed and touched Carol's arm. "Well, we've all got 'em! You make sure they come over to see me when they come back in!"

"Definitely! They like you. You say things their Gram back in New Hampshire would never say."

Marion looked well. Her hands shook a little as she handled the girls' photos, but she seemed alert and able to hold up her end of a conversation.

Helen turned toward Matt and spoke quietly about Marion. "She's doing okay, but I think she's gone downhill the last couple of years. She still lives at home, but I worry about her. I live three hours away and my brother lives in Texas so we can't check on her as much as we'd like to. She has a friend living with her, which helps…but her friend is old too!"

Matt nodded. "Well, at least neither one of them is alone. I'm sure they keep an eye on each other."

"Yeah, it helps a little. At least one of them can call for the ambulance if something happens to the other." Although Helen's words sounded callous, they actually exposed her genuine concern for her mother's wellbeing. As she spoke, she became emotional. She dabbed tears from the corners of her eyes. Matt gave her an empathetic pat on the arm.

"Thanks. I'm all right," Helen said to Matt. "It's just the timing. I've been thinking about Mom a lot lately, and now with Aunt Lilla gone…Well, it makes me think about bringing Mom down to live with Bill and me. I'm torn about when to do it. She just doesn't want to leave her house. Too many memories.

"And I don't think her friend, Cindy, has anywhere else to go. She was broke so Mom took her in. It worked out great for both of them. Neither one has to live alone. She's a little odd, but Mom seems to like her. When Cindy can, she gives Mom money toward the bills…utilities, and taxes, and stuff. But, it's really time to start the ball rolling so Mom can live with us. We'll help Cindy find someplace else to live, too. I'll probably talk to Mom and Cindy about all of this in a month or two. I just can't spring this on them so close to Aunt Lilla's funeral."

"Mmm, funerals really make you think, don't they?" Matt said quietly. "About our parents…ourselves. Now we're gonna be the 'old people' at family parties." Matt suddenly laughed and remarked, "Hey, remember the time we broke that huge branch on Aunt Lilla's tree? We were at their house for an anniversary or something."

"Awww," Helen sucked in her breath. Her eyes widened and her mouth curved into a grin as she remembered the childhood ruckus. "Oh my God! That's right! Four of us were hanging on that thing. I can't believe none of us cracked our heads when it came down."

"Yeah, heh heh, and then we dragged it away and threw it over the bank so nobody would know. Jesus, I can't believe nobody saw it from the house." Matt shook his head when he remembered how lucky they'd been to pull it off.

That's what happened to my crabapple tree! To this day, I thought the kids down the street broke it. I always wondered where the branch went!

"Oh, I know!" Helen exclaimed. "Can you imagine if Aunt Lilla ever found out someone broke something in her garden?"

It's probably lucky for all of us I didn't find out until now!

Matt raised his eyebrows. "No way. Those gardens were her life! We would have been in such wicked trouble."

"Yeah. I think I knew not to step on her flowers even before I learned to walk," Helen chuckled. "But I guess if she wasn't so particular, she wouldn't have been so famous in her own right."

"It was pretty cool when they were on T.V."

"Yeah, remember when we all rode in that parade with them? We got to throw candy at everybody."

Matt burst into laughter as another thought struck him. He spoke between fits, "Remember? Ha ha! We ran out of candy almost near the end of the parade, and Aunt Lilla stopped the whole thing so we could get more candy? Uncle Sam held back the whole parade behind us and sent some poor flute player or something into a store to buy more candy! When that poor guy got back with the candy his hat was all crooked. He must have bumped it on the doorway of the store." Matt laughed and finished his story. "Then, Aunt Lilla said she just did that so we would have lots of leftover candy for ourselves!"

"Oh, yeah! She said it wasn't fair for us to give away candy all day and not get to have any of it," Helen laughed quite hard.

"Yeah, right," Matt laughed. "She said it was for us, but did you see her go after those root beer barrels?"

"Oh that's right," sighed Helen. "That was such a fun day."

"The best," Matt replied.

Man, that was a great day. Sam and I had all of our nieces and nephews on the float with us. We had a ball!

Matt continued, "We hated that long drive from New Hampshire, but when we got here we always had so much fun with you and Tom and the other cousins. It's nice so many of us could make it today since everyone's parents are either gone or can't travel."

Matt and Helen both fell silent. Their thoughts drifted as they gazed across the room. They were probably thinking of Matt's last words, and making memories of how everybody looked and talked, the generations gathered together on that day.

I, on the other hand, still dwelled on Helen's last words about Cindy. I would love to throw her out on the street with her bag of "chocolate covered peanuts" and see how long she would last.

The crowd started to thin out. The funeral parlor was closing up for the night. I went back to Marion's house to see if Cindy was up to any mischief while everyone was still out. She was still in bed. No guilty conscience kept that lady up at night.

I realized I was still holding my arms from when I was eavesdropping at the funeral parlor. I loosened my hands, and my energy released with a small burst of light. It felt good to relax. Holding that energy back for so long made me feel weak, like after I watched Amelia's whole life that first time. I didn't need to hide myself any longer that night. I wouldn't have minded if Cindy woke up and saw me standing there so I could give her a little scare…just a little.

Helen, Bill, and Marion arrived from the funeral parlor around ten o'clock. They all looked tired. They talked a little about the funeral, scheduled for eleven o'clock the next morning. Saying their good nights, they retreated to their bedrooms. Helen and Bill watched television in bed and Marion read for a while. Before Marion went to sleep, she closed her bedroom door, which gave a jingle.

Hanging on the doorknob was the most God-awful Christmas decoration I've ever seen - a red felt panel with a strand of bells running down the middle. The bells were painted white with red letters that spelled "Merry Christmas." On the bottom of this monstrosity was a picture of an ugly reindeer with a red bell glued onto the tip of its nose. It reminded me of the ugly junk I used to snicker at in my great grandmother's house. Marion always had better taste then that, but I guess leaving tacky Christmas decorations up all year is just one of the signs of getting old.

Shortly after Marion closed her door and fell asleep, Helen and Bill turned off their T.V. and went to sleep as well. I really didn't feel like staying around all night listening to everyone snore, so I headed back to the cemetery to catch up with Amelia.

****

"Well, I don't have to guess where you've been," she said.

"Oh, am I that transparent?" I asked.

"Well, actually, you are!" she quipped. We both laughed. "When I didn't see you, I figured you went to see your family. How was everything? Did you revisit your body?"

"Yeah, I mean I went to the funeral parlor to see my body. I didn't try to crawl back in or anything. Seeing my body didn't really bother me as I thought it would. Maybe this whole thing still hasn't sunk in yet. It was nice to see so many friends and family, but it would have been nicer to be alive and really with them."

I raised my arms in an exasperated gesture. "Oh! I just found out my brother had a stroke! He's okay and everything, but I was sad to hear he's been ill. Thank God, you showed me how to keep my feelings to myself. I held my hands and arms together really tightly. As far as I know, no one saw me."

Amelia nodded casually. "This happens all the time. Almost every spirit I know went to their own funeral to say goodbye to their families. And to themselves in a way. I knew you would have to see your people, too. You're quite peaceful compared to some others I've seen. Some spirits get hysterical – they truly go mad! Sometimes I can't decide if they're upset from seeing their dead body or because this is all they get after a lifetime of hardship." She opened her arms wide to present the no-man's land of the cemetery.

"I'm not as upset as I am bewildered...about being stuck here," I replied. "I'm still hoping this is very temporary. I'm sure Sam and I will be together again, preferably sooner rather than later.

"If he was still alive and I had to watch him grieve, things would be different. I would be a mess. It wasn't all that hard to stay calm at the funeral parlor," I shrugged. "Everyone came to grieve for an aunt, a great aunt, a sister-in-law, a friend. They were sad, but it's not the same as if I was their mother or wife. It felt as if I were wandering through a family reunion. I almost forgot why everyone was there."

"Well, you'll remember when you go to the actual funeral. Do you know when and where it will be?"

"Yeah, it's tomorrow. It's just a little service at the funeral parlor. I told my niece to keep everything short and simple. I don't want her to have to manage a huge funeral."

"Just remember – hold tight!" Amelia reminded me as she connected her arms together. She smiled and floated onto the early morning fog that billowed through the cemetery.

Chapter Five: Saying Goodbye

Well, only a few more hours until my funeral. I wanted to get that part over with before moving on. I felt tethered to my earthly existence. My spirit wouldn't feel free until my body was buried.

The morning was overcast and apparently cool as I watched the day break over my gravesite. Joggers wore sweatshirts, and I could see their breath. They glanced at the freshly dug grave as they passed. Maybe it inspired them to go that extra mile.

As I watched the joggers, the spirit of a little boy sidled next to me. Looking first at my grave, he then inspected my face. I nodded to acknowledge him and to let him know that, yes, the grave was for me. The boy had dark, curly hair, and was dressed in a little Sunday suit with short pants. We stood next to each other, as we exchanged small thoughts. I was careful not to frighten him by asking too many questions.

After I told him my name was Lilla, he told me his name was John and he was six years old. He enjoyed watching the men work with their machines. He'd never seen anything like that when he was alive, so whenever a grave was prepared, he was usually nearby. I told him I liked to watch the machines, too. He thought it was funny that a lady likes machines. We looked at the excavator and the truck for a while, and he told me stories of the different machines he'd seen in the cemetery or the ones used to build neighborhood homes and the nearby hospital.

After Amelia and Harvey had taught me how to exchange visions of our lives, I wanted to know everything about everyone, especially the ones who died so long ago. To me, it was a wonderful game. I assumed everyone else must've thought so, too. Confidently, I bent down and held out my hands, but when I reached over to take John's left hand in mine, he pulled away. He backed away until he moved around to the other side of my grave. I stayed put, so he didn't think I was chasing him.

Standing up, I told him it was okay. He could watch the men work and I wouldn't bother him. In fact, I told him, I was going away for a while, but I would come back later and watch with him.

I asked him if that would be okay, to which he nodded slowly. I felt a little better. We gave each other a little wave, before I shot over to Marion's house.

The morning routine was in full swing. Marion, Helen, and Bill were getting ready upstairs, going back and forth from the bedrooms to the bathroom. Cindy reclined in the big easy chair in front of the television, gorging loudly on eggs, bacon and toast. Clad only in a plaid flannel nightgown and tattered brown slippers, she had wrapped a blanket around herself while trying to eat her breakfast, using her hand as it protruded from the blanket. Toast crumbs sprinkled the blanket and her slippers. I guessed she didn't plan on coming to the funeral, which suited me just fine.

Helen came downstairs and asked, "Cindy, are you sure you don't want to come with us? You're perfectly welcome. It's fine if you want to stay here, too. I feel badly leaving you here all alone."

Still chewing, Cindy began to reply, "Oh don't wor—" In the middle of her sentence she choked on some toast crumbs. She sputtered, holding up one finger, she grabbed her coffee with her other hand and washed down her food with several loud gulps. "Ahhh," she exhaled loudly after swallowing.

Cindy continued in a raspy voice, "Sorry 'bout that. Naw, naw. I'll be fine. This is family time. You go on and be together without worrying about me tagging along. I never met your aunt. Sounds like she was a good woman. I'll be okay."

Helen went into the kitchen to pour a cup of coffee. When she came into the living room to let Cindy know they would be leaving soon, Cindy noticed Helen wearing the earrings that she tried stealing the previous night. She sat there dumbfounded, with her mouth agape.

Helen asked, "Is something wrong? Is my dress buttoned okay? Oh Jeez! I bet I left the price tag on. I just grabbed this at the outlet on my way up here the other day." Helen reached under each armpit looking for tags.

Cindy waited for the bomb to fall. I'm sure she thought Helen was playing games before accusing her of stealing. She managed to choke down her mouthful of food and squeak out, "Oh, you're fine. Look fine."

I could tell Cindy was waiting for Helen to turn on her, but Helen maintained her warm disposition. Helen finished her coffee and went back to the kitchen. Bill and Marion eventually worked their way downstairs to join her for breakfast. When Cindy was sure they were all downstairs, she pushed her T.V. tray aside and threw off her blanket, sending toast crumbs flying all over the carpet. She tried to sneak upstairs when Bill spotted her.

"Good morning, Cindy!" he greeted her with his booming voice. Bill was a big man, whose voice commanded attention. Cindy jumped about a foot. It was really funny. Too bad they didn't know why she was so nervous. I bet she thought Helen asked Bill to say something about the earrings. Cindy had one foot on the stairs, ready to bolt if necessary.

"Oh, sorry about that! I didn't mean to scare you. Do you want some breakfast?" Bill offered. He was too nice.

"No, no thanks," Cindy said, rather she gasped. It was such fun, watching her sweat. "Oh, it's… I mean, I ate already. I'm… um… just going up to get dressed. See you later."

"Okay, then. Take care and we'll see you later!" Bill answered, and turned his attention to his cereal. He, Marion, and Helen talked about how good everyone looked the day before. Helen informed them about my brother's stroke. Marion agreed it was sad, and she hoped nothing like that happened to her because she might not be able to stay in her own house. Helen and Bill exchanged nervous glances. Marion didn't see it, but Cindy did. She was watching and listening as she inched her way up the stairs. Earlier, while Marion took a shower, Helen and Bill had spoken quietly about the future of that household. I suspected Cindy had heard, and now I was sure.

I watched Cindy as she nervously watched Helen and Bill. In her eyes I saw her concern for her future if Marion moved to Pennsylvania to live with Helen. I wished Marion could walk away from her house right then.

Cindy silently went to her room as I followed her. She closed her door and headed straight to the shoes in the bottom of the closet. Predictable. She checked to ensure the earrings were really gone from inside her loafers. Sitting on the floor with her legs crossed, Indian style, she stared into space.

Her lips moved, as she muttered to herself. If she was confused then, just wait until she saw what would happen next. I was looking forward to spending some more time alone with her, but I had things to do first.

Downstairs, the others cleaned their dishes and prepared to leave. I slipped through Cindy's bedroom wall and down to the foyer as Helen and Marion were deciding if they needed coats or not. They decided to wear light jackets because it was still cool and cloudy. It didn't look like the sun would come out that day. They thought the chapel might be cool, too, because of the stone walls.

Chapel? My funeral service was supposed to be right at the funeral parlor. Maybe they were talking about the room where I saw my body the night before. I think they called that room by some sort of chapel name. That must be it, just the name of the room.

Bill waited in the car while Helen and Marion yelled their goodbyes to Cindy. They listened for a response, but when they didn't hear anything, they looked at each other and shrugged. Marion started walking out the door, but Helen hesitated.

"Should I check on her?" asked Helen, but Marion was already getting into the car.

"No," Marion answered tersely. "She probably went back to bed. Let's go."

Marion and Cindy didn't have much of a friendship. Marion didn't seem to care too much where or how Cindy spent her days. Maybe their only bond was a convenient living situation. I wondered if Helen felt the same as I did. She glanced at the upstairs window as she walked to the car. I don't think she liked Cindy having the house to herself.

I wanted to shout to Helen. "Do it! Do it! Kick her out!"

When Marion and Helen finally entered the car, Bill pulled out of the driveway and headed toward the funeral parlor. When they arrived, everyone was milling around the parking lot, waiting for them. There were many handshakes and hugs as everyone primed up for the main event. Instead of going into the building, though, they all returned to their vehicles and filed into formation behind Helen and Bill's car. A hearse appeared from around the other side of the building. It pulled out of the parking lot, followed by a winding line of cars.

Sure enough, the procession headed from the funeral parlor straight into the cemetery and the Sisters of Mary Chapel. The large wooden doors had been propped open to air out the tomblike structure. Talk about a wasted trip! If I had known I'd end up right back here for my funeral, I never would have bothered going to Marion's house that morning.

The idea of my funeral being held at this chapel annoyed the heck out of me. Too much fuss! I didn't need this show! It would have been worse if I hadn't noticed Amelia passing at a safe distance. She motioned for me to clasp my arms and hands together. Oops. I had forgotten! I gave her a little wave of gratitude before connecting my arms. As they brought my casket inside the chapel, cars were still parking alongside the edge of the narrow cemetery roads.

I didn't think everyone would fit into the tiny chapel, but somehow they managed to squeeze inside. The wooden doors remained open, so I watched from the outside until the service started. Despite the pomp of the procession, it was very informal. I was never big on going to church and didn't even know the name of the minister at my own funeral. He was probably from Marion's church.

"Good morning," he began. "Thank you all for coming to celebrate the life of Lilla Woodworth, the Lilac Lady. I don't need to explain why we're meeting here today in the lovely Sisters of Mary Chapel. You saw for yourselves. If you passed Highland Park, you drove by the pansy bed and the forest of lilac bushes. You probably drove across the purple crosswalks, and turned when you saw the purple street signs for Highland Ave. As you entered the gates, you might have admired the gardens right here in the cemetery.

"Lilla and her husband Sam created gracious gardens all over Rochester, but especially right here in this neighborhood. Lilla and Sam loved to share their gift of gardening. I have a couple of their books on my shelf. I remember listening to their radio shows, too. Don't tell anybody but I'm not as young as I look."

When the crowd finished chuckling, the pastor continued. "Marion asked me to speak today, but the real testimony about how many lives Lilla touched is right here." The pastor swept his outstretched arm across his audience.

"Please, let me step aside and welcome all those who wish to come forward to share their memories of Lilla."

It was nice to hear the pastor's words about my life in the public eye and the work Sam and I had put into the grounds surrounding the chapel. He didn't go on for too long before my friends and family took over. The others paid tribute to my personal life and how they knew me. While they spoke, my thoughts wandered as I recalled memories of each person in the room. Every now and then, I'd shake myself back into the moment so I could catch their words.

"...always remembered everyone's birthdays, anniversaries, and even the kids' college graduations. I don't know how she kept track of all of that stuff. She remembered our anniversary better than me!"

That was my nephew on Sam's side, Alex, providing a little humor for everyone. Those cards were my pleasure. Alex always included us in his family's activities. He and Samantha raised such nice kids!

A few minutes later, I snapped out of my daydream to see a friend from the garden club standing at the lectern. She was quite young when she volunteered with us. I had gladly taken her under my wing because she reminded me of myself when my parents' friends let me help them in their gardens. "...it's been a long time since I've seen Mrs. Woodworth. She and Mr. Woodworth taught me about gardening...to appreciate the outdoors...taking care of so many plants. They really opened up a new world for me. I think of them whenever I'm in my own garden. She gave me some of my favorite peonies from her heirloom collection..."

She still has those! How sweet! Maybe I'll swing by her house next year to see them. Oh God, did I just say I would still be here in a year? Deep down have I given up already? Stop it! I can worry about that when after this. Right now, I need to pay attention to what they're saying before I miss the rest of my funeral! There's Kathy, my old neighbor. I think she still lives in the same house.

"...loved good food even if she couldn't cook," Kathy paused as the audience snickered. "She always came over to give her official report when they tried a new restaurant. Most of you know Sam was the cook in their house. He was her gold standard. Lilla rated every restaurant based on how it compared to Sam's food..."

Listening to people I hadn't seen in years choked me up. I moved around the side of the seats and cautiously forward as the speakers continued, to see everyone's faces, together for one last time. I gripped my arms more firmly now than ever before - this was a very sad time for me to bid farewell to my family and friends. I would miss sharing their world. I took a picture in my mind of all of the people packed into the chapel…Sam's family, my family, Peggy, Nurse Becky, were more people from our gardening shows and horticulture clubs.

Spooky Marcie and some of her friends stood behind the back row. I didn't know how sensitive they were to my presence. I made a mental note to myself not to get too close but it was too late. Three women, and one dark mysterious man, honed in on me. In fact, every one of Marcie's friends stared right at me. Not Marcie, though. I could see her searching the room incessantly during the speeches, skipping right over the actual corner where I rested. Poor Marcie…apparently not as gifted as her friends. She couldn't sense me from this far away.

The man in Marcie's group gave me the willies. He kept staring directly at me. I thought maybe he didn't really see me. I stayed completely still and held my arms tighter, but he continued looking right at my face. He saw me looking back at him, and nodded at me, a slow deliberate acknowledgement of my presence. I nodded once, slowly, in his direction. Spooky Marcie had nothing on this guy – he was creepy, even for me. I thought it best to get out of the chapel before he pointed me out to everyone in the entire place.

The service was almost over. The mayor said a few words about this cemetery being part of Rochester's history. He thanked the Lilac Lady (and her husband) for working so hard to preserve the past so future generations could appreciate its beauty. If this hadn't been a funeral, he would have gotten a round of applause.

In front of Marcie's friend's watchful eye, I didn't want to try anything fancy. He really didn't need to see me get stuck trying to go through one of those stone walls. I wouldn't provide him with such amusement at my expense. Inching my way toward the open doorway at the front of the chapel, I stuck close to the wall, as far away from Marcie and her group as I could manage. That man stared at me until I was nearly out.

There were a few people between us now, so I knew he couldn't see me anymore. I still held my arms in front of me, hoping nobody else would see me. I figured I would hide behind the chapel as soon as I left, so I went through the doorway and quickly turned to go around the corner of the chapel. What happened next guaranteed the legend of Rochester's Lilac Lady would continue whether I wanted it to or not.

I zipped out of the chapel doors quickly, with my arms still clasped, not realizing a news team had come to record a human-interest blurb about the Lilac Lady's funeral. I had been looking behind me to make sure the creepy guy wasn't following me. When I turned around, I was right in front of a news guy adjusting his camera. It startled me so much that I gasped and my hands flew up to cover my mouth. I completely forgot I was holding back so much energy. My arms flew open with a flash, right into the lens of the camera. The poor cameraman jumped back and put his hands over his left eye. He hunched over and squirmed in pain.

"Holy Jesus! Jackie, get over here!" he yelled.

His coworker came running from the news truck, which was double-parked next to the hearse. I went around the side of the chapel to get away from the mess I just caused. I still had to watch, but from a safer spot.

"Oh my, God! Rick, what happened?" Jackie asked. She was trying to pry his hand off his eye so she could see how to help him. Even though he had just called for her, he wouldn't let her touch him. He pushed her hand away and slowly lifted his hand off his eye. He cupped his hand in front of his face to shield his eye from full daylight.

His coworker, Jackie, bent down to see his face and eye. He let her move his hand back a little, but his hands were still in the way, in case she got too pushy. Rick finally pulled his hands away from his face for Jackie to see his eye, watery and red. He squinted to block the daylight. At least it was cloudy that day. It would have been worse for him if the sun had been out.

After a few minutes, Rick squinted. He blinked at the daylight, and it looked like his eye might be feeling better. Jackie backed away, letting him nurse his wound.

She was probably waiting until he admitted he needed real medical attention or decided he was okay and it was just a scare. Rick put his hand on Jackie's shoulder and leaned close to her. He lifted his hand to point at the camera but his mouth hung open while he tried to find the right words. Squinting profusely with his sore eye, he looked more like Popeye every minute.

"I…saw something," he said quietly into Jackie's ear. "I was recording, queuing up the camera, and a flash blinded me."

"Are you sure it wasn't a bird?" Jackie asked. Rick pulled his hand off her shoulder and gave her an annoyed look.

"Jesus, I'm almost blind now, but I could see fine then! No, it wasn't a stupid bird! I know a bird when I see one." The more defensive Rick became, the more amused Jackie looked. She bit her lip to keep the edges of her mouth from curling up into a smile.

"All right. Calm down. Can you see how many fingers I'm holding up?"

Rick hunched over a little, so Jackie put one arm gently across his shoulders and held her other hand low where Rick could see it. She had to reach up from below so he could see her hand curled into a fist, with only her middle finger showing.

"Very funny, jerk. Get that thing away from me – I don't know where it's been!" Rick said, and he pushed her hand away.

"Okay, okay," Jackie laughed. "Just checking to see if you really do know what a bird looks like."

"Very funny. Okay, smartass, let's see what really went on!"

Rick stormed back to the camera. They both hovered over it while he checked his recording. Jackie cast a doubtful glance at Rick, but he ignored her.

"Okay, here's the beginning…wait…wait…okay, there!" Rick stood back and gave Jackie a big "I told you so" look, but she didn't see his face because she was staring intensely at the footage. The camera had kept recording after the flash, while Rick was grabbing his eye. Jackie stood up and looked at Rick, than back at the camera.

"Whoa! You didn't see everything," Jackie said as she took Rick by the shoulders and held him behind the camera. "Watch it again."

Rick watched the recording again, but he didn't show much of a reaction while the flash replayed. After a minute, though, his eyes got wide, even his squinty one. He looked at Jackie, who stared back at him. I stared at both of them from the shadows, with my arms firmly gripped in my circle of protection.

"I don't know," Jackie shrugged and shook her head. "Did it look like a person to you?"

"Yeah, but only if it looked like a person to you. It's hard to say, it disappeared so fast." They were feeling each other out to make sure neither one was crazy.

Shit. How much did they see? Yup, you did it again, Lilla. Just like the time I made fun of the coffee at the station, not realizing we were still on the air.

Discretion was never my thing. Maybe I should find an abandoned house to haunt. If I became the official resident ghost, I wouldn't need to hide. Thrill seekers could hunt for me in the shadows. They could see me, I could scare them, and everyone would get what they came for. No, I really didn't want that kind of freak show existence. I wanted to get through the funeral, say goodbye to everyone in the family, and move on without a ruckus.

Speaking of goodbyes, I heard movement from inside the chapel. The mayor finished his speech, and the minister was releasing the mourners. Rick and Jackie didn't have any more time to debate the thing in the camera. They both agreed they would save it to review later. Caught off guard when the chapel started emptying out, they hurriedly got ready to record the events. They filmed my casket being carried out of the chapel, and caught some shots of grieving mourners. Dull compared to their first footage.

Using my gravesite and mourners as her backdrop, Jackie stepped in front of the camera to say a few words about the Lilac Lady and Mount Hope Cemetery. This piece would trail the late night newscast, if they had time for it after the real news.

I went up and over the chapel roof to get closer to my gravesite without getting near the camera. I descended into the privacy of some bushes. Hiding myself in their branches, I could see and hear well enough. The pallbearers, my nephews and great nephews, carried my coffin over to the gravesite and laid it on support beams over the hole.

Everyone bowed their heads for their own silent prayers. The minister thanked everyone for attending and relayed a message from Helen, inviting everyone to Marion's house for lunch. My funeral was over. As my family and friends turned away from my casket, I felt alone. It was the end of my existence to them. I was only a memory that would fade in time. People settled into their vehicles and followed Bill's car to Marion's house.

Jackie and Rick were the only ones left besides the cemetery crew. They futilely tried to recapture that magic moment. The camera was filming as they walked around the chapel doors and over to my grave. The prospect of being captured on film again while I watched my own burial sickened me. I decided to go to Marion's house for that one last family gathering.

I got there just as the first car pulled up to the house. Helen must have had food delivered while they were at the funeral. The table was laid out with cold cuts, rolls, lasagna, salads, and cookies. And guess who was already helping herself?

Cindy rolled a slice of ham and dipped it right into the dish of mayonnaise. She dipped the ham into the mayonnaise between each bite. Then she picked her teeth, before using the same hand to paw through the cookies.

She was just biting into a cookie when the door opened and people started piling in. Cindy met Helen in the foyer. "Mmm. Mmm…sorry," Cindy said, while spitting cookie crumbs. "Hope you don't mind. I just couldn't resist having one of those delicious cookies."

"Oh, no! That's what they're for! Did you want some lunch, too? Help yourself to the rest of the food. You can meet some of the family."

"Oh, you're so generous, but really, I wouldn't want to intrude. I'm not really hungry."

"Are you sure? There's plenty to go around."

"Yup. Yup, I'm okay. I might grab some leftovers later. I'm going up to my room to catch up on some reading," Cindy smiled stiffly. Did it look as fake to Helen as it did to me? She motioned to the people streaming through the door. "I can bring their coats upstairs for you. I'll just put them on the bed in your room, if that's okay."

"Oh! That would be great! Thank you so much! And if you get hungry, please come on down for some food!"

"Sure thing. Thank you!" Cindy plastered on her best smile and gathered everyone's coats from their arms as they walked in the door.

Most people had worn jackets because the morning had been so cool. Cindy took an armload of coats up to Helen's room and went right to work. Her hands rifled through the pockets before the coats even hit the bed. She went through the ladies' jackets first, finding a couple of dollars and lots of used tissues. Sticking her hand into other people's snot-rags probably didn't even faze her. I prayed she wouldn't put her hands all over the food again.

Then she went through the men's coats. I think she took a couple of fives, but that's about it. Fortunately, nobody had the misfortune to leave any wallets in those pockets. She stuck her loot down the front of her shirt, and made sure nobody was in the upstairs hallway. She went to her room and closed her door so she could add the money to her bag of chocolate covered peanuts. Then she lay on her bed and pulled a National Enquirer out from under her pillow to catch up on the latest news.

I was so irritated with Cindy. It was hard to tear myself away because she was such a train wreck, but I finally went down to see the people that really mattered. Luckily, Marcie and her friends didn't show up or I would have had to be extra careful where I went. As it was, I drifted freely from room to room, while both sides of the family chatted and made small talk about upcoming events in all of their lives. Mostly, they were finishing conversations from the night before.

Marion had corralled the twins, Shelly and Kelly, and had placed one on each side of her. They ate their lunch with her and told her about school and their soccer team. They were nice girls and didn't seem to mind humoring Marion.

"Now you two smile! See there are those dimples…you are Shelly, right?" The girl on Marion's left nodded. "Aha! I'm right! Your mother doesn't know how I do it. I just know, that's all! And you," she said to the other girl, "I know you're Kelly because your eyes are just a little rounder than your sister's."

Well, I'll be damned! She could tell them apart better than me, and they're my own flesh and blood!

It was wonderful to see so much activity in Marion's house. She enjoyed it, as well. Several kids chased each other all over the house. One of my grandnephews must have stumbled across a pile of my belongings. He ran through the house holding my cane.

Ah, my cane! God, I loved that thing!

Helen helped me cut the wood for that cane from my backyard. When I could no longer care for my house and garden the way they deserved, I knew it was time to go. The last thing I did before selling my house was to take a little piece of my garden with me. Helen helped me get to my walking stick bush with its gnarly, twisted branches. She cut one of the sturdier limbs and brought it to an artist friend of mine. He sanded and polished it into a twisted cane and topped it with a brass dragonhead.

When I showed up at Winfield Acres wielding the wicked cane I felt like a real "bad ass." Then they stuck me in a wheelchair and took me to my sterile room. Sigh. So much for my delusions of the geriatric wild child. Still, my cane and I did turn heads, especially when I paired up with tattooed Cora.

I was glad my cane didn't disappear into the woodwork at Winfield Acres. It was meant for bigger things, like entertaining the masses at Marion's house. That little guy who found it treated everyone to a comical soft shoe routine he must have seen in an old movie. His mother chided him as everybody else stifled guilty giggles. Hey, I thought it was funny, too. Who doesn't need a little innocent comic relief now and then? Nobody argued when he asked to take the cane home. It was one less thing for Helen to tote to the thrift store. I hoped he would enjoy it and treasure it as much as I did.

More than likely, this would be the last time many of these people ever saw each other. The girls were heading back to New Hampshire late that afternoon and probably wouldn't make it back this way again. They would have no reason to, really. They might call Helen to ask about Marion occasionally, but she was Sam's sister and my side of the family probably wouldn't travel to these parts again. I was the last bond between these two families. Now that I was buried, they would move on with their separate lives.

The afternoon went too quickly for me. The two sides of the family, Sam's and mine, circulated amongst each other. They had said goodbye to me and were now saying goodbye to each other.

"Hey," Helen said as she hugged my nephew, Matt. "I Hope everything goes okay for your dad and that he gets better soon."

Matt squeezed her hand. "Thanks. He's definitely better every day. When he's stronger, we really have to talk to him and Mom about the house and stuff. I'm not looking forward to that conversation."

Helen looked over to where Marion was handing out everyone's jackets. "Yeah, I'm right there with you on that one. Keep us posted."

"Yeah, you too. Your mom looks great," Matt nodded toward Marion. "Hope things go okay for you, too. Take care."

"You, too," Helen replied. They understood the difficult decisions facing both of them. They tried to act upbeat as other family members filed past.

Everybody wished each other well and parted with hugs and kisses. As the cars drove away, the passengers waved goodbye to Helen, Bill, and Marion, who waved back from the doorway. The departing guests couldn't see me, but just the same, I stood behind Helen and waved to them, too. I pretended for just a few minutes that their waves were for me, and that my family would return soon for another visit. I moved away from behind Helen to the edge of the driveway. I turned and gave my own wave to Helen, Bill, and Marion before heading back to the cemetery.

Chapter Six: Catharsis

I knew I had missed my burial. Just as well. As much as it traumatized me when they dug the hole, I think it would have been worse to watch them toss that dirt back over my body. It meant much more to me to spend the afternoon at Marion's house. I could sit and stare at my grave for all eternity, but today had been my last chance to see my family together. When I returned to my gravesite, the burial crew was finishing. They patted the mound of dirt over my grave and loaded their tools into the truck. One worker got in the truck and drove away. The others followed in a bucket loader.

My new friend, John, followed behind them. He waved to me. I forced a smile and nodded. I didn't come back to watch the burial with him as I promised, but he wasn't upset in the least. Kids go with the flow. He was probably too busy watching the workers to notice I hadn't shown up.

It was getting dark and the crew was probably tired and ready to go home for dinner. Things were quiet. No joggers, dogs, or cars in sight, which left me alone to obsess over my little pile of dirt. I sighed heavily with disappointment because I was still here. Apparently, my finished burial wasn't enough to set me free from this earth. Sitting on a tree branch, I looked down where my body now rested next to Sam's. Was he looking down on it too, wondering where I was? I should be with him by now.

Oh, Sam! I couldn't agree with you more.

"Hello," said a soft voice behind me. Jodi flew over and sat next to me on the tree branch, on my left. Her good side facing me, which I'm sure was intentional. She knew I had a hard time looking at the gnarled left side of her face and body.

"Hi. Fancy meeting you here," I tried to be clever, but ended up blurting the first stupid cliché that came to mind, with the added bonus of unintentional sarcasm. I was so self-absorbed, I couldn't think of anything else. Jodi didn't press me for any conversation or try to play games.

She seemed quieter and more thoughtful than my first impression of her. I guess she came to keep me company. Every spirit I've met so far, even Jodi, has probably gone through this phase of wondering what's next for them.

Even though it was so long ago for her, she must still carry a flicker of empathy for new spirits trying to figure out what's happening.

"I know this sucks for you," she said gently as we peered down at Sam's gravestone. "I know it's hard to believe, but it gets easier. I was fourteen when I croaked. God, that was a scar time! I didn't leave my friggin' grave for three months. I didn't know what else to do. I was afraid I would miss God when He came to take me to heaven, so I waited and waited. My mother visited my grave every day and cried oh so much. I thought her prayers would remind God I was here, so I waited to make sure He found me. He never came for me, though."

Jodi wasn't helping me feel better, yet this was the first time we'd held a real conversation. Now that she was sitting still, I could see she had been quite a young lady in her day. Her dress wasn't as fancy as the ones I'd seen in old portraits hanging on the walls of the nicer historic homes, but she was mindful of her appearance.

Constantly smoothing her dress and tending to the dainty curls that cascaded down her face, she must have been right on the cusp of womanhood when she died. She was sentenced to walk this fence forever: that between girl and woman and that between life and eternal life.

No wonder I never knew what to expect from her. I would have to grant her more patience. She still had a playful girl inside and not enough maturity to know when she was being downright rotten. Interested in hearing more of her story, I continued listening. I hoped I could find out what disfigured her.

"I decided…if God couldn't find me, I would find Him. So I went to church looking for Him. I visited every church in town over and over, all of the time. Of course, it was a long time ago, and there wasn't nearly the number of churches in town as there are now. So, then, I went to churches in other towns. I went from church to church, and still didn't find God so He could take me to heaven.

"I busted my ass and got nowhere. It drove me daft, I tell you! I didn't want to turn into a crazy ghost hiding under children's beds. I started to see how different everything was since I wasn't alive anymore. Some things were unfortunate, like not being able to pick anything up, but I could fly!"

"And pass through walls! It was far out! I was having fun doing things I couldn't do before. I went wherever I wanted, and got there damn quick, too. I practiced lifting things until I could move anything I wanted. Soon I was having so much fun I didn't give a bird-turd about finding heaven, so I stopped looking. I wasn't scared or worried anymore, you know?"

Jodi had become quite the little chatterbox. She seemed so much more comfortable around me, so I let her run with it. "I knew I was dead for a long time because after a while the rest of my family became old and boring. I wanted to do young things so I took off again but I didn't go to churches anymore. I found parties in the back rooms of those fancy houses on East Avenue. I didn't even need the secret word to get in. I just walked right through the walls. You should've seen the crazy dresses on those girls! They wore long necklaces and these super cool things around their heads. They also wore lots of lipstick. It was really red. That was the bee's knees, all right." Jodi gazed into space, and I along with her. We both imagined what life would have been like in the '20s.

Jodi sighed, before continuing, "Yeah, those times were the cat's meow. Then they kind of died out, and I ended up going all over the place."

Jodi ran down the list of her other haunts in a very teenage-like manner. The raising inflection of her voice at the end of each sentence made it sound like a question. "So then I started going to school dances to hang out with kids like me. Boy, have they changed! Oh, sometimes I go to this diner over on Main Street? I've been going there for almost eighty years. It's the best at two in the morning after the bars let out. Those guys are shitfaced!" Jodi shook her head and snickered.

"Jodi!" I exclaimed. I raised my eyebrows and my jaw dropped a little.

"What?" she said.

"Well, I don't know," I said. "I guess I'm not used to hearing young ladies like you speak like that."

"Oh, sorry," she smiled sheepishly. "My mother would roll over in her grave if she heard me, too. I guess I forget since I hear so much of it when I'm at some of the school dances or the strip clubs."

"The what!" I cried.

"Oh. Sorry, didn't mean that. Just kidding." Jodi looked away sheepishly.

"Uh huh," I rolled my eyes. I really didn't have anything to say about that. I didn't want to know and Jodi was just as happy to forget about that slipup, too.

"Oh. Uh," she moved right along. "There are so many nice things to see all over town, too. I go into people's houses, and the museums, and to restaurants. I follow people to their jobs and to parties. Sometimes they can be such assholes but most of the time they're pretty funny.

"Everything's changed so much since I died. I never get bored. Some spirits go all over the world, like Doctor Klinck. You haven't met him yet. He's the coolest. He's so very adventurous! He's only here sometimes. He goes all over the world! Then he comes back to visit Mrs. Klinck's grave and tell her about everything he saw and did. He lets us listen, too. He has such killer stories! Mrs. Klinck always wanted to travel, but she died before she had the chance to…Oh, crap! I'm sorry! I didn't mean to ramble on. I hope I didn't upset you!"

I couldn't understand why Jodi abruptly ended her story and became apologetic. Maybe because that doctor's spirit was separated from his wife's in a similar fashion as mine and Sam's. The truth was, I was so caught up in her childish sincerity peppered with vulgarity that I wasn't bothered in the least. Her storytelling revealed her compassionate side. It must have been hard to become a spirit during her teenage years.

It was comforting to hear from someone who'd been through this, to give me hope that this horrible emptiness would lessen in time. I didn't feel much better yet, but I'd try to believe the words from someone who had been there. After her initial anger she embraced her spirited existence and used it to grow and learn instead of suffer. Initially, I thought she was a nuisance, but now I could see she still possessed a playful youth that had been cut short. She challenged me to appreciate the things I'd gained, not the things I'd lost. I mean, really…flying, going through walls, listening in on everyone's conversations. This stuff was awesome!

I was still miserable in my predicament, but hopefully there would be better days ahead. It was nice of Jodi to sit and talk to me. Her words were encouraging. Sitting in the cemetery would become dreary at some point but I wasn't ready to leave just yet. It would feel too much like I was abandoning Sam's memory. I would have to work up to traveling the way the others did. It was good that Jodi found peace with this existence, and hopefully I could do the same someday.

"Wow," I responded to Jodi's story when she finished speaking. She still looked nervous about how I might react to the part about Dr. Klinck's separation from his wife. I smiled to reassure her. "That is so interesting, Jodi. No, believe it or not, I'm not upset by any of that. Well," I paused. "I'm sad to hear it because it sounds like a lot of spirits are stuck here when they die and the rest of their family made it to the other side without them. If you haven't found your way out of here, I'm starting to think I might be here longer than I imagined.

"Dr. Klinck sounds interesting." I returned to a more cheerful topic. "I really would like to meet him and find out what happens to spirits like us. I don't expect him to take me to my husband or anything, but maybe he's seen something that could help me."

Jodi nodded. We sat in silence for a bit. I didn't know how much more information Jodi was willing to share, but I wanted to ask her something she skipped over in her story. I hoped I didn't send her scurrying away.

Finally, I asked, "Jodi?"

"Yeah?"

"How did you die, anyway?"

"Oh, my horse threw me and I broke my neck," she answered quickly.

At first, I thought she was kidding because she said it so nonchalantly, and besides, no fall from a horse could disfigure anybody's face like that. I wondered how Jodi could look the way she did from a broken neck. Then I remembered Amelia. She died of smallpox but her spirit looked perfectly fine, no sign of those horrible pox marks.

"It's not from falling off my horse," Jodi replied to my unspoken thoughts.

"What?" My eyes widened in surprise.

"This." She tilted her head revealing her gnarled face and arm. "It's not from falling off the horse. It happened…after."

Oh! I must have been thinking too loudly. Jodi had read my thoughts. I felt terrible. "Oh, gee! Honey, I'm so sorry! I'm terrible. I didn't mean to think such things. I hope I didn't hurt your feelings!"

Jodi patted my arm. "Nah. It's cool. I'm okay. You're just being honest. Sometimes I forget about how gross I look until I see other spirits gawking at me, and then they make a face. It doesn't bother me until then. If I want to forget about my looks for a while, I hang out with the living. They can't see me, so nobody gets scared. That's the main reason I go to all of those places. Nobody stares at me. Don't worry – I've been like this for a long time."

"I still feel bad, especially for that time when I met you. I know I upset you, but then I wondered if I scared you, too. I had no idea what I looked like."

"Well, don't worry. You're not horrid at all, even if you did scare those people out of the cemetery! You really know how to jump out of the bushes, but your 'Boo!' needs a little work!" Jodi laughed so hard it took her a couple of minutes to compose herself.

"No, really," she continued as her giggles died down. "You look like you did when you used to work here."

"Oh, you mean with messy hair and dirty handprints on my slacks?" I joked.

"Yeah, like that!" Jodi nodded.

Kids are too damned honest.

"Oh, God," I sighed and rolled my eyes. "No wonder everyone's been running away. I really look like that?"

"Well…um." Jodi paused. "Um…That was what, like, fifty years ago? Maybe I only see you that way. And maybe Harvey and Amelia. You might look different to people who knew you in different places.

"I think we appear in whatever form people recognize us. I kicked off so young nobody ever saw me as a grown up. I don't know if I will ever look like an old lady, since I never got a chance to be one. Maybe, someday I'll try to look like an old hag, just for fun. If someone knew you when you were old, maybe that's how they'd see you now."

Jodie shrugged, and then continued. "Like Amelia? I don't see smallpox on her. I'm glad, too," Jodi confessed. "Those things are nasty! Maybe her husband or a doctor who saw her after she was sick might see the pox, but I only see her the way she was before she got sick. Harvey saw her when she was sick. He told me he sees her with the smallpox sometimes, and other times without them. I know that doesn't tell you why you see me like this. Let's just say it was a crummy time for me. I don't like talking about it, if that's all right with you. Hope you're not mad about that."

"Mad? How could I be mad about that?" I tried to put my hand over her good hand as a gesture of comfort, but it went right through to rest on the tree branch. Well, at least I tried. I looked at Jodi and we laughed. "I don't want to make you uncomfortable. You don't need to tell me what happened, but…your hand. Can you still hold hands with other spirits, you know, to connect with them and see into their past?"

Jodi's eyes widened. She had been resting her bad hand in her lap, but when I asked about grasping hands, she moved her shriveled left hand from her lap way over to her other side, as far from me as possible. Maybe she was afraid I was going to grab it or something. Her body language said enough, so I pretty much knew the answer to my question. "Nobody's really tried it," she said. "I'll punch 'em in the eye if they do try."

All righty, then, I thought. She has a scrappy side, too. A little bit shocked, I nervously chuckled, but she just went right on…"I'll tell them about myself, and they can tell me about themselves if they want to, but I don't want to see everything they've seen. It's not always good." Jodi made a sweeping motion over the grounds below us with her good hand. "This might not be heaven, but it's better than the shit that happened to some of those poor suckers."

"Definitely," I agreed. "You're right. I bet some of the stuff people go through is too hard to watch, even for a short time. I was lucky to have Sam, and to have led such a good long life. I look at those kids' spirits who are even younger than you are. I wonder about their lives, and what happened to them, and why they died so young. So far, none of them has let me get close enough to them to see the memories in their minds."

"Are they just shy or are they afraid of me? It would be interesting to know what their lives were like in their living days."

Jodi thought for a minute before speaking. I think she was trying to find a nice way of telling me to back off, and not interrogate everyone I met. "I know you don't mean any harm but all of those things grownups do – they really spook the kids. Kids don't know what's going on. They never saw the world the way grownups do. It's a hell of a place to watch sometimes."

Wow, Jodi was certainly a character – at two hundred years old, she had the wackiest combination of insight and slang I'd ever heard seen. She made sense though, and she had been around for a long time. Possibly, she could teach me a thing or two, so I kept listening.

"I mean, think about it, you're showing them your great life. At first, it's all flowers and TV shows, and then, bang! They watch you die! It scares the daylights out of them! Half of them don't even know they're dead or what happened to them.

"See that one under that maple tree?" Jodi pointed to the cutest little ghost darting around the tree branches. I nodded, and Jodi continued, "That's Melissa. Well, her family came to bury her back in the twenties. She came with them, but she was already a spirit, like what you see now. She stood next to them, holding her father's hand, even though he didn't feel a thing. She thought they all came here together. She went chasing after a rabbit. Then her family left to go home, she ran after them but they left without her.

"She stood there and cried for days after they left her alone in the cemetery. Because she was dead, she could see me. I was dead, but I didn't look so scary back then. It was before my…second accident. She asked me to help her get home. I didn't really want to, but she was hysterical. She was getting on our nerves, so I took her back to her house." Jodi rolled her eyes. "She didn't know about flying or anything yet so we walked the whole way! It took hours! Then we had to wait outside the door for someone to come out because she didn't know she could go through things! It was friggin' ridiculous!

"When we finally got inside she tugged on everyone's clothes trying to get their attention, but they had no idea we were there. Of course, they ignored us. They wouldn't say anything to her. They just walked around the house, crying and carrying on.

"When we went to her room, all of her toys were gone. Finally, she came back here with me. Probably because I was the only one who talked to her. Some of the other kids asked her to play with 'em. They knew what to say to make her feel better because the same things happened to them. Now we are her family, but I still don't think she understands she's dead.

"The poor dears, most of them think their parents abandoned them. They're afraid of grownups after that, especially if they think one is reaching out to grab them. Even if their parents have been gone for years they remember they always told them to watch out for strangers."

My feelings were hurt they thought I would harm any of them. "Well, thanks, I feel like a witch or something now."

Jodi chuckled, "Nah, they know you're not. They think you're nice. It's just too much for them to visit all of your memories at once. That's all. A lot of them saw you here a long time ago, when you were alive. They know that people called you the Lilac Lady and that you like flowers," Jodi shrugged.
"That's good enough for them. Just play with them and they're happy."

Almost on cue, a flash sped past the tree where we sat and zipped behind a humongous gravestone.

"What the heck was that?" I asked.

"You remember that little brother and sister, Jimmy and Cathy? That was them."

"No way! It didn't even look like a person, it was so fast!"

"Cool! They'll be psyched you're impressed. I've seen you flying around like crazy, man! Shit, you can keep up with that. Hey, wanna sneak up on them?"

Jodi was up for an adventure and I was ready for a change of pace after our serious conversation. Jimmy and Cathy peeked over the gravestone, and then ducked behind it. I was happy Jodi invited me along, rather than challenging me to another one of her mean tests. Besides, I knew I could keep up now. A playful fright might cheer me up.

I figured I had better learn how to make the most of this time on earth, especially if it turned into forever, God forbid. Isn't that funny?

When we're alive, we try to make the most of our time on earth because we don't know how short our time may be. Yet here I was, dead, worrying about how long my time here might drag on.

As far as I knew, the plan was to swoop down to the bottom of the tree and move along the ground toward Jimmy and Cathy. If they were looking for us in the branches, they would be surprised when we jumped up from behind the next gravestone.

Drawing a deep breath, I said, "Let's do it." We waited until Jimmy and Cathy ducked down before making our move.

"This way!" Jodi flew behind the tree and straight down the side of the tree trunk. Of course, I followed close on her heels. When she got to the bottom of the tree she didn't swerve like she was supposed to. She dove straight into the ground, and so did I because I was so close behind her and couldn't avoid it. When I realized I was going to plummet into the earth I closed my eyes and waited for the thud. The impact never came. Opening my eyes, I thought I had stopped myself at the base of the tree, but I found myself inside the ground, surrounded by soil and tree roots.

My movements became slow and labored, worse than being underwater. I hated it! I felt claustrophobic, like I was drowning in sand, even though I didn't need to breathe. I could barely see Jodi looking back to check on me. Everything was grainy and murky and sounds were muffled and distorted. Jodi waited for me as I inched my way along underground. It was so hard to move. I didn't think I was actually moving through the dirt and stones. I think I had to displace them with my body as I went along, like a live person trying to swim in mud or Jello.

Oh, when would I learn? Was Jodi trying to scare Jimmy and Cathy…or me?

Who was playing tricks on whom? I wanted to go back to the tree branch, but I thought I might already be past the halfway point to Jimmy and Cathy, so I kept following Jodi. Jodi saw I was having trouble, and came back to take my hand and hurry me along. She pulled me quicker than I had managed on my own, but it was worse because she dragged me straight through a grave. I couldn't even see it before I realized what was happening. I was afraid I would be stuck underground with my body if I let go of Jodi's hand, so I held on and let her take me through the old grave.

The casket had been crushed by the weight of the dirt. We went straight through its decayed walls. Through the dust that remained inside. It was macabre. I felt like the soil was crushing my spirit as well. I wanted Jodi go on without me. I had to escape this suffocation. Just as I let go of Jodi's hand we broke the surface and rose out of the ground right behind Jimmy and Cathy.

Forgetting I no longer needed to breathe, I gasped for air like I had been dragged out of a riptide. Moving my limbs through the earth took so much effort, but now I was free. I flew into the night air, feeling light once again! It was more liberating than when I died and left my body for the first time. I hoped I would never be reincarnated as an earthworm. I was so happy to return to the surface I forgot why we had gone through the dirt in the first place, until I heard Jodi screaming like a banshee.

She scared me more than she scared the kids. I thought she was dying all over again. The sound she made was positively demonic, while she grimaced with her twisted face so she looked even freakier than before. I thought she was going overboard terrifying those poor kids, but apparently this was how they played. Jimmy and Cathy didn't even flinch. They practically yawned. They wondered what took us so long and then zipped away.

I looked at Jodi and rolled my eyes. "You dragged me through hell for that?! Just for one scream?" I cried to Jodi.

"Well, yeah!" Jodi laughed. She was having a great time.

I clicked my tongue in exasperation. "They didn't even care! That was definitely not worth it. I was suffocating under there, and besides, it was just gross going through that poor person's grave!"

"Oh, lighten up, will ya? You know you're right in the ground over there. We're dead! Hello! We are in…the…ground! It's what they do with us."

"Ha!" I replied. "No way I'm doing that again. Go by yourself next time. Moving around those rocks was harder than it ever was to move my own body. It was like quicksand!"

Jody harrumphed and rolled her eyes. "Whatever. It wasn't that bad."

Tired of arguing for the time being, I remained silent. I was relieved to have my free spirit back. Lifting my arms straight out by my sides I shook them vigorously.

Then I flew around the tree and perched on Sam's headstone. Mine hadn't been installed yet, but I would have chosen to rest on Sam's even if I did have my own. So far, that was the closest I could manage to get to him.

Jodi sat on my stone bench. I really shouldn't call it mine anymore now that I was dead. It belonged to anybody who wanted to sit on it. She flicked her good hand back and forth a few times as if she was dismissing a silly notion. "Well, I guess I'm not as scary as I thought – at least not to them." Jodi sighed nonchalantly. "I'll try harder next time. I didn't think to tell you how different it feels underground. I like to go there sometimes because it's nice and quiet. It's too bad you don't want to do it again."

"No, thanks. I'll rest up here from now on and let my body rest in peace down there," I nodded toward my mounded grave. The image of the body through which Jodi and I had passed kept playing over in my mind, except the person in the coffin would change into Sam, then into me. It wouldn't stop. Maybe my body wanted to get out of the ground, too, like in those zombie movies. Who could blame it? What a horrible place!

Noticing me staring at my grave, Jodi lifted herself off the bench and hovered near the tree. If she had read my thoughts, she knew I started to feel sad again. "Lilla?"

"Hmm?" I replied. Actually, I think Jodi called my name three or four times before I heard her through the fog of my daydream.

"I'm going to Laverne's place. Laverne sells bikes – just got some new ones in. Wanna come see 'em with me?" Jodi backed into the night as she talked. She was being polite by inviting me to come along, but we both knew I was going to remain where I was for the time being.

"No, I think I'll stay here for a while. You have fun. I'll see you later." Forcing a little grin, I waved. Jodi smiled gently back and disappeared down a side street to go see her friend Laverne. I stayed on Sam's grave all night and halfway into the next day. Finally, I floated up to the treetop so I wouldn't get too close to the curious pedestrians who stopped in front of my grave. If I had to listen to one more person remark how that spot was finally filled, I might be driven to start scaring people again.

Gee, do they have to get so emotional? I thought sarcastically. It sounded like they'd been waiting years for me to die.

For three days, I sat in that tree, thinking about all kinds of things. Not just about my days with Sam but my entire life. I was tried to remember everyone I'd ever met and guess what might have happened to them when they died. Were they in heaven? Hell? Or, were they like me? Would we run into each other somewhere in the treetops trying to figure out what happened to us? I wondered what would become of all of the people who passed by every day.

My second day, I watched the cemetery workers erect my headstone. When Sam died, I ordered matching headstones for both of us. Now mine was in place. I checked the inscription to make sure the engravers got everything right. Yup, my name was spelled correctly, and the dates were right, 1940-2028. Even the inscription was the one I had written. I had them detail my date of death as the day I reunited with my husband. I'd always been a hopeless romantic. My epitaph, "…when she joined her husband in eternal peace." sounded beautiful at the time, but now it was a painful lie. I moped in my treetop, feeling sorry for myself as I listened to people who read it comment how sweet and sad it was.

Jodi and Amelia checked on me once in a while, keeping a polite distance. I needed time alone to gather my thoughts. I took solace in knowing when I was ready, I just had to give them a wave and my friends would rejoin me. They knew from experience that I needed time to grieve for my old life before I could embrace my new one.

I missed my life, my "real" life. I missed ice cream. I missed walking in gardens. I missed fixing up our home and showing it off to our friends on holidays. I missed having a daily schedule. I even missed those stupid Wednesday night card games at The Home. I no longer had a body to do these things, and I no longer lived anywhere to do them anymore. My spirit felt light and unencumbered, yet I yearned for a permanent place to "be." I struggled with conflicting feelings of freedom and abandonment.

On third day after my burial, I wouldn't necessarily say I rose from the dead, or anything even remotely as spectacular, but I did go through some sort of catharsis and felt so much better about everything.

I reminisced about my life. I was happy with the directions I took and the years I was blessed with Sam's presence. I would always wait for our reunion, but until that happened I would settle for occasional stops in our grotto to bask in his memory.

I accepted my new immortal life and freedom from my mortal self. Who cares if I couldn't eat ice cream anymore? I used to eat too much of it, anyway. Fixing up the house was great, but then I'd have to clean around all the new bric-a-brac. Now I swoop into other people's homes to gawk at their décor. I could even watch them clean to remind myself of things I would never miss.

Maybe the reunion wouldn't happen here, but somewhere in another part of the world. My new freedom could take me so many places. Who knew? Sam might look down to see me passing by one day and whisk me off to our grotto in the sky, where I wouldn't even have to pull any weeds! Okay, put the violins away. I know I'm getting corny and sappy, even for me, but it makes it easier to think about my time on earth as an adventure, not a sentence.

I needed a break from watching the grass grow over my grave. I was ready to hang around with Amelia and Jodi, but they were nowhere to be found. They grew bored waiting for me, no doubt. Who could blame them? I floated around the cemetery, but it looked different than before. When I first went to Mount Hope after I died, I was confused and searching for answers and for Sam. Everything revolved around me and my problems. It was like when I was underground with Jodi — I couldn't see anything around me and I didn't care what else was out there. I couldn't see past my own immediate situation.

Wandering through the rows of tombstones, I regained my awareness of the world surrounding me. The early morning light cast long rectangular shadows on ground. The grass looked dry in the sunlit areas but dewy and cool in the shadows of the headstones.

I followed a pathway through a grove of trees to the bottom of a gully, surrounded by a Millionaire's Row, a crypt-lined village of Rochester's who's who. Once upon a time, this was one of my favorite summertime hideouts. I often sat on one of the mausoleum steps to eat my lunch, imagining I was the sole occupant of my own little village.

Some of the mausoleums looked like mini Parthenons. They adorned beautiful columns and ornate bars covered their windows. Others, plain cubes with straight iron bars on the windows could have been small jails plucked right out of the Old West. I almost pictured a sheriff leaning back on his chair, whittling a new pipe.

I hoped I would run into Amelia or Jodi, but they weren't anywhere near the mausoleums. Nobody really went down there, which is why I liked going there when I wanted a break from the garden club chatter. Actually, it was a little too quiet for me on this particular day. I was tired of being alone. I wanted to hear some conversation besides my own thoughts running through my head. Three days of that was more than enough. Even old Harvey would be a welcome sight, but I hadn't seen him for a day or two. Everyone must be off doing whatever it is they do.

A change of scenery sounded good to me, too. Since I didn't find anyone in the cemetery, I could go to Marion's house to check on her. I thought about her a few times while I sat in the tree mourning for myself. I wondered how she was doing, so I popped myself into her living room.

I could tell I was feeling better because the ability to wish myself anywhere instantly was incredibly fun to me. This was the first time I didn't wallow about how Sam wasn't here sharing this moment with me. I thought of him, of course, but until we could meet again, I would embrace my new gifts and make the most of my new life.

Tracy Fontaine

<u>Chapter Seven: Marion's Magic Moment</u>

Marion's house looked great. Dusty corners had been swept clean and the kitchen was spotless. Helen and Bill probably cleaned the dickens out of the whole place after the funeral crowd departed. I wondered if they stayed long enough to see the real Cindy, but she probably behaved herself in front of them. It must have tormented her, unless she stayed in her room the entire time guarding her bag of "candy." I hoped I didn't see her. I only wanted to check that Marion was okay.

Soon after I arrived, Marion wandered into the kitchen to make her lunch. It was good to see her eating. She'd always been thin as a rail and couldn't afford to lose any appetite she had. I used to tease her about how jealous I was that she retained her figure so well. We were both around 5'5" and about the same size until we hit our fifties. I packed on a couple of pounds here and there, while she remained svelte. It's hard to fight those genes. My family was on the stocky side, while all of Marion and Sam's relatives were tall and trim.

I wondered if she had considered the eventuality of moving in with Helen and Bill. She seemed okay on her own for now. At least she could make her own meals and keep the house in decent shape, with the exception of Cindy's filthy bedroom. Every now and then, though, I could tell Marion had slowed down. It looked like her arthritis bothered her when she spread mayonnaise on her bread. She fixed herself a ham sandwich and dolloped a scoop of potato salad onto her plate when we both heard a jingling sound upstairs. Marion slammed the potato salad bowl onto the table and marched to the bottom of the stairway.

"Get out of my room!" She yelled up to the open doorway of her bedroom.

Cindy must have gone into her room and bumped into something. Then I remembered the awful Christmas banner hanging on Marion's door. It wasn't just some leftover piece of Christmas crap. It was her alarm! Was it really worth it for Marion to stay in this house if she had to put up with that? She must have been the only one who knew how her roommate behaved.

She waited at the bottom of the stairs to make sure Cindy was empty-handed when she left Marion's room. A moment later we heard the door jingle again as Cindy came out and closed it behind her. She gave Marion a smug look before turning toward her own room down the hall.

"I'm warning you for the last time. Stay out of my room!" Marion sounded brave, but her quivering lips exposed the anxiety she really felt. Would she be able to pull it off? Not this time.

Cindy whipped around to sneer at Marion. "Oh, you're one to talk," she hissed. "You better stay the hell out of my room. I know about that shit you pulled, taking those earrings out of my closet!"

"What earrings? I don't know what you're talking about." Marion replied with confusion.

I felt bad. When I removed Helen's earrings from Cindy's closet and placed them back in Helen's room, I thought it was funny. Especially when Helen wore them right in front of Cindy. It never occurred to me Marion would be blamed for that.

Cindy ignored Marion's plea of innocence and kept talking. "Anyway, what happens if I don't stay out of your room, huh? You'll tell Helen? Then what do you think'll happen? She'll sell this house and drag you down to Pennsylvania so fast your head'll spin! Don't think I didn't hear them talking about it, either!"

Marion was speechless. Cindy won. She waited defiantly with her hands on her hips for a response, but Marion had nothing else to say. She had heard Helen and Bill talking, too, and knew it was only a matter of time. Cindy ducked into her own room and violently slammed the door. Dejected, Marion went back into the kitchen and tried to eat her lunch, but she only picked at it a little before throwing it into the trash. She went into the living room, pausing at the bottom of the stairs to look up and mutter, "Foul-mouthed witch," at the spot where her roommate had been standing.

She pushed the ottoman over to the large end table where her family photos had been on display for years. Sitting silently, she held them, one by one. Marion and Don, their children, their grandchildren. Moments captured in the past, but the memories still lived in that house. I remembered doing the same thing when I convinced myself it was time to leave my home of fifty years.

It was too emotional for me to watch Marion. I felt like I was intruding on her very private moment, so I returned to the cemetery.

I wanted to find Amelia and Jodi because I had been such a sourpuss these last three days. They were kind to give me time to collect my thoughts and I wanted to let them know they didn't have to tiptoe around me anymore. I saw Harvey first. He was checking one of the new trees planted near the main entrance. Rubbing his chin, he looked at the tree from different angles, trying to decide whether he approved of the selection, as though he had any say in the matter.

"Hi, Harvey!" I gave him my most chipper greeting yet. He greeted me with a quick nod.

"They're over there." He pointed over his shoulder toward the river's edge and returned to his business with the tree.

Jeepers, people sure are on the ball here.

I could really get lazy, what with people answering my questions before I asked them. I thanked him quickly and flew over to the river. Amelia and Jodi saw me coming and rushed over to welcome me back. It was somewhat embarrassing because I felt silly for having been so morose.

"Hey, look's who's back from the living!" Amelia exclaimed.

"Yup. Here I am! Back home, I guess," I shrugged, trying to sound more upbeat than I felt. "Sorry I've been so mopey," I grinned.

"It's okay. I was worse than you. Believe me," Amelia said.

"Boy, were you!" Jodi chimed in. Amelia glared at her. "Well, you were! You were a nutcase!" Jodi exclaimed to Amelia. Then she said to me, "Who wouldn't be pissed about this? I think you're doing great. We're glad you're back here."

"Aw, thanks," I replied to them. "I mean it. You've both been so nice. I guess you've seen it all."

"Pretty much," said Amelia. "We looked for you earlier but we couldn't find you. We didn't know if you had left for good."

"No, I don't want to go too far away. I can't leave the places Sam and I shared when we were both still alive. Not yet, at least. I went to his sister's house - you know...my sister-in-law, Marion. I wanted to see how she's doing. I'm worried about her. I mean, she's fine."

"If it was just her it would be no problem, but it's her roommate. She's scary. She steals from everyone who goes into that house. Today I got the feeling she could really hurt Marion if she wanted to. I wouldn't put it past her. I'm thinking about going back for a few nights to make sure her roommate doesn't do anything to her while she's sleeping. What do you think? Is that butting in too much?"

"Oh, not at all! It's pretty normal…well as normal as we get around here. I did that after I died," Amelia said.

"I did it, too," agreed Jodi. "I missed my family so I'd visit them sometimes."

"Good. That makes me feel better. I think I will go back there, at least for a few nights to make sure Marion is safe. So if you're looking for me at night, that's where I'll be."

"Sure," Amelia smiled softly. "We'll keep our fingers crossed for both of you."

My new friends were such comfort. They'd been through this and understood it all too well. If you're in shock and not quite ready to let go of your life here on earth it helps to spend time with your family. It's as much a transition for the dead person as it is for their living relatives. I thought I was doing it for Marion, but it would be nice to spend time in Marion's house as well, before it belonged to somebody else. Many of my memories continued to live there, too.

So Amelia, Jodi, and I spent our days together, and went our separate ways at night. I went to Marion's house while they did their own things. Amelia liked to meander through the city streets and Jodi had been going to her friend Laverne's place at night. I had open invitations to join either one of them if I wanted, but I didn't dare leave Marion alone right now.

Nothing happened while I patrolled Marion's house. I considered taking Amelia up on her offer soon. However, Marion, not Cindy, began doing strange things. She started getting up in the middle of the night and bringing her belongings out to her garage. The first night it was family photos and scrapbooks. The next night it was some of her jewelry and a few books from the living room bookcase. A few nights later, she wrapped up her miniature teacup collection and brought that to the garage.

She had hidden the first few things on a shelf under a tarp, but when she brought her teacups to the garage, she put them right into a box. She took everything off the garage shelf placing them neatly into labeled boxes. Apparently, Marion decided it was time to go, but she must not have told Cindy. She was probably smart to keep it to herself as long as she could, but I couldn't wait for the day when someone finally told Cindy to get lost. I hoped I would be there to see it! I was really proud of Marion and happy for Helen that she would have Marion safe with her.

After a week, Marion's house started showing some bare spots where knick-knacks and pictures had been. Maybe I noticed it because I saw her packing those items into the boxes in her garage. I wondered if Cindy had noticed. If she did, she probably thought Marion was hoarding them in her room so she couldn't steal them. As long as there was food in the fridge and the T.V. worked, I was sure Cindy wouldn't suspect a thing.

Marion was doing a great job at keeping her secret until she tried to move the clock from the mantel. I knew it would be too heavy for her, but I couldn't interfere and risk her seeing me. She dragged it off the mantel into her arms. By that point, she knew it was too heavy, but there was no way she could lift it back onto the mantel. She labored across the living room toward the garage door. Just as she was about to go into the garage, she tripped over the little threshold in the doorway. She lost her grip and the whole clock crashed onto the garage floor, with Marion falling down right next to it.

Fortunately, she landed on her hands and knees on the welcome mat. She didn't appear to be hurt. Marion winced, and I winced for her as a bedroom door flung open upstairs. We both froze and waited breathlessly for the inevitable. Sure enough, in less than a minute Cindy's footsteps thundered down the stairs and through the living room. Marion scrambled to her feet as Cindy neared the garage door.

Personally, if I heard a loud noise in my garage at night I sure as heck would think twice before pushing the door wide open. I mean, wouldn't you at least ask who's there? Maybe threaten to call the cops? Not Cindy. I guess she was scary enough in her own right to hold her own against a burglar.

When she flung the door open, I think she was itching for a fight. There stood little Marion, all quiet and shifty-eyed.

Cindy hadn't bothered throwing a robe over her tight, plaid flannel pajamas. The pajama top strained to contain the folds of flesh that peaked out between every button. Two of her chins hung over the collar. The bottoms were too short, revealing gray mottled socks, which might have been white at one time.

Marion was so nervous, visibly shaking. Cindy stared down at the broken clock pieces on the garage floor. "What the hell are you doing down here? Jesus Christ, I thought we were getting robbed!"

"Oh, I couldn't sleep, so I was just straightening some stuff up. It slipped out of my hands." Marion shifted from one foot to the other. Her eyes darted to the neatly labeled pile of boxes next to the broken clock. Cindy followed Marion's eyes and noticed the boxes that Marion had stacked over the past several weeks. Cindy's eyes narrowed and she stepped into the garage, lifting her feet over the obstacle course that used to be a clock. She read the writing on the wall of boxes.

"China, books, pictures…summer clothes…dishes." Cindy read slowly, then turned to address Marion. Very flatly and slowly, she asked, "What is this?"

Marion sighed. I hoped she could conjure up another lie or two to buy more time for herself, even if Cindy didn't quite believe her. Instead, she spilled her guts. In a tired, detached voice, she put it all out there. "I know it's time for me to go and live with Helen. I didn't know how to tell you, but now I don't care. Let's face it Cindy, you're an ass and I can't stand you. I'm too old for your nonsense and you're not worth it."

I couldn't believe Marion was saying that. Her voice didn't quaver and she looked so relieved to have it out in the open. She even stood a little taller and looked Cindy in the eyes. Cindy's face reddened. I was afraid Marion pushed her a little too far.

Cindy clicked her tongue, leaned on one leg, and crossed her arms like a child about to have a temper tantrum. "Oh, so you're really going to move to Pennsyltucky?" She taunted Marion.

"You got it. Helen wants me to call when I'm ready." She glanced at the boxes and nodded smugly. "Hmm…I think I'll call her tomorrow."

"Well, that's just great. What am I supposed to do? Where am I gonna live?" Cindy demanded.

"I don't know, and I don't care but you better start looking, because I'm going to Pennsylvania so fast your head will spin!" Marion threw Cindy's words right back in her face. She was a little too sassy. I was nervous for her. I thought Marion should be a little more careful, at least until Helen showed up.

Cindy's restraint visibly crumbled. She understood this was a done deal. She couldn't intimidate Marion and go hide in her room anymore. She glared at Marion so intently; I became very concerned. Marion had kept quiet for God knows how many years, but once she reached her breaking point she couldn't stop herself. Then she pushed Cindy's last button.

Marion looked at Cindy and threatened her so sweetly. "Cindy, help yourself to an empty box if you want because if I were you, I'd start packing, too." Realizing she'd gone too far, Marion pulled back after uttering those last words.

Cindy yelled out, "You stupid bitch!" and grabbed a piece of glass from the broken clock face on the floor. Raising her arm over her head, she jabbed at Marion's face with it. Marion didn't have time to protect herself.

I could no longer just watch from the shadows. I needed to step in. When Cindy was less than a foot from Marion, I reached out and blocked her arm, but just barely. My hand hadn't been able to block the skin and muscles on Cindy's arm. Instead, it rested inside her arm, against the solid surface of bone.

It was a real showstopper. I was so angry and worried for Marion's safety that I let my guard down and showed up as plain as day. Both of them stared right at me. Cindy dropped the glass but didn't relax her arm. She gaped in horror at my fingers interwoven with the flesh of her arm. She tried to shield herself from me. My hand still rested against her arm in case she took another swing at Marion, but she forgot about Marion altogether when she saw me. I'm sure she thought I was here to kill her.

Cindy started hyperventilating and screamed, "Oh my God! Oh, God! Get…get away from me! Get away from me! Help!"

She pulled her arm back and tried to run away, but she tripped over the clock pieces and fell. Her head hit the floor with a nauseating crack. She didn't move. I stared down at her and wondered if I killed her. I didn't like her, but I never wanted to kill anybody. It was a horrible feeling. I felt sick as I stared at Cindy, lying still on the floor. I couldn't help feeling, selfishly, that if she was dead, would she return as a spirit to haunt me?

"Lilla? Is that you?" I heard a faint whisper. Marion. She saw me and actually recognized me. She looked afraid. Who could blame her after I had just killed her roommate? I looked in her eyes, but didn't acknowledge her. I pretended that if I didn't see her, she couldn't see me.

I didn't know what to do, but I knew I shouldn't stay there. While Marion stared at me, her roommate's life ebbed away on the floor. I didn't want to abandon Marion, but she needed to stop staring at me and get help for Cindy in case she was still alive. Reluctantly, I disappeared from her garage and hovered just outside the back of the house.

I saw Marion peering out of her garage windows, looking for me. I don't know how much time she spent looking for me in the rest of the house, but at some point she must have called an ambulance. After what seemed like a long time, paramedics showed up and took Cindy away. So far, so good. At least they didn't have to call the coroner. I hoped for the best, that she wouldn't die. I wanted her out of Marion's life, but not like that.

The commotion brought curious neighbors running. Some of them stayed at Marion's house for a while after the ambulance left. I'm sure Marion called Helen and Bill, but I hoped the neighbors would keep an eye on her until Helen could get there. Eventually, the neighbors returned home to get ready for work that day.

It was almost six in the morning. I peeked in one last time and saw Marion sleeping in her bed with her bedroom door open. It's funny, but even if Marion had to stay alone for a few days, I had no doubt she was better off than when Cindy roamed around. I bet Marion slept more soundly than she had in a long time. For the first time since my funeral, I felt I didn't need to worry about her.

I slipped over to the cemetery to tell Amelia what happened. She was happy for Marion, too, even though she'd never met her. Jodi came along with a bunch of hideous plastic flowers she plundered from the garbage pile. She looked like a young woman, but because of her disfigurement and precocious language, I tended to forget she was only fourteen when she died, still prone to childish impulses like picking treasures out of the trash.

Some things never change. I did the same thing when I was a kid. My cousins and I played in a cemetery and found a pile of junk. We brought our loot home to our mothers - faded, dirty bouquets of plastic funeral flowers and a banner with "Grandma" written in gold. To say our mothers were not impressed was putting it mildly.

First, they said a quick prayer so we would be forgiven for desecrating the cemetery. Then they told us to take those germy, dirty things back to the cemetery and come home for a good scrubbing. Jodi was a little older than we were when we did that, but I could understand the attraction to the colorful cemetery trash pile. I should have known she had bigger plans, though. She went to a very prominent grave near one of the access roads and carefully arranged the faded flowers with the missing petals. It looked like a loving family with poor taste had placed them there years ago.

"Now, all we have to do is wait," Jodi said.

"What are we waiting for?" I asked.

"For Harvey, of course," Jodi replied, annoyed I didn't understand yet.

Apparently, even though Harvey had been dead for a hundred years, he still went crazy when he saw plastic flowers. He hated them even more than marigolds. Poor Harvey. Jodi knew her victim came down this road at least once a night. After a hundred years, he'd settled into a predictable routine. As spirits, we had all of the freedom imaginable, but Harvey preferred sticking to a schedule. That's what gave him purpose; he pretended he was a living person, with appointments that mattered to someone.

Sure enough, I felt him approaching. He was even a little early that day. He came out of a clump of rose bushes and turned down the road toward us, so we ducked behind a large monument. He went straight to the ugly arrangement and yanked out every plastic flower, stem, and leaf.

117

Jodi had only lightly set them in the soil, so they came out easily. Dirt flew everywhere. I still had trouble reading thoughts of others who weren't communicating directly to me, but Harvey's brain spewed such a tirade even I understood most of it.

"What the…What's going on here?…ugly junk…nobody appreciates the good stuff anymore, the real stuff…add insult to injury…"

He spouted off while Amelia, Jodi, and I listened from behind the monument. He sprinkled an occasional obscenity here and there, but not nearly as much as I expected from such a gruff looking man. Maybe after all these years, some of that polite shoe salesman still dwelled somewhere in his soul.

Arms flailing, he was quite a sight. That Harvey. He became so worked up over the smallest things that upset his perfect world. Just when I started thinking how it was easier to fool Harvey than it was to fool me, he came right over to us with his fists full of mangled plastic flowers. Some of the broken fragments fell through his ghostly hands, landing on the ground beside us.

"I couldn't begin to guess which one of you put these out. Don't you have any respect for the dead? They don't want to look at this stuff. It's horrid. Just horrid!" He looked right at Jodi, who didn't even try feigning innocence. We all laughed out loud, except for Harvey.

"I'm puttin' these back in the garbage! And you leave'em be!" He floated away in a huff, carrying the tacky decoration with him. As he faded into the night, so did his words. He was still going on about filthy junk, and how only real flowers are proper. We listened until he was too far away to hear or see. Then we burst into laughter again.

"How did he ever know it was you?" I asked Jodi.

"Oh yeah, whenever I find something really crusty, I fetch it back for 'im. It's fun. He's not such a bad old codger. I know he's not really pissed. It gives him something to fix. He says the same thing every time, but it still makes me laugh."

It made me laugh, too. I felt good that day and was coming out of my funk. I was happy Marion was okay about living with Helen and I was glad her roommate was gone. I checked on Marion once that night. She was sleeping the most peacefully yet.

I went to her house a few times over the next couple of days and watched her pack more of her things. Now she did it in broad daylight. She took down the ugly Christmas banner alarm from her door and threw it into Cindy's room, which, for the most part, remained untouched. I didn't know what they were planning to do with the junk in that room. They should have a bonfire or something.

Two days after Cindy had been taken away in the ambulance, two cars pulled into Marion's driveway. One was Helen's and the other one belonged to a realtor. Helen, the realtor, and Marion walked through the rooms, summing up the good and bad selling points of Marion's old but tidy Cape Cod house. The furnace was old and the house needed painting both inside and out, but the neighborhood itself had held up okay which, according to the realtor, was its best feature. She assured Marion and Helen that they could get a fair price and a quick sale. The idea of slapping a price tag on a house full of their memories probably caused mixed emotions for both Helen and Marion.

As I followed them room to room, Marion conducted the tour. "This is my room, and that's Helen's room…and Tom's room is down the hall on the left." Even though neither Helen nor Tom had lived in that house for years, those rooms would always be theirs as far as Marion was concerned.

Marion answered the realtor's questions about the last time any work had been done in the house. "Hmm. It's been a long time since we painted up here, maybe thirty years ago." Marion's face looked apologetic. Her look changed to cheer as she looked at the floor and said, "I did just get new carpets through the whole house a few years ago."

"Mom, that was like twenty five years ago," Helen chortled.

Marion stopped to think for a minute. "Mercy, has it been that long?" she wondered aloud.

"At least," Helen raised her eyebrows. Then she sighed. "We should probably paint and put down some new carpet, right? What do you think?" She winced as she waited for the realtor to answer.

"I don't think I'd worry about it."
"Really?" Helen leaned against the wall, visibly relieved. Marion smiled but Helen was the happier of the two since she and her husband would no doubt have had to do all of the work.

"Oh, great!" Helen exhaled. "That is such a relief! I mean, I totally expected we'd have to paint!"

The realtor replied, "I wouldn't just yet. I've never had trouble selling houses around here. Actually, they've been selling really well in the past year. You should see one I sold last week for the exact asking price! Chipped plaster, broken moldings. People are buying.

"The only things I would recommend are to give the walls a good once-over. You know, just scrub them down. Then, steam clean the carpets and you'll be good to go. This neighborhood will sell the house for you."

Marion put her hand across Helen's back. "You have your father to thank for that!" she said with a gleam in her eye. Then she turned to the realtor and said, "Don had such a knack for that kind of thing. He always knew a good buy."

"You're definitely in good shape here. Just take care of those couple of things and you'll be fine." The realtor put her hand on Marion's arm. "We'll see how it goes. This house has a great layout. It's a real family home. Someone will fall in love with it quickly."

I was impressed with the realtor's sensitivity. Marion smiled and dabbed a tear from the corner of her eye. She nodded silently.

The three women paused in front of the door to Cindy's room.

"Uh…How is she doing, anyway?" The realtor's cautious question indicated she'd been briefed.

"Oh, she's got a broken hip," Helen replied. "When the hospital discharges her they'll move her to a rehab center until she can get around her own place well enough."

I hadn't killed her after all! Phew!

Helen reached for the doorknob, pausing before she turned it. "I'm sorry I haven't had a chance to do anything in here yet. Things have been so crazy. Tomorrow I'm going to clean it out and take her stuff to Social Services. They're taking care of everything now."

"No problem. I'm sure you'll have everything sorted out by the time the listing goes through."

"Yes, definitely!" Helen assured the realtor as she opened the door.

While the items from the rest of the house had been packed and pared down to the bare necessities by Marion, Cindy's room remained virtually untouched. The bed was still unmade.

Beyond Lilla

Clothes and magazines littered the floor. The Christmas banner lay across the dresser where Marion had thrown it. That must have made the realtor wonder what went on in that room.

None of the three women wanted to go into this unkempt lair. I'd have to guess the room probably smelled pretty rank, too. For the first time since I died, I was thankful my sniffer didn't work. The realtor assessed this room from the hallway. Despite Helen's gentle warnings, I think she was still taken aback at how disheveled this room was compared to the rest of the house.

Helen cleared her throat and said, "Yeah...um...it's pretty bad. You know, I think I'll start on it today if I have time. I promise by tomorrow night you won't recognize it. Whether I pack or toss things, they'll all be gone before any buyers come through." Helen was already closing the door as she spoke that last line, obviously embarrassed by the sight of that room.

Helen ushered the realtor back downstairs, with Marion following as best she could. They walked around the outside of the house and the yard and talked about the going rate for the neighborhood. Helen thanked the realtor and told her she was happy to get the ball rolling. The realtor drove away, but promised to return soon with a contract and a sign for the front yard.

Helen went back inside the house and changed into jeans and an old sweatshirt. Time to get to work. She headed up to Cindy's room to start sifting through the piles of junk, but before she started, she also donned a pair of rubber gloves. I couldn't blame her. I wouldn't want to touch any of that stuff with my bare hands, either. Marion watched from the bedroom doorway. I think she was a little afraid of Cindy's leftover aura. She would be glad when all of that stuff was gone and the room would revert from "Cindy's room" back to "Tom's room."

Marion brought up some boxes for the clothes, while Helen folded and sorted them into piles of shirts, pants and sweaters. It took Helen almost an hour before the floor was completely visible and she could walk from one side of the room to the other.

"Well, that's a start," she said to Marion as she looked around for the next mess to tackle.

She lifted the Christmas banner off the dresser and held it at arm's length. She scrutinized the sappy reindeer face with missing paint. "I wonder how much lead is in this thing…or was in this thing before the paint flaked off?"

She shook the banner. As it jingled, even more paint flaked from the ugly bells onto the floor. "Look, Mom! Snow! If you hurry you can catch it on your tongue!" She and Marion both laughed. "God! This is so ugly!" Then she turned to Marion and said "Hey, wait a minute…Mom, isn't this yours?"

"Yeah, it used to be, but I think Cindy should have it. Put it in that box with her clothes. Sort of a housewarming for her new place. Unless you want it. It could be a valuable heirloom someday."

"No, I think I'll pass. I wouldn't want to be responsible for such a priceless treasure." I'm sure Helen was relieved the banner wasn't going to become part of her household.

Marion and Helen both laughed as they folded the ugly banner and tucked it into a box of clothes. Someday when Cindy opened this box, the banner would jingle warmly, "Hello, remember me?" At which point she'll tear it to shreds.

Over the next couple of days things moved right along at Marion's house. Cindy's room was tidy and full of boxes marked with her name. The "For Sale" sign was up and people were already driving past the house, slowing down for a better look. Helen's husband Bill and their son John showed up with a U-Haul one Saturday around noon. Helen and Marion had made a large lunch, obviously expecting Bill and John at that time. They met them in the foyer, which was piled high with bags and boxes that were to be dropped off at a donation center.

Most of the items were Helen's and Tom's things from the attic, toys and clothes that had been stored and forgotten for forty years. Marion didn't want to throw them away without asking the "kids." Helen assured her it was okay to get rid of the old banking game that was missing all of the play money, as well as her stretch pants from 1988. She wouldn't be able to fit into them anymore, nor would she want to. They were authentic vintage, now, so let the kids at the thrift stores have dibs on them.

Helen did take a couple of her old dolls and Tom's Matchbox cars, which she would send to him in Texas. After so many years, it was easy to toss away most of the dusty worn relics.

Bill and John maneuvered their way around the donation pile and greeted Helen and Marion. Then they all sat down to lunch and planned how they would remove most of the items from the house that day. Bill, John, and one of Marion's neighbors would load up the U-Haul. Helen and Marion would make a trip to the donation center, then come back for Cindy's stuff and take it to her. There was a quiet moment, when Helen said something about wanting to leave Cindy's boxes for the trash man or maybe burn them. I did a double take. What was this hostility I was hearing? Marion must have told Helen everything that went on around there.

"Dear," Bill said and raised his eyebrows to indicate he didn't want to hear that tired old story again. Helen looked back at him with her mouth open as though she couldn't believe he wasn't as riled as she was.

"Ugh! She doesn't deserve to get any of her things! We have been way too nice to her." Helen spoke tersely before biting into her sandwich.

"Why? What's going on?" John asked, with his mouth full. He glanced back and forth to both parents. He didn't want to waste time swallowing before asking or he might have missed the moment.

Bill sighed and rolled his eyes because he knew his wife didn't need much prodding. Helen launched into her story of Cindy the cheater, liar, and thief, for which even I was unprepared. This was getting good.

"Well, first of all," Helen leaned toward John for dramatic effect and because he was the only one for whom this was news. "She wasn't as poor as she pretended. Not by a long shot. She has over fifty thousand dollars in a savings account. Fifty thousand! Oh, and she even owns some decent stock. She's just as cheap and selfish as they come. Or, maybe just crazy. Oh! Guess what I found in her room."

Of course, John wouldn't know the answer. He didn't even dare to guess. I was afraid it was going to be something like a dead cat.

"Grandpa's wedding ring and my pearl earrings in her dresser drawer!" Marion shouted, slapping her hand on the table, making everyone jump. "Took'em right out of my room. I know she did!"

Bill sat silently while both women vied for John's attention, as they rattled off the things Cindy had done.

"There was a bag of money in her drawer. It had almost nine hundred dollars in it!" Helen added. "I know she took some from us."

"Come on, Helen, you don't know where she got it from. She could have been saving her own money." Bill was being too nice. Was it diplomacy or naiveté? I couldn't decide.

"No way." Helen stuck by her accusation. "Every time I came here, I ran short of money. I always knew I had more when I got here than when I left."

"It's true. You're right. She was sneaky," Marion defended Helen and patted her hand as she spoke.

"Wow, that's pretty bad, Grandma," John agreed. "Why'd you let her live here in the first place?"

Marion felt stupid for letting Cindy bully her around, but the way she explained it, anybody would have been fooled. "Well, sweetie, she was so nice at first. She went to church every Sunday…and bingo on Tuesdays. That's where I met 'er. We'd talk and laugh so hard! We had such a good time. She told me she was having a hard time making ends meet, so I said 'Why don't you come live with me?' So she did.

"Right after that, she got really mean. She'd change the T.V. channels without asking, and she ate me out of house and home. She just wanted somewhere to live cheap, and a landlady she could intimidate. Boy, I'm sure glad she's gone!"

"Sounds like you're coming to Pennsylvania just in time. So what's she doing now?"

Sensing Bill was tired of hearing her story, Helen spoke briskly. "Well, she's still in the hospital, but then she goes to a nursing home to recoup from her broken hip. That's where Social Services told me to bring her things. They can worry about storing them for her. After that, who knows? Someone's working with her to set her up in either a home or a senior apartment. All I know is, we're done."

"Good, let's keep it that way, all right?" Bill's voice was large and his word was final.

Everyone was quiet while searching for something else to talk about. Then Marion brought up something even better. Me.

"You know, I have a guardian angel," Marion positively beamed as she loudly whispered her secret. She looked around the table wryly, waiting to see who would bite first.

I had been hovering all over the kitchen. I knew nobody had seen me, not even Marion. I was as surprised as everyone else was when she blurted that. I snuck through the kitchen wall into the living room in case the mere mention of my name might make me materialize. If any of them tried to be funny and said they could see me, I didn't want to wonder if they were just joshing or if it was for real.

Helen, Bill, and John rolled their eyes and laughed to each other at goofy Grandma. Good for me, bad for poor Marion.

"Mom, really," Helen tried to stifle her mother's crazy talk. She'd had listened to it all week and hoped Marion would tire of the subject. However, old folks like me and Marion don't have a lot of other things to do but obsess on anything even remotely out of the ordinary.

"You know who it is?" Marion ignored Helen and spoke excitedly to Bill and John. "It's your Aunt Lilla!" she exclaimed.

"She thinks she saw Aunt Lilla," Helen whispered loudly across the table to Bill and John, without actually leaning over to them. She was trying to convey how foolish Marion's idea would sound to others, hoping to shame Marion into shutting up.

There was another moment of silence while everyone tried to think of good reactions.

"That's cool, Grandma. What was she doing?" John really didn't know what else to say. He was just being polite, but Helen was annoyed that he egged his grandmother on.

"She saved me from Cindy. She's my guardian angel. I saw her, you know."

I saw "The Look" flash between Bill and John. You know, the "Grandma's nuts" look. Grandma said something comical at her own expense and she was the only one who didn't realize it.

Believe me, we old folks see more than you think we do. We merely choose to ignore it. If Marion caught it this time, she let it pass. She did quiet down, but not like they'd hurt her feelings or anything. She had her say and they didn't have to believe her if they didn't want to. She knew it was true but also knew better than to try to discuss it further.

"Okay, let's clean off the table and get busy." Helen ended the conversation and hustled everyone away from the table. They had eaten on paper plates because the regular dishes had been packed, so she swept everything into a garbage bag.

For the rest of the day, everyone worked doggedly to empty out the house. Helen made two trips to the thrift store, and another trip to get rid of Cindy's belongings. I didn't follow her to see if she really took them to the nursing facility or if she just dumped them in the river. I guess at that point neither one of us cared. Cindy and her stuff were gone.

The U-Haul was stacked like a block of Legos. You couldn't squeeze a piece of paper between the sofa and the dressers. The men in the neighborhood had drifted over and elevated it to a science. Two men carried something into the U-Haul while three men stood outside discussing the best way to stack it on top of the piles that were already inside. I think Bill appreciated most of the suggestions -- I only saw him grimace a couple of times. Overall, I'm sure the extra help made things go more quickly.

Around seven o'clock, the commotion died down, and I realized the house was almost empty. There were a few items that Helen and Bill would come back for in a week or two, but for the most part, they were ready to hit the road. Helen and Marion strolled around the rooms, arm in arm. They both dabbed occasional tears rolling down their cheeks. Their voices echoed down the bare hallway. "Are you okay, Mom?"

"Oh, yes, yes," Marion sniffled. "These empty rooms remind me of when your father and I first bought this house. It was so long ago," Marion sighed and blew her nose. She composed herself and said, "The longer I stand here, the harder it gets. We better get going. You have a long drive. And Bill has to drive that big truck."

"Yeah, we should go." Helen put her arm around Marion as they walked out the door, locking it behind them. On the way to the car, Helen continued in a soothing voice, "Boy, you wouldn't believe all the cool things I found back home, Mom. I started looking at clubs for seniors. There is so much fun stuff going on all the time! Oh, and I'm going to get you together with my friend Megan's mom and some of our friends from church."

"Oh, don't worry about me. Anybody will be better than you know who." Marion cracked a sad smile as she walked past Bill. He shook his head and patted her gently on her back. Marion and Helen giggled. They could swap Cindy stories the whole way to Pennsylvania without Bill changing the subject just when it was getting good.

Bill and John checked the latches on the U-Haul door and hopped into the seats in the cab. They started the truck and slowly pulled out onto the road. Helen and Marion situated themselves into Helen's car. After Helen helped Marion with her seat belt, she pulled out of the driveway behind the U-Haul. Both vehicles rolled down the street and Marion was on her way to her safe new life. She was sad to leave and so was I. I was going to miss coming to her house. This was one of the last connections to my life where I could almost touch the old days. It was good because things would be better for her and Helen this way.

Helen must have been excited bringing Marion down to Pennsylvania to live with her. She would get to introduce all of her friends to her kooky mother who talked about ghosts and guardian angels. Now that would be some fine entertainment.

I watched the U-Haul and the car turn onto the street that would take them to the highway. I suppose I could have watched them travel all the way to Pennsylvania, but that would have been excruciatingly slow for me. I had gotten used to moving so quickly; following a moving van through the Pennsylvania hills would feel like an eternity. I blew a kiss to the car; a good luck wish to Marion from her guardian angel.

Tracy Fontaine

Chapter Eight: Meet and Greet

Once I dealt with the fact that this was how things were for the time being, my afterlife wasn't so bad. The timing helped me cope a little. Fall had always been my favorite time of year. Even though leaves and grasses withered into winter hibernation, their colors and earthy scents invigorated me and Sam. As dried remnants of summer blew across yards, we'd feverishly prepare new radio spots and write chapter after chapter for our "how-to" books. We fed off each other's energy.

If I had to die and then suffer the added shock of realizing I wasn't going to The Promised Land, this was the time of year to do it. Fall put me in the best of spirits no matter how bleak the events in my life. Although I couldn't "smell" fall, at least I could see it. Dry leaves fluttered across the cemetery. Walkers wore cozy sweaters. Red leaves glowed against dark skies. The fall season pulled me out of my post-death depression. My eyes awakened to the changing plants as well as the rest of the world around me.

Up until that point, I had been so self-absorbed, I hadn't even noticed the others. Creatures like me, Jodi, Amelia, and Harvey, floated all over the place. So many of them! Not once when I was alive did I ever imagine this invisible world of the dead intertwined throughout the midst of us living breathing people. Each one had their own gig. Some hovered over their graves or the grave of a loved one. Some wrung their hands and looked to the heavens for salvation; that could have been me if I hadn't snapped out of my funk when I did.

Others flitted nervously, haunted by visions only they could see. A few lurked mysteriously in the shadows, eyeing both the living and the dead suspiciously. Crazy in life…crazier in death, no doubt. Many spirits remained isolated in their own worlds. They traveled among us, but existed in a universe of one, paying no mind to any others, always deep in thought. Sometimes they mumbled and I wondered if they were talking to themselves or to other spirits in yet another dimension. They were so engrossed, it was impossible for me to ask them any questions, so I did what everybody else did and just ignored them.

With the exception of the oddball spirit, most everyone exchanged greetings in passing. Usually a familial nod, but chitchat was not uncommon. Thus, everybody got to know one another. "What's your name? How'd you die…and when? Are you from around here? Have family nearby?" You know, the usual small talk. I never knew what to say to that last question about the family. Were they talking about living relatives…or dead ones buried nearby?

I met hundreds of souls. They were everywhere! After a while, it became hard to keep everyone straight. Like Henrietta, Blanche, and Eduardo. They all died in separate car accidents, but I couldn't remember who died where, when, or under what circumstances. Then there was Buell and Max: They died in The Civil War, but I couldn't tell you on which battlefield or if they died from gunshots or canon blasts. If I stood near them, I could read their memories, which helped a little. From a distance, though, it was hard to read their thoughts. I laughed at myself when I realized I was squinting to "see" into their minds better!

For the most part, I settled in comfortably with Amelia, Jodi, and Harvey. I don't know if it was because they were the first souls I met, or if we bonded because we all had some sort of connection to this cemetery during our lifetimes. Amelia in her house next door, practically living within the cemetery gates, sneaking in to write her stories; Harvey, so distraught by the tragic deaths of his wife and son, that he actually did live in the cemetery; And Jodi…I'm not sure if she had any particular attachment to this place other than she was probably one of the oldest souls here. Maybe because Amelia and I never had children of our own, we became Jodie's Auntie figures.

A few other characters came around regularly. Nolan was notable and easy to remember because his soul appeared without legs. My mnemonic device was "No-lan has no legs." Stricken with polio as a child, he'd been confined to a wheelchair. He was a successful realtor around Rochester and liked to joke that he stood on "his own two wheels." After he died, he discovered he could float through the air as quickly as anybody else could. He didn't need his legs to get by when he was alive so I guess he didn't see them as part of his identity in death, either.

Mr. and Mrs. Judson were nice, too, always tending to the graves of their three children, who must have been able to move on, as I never did see them. Two of the children died before their first birthdays. The third child died at seventeen, from an infection that set into his foot after a farming accident. Fresh flowers always graced the Judson children's graves. Just a bud or two, whatever the Judsons could borrow from another grave or from a neighborhood garden. Every now and then, if I passed some unattended flowers, I'd pluck one for Mrs. Judson. She always thanked me warmly, and had me wait while she placed it on the graves.

Then there was Victoria, with her incessant mumbling of, "Who is John Galt? Who is John Galt?" If you were unlucky enough to make eye contact, she'd whoosh right over to your face and demand to know, "Who is John Galt?" I made that mistake once. Before I knew her, I waved hello from across the pond, and without warning came face to face with Victoria who asked sternly, "Who is John Galt?"

"Who?" I asked, which was stupid, I thought, because if she knew the answer to that question, she wouldn't have asked it in the first place.

"Who is John Galt?" she demanded again.

"I...uh..." I stammered, trying to come up with either an answer or a way to get away from her. Thankfully, Harvey was eavesdropping nearby.

"Aw, c'mon. You're not gonna start that again, are ya?" he asked Victoria.

"Why not? More people around here should know the answer to that question. Just like they should know the difference between a fiddle and a violin." She turned to Harvey, "You do know the difference between a fiddle and a violin, don't you?" she asked Harvey the former fiddle player. Without waiting for his response she sneered, "A violin plays music."

"Shut up, Vicky." The only insult Harvey could fling back was to shorten her name to its less regal version. Apparently, it was enough. Victoria reeled around and disappeared in a huff.

"Thank you, Harvey!" I thought loudly, hoping he would hear me. I avoided Victoria from then on.

As for the children, Althea was one of my favorites. She was probably only about four, and was so darn cute! She told the strangest stories, hodgepodging her real life in the past with things she saw after she died. One day she followed me around for hours talking about how she wanted to be in pictures.

"Oh, Mary Pickford! I'm going to be in pictures like her someday. And Shirley Temple! She's little like me…but I can dance like her. Watch this! 'On the good ship Lollipop,'" she sang and did a little dance for me. I think it would have been a tap dance if she were able to make sounds and wear shoes. "I asked Mother to get a VCR so I could watch Shirley and practice to be like her…then…then I could sing on the internet for the whole world and be famous and then I would be in a picture with Shirley…" Althea paused and sighed. "Aww, but then the war came. You know, the second one? And Mother said we had to 'tighten our belts.' We couldn't get our VCR…and I could only sing to the Victrola again. Like this. Hey, listen!" Althea thrust her chest out and marched away singing, "…animal crackers in my soup."

I smiled and nodded while she told her disjointed stories. I contained my laughter until she walked away so she didn't think I was making fun of her. She cracked me up! What especially endeared Althea to me were the pet names she used for everybody. She called me Lima, mostly because she just couldn't say Lilla. Whenever I heard someone call out for Lima, I knew she was looking for me.

I finally met one of her other friends, Teddy Bear. I couldn't understand the weird story she kept telling me about her teddy bear. It took me two days to realize Teddy had been a real person, a full-grown soldier in World War II. If Amelia was the big sister/auntie to the children's souls around here, Teddy was the big brother/uncle. They loved him, and he loved to roughhouse with them. He was an all-around nice guy – and polite! He always appeared in uniform, so to me he became Soldier Teddy.

Like many restless spirits, Teddy disappeared for stretches at a time. I thought he might be revisiting places where he served as a soldier. Wherever he went, he always returned to Mount Hope Cemetery. He told me he felt such peace here. Once he thanked me for building it!

That cracked me up. He was way off the mark there, but I thanked him for his exaggerated compliment. He must have forgotten he was there way before me. I hoped Harvey didn't hear that – he'd have a cow after dedicating his whole life to this place! I stressed to Teddy that I just pulled a few weeds and planted a few bushes.

I thought it would be interesting to look into each other's pasts, so he could see my life with Sam and I could look into his soldier's world. We linked hands and he took me through his earliest memories. Most of it was pretty basic…boy is born, goes to school, hates girls, likes girls, rides a bike, drives a car, works at a gas station, and then…goes to war. It occurred so suddenly. There he was, sitting in the back of a military vehicle with other soldiers. They were riding on rough water, pitching and rolling, heading toward the beach where most of the soldiers in his landing craft would die.

"Whoa! That's all for me!" I exclaimed, yanking my hands and arms back.

I didn't want to work through what would happen next. As I discovered when I struggle to share Amelia's memories, when we share memories that way, it's even deeper than watching a movie. We don't just feel that person's pain – we relive it. We hear, smell, and taste everything just as they did when they lived it during their lives. Before I pulled away, I felt Soldier Teddy's nervous, wet hands tighten their grip on his weapon. His stomach had knotted up and his heart pounded like it was going to explode.

Teddy's death in that WWII battle struck an almost forgotten memory for me of Nana, my crazy grandma. I thought if I watched it too closely through his eyes, I would lose my mind like Nana. She was never right after my Uncle Ralph died in WWII. I couldn't take that chance.

I was a baby at the time, so I never really knew Nana when she was in her right mind. I never knew exactly when or how Uncle Ralph died, but I had a feeling it was that singular event which sent Nana's brain into a tailspin. All my life, every family event was recollected in terms of "before" or "after" that time. Because everyone in the family kept it so hushed, I was always afraid to ask.

Ever since I could remember, Nana rambled on about the fates suffered by our soldiers who faced the horrors of war. She endlessly bashed the Japanese and the Germans. Her legacy to me was paranoia of both.

When I went to an integrated college in North Carolina, everyone else in the country was concerned about how the Blacks and Whites were getting along, but Nana warned me to watch out for the Japanese. Fortunately, by the time I reached my thirties, my fear of Japanese people faded into a mild curiosity.

I wish I could say the same about the wartime scenes themselves. The way Nana fabricated her war stories with such detail and conviction; you'd swear she'd been on the front line herself. She frightened me so much; I could never stomach war movies, not even the comedies. There was no way I could go on a tour of duty through an actual battle scene in Teddy's head. I hoped he didn't think I was a heel. He had probably already read my thoughts, like everyone else around here, so maybe he knew my reasons. I apologized anyway, for pulling away so abruptly. I told him he was more than welcome to tell me about it. We made a deal, though. If it started upsetting me, I reserved the right to ask him to stop.

So, with a "Yes, ma'am. Thank you, ma'am," Teddy picked up where he left off, with his unit arriving on the beaches of Normandy. As the soldiers left their amphibious vehicles, the weight of their backpacks dragged them down into the water. Many of them drowned before ever setting foot on the beach. Teddy managed to make it to solid ground, quite possibly by stepping on the bodies of fallen soldiers. He wasn't sure how he made it that far. Like so many of the men around him, he was trying to survive and couldn't even think about firing at the enemy yet.

Nothing could have prepared him for the mass confusion. It was impossible to see through the smoke from the gunfire, and even harder to hear any commands. Voices of the injured and voices of those shouting orders melded indiscernibly into the deafening din of battle. With bullets whizzing right by his head, Soldier Teddy managed to get his feet on solid ground and ran about twenty feet when a piece of shrapnel hit his helmet so hard it knocked him to the ground.

After what felt like an eternity, but was probably only a minute or two, Teddy rose to continue toward the safer, sheltered area of the beach. However, things were not the same. His gear was lighter. He could see the beach more clearly, and make out distinct voices. Then he saw his body, lying exactly where it had fallen. A piece of shrapnel hadn't just clipped him. A bullet had completely pierced his helmet with such a clean fatal shot that he died instantly.

Teddy screamed "No!" about a dozen times, as he pounded on his body to revive it. Looking around the beach, he saw many more soldiers than before. The live ones struggled toward safety, but he also saw the ones who didn't survive. For every corpse lying on the beach, there was a soul grieving at its loss. Some tried to revive their bodies by tugging at them, as Teddy had done and failed. Some desperate souls tried crawling back into their bodies to reanimate them from the inside.

Teddy said it was terribly gruesome. I told him I was glad I chose to listen to his story rather than experience it through his mind. The imagery conjured up by his description was all I could bear. I didn't need to taste the blood of that scene.

Soldiers continued pouring onto the beach. They forged their way through the water onto the sand. Blinded by smoke, sweat, blood and salt water, they grasped at any solid footing they could find. Teddy knelt next to his body as men staggered over it. He screamed for help. His ghostly hands grasped futilely at any passing soldier. The living soldiers heard and felt nothing from Teddy. Even if they did, it was nearly impossible to help the wounded. As Teddy watched them struggle on to meet their own destinies, he knew they couldn't help one dead soldier among the hundreds of other bodies.

As he recounted the tale of his brave death, Teddy's last battle replayed vividly in his own head. He grew quieter and quieter as his story unfolded, until I could barely hear the end. I wanted to comfort him by patting his shoulder, but I was afraid if I made any physical contact, Teddy's frightful memories would travel from his brain into mine. I knew I was being selfish, but I was apprehensive of what would happen if I gazed upon the horrors. Those visions destroyed Nana, and she had only heard about it on the radio and when she was notified of Uncle Ralph's death.

I did the best I could…with the first clichés that came to mind. "Oh, Teddy," I said as quietly as he had spoken, "I'm so sorry…that must have been terrifying."

Teddy released a nervous twitter. As pathetic as my condolence was, it gave him a break from his story and a chance to collect himself. He cleared his throat. "Really, I'm fine," he replied. His voice returned to its normal tone, the emotional quivering gone. "I'm fine now," he continued, "but I was anything but…on that day."

Please don't cry. I can't take it when soldiers cry. I thought to myself. At least I thought I had thought it to myself. Will I ever learn?

"Nah, I won't cry on ya!" Teddy replied to my thoughts. "Actually, and this is the part I feel the guiltiest about…" Teddy paused and grew somber. "I left. I left the fight. I left my buddies. I never went back until years later. It was too late to help myself, and I couldn't help anyone else, either. Boy, if I could've shot at least one German to give even one G.I. a chance to make it, I would have. But, I couldn't do it. I couldn't lift my weapon…you know how it is."

"Boy, do I," I rolled my eyes when I responded. That's one part of his story I could relate to, feeling as useless as a newborn when I crossed over into this new life. "So, where did you go until they brought your body back here?" I ventured to ask. I hoped I wouldn't upset him. If I hadn't asked him outright, Teddy would have "heard" the question in my head anyway.

"Well, you know…I'm not even buried here. My body is in one of those big cemeteries over in France. I'll tell you what though – I thought the same thing. I…I just couldn't keep watching everyone die on the front line, so I came back here. Well not here." He motioned at the surrounding cemetery.

"I came back to Rochester. I figured my body would get here eventually. I didn't go back to my house until I was sure the War Department already told my folks. I couldn't bear to see 'em get the news. I guess things just worked out kind 'a strange. Lots of fellas like me are buried over there. I don't know what happened to them after that…if they went to heaven or back to wherever it was they called home when they were alive.

Once in a while I go over to see my grave, but I spend most of my time right here. I guess it's just where I feel the happiest. Well, anyway, that's my story. I'm sure you've heard enough."

Teddy sighed. At the beginning of his story I was concerned because he seemed so introspective, but by the end he seemed almost bored. He casually leaned against a monument and spoke in the blasé manner of someone who has repeated a story umpteen times. Then his head and shoulders jerked slightly to attention. An expression of discovery washed over his face as something dawned on him. "You know, me not being buried here, but still spending most of my time here? It's sort of like…" he trailed off. He must have decided it wasn't important.

"Hello, Ted! Hello, Lilla!" Amelia bobbed out of the bushes, unusually chipper.

"Oh, hi Amelia," Teddy and I said at the same time.

"Teddy was telling me about the war and how he got here," I said. "Well, how he's here now, but his body's no…" I became flustered before I finished the sentence because I didn't know how much he'd told the others. "Oh! Sorry, Teddy. Maybe I shouldn't have mentioned that?"

"Don't worry about it. Everyone knows I'm not buried here, but they don't care. Rochester was all I knew before I died, so I'll always come back here. That's why we're all here, right Amelia?"

After a pause, Amelia hesitantly agreed with Teddy. "That's right, Teddy." She shot him an annoyed look. Maybe his combat story was too violent for her delicate ears. Whatever the case, her gentle tug on my elbow told me she wanted to part company with Teddy, and wanted me to come along, too.

"Lilla, there's a new vintage store on East Avenue. I think they may have just closed for the night. Come with me to look at the dresses."

"Sure, that sounds nice," I replied. It did sound nice. I needed to see something pretty to get Teddy's war images out of my head. Of course I felt guilty ditching Teddy to look at stupid dresses after he just finished telling me about his battlefield death, but I think he'd had enough, too. I smiled gently at him. "Teddy, thank you for sharing so much of your life with me. It was so special to share that part of you."

"Yes, Mrs. Woodworth, you too. Thanks for listening to a young old vet," Teddy nodded toward me while glancing at Amelia. He good naturedly took her hint, and left us before we had to leave him. A couple of youngsters jumped out at him as he drifted into the back part of the cemetery, and I faintly heard the beginnings of a game of tag.

Amelia and I checked on that vintage store, but it wasn't my cup of tea. Most of the stuff was from the 80s, shoulder pads and baggy shirts. Yuck! What were we thinking back then? After that wasted trip, I was all too happy to get back to Mount Hope. I thought I had pretty much met everyone, but that place is so huge! New spirits kept coming out of the woodwork, all willing to share their past life stories. It was like listening my way through a library.

Mrs. Nester's spirit took me on a field trip to her old house so she could give me a tour of the gardens she planted many years ago. She asked me many questions about the new plants the current owners added. I wanted desperately to ask her if she'd ever looked for a way to move on, but I never got a word in edgewise.

Then there was Benny, large and slow, but very sweet. He showed me his parents' grave, where he sat and talked to them all day, every day. As far as he was concerned, they were there, too. I wanted to know if he'd ever tried looking for them elsewhere but I didn't dare upset the world he created for himself, so I never mentioned my question to him, either.

This was how it went. When meeting all of these characters, what I really wanted to ask them was, "How the heck do I get out of here?" I wanted to know if they were happy, or clueless. Did they wonder if there might be more? For the most part, though, everyone was so nice that it just didn't seem appropriate. If they were at peace with their lot, I didn't want to make them restless.

As for the not-so-nice folks, I wouldn't have trusted their answers at all. I maintained a low profile and blended in with the average crowd. I always kept an ear out for a clue about any spirits who got their wings and flew the coop. I never noticed anybody ever trying to leave, though. Either they stuck around on purpose to take care of some unfinished business, or they had tried to leave but never made it. By now, they resigned themselves to staying here forever. Ugh! I mean, I adored the beauty of this historical cemetery.

The time Sam and I devoted to restoring it had come from the heart. But I didn't do that because I wanted to stick around here forever after I died.

I wondered if Amelia felt any of the disappointment I had about staying here. Sometimes she stood at the southern edge of the Mount Hope Cemetery, just stood there staring past the traffic. She didn't look around as if she were waiting for someone, though. She looked distant, like she longed to be elsewhere. She never shared it and I never asked. God bless anyone who could keep secrets around here.

So far, anything that had crossed my mind was an open book for everyone to read. I hadn't yet learned to cloak my thoughts. Whatever Amelia thought about at the edge of the cemetery I guessed she would tell me someday, or, maybe not. I thought I came close to figuring it out once but stranger things sidetracked me.

A few weeks after my funeral, when I was starting to reach out and meet some of the others, I had a bit of a run-in with some unsettled souls. Every time I passed the South Entrance of the cemetery, I noticed this little group of spirits just outside the gate. Their faces peered between their hands which were wrapped around the bars of the gate. Even my weak beginner's perception sensed them watching me. I felt their eyes burning into my back every time I passed. I guessed there were about a dozen of them, mostly adult men and women, but there a few children, too. A couple of women held ghostly babies in their arms.

I usually looked the other way when I passed them, but on one particularly gloomy fall day, I was too busy marveling at the massive storm clouds moving in from the west. While gazing at the sky, I went through the gate and plowed right through them. I was in for it now. Whatever they had in store for me, I hoped it was quick. One very old woman barreled up from the back to shake her fist in my face. Her short hunched body was covered in a huge scarf tied tightly under her chin.

"Yah! Yah!" She cried as her entire head bobbed way up and then way down. Apparently, she was arguing with me. About what, I had no idea. My mouth hung open in a silent stupor. Then the rest of the group pushed in front of her so they could take their turns.

A woman to my left nudged closer, until I felt her arm touching mine. Her spirit looked worn and frail, but I sensed that when she died she hadn't been as old as she looked.

As terrified as I was, I managed to squeak out, "Hello…uh, my name is Lilla." Almost on cue, the sky released torrents of driving rain, thunder and lightning, paralleling our own storm on the grounds of Mount Hope.

"We know who you are," said one man in back. He wore an eye patch and tattered clothing.

"Yeah," chimed the others.

"Yah!" from the old lady in back. "Yah!"

"Who wouldn't know 'The Queen of Rochester' or whatever it is you call yourself?" snarled the woman standing uncomfortably close to my left side.

The words "Lilac Lady" formed in my mind, but I dared not speak them. I knew it didn't matter, though. As soon as the thoughts formed in my head, these others could read them, and no matter how I tried to mask my correction, I'm sure I still looked like a jerk.

The man with the eye patch spoke coldly from the back. "So you finally showed up. It must be nice to have a place all laid out, just waiting for you. Now the party can start! The Queen is here!" he roared with slurred speech. "I guess we'll never get our invitation to this party, so you won't mind if we just invite ourselves, will you?"

"Yah! Yah!"

"I…I don't own this place," I said cautiously, trying to set them straight. "I don't care who comes here! Jeepers! You were here before me – I don't even want to be here, and I promise not to bother you if you…" I babbled as I backed up, but they moved along with me, inching closer.

"Bother? Well, you couldn't bother with us forty years ago, why should it be any different now?" remarked a woman holding a baby.

"Forty years ago?" I wondered. "What on earth did I do to you people forty years ago? Did I even know you?" While I was racking my brain, along came Amelia and Jodi. My cavalry was here, thank God. Muscling in, they firmly planted themselves between me and the mob.

"What's wrong with all of you?" Amelia screamed at the angry group.

"Yah!" said the old lady again, shaking her fist. I couldn't tell if she was agreeing with or arguing against Amelia.

Amelia continued lambasting them. "Don't blame Lilla – she did the best she could. She couldn't get to everyone. There were just too many of you! If it weren't for her, nobody would have known about any of you at all! It's not her fault they left you there in the first place or that you're The Forgotten! Now leave her alone!"

As the mob backed off, the man with the eye patch yelled, "Have it your way. We just wanted her to know we haven't forgotten. And besides…" He winked slyly at Amelia, "I'd rather be a Forgotten, than a Stolen, any day."

The visibly shaken Amelia just stared, mouth agape, eyes darting from the meddlesome spirits to me, and back again.

Jodi swooped in front of Amelia so quickly it made both of us jump. "Shut your pie hole, you…you scalawag!" She yelled to the man's back as he and his friends disappeared down the side street on the other side of Mount Hope Boulevard.

I shook with fear. Apparently, I was the only one who didn't know what was going on. To think they're mad at me for something that happened forty years ago! Something I couldn't even remember! "Amelia, who are they? Should I know them? You've gotta tell me what happened," I pleaded.

Amelia led me to Section Y, way in the back of the cemetery, and pointed to a plain grassy patch containing paupers' graves. Memories flooded back about the bodies at this section marked by a single large stone flowerpot.

"Oh, my God. This is them? The people buried right here?" my shaky voice squeaked out.

"No. It's not. But they wish it were." Amelia replied flatly, waiting for me to put the pieces together.

Feeling sick to my stomach, I think I lost my breath for a second. Gasping, I replied, "You mean…" I looked past the gate and nodded toward Highland Park. "It's them?"

"Yeah." Jodi whispered, so they wouldn't hear.

I shuddered. The creepiest thing to happen to me during my lifetime returned to haunt me. Back in '84, Sam and I had just started a huge project over in Highland Park. Because it was a city contract, we had lots of workers and equipment at our disposal.

Everything was going great…until the bodies started showing up. Well, not whole bodies, just skeletons, really. Their pine boxes and flesh had dissolved into the ground long ago. Hundreds of them, maybe a thousand, lay in old graves on the very hill in the park where we worked.

Most of their forgotten bodies probably came from the asylums, prisons, and orphanages that lined South Avenue back in the early to mid-1800s. These poor people with no families or money had been buried in paupers' graves in plain boxes, some stacked on top of each other. Any tiny markers had long since disappeared, and these folks were completely forgotten until 1984.

The work crew found them when we were digging. We notified the city of Rochester and they took over after the discovery. Sam and I had nothing to do with any decisions about what happened to those bodies. Someone from the press heard Sam say something about how sad it was to be forgotten. The next day the newspaper started calling them The Forgotten and the name stuck.

I can't believe any of those spirits would hold that against us! The city removed three hundred bodies. They catalogued them by age and sex, and reburied them twenty years later in Mount Hope Cemetery. Our Mount Hope volunteers rescued some large planters that were left over from one of the city projects. We used those planters to mark several pauper sections. It was the least we could do for them.

As for the rest of The Forgotten who were left behind, the city didn't feel right about digging up everyone. They really didn't know how many bodies there were. Maybe city officials felt they wouldn't be able to find them all. Maybe they didn't want to disturb that many bodies, so they left the rest of them in Highland Park. As many as seven hundred more skeletons might still be there to this day.

We'll never know their names, but I think the bodies left behind might have some sort of marker and a little more dignity than before. It sounded like those souls still considered themselves forgotten, and blamed me and Sam. For heaven's sake, I didn't make any of those decisions! God, I hoped all of the "Forgottens" didn't decide to come after me!

"Don't worry about any of them. They're just bullshitting you," Jodi spoke so gently I could barely hear her. She knew I was scared.

"She's right," Amelia agreed. "I don't think they'll bother you anymore, now that they've said their piece."

For the most part, Amelia and Jodi were right. That group never did stalk me after that. I think they wanted me to remember them, which I definitely did ever since that day, albeit with a twinge of fear. I avoided the South Entrance when I could, and made sure never to go near their burial area in Highland Park. It's funny, after all those years, they're not really forgotten; they're remembered by us other dead folks. That's something, anyway.

One thing still stuck in my craw, though. Just because The Forgotten, as everyone called them, were left behind in Highland Park, I still thought it was bitter of them to say we stole those three hundred bodies that were moved to Mount Hope.

The day after my encounter, I ranted to Amelia, "You know, I still have a problem with those Forgotten people. They called the bodies that were moved over here 'The Stolens.' What the heck?" I said. "I mean, the city was just trying to do the right thing for as many of them as they could. The city could have easily left them all in the park, and they'd probably still be mad."

After a few minutes passed, Amelia explained. "Lilla, when they talked about being stolen, they didn't mean those bodies from Highland Park."

"Really?" I asked. "Then what were they talking about?"

Amelia drew a big breath before she said, "They were talking about me."

"You? Really? Why?"

"It's not a strange story, but it's better if you hear the true story from me. Some others think they know what happened, but they're just spreading troublesome rumors. I'm not buried here in this cemetery."

Amelia took a long time to elaborate. By the time she answered, I felt her efforts to shield some of her thoughts from me. She was going to tell me something, but once again, I was only privy to some information, not all. Everyone was so mysterious around here, but I had learned to take what information I could get. I let Amelia tell me what she wanted me to learn.

Even though she said she wanted to tell me so I would hear the true story I figured that was only part of it. She probably wanted to head off anybody else who might tell me too much of her story. Whatever the case, I was upset to hear that Amelia's body had been stolen. How horrid! I envisioned grave robbers with lanterns, tearing at Amelia's casket, looting, pillaging her body already ravaged by small pox. It bothered me greatly to think that had happened to my very good friend.

"Oh, no, stop that, Lilla! Don't upset yourself! It was nothing like that!" Amelia calmed me as soon as she saw the crazy images playing in my head. "I wasn't stolen. Really, I wasn't," Amelia insisted. She patted my hand to comfort me, but her touch was deliberately short, to prevent me from sensing more information than she wanted to share.

She continued with what she wanted me to know. "It's true. I'm not buried here in Mount Hope. It was a decision made by my husband, Joseph...and my family, perhaps because I was the last born. Even as a married lady, with no children of my own, I was always the baby of my family.

"Because of my small pox, Joseph had to bury me as quickly as possible. My poor mother was inconsolable. Her baby was in the cold ground, way up in the epidemic city of Rochester. Mother and Father asked Joseph if I could be buried in the little cemetery back home, next to two of my brothers. Joseph agreed, but nobody in Rochester or the little towns along the way would ever let a small pox body pass through.

"So Joseph paid some grave diggers to dig me up in secret at night and drive my body back home. They hid me under a pile of blankets and vegetables, which my family burned after they buried me."

"Oh, gee," I remarked, not really knowing what to say. "I...I'm really sad they moved you...Do you think it's better, being buried with your family, back in your old home town? Would you rather be here with Joseph? Do you ever go to the place where you're actually buried?"

"No, I never went back home after I left. Not when I was living, and not when I died. I'm happy to stay here. Everyone else in my family has been dead and gone for so long that there's no reason to return now."

"I've seen you looking out that way, toward your old home. I thought you were just thinking about when you were still a kid. I guess that explains the real reason."

"It's probably both," Amelia shrugged.

She conveyed to me that this was over and done a long time ago. Apparently, it didn't bother her. She finished up by implying there was no need for further questions, especially if I intended to ask the others about her story.

"Lilla, I wanted to tell you myself, so you wouldn't be inclined to ask the others. Just about everyone here knows about this. I think you're the last one left to tell. You'd be surprised at how many life and death stories each of us keeps in our minds. Not all are fit to share, so mind your curiosity. It's not polite to ask spirits about other spirits. If there is something you must know, it's better to ask them directly. They'd rather answer it themselves."

Amelia's voice became quieter and quieter as she spoke. Finally, she leaned in and whispered, "Either that, or they'll drag you straight to hell and you won't be able to come back. It happened to five spirits last year."

I gulped, wide-eyed and terrified, until she giggled in my ear. "Argh!" I cried and pulled away to check her expression. I needed to gauge if this was some kind of joke.

She wasn't laughing. With her head bowed, her forehead creased as she gazed out of the upper parts of her eyes. Her pursed lips formed a straight line. Her school-marm appearance implied I should believe her story and heed her advice. As soon as she sensed my understanding, she nodded and took off in a flash into the crisp fall sunlight.

God! I was so confused! Teddy wasn't buried here. Amelia used to be buried here, but wasn't any more. The Forgotten were never buried here and wouldn't let me forget it. Jeez, was anyone really buried here, or were they ectoplasmic tourists just passing through? Well, I was buried here, permanently, I'd say.

So I wasn't going to bother with anybody else's bodies but mine and Sam's. I decided whatever brought people to these parts was their business. They were free to tell me all the stories they wanted, but I would heed Amelia's advice, and not delve too deeply where I wasn't invited. That was going to be a challenge.

Chapter Nine: Halloween

It was only about a month after I died when I began losing touch with the passage of time. The middle of fall came out of nowhere. I had spent so much time up in that tree and inside Marion's house, I didn't notice the leaves had covered the ground with a crisp autumn blanket. For the first time, I couldn't enjoy the things that made this my favorite time of the year. I hadn't felt the temperatures cool, first at night, then during the daytime as well. I used to relish pulling my sweaters out of storage in the spare bedroom and whipping up fresh apple crisp and corn chowder, Sam's favorites.

Between my funeral and Marion's situation, I had missed some of the best colors… glowing fields of golden rod, red tassels on the cornstalks, and burning red sumac bushes. Everything was already brown and crunchy, but I was determined to salvage what was left of my favorite season.

I was sad I couldn't smell October's unique scent. Sure, it was decaying plants dying off for the winter but I still loved it. I also missed the faint smoky smell wafting through the air as people cozied up in front of their fireplaces. What I missed most was walking through crunchy leaves. That was the essence of fall. I used to go out of my way to avoid sidewalks swept clean by fanatical housekeepers, choosing instead to walk on the leaf-covered lawns. During my living years, October delivered a sensual feast for my whole being. Cool breezes and warm sunlight competed for attention on my skin. Earthy scents foretold winter's impending arrival as the world readied to hibernate. Leaves crackled and crunched underfoot.

It wasn't fair I was forced to remain on the earth without being able to indulge in its simple pleasures. I knew I couldn't recapture brisk temperatures or earthy scents without a living, breathing body, but I could at least shuffle around in the leaves. Actually, that did take a little more effort than I anticipated.

If I glided through the leaves the same way I slipped through walls, I didn't stir a thing. Complete silence felt eerie when I knew I was traipsing through piles of leaves. I rolled a rock across a patch of leaves in an attempt to recreate a little sound. It wasn't the same, though, and I didn't want to keep moving rocks all over the place.

It seemed so primitive when my spirit was getting stronger every day. I couldn't believe I was even thinking that. Was I mentally preparing myself to embrace the spirit world because I suspected I would be here for a while? Conceding to being stuck here really bothered me.

Playing in the leaves would be a great way to steer myself away from too much deep thought. Perhaps, since I was already able to lift things by focusing energy on my hands, I could redirect that same energy to my feet to rustle leaves. It made perfect sense. Stiffly, I moved one straight leg in front of the other, trying to force myself to crush the dry leaves underneath my feet. "Physical therapy for the physiqueless," I laughed to myself. Miraculously, I managed to create that crunchy sound for which I longed. At first, every step was slow and deliberate, but I gradually progressed into a pace similar to what my elderly body might have managed.

During blustery October nights, I trudged up and down the cemetery lawns, purposefully crunching leaves wherever I went. In daytime I moved silently, so as not to frighten the living. They wouldn't understand I was enjoying some harmless fun. Busy winds whipped leaves right through me. At first, I held my arms in front of my face to shield my eyes, but I soon realized it was unnecessary since I no longer possessed flesh or eyes.

Talk about weird! Debris passed through my face without resistance, and rain pattered straight through my body to the ground. No more wet hair or clothes. It was freaky, but fun. I understood what it meant to be a spirit without any boundaries or limitations. I couldn't imagine ever having been compressed and stuffed into the confines of the tiny human body I had occupied for eighty-eight years.

As my spirit grew "larger," those spectacular autumn days grew shorter. Finally, the best day of all arrived: Halloween. The one day of the year when the veil, separating the living and the dead, became its thinnest and most permeable. When I was alive, Halloween was one of the best holidays. Okay, technically, it's not really a holiday, but since October has always been my favorite time of year, Halloween was just as important as Christmas to me.

What wasn't to love about decorations, costume parties, and ghost stories? It was all fun. I never thought about real hauntings or actually seeing dead people. I left that to Spooky Marcie and her friends.

Now that I had crossed over into the spirit world, would Halloween take on a new meaning? Was I supposed to do something in reverence to the living or the dead, maybe jump out and scare a few people? Dare I hope the veil would become thin enough for me to crawl through and find Sam? Maybe he would find me and pull me through.

Never let it be said that Lilla Woodworth doesn't have a vivid imagination. I pictured throngs of spirits popping up or coming down from wherever it is they spend their eternities and we would have the largest Halloween party ever. The cemetery might get so full of dead revelers that our crowd would spill into the street, which would be fine since the living couldn't see us anyway. Trick-or-treaters would walk right through us.

"I'm really looking forward to Halloween," I said to Amelia two days before the big event. "Is there anything I need to do to get ready?"

She looked puzzled as she tilted her head. "Get ready?" she asked. "For what?"

"Well, I don't know...but isn't there anything I should know? You know, if a lot of spirits come back that night. I mean, are they celebrating? Is it like a party? Does a cemetery like this get kind of crazy? Do they look like their regular living selves or are they weird looking, like they're in costume?" I grilled her faster than she could answer.

Amelia looked sympathetic when I described the Mardi Gras type of party that had everything going for it except beads. "Goodness, Lilla, I'm sorry to disappoint you," she giggled as she spoke, "I've never seen a Halloween like that one! I've never seen any extra spirits around here on that day that we don't already see every day in Mount Hope."

"Really?" I asked. "Do you even feel anything? Or see lights, like the other side is calling to you?"

"No, not really. Maybe some spirits who've gone on to the farther places use this day to return briefly, but I've never seen them. At least not around here."

"Hmm," I pondered it for a minute. 'Maybe it's because we're stuck here. Maybe we're more attached to the living than the dead people who've actually crossed all the way over to the other side."

"It's hard to say. Who knows?" Amelia shrugged and gestured upward with her hands. "Any of that could be right."

I sighed. "I can't believe nothing goes on that night! What a rip-off!"

Amelia laughed at me for trying so hard to find some sort of Halloween craziness. Sadly, I accepted the fact that Halloween was just another night. Celebrations were more for the living to pay homage to the dead. For some it was a solemn religious ceremony, but for most it was party time. I had fallen through the cracks again. I would be summoned by neither the living nor the dead. No! This was Halloween, and I would find a way to enjoy it!

For a while, I watched the trick-or-treaters run past the cemetery fence. They dared each other to walk into the cemetery. As they approached the gate, someone from each group smartly claimed that although they weren't afraid to enter the cemetery, they didn't have time. They had more streets to cover before heading home. There were promises to do it next year Amelia and I took bets on which one would chicken out first.

Eventually even the older kids finished trick-or-treating for the night and porch lights were turned off. People either ran out of candy or went to bed.

"Is that it?" I asked Amelia. "That was dull. I was secretly hoping it would be a bigger night for us. You weren't kidding about nothing happening. There isn't even any toilet paper in the trees!"

"Just because it's Halloween and we're dead doesn't mean the world turns into a giant fair for us," Amelia laughed at my disappointment. "We can still find our own fun. When Jodi gets here we'll go someplace."

"Where?"

"Someplace we like to go to once in a while. Halloween is the best time to go," Amelia said. She glanced around for Jodi.

"Really? Oh tell me what it is!"

Halloween could still be saved!

Abruptly, Jodi showed up, saving Amelia from giving away her surprise.

"Are you ready? You know where we're going, right?" Amelia asked Jodi.

"You bet!" Jodi replied, grinning at me, "Only, can we stop at Laverne's on our way. Please?"

Amelia frowned slightly. "All right. It's not exactly on the way but we can stop there for a minute. It is Halloween, and I know you want to see what everybody's doing tonight."

"Hooray! Let's go!" Jodi took off so quick we almost lost her at the end of the first street.

Since I didn't know where we were going, I couldn't just wish myself there. The three of us took "the long way," drifting through the air over the city. We didn't have to follow every street and sidewalk like when we were alive, though. We passed over houses and neighborhoods in any direction we chose. I enjoyed it, and it gave me a chance to float through this perfectly spooky October night. Gusty wind tugged the last of the rattling leaves from the barren trees and tossed them across lawns.

We moved quickly toward the outskirts of the city, eventually stopping in a parking lot front of a bar. Even on this cold Rochester October night, a dozen motorcycles lined the parking lot, with more rumbling in from the street. "Verne's Place" flickered from a neon sign above the bustling doorway.

"Verne's Place?!" I looked at Jodi, my mouth hanging open. "This is Laverne's? You're kidding, right?" I chuckled, waiting for Jodi to confess she was teasing me.

Amelia sneered as she rolled her eyes. "No, this is Laverne's."

Jodi laughed and tilted her head toward Amelia. "She doesn't like this place. I think it's a blast! This is the last chance I have to see everyone 'til next year. Most of them'll put their bikes away tomorrow." She motioned for us to follow her. "Come over here to see this bike he just got in. It's used, but it's the shit!"

We followed her past several groups of people in the parking lot. Everyone was having a good time. One woman slapped a nearby man on the back in jest. "You dumbass!" she laughed. "You are so full of shit!"

"No way, man!" he replied. "I'm tellin' you he did her out behind Grover's barn and they both got poison ivy all over their business! Hey, don't believe me. Go ask Allen why he didn't ride all week. He's one itchy motherfucker. Can't ride and scratch at the same time!" The whole group laughed loudly.

Well, that told me where Jodi got some of her naughty language. She beckoned us to a storefront on the other side of the bar. I didn't mind moving past these conversations. Judging by Amelia's sour face, neither did she.

"Jodi," I said with wide eyes. "I can't believe this is Laverne's! I thought Laverne was a girl!"

"No way," Jodi laughed. He's an old dude. He goes by Verne 'cause it sounds tougher. I'm the only one who calls him Laverne I just like the way it sounds. La-verrrne. Almost like an engine revving."

"I thought you said Laverne sold bicycles."

"Bicycles!" Jodi laughed. "No, I said bikes! Motorcycles! Not pansy-ass bicycles!"

"Yeah, I get it, now," I chuckled at our miscommunication.

Amelia hovered near the edge of the parking lot. "Well, have you seen enough of the famous Verne's for one night?" she asked me. Impatiently, she started floating down the street before I even answered.

After experiencing Verne's first hand, I knew Amelia had enough even before we landed here. "Yeah, I'm ready to go see what the rest of Halloween is about." I turned to Jodi. "How about you?"

Jodi sighed. "All right. I'm coming. I just wanted to check this out tonight."

Jodi and I caught up with Amelia. The three of us flew over the rooftops, back to the middle of the city. We ended up at a dead end street, perfect for Halloween. Old Victorian houses, well maintained and artfully decorated, had been converted into small shops and offices. Suddenly I recognized the street. I used to shop there sometimes.

Cute signs advertised a doctors' offices, a gourmet bakery, a small music store, and a women's boutique. The outdoor public market was on the other side of the fence toward the end of the street.

The original homeowners blocked the street with a fence for more privacy, to prevent people on their way to the market from wandering through their yards. When businesses moved in, the shopkeepers planned to tear down the fence, hoping to attract patrons visiting the market.

I could see that still hadn't happened. Too bad. The shops were cute and it was a nice street, if you didn't mind the smell of fish wafting through the fence. I think some of the market dumpsters were right on the other side of the fence. I remembered the pungent odors on hot summer days. That was probably why there were no outdoor cafés around here, even though they'd look perfect in this neighborhood.

I found myself instinctively trying to block out the smells by not breathing through my nose, a survival tactic I used here over thirty years ago. That is until I remembered I didn't breathe, much less smell anything anymore. Besides, tonight was definitely not a hot summer day.

Amelia, Jodi, and I headed for the house at the end of the street. Wind chimes on the porch filled the air with ethereal music. Gargoyles and fairies were carved right into the porch railings. What an enchanting house! Right out of a fairy tale. I was glad we came. I think it used to be a coffee shop but now housed a bustling store full of psychic stuff. According to their sign, they were going to be open all night. At least this was a big night for somebody.

Shoppers pored over crystals, minerals, spell books, jewelry, and flowing dresses. It was fun to guess which customers were regulars and which ones were only curious. Amelia was right; Halloween really was a party for the living to explore the spiritual world, more than it was for the dead to jump back into the world of the living. We'd already lived our lives. To these people, the afterlife where we dwelt was a magical place full of wonder.

Keep dreaming. I thought sourly to the living customers. Maybe you'll have better luck than me when you get here.

Extending from the back of the store, a short hallway led to several rooms. A woman in a long lacy black dress came out of a back room to announce it was almost eleven o'clock for those who had come for the meetings.

Most of the customers filed back to two of the rooms, sorting themselves into distinct groups, diehards and dabblers, I decided.

People wearing robes and carrying small identical books entered the room on the left. Everybody else wearing regular street clothes entered the room on the right. A few of them sported funky crystal and silver jewelry, but, for the most part, they blended in with the rest of the regular people. They were just your garden-variety curiosity seekers. Not much to see there. The other group looked much more interesting! I loved their hooded robes, so I started following them to see what they were doing.

Amelia held me back. "Oh no, not in there. It's boring, almost like church." She made a sour face. "This side is much more fun," and she and Jodi went into the room on the right.

I stood in the hallway. I really wanted to go with the robed people. The people in the regular clothes looked so average. How could they be nearly as interesting as the robed crowd? I hesitated too long. After the last people entered the rooms, both doors closed, leaving me alone in the hallway. I figured I might as well go into the room where Jodi and Amelia went. If I didn't like it, I could always go across the hall to the other room.

I slipped through the door into a room where chairs were arranged in a circle. The only light was the glow from candles on a low table in the center of the room. I waited for people to seat themselves while the group leader checked her roster. Jodi and Amelia hovered in the darkest corner of the room. They motioned for me to join them. On my way across the room, I passed very close to the group leader.

"Mmm! Lilacs," she said pleasantly. I stopped short. Was she talking to me? When I was alive, I lived and breathed lilacs. Maybe I had sent her some sort of aura or something. When someone mentioned lilacs, I usually stopped to join the conversation but not this time. I didn't even dare turn in her direction. I looked cautiously out of the corner of my eye. She wasn't looking at me specifically but scanned the room to get a better feel of where the scent might have originated.

"Is someone wearing lilac perfume?" she asked the room. Jodi and Amelia waved me out of my stupor. I immediately joined them, hopefully out of range of anybody's hyperactive sense of smell.

The group looked at the leader blankly and a few women said they were wearing perfume, but not lilac.

"Oh, it must be one someone's perfume that just reminds me of lilacs. Whatever it is, it smells good." The group leader was satisfied someone's perfume was close enough to lilacs and didn't seem interested in pursuing the subject any further, thank goodness. She moved on to address the people in the group about loved ones who'd been lost. She softly recounted stories of family members and friends who'd entered the spirit world, but still had undelivered messages for their living acquaintances. She encouraged the others to open their thoughts and invite the departed into their minds and into this room. We were at a séance.

This was a first for me and I was a little worried. We hadn't been chosen to visit by anybody. Nobody in this room knew we existed or that we decided to visit for the hell of it. This had to be the ultimate form of party crashing.

The room fell silent as the group waited for their ghostly visitors, wondering who would be the first to hear from the great beyond. The air around us fluttered. Jodi, Amelia, and I weren't the only spirits in the room. Two women's apparitions and that of an elderly gentleman materialized near the other side of the room. They moved forward together, unseen by the living, except possibly the group leader. Then they separated, moving around the outside of the circle of chairs, until each one of them focused on an individual and remained close to that person's chair.

The woman who'd given the introduction remained silent, except for her slow rhythmic breathing. She concentrated on sensing any otherworldly presence in the room. Her breaths became longer, more controlled and deep. She sat a little straighter in her chair when the three newcomers appeared. She turned toward a seated woman who wore jeans and a pink cardigan.

"Hello? Donna?" The leader addressed the woman to get her attention.

"Yes?" Donna answered as her face registered surprise.

The leader spoke haltingly as she interpreted the information to her.

"There's an elderly woman near you. She's tall. She has reddish hair. Umm…She has reading glasses on a chain around her neck…She wants to let you know…thanks for making her laugh. Oh…and for taking care of Max." The group leader smiled and nodded. Already I could see a flood of recognition wash over Donna's face.

The group leader continued, "Your visitor thanks you. Does this make sense to you?"

"Yes! Thank you!" the woman smiled.

The message had been delivered. A cryptic conversation understood by the one for whom it was intended. I suppose if I had been better at reading thoughts I might have known more details about what transpired between them. Amelia and Jodi were stronger than I was. Maybe they understood more of the message than I did.

Amelia drifted from our group in the corner until she was very close to the red-haired spirit. This spirit looked at Amelia as if to ask, "Who is this spirit and why is she here?" Amelia smirked and held her ground while the red-haired spirit became irritated. The group leader spoke to Donna again.

"Ma'am? I think there's a second spirit here to see you as well…She's…an older spirit from quite a while ago…definitely several generations back…"

Amelia laughed, while the red-haired spirit flailed her arms to swoosh Amelia away. This was her person and Amelia was interrupting. It was quite a sight to see the two spirits vying for the same space and passing through some parts of each other as they jostled for the position behind Donna. The group leader raised her eyebrows a little. Could she actually see what was happening or merely sense it? How could she describe this scene and expect her paying customers to take it seriously? She minimized Amelia's presence.

"I don't think she has a message…She's just from the past…maybe just visiting." The group leader was done with Donna and her ghostly entourage. She rolled her head to clear it and stretch her neck out a little. Next, she spoke to an Asian woman about the man standing behind her.

Amelia came back to the corner with Jodi and me. Although I didn't agree with Amelia interfering, the three of us were in stitches. The red-haired spirit didn't budge from the piece of air she had claimed until she was sure Amelia was done pestering her lady, Donna. She threw an irritated glance toward the three of us and floated out of the room, back to wherever she had come from.

The gentleman's spirit stood behind the Asian woman. He had more to say than that first spirit, which helped me understand more easily. The group leader conveyed his message. He told his daughter to keep practicing. He had faith in her and wanted her to keep studying and perfecting it. The Asian woman filled in the blanks by telling the group leader she knew he was talking about her singing and this was a special message. The man's spirit looked pleased and nodded to the group leader before fading away.

Amelia didn't bother this gentle spirit. He seemed too sweet to tease. Besides, she was already poised next to the second of the two women who had arrived with the old man's spirit. This woman looked young, somewhere between Jodi and Amelia. She hovered closely behind a young man. This woman wasn't nearly as territorial as the red-haired spirit. Amelia wasn't as aggressive as before because there was sadness about this woman.

She moved in front of the man in the chair. He couldn't see her, but she bent down to look in his face. She smiled gently, and stood up next to his chair, with her hand on his shoulder. I know Amelia had planned to confuse the group again, but for some reason she didn't feel right when she felt the girl's angst. Amelia touched the woman's spirit on her shoulder, and then backed away to give the group leader an uncluttered pathway to communicate.

"Sir? The man wearing black. Mark, right?" The leader looked over at the man, who was dressed completely in black, from head to toe. Even his hair was dyed jet black. He was accompanied by four friends, two guys, and two girls, all wearing black. None of them could have been over twenty. Like me, they were looking for something exciting to do on Halloween. Before the séance, while waiting in the little shop out front, they had joked about ghosts.

The group leader had to point slightly to get the attention of the correct black-clad person.

"Me? Oh, yeah." Mark pointed to himself. He shifted in his chair and looked a little surprised, even nervous.

"Yes, I think this is for you. There's someone who wants to tell you something."

"Uh-oh, now you're in trouble," one of the girls from his group quietly muttered to him out of the corner of her mouth. The man and his friends chuckled.

Ignoring their titters, the leader continued. "It's a young lady, with long curly hair…very petite build…very cute…nice smile."

The man sat erect. "What's her name?" he asked, his voice quivering a little.

"She hasn't said anything about…Oh…mmm hmm…" The group leader spoke to Mark, then to the spirit, then back to him. "It's something…like…Tina…Katrina…Does that sound like someone you might have known?"

The young rugged man, who'd been so jovial minutes before, hunched over, with his head buried in his hands and his elbows resting on his knees. He sighed heavily.

The girl sitting next to him leaned over, passing through the spirit of the young woman, and spoke quietly. "Oh, my God. It sounds like his sister, Katy. He was the only one who called her Tina. She ran away three years ago."

The man lifted his head out of his hands and looked at the group leader. Tears pooled in his eyes. "Why is she here? Does this mean she's dead?" His question was barely audible as he blinked to hold back his tears.

Everyone in the room felt the emotional tension. Several women wiped tears from their eyes. The group leader tried hard to find the gentlest way to tell this man his sister was dead. I was sure this was an unusual and difficult situation for her and for everyone else in the room. Even Jodi and Amelia were silent.

"Well." The group leader had to clear her throat and paused before she continued. Her voice came out a little shaky, and she spoke more quickly than. "Well, I thought she may have crossed over, but I could be mistaken. It could just be a strong emotional connection between you that I feel over a distance."

"She really, really wants you to know she's okay. Please don't worry. She's happy and loves you and Mom and Dad. Things were tough at first...but wherever she is...it's the most beautiful place."

There was nothing more the dainty spirit could or would say. In a tiny flash that only Jodi, Amelia and I could see, she was gone. She left before anyone could find out what happened between the time she left home and her appearance in this room.

The five friends looked at each other in silence. They rose from their seats and put their arms around the young man's shoulders. They stayed close together, as they all walked out of the room.

On her way out, one of the girls stopped in front of the group leader. "This is bullshit," she hissed.

The group leader, with tears in her eyes touched the girl's hand. "I'm sorry," she said. "He doesn't have to believe any of it. Please understand. His sister was trying to let him know she's okay wherever she is. She was trying to send a message of love, not despair."

"There's no way Katy's dead. If you're fucking messing with him, this is one sick joke." The girl pulled her hand away and went out the door. She slammed it loudly behind her.

Trying to regain their composure, the remaining customers avoided eye contact with their neighbors in this shrinking circle. The only sound in the room for the next few minutes was the occasional blowing of a nose. Amelia, Jodi, and I remained very still in the corner, just as mystified as the people in the chairs.

I wished I could have seen what had happened to the young woman whose spirit had upset her brother so much. I was hoping for the chance to touch her on the arm to see the visions of her past and how she died. Poor thing. Why was her life cut short without her family ever knowing what happened to her? She had left as soon as her brother broke down. How would her family deal with this? Would they believe it? I know if I were them, I would refuse to give up hope that she's still alive and would come home someday. I wanted to believe it for them, despite what I'd seen here tonight.

I deadpanned to Amelia, "Gee, I can't remember when I've had so much fun. This is even better than the giant cemetery party from my imagination. You sure know how to have a good time."

"Oh, stop!" Amelia chastised me. "We come here all the time; this never happened before!"

"Yeah! She's right!" Jodi defended Amelia. "It's usually way cooler than this."

Jodi was probably right. For the most part, I bet everyone usually left feeling closer to a deceased loved one, or at least made some much happier connection.

The group leader finally asked, "How's everyone doing? Do you want to call it quits for tonight? If you want to leave, I understand. I'll put your name on a list and you can come back another time, no charge. Or…anyone who wants to can stay for a while longer…if you want. I'll leave it up to you."

The eight remaining people stayed in their seats. With shrugs and murmurs, they nodded collectively that they wished to continue. The room grew quiet again as everyone refocused. It took longer than the first waiting period. Maybe other spirits might have been afraid to come into this room until the negative energy was gone. Honestly, I don't know why we stayed. I guess it was like a bad movie. It had to get better sometime, right? We waited for a few minutes, wondering if anyone else would come.

Trying to capture anything that might entertain her remaining guests, the group leader threw out her psychic net, dragging it through every corner of the room, including ours. I started to tingle all over. When my foot used to fall asleep, I'd stomp on the floor to wake it up. Here at the séance, my whole being felt like it was being teased by pins and needles. It reminded me of the days when I had real flesh, only I didn't have flesh any more. I knew slamming myself into the wall wouldn't work because I'd go right through.

Something felt wrong; I shouldn't feel sensations like this anymore. I looked at Amelia and lifted my hand out to her for help. I was afraid I was about to be pulled away to another world or disintegrate completely.

"Amelia, what's wrong? I feel funny…Do you feel it? Jodi, do you feel it?"

"It's fine. You'll be all right," Amelia reassured me. "It feels this way when they call to us."

"Are you sure you feel it? It's so strange," I asked my friends. I squeezed my arms to try to rub that sensation away. Amelia and Jodi remained calm. I had a hard time believing they also felt the prickly feeling as strongly as I did.

Jodi told me quietly, "It's like this every time I come if they talk to me. I like it! It kind of tickles, like I've been messing in the barley broth." She giggled. "Listen! You can hear the woman talk about you. Usually she's righter than right. There are some fakes out there. They just make things up so they can sell stuff! But this one's good." Jodi and Amelia turned their attention toward the group leader as she peered over to our corner.

"We have three ladies with us in this room…They are from the past…all different times…They might not have known each other when they lived on earth," the group leader smiled so nicely over to our corner. Didn't she know I wanted her to finish up so the prickly feeling would stop? I fidgeted to shake her away, but she continued, "Two of them have been here before…I don't feel any messages coming across…"

The only message I wanted to send was, "Please leave me alone." She didn't hear me.

"Two of the spirits are quite old. They've been around for a long time. There's a young girl, maybe from the 1800s, from right here in Rochester. One of the women with her is from nearby also. I think the third woman is much younger…a newer spirit. They're just spending time with us tonight."

Jodi stayed noticeably in the shadows behind me and Amelia. I waited to hear if the group leader tried to describe us in more detail, if she'd mention Jodi's disturbing appearance. She only nodded at us and smiled around at the members of the group. She no longer looked at us, but around the room for a new spirit with which to communicate. The tingling sensation gradually disappeared, for which I was thankful.

Well, this had been interesting but I'd had enough. I turned to tell Jodi and Amelia that I was leaving, when Amelia got bowled over by the whoosh of a boy.

"Mommy! Mommy!" shouted an exuberant child. His spirit rushed into the room so quickly he couldn't stop. He went out through the back wall and had to turn around and come back in.

"Oh, Mommy!" The little boy exclaimed again as he stood near a woman right next to the group leader. He leaned very close to the woman and put his head on her shoulder. He rubbed his little hand on her arm. She was unaware of any of this until the group leader turned and spoke to her.

She smiled at the vision of the child. "Ma'am, there's a child standing with you…a little boy."

"Frances," the woman interrupted. "It has to be. Is it?"

"He says he feels much better now. He's happy he doesn't have to stay in bed anymore…he plays with Grandpa Tobin all the time…He's touching your arm and shoulder."

"Yes, that's him. That's my son! He had cancer. He died almost ten years ago. I can feel him around me sometimes." Did she really feel his presence or was it just wishful thinking? She looked around and right through her son's soul. "I can't tell if he's really here. I wish I could feel him now."

Jodi granted this woman her wish. Little Frances still caressed his mother's arm, even though she couldn't feel it. Both mother and son wanted desperately to meet somewhere in the middle of their two worlds, but neither one could find the bridge. Jodi stepped out of the corner and held out her gnarled hand to the tyke. She tilted her gruesome face near Frances knowing it would cause him to panic.

"Mommy!" He shrieked and clung to his mother's neck. His frantic state triggered a connection I'm sure his mother will treasure for the rest of her life.

"Oh, Frances! I love you!" She gasped and put her hand up to her neck. For a moment, the flesh of her hand and Frances' ghostly arm occupied the same space and both of them knew it.

Frances looked at Jodi, and then at his mother. "I love you too, Mommy. Bye, Mommy!"

With that he was gone, most likely to escape from Jodi. I thought Jodi's feelings would have been hurt but instead she smiled and said she still had a few tricks up her sleeve. At first, I thought it had been an accident but she knew what she was doing.

We looked at Frances' mother, smiling through her tears. "He was here – I felt him!" she exclaimed as she wiped a tear from her cheek. "Thank you. Thank you," she whispered to the group leader.

Everyone smiled for Frances' mother. The group leader gave her a hug. It was a much-needed lift after that guy found out about his sister. Yet the atmosphere was still very serious and emotional. It wasn't the barrel of laughs I had pictured. Who knew what the next spirit would have to say? It could be someone with a whole slew of problems. We decided to leave before they finished their séance.

That little boy was so chipper. I thought it would be a good time to quit while we were ahead. Even Jodi and Amelia were ready to wrap it up for the night. You know, this was the first time ever I looked forward to the end of Halloween.

"Jodi," I asked, as we floated through the wall out into the Halloween night, "you scared that kid on purpose?"

"With a name like Frances, he'd be a rather weak little thing. Those little pats on his mother's arm wouldn't have done a blasted thing! He needed a little…encouragement."

"Now there's a girl who knows how to use her looks!" Amelia winked at Jodi, who winked back with her good eye. They both laughed.

I couldn't believe Amelia had said that, but if Jodi thought it was funny, than I guess it was okay. I also smiled and snickered a little. It was Halloween after all, the one night a year when freaks get to be themselves.

Tracy Fontaine

Chapter Ten: Presenting the Lilac Lady

It was bound to happen eventually. The first cemetery tour invaded my gravesite the day after Halloween. It was my just desserts for crashing the séance the night before. About thirty people trailed behind a middle-aged woman. She started speaking before they arrived at my and Sam's graves, so I didn't hear the first part of her speech. As soon as I saw them, I cloaked myself and hid in the bare branches of a nearby tree.

"She's the last one to be buried here in Mount Hope," she said as the group convened near my grave. "Lilla Woodworth. You can see how the grave is still sort of fresh. She was buried about a month ago. Her husband, Sam, is right there." She backed away while the group milled about to take photos and read our inscriptions. "Remember on the tour today, all of the places where I mentioned the Lilac Lady and her husband?" she continued. "Here they are. They had a radio show, and a television show. They wrote some books, too. I think there might be one they did about the cemetery back at the office if anyone is interested in looking at it when we get back."

The tour guide started leading the group down the road. At least my portion of the tour had been brief. That wasn't so bad.

Suddenly she stopped and turned to them. "Oh. About their radio show, I have a family connection to that. My Uncle Paul started that show. Actually, he was my great uncle. He was a friend of theirs. They went on the show with him sometimes. You know, I think my uncle was the first one to start calling her 'The Lilac Lady.' When he retired, they took over for him.

"Now before anyone starts doing the math..." She looked slyly at her followers. "I was very young when that all happened. I don't even remember it." The group laughed as they resumed walking to their next stop.

I stayed in the tree, arms folded, mouth agape. Her Uncle Paul retired? We were friends with that guy? Was she kidding? Either she must have been too young to understand what happened, or her uncle told it differently to his family. I wished I could shout the real story to the crowd that before they disappeared over the hill.

I looked down to see if Sam was rolling over in his grave. There was so much I wanted to tell those people about how we got our start.

After graduating from Watson, Sam and I headed back here to Rochester, New York and were married that summer at Sam's grandparents' house. We kept the ceremony simple so we could save money for a down payment on a house.

I managed a garden supply store and Sam took a job with a landscaping company. We dreamed of having our own business someday. We took any gardening opportunities we could find to hone our skills and meet as many people in the field as we could. We volunteered for anything from tending gardens in the highway medians to filing paperwork at the county land management offices.

On Saturday mornings, we'd head over to watch the broadcast of The Paul Franklin Show at the radio station, Mr. Franklin being that tour guide's great uncle. Listeners called the station and a panel of gardening experts answered their questions over the air. People in the studio audience could ask questions and comment on the panel's responses.

It was fun to see the panel members temper their emotions when they disagreed with their host, Mr. Franklin. Lucky for them, radio listeners couldn't see the panel's sour expressions. Their radio voices sent only flowery joy over the airwaves.

Paul Franklin himself tried everyone's patience. The guests on his panel often rolled their eyes at some of his answers to listeners' questions. However, they didn't dare contradict him too strongly lest they not be invited back to the show. Even if they had to sell out a little to Mr. Franklin, it was still worth it if they could get a plug in for their own businesses.

"How did that guy ever get his own show?" Sam asked me almost every week as we giggled from the back row. "His brother must own the station."

As Mr. Franklin spewed bizarre answers, Sam and I whispered our versions to each other. Old school regulars in the audience turned to leer at us "mouthy kids." This was until the panelists tactfully expressed opinions very similar to ours. We'd smirk and congratulate each other on our smarts.

Our big break came about six years after we graduated from Watson. It was the spring of '68. To think Sam and I almost skipped the show that day to do housework. We had bought an old Tudor-style house with lots of gardens. I was itching to plant a bunch of lilacs that weekend, and I wanted to get an early start in the yard that day. We planned to go straight home after our trip to the market, but Sam wanted to stop into the show since we would drive right past the studio anyway.

"I don't know, Sam," I sighed. I looked up at the clouds moving in. "It's supposed to rain later. I was hoping we could get everything in before then. Besides, the panel hasn't been there in weeks. I can't take much more of Franklin doing the show by himself."

"C'mon," Sam said as he pulled into the parking lot. "We'll sit in the back, and if you get antsy we'll duck out during a commercial. Besides…" Sam nuzzled my cheek and whispered, "I think they might just be talking lilacs today."

"Oh?" I giggled because his breath tickled my ear.

Sam knew I'd cave for anything about lilacs. That's how we ended up going to the studio and taking our usual spots in the back row. Little did we anticipate that we would be the show.

Shortly after Mr. Franklin introduced lilacs as the show's topic, he received his first call. The listener cleared his throat to get ready to ask his question.

"Go ahead, sir. Do ya have something going on with lilacs? I'm ready any time you are," Mr. Franklin prompted the caller.

"Uh…yeah," said the man on the line. He sounded like he might be about our age. "Well, see…I've got some lilacs that aren't doing so hot. I planted them about three years ago. They're kind of scrawny. They barely flower…they're under some pine trees. I'm pretty sure they need more sun…but besides that…my brother-in-law said the pine trees might make the soil too acidic. Which is the worse problem? The pine trees themselves, or the shade?"

"You worry too much. Just fertilize 'em. They'll be fine," Mr. Franklin said. "Next caller."

"Oh, Paul? Oh, um…Mr. Franklin?" The first listener hadn't hung up. He blurted out one last question to Mr. Franklin before they disconnected his call.

"Um. I just bought three new lilacs. They're a different variety. If I plant the new ones in the sun, will they still be okay near the pine trees?"

Franklin's eyes shot over to the control booth. Click. On his queue, the studio ended the call. Franklin clicked his tongue and sighed loudly. He leaned back in his chair and drummed his fingers on the table.

After a few long silent minutes, he sighed. "Go ahead and plant them…under the pine trees away from the pine trees, wherever you like'll be fine. Don't worry about the pH. Nature'll know what to do." The listener probably heard Franklin chortle, but fortunately he couldn't see him roll his eyes.

"Ugh!" I exclaimed quietly to Sam. "That was so rude! What the heck kind of answer was that?"

"Hmm. That's messed up, all right," Sam agreed.

"He'll never have decent lilacs if he listens to Franklin!"

"Yeah, it's too bad we couldn't talk to him ourselves. I know! I'll hold Franklin down. You grab the microphone and yell out a real answer."

"Don't tempt me. You have no idea how good that sounds," I said and giggled at the thought of hijacking his show.

Sam nudged me with his shoulder. "You really wanna do it?" I looked at him in shock. "Oh, not the part where I hold him down, you goof!" Sam teased. "Just the part where you get to talk into the microphone."

"Oh, that would be neat, wouldn't it?" I mused. "If the rest of the panel was there, I'd do it. At least they'd back me up. But I'm not going up there alone with Mr. Franklin."

"Go on," Sam said. He nudged me a little harder to make me stand up. "If you don't say something now, you'll regret it for the rest of the weekend. Maybe longer."

While I mulled over the possibilities, the man in front of us turned around. It was Mr. Burnside. That's what Sam and I called him because he had bushy sideburns. We had secret names for almost all of the regulars.

Mr. Burnside swung his arm over the back of his chair like my father did when he was driving. It meant either my brother or I was about to be spanked for fighting.

"You two," Mr. Burnside said in a low serious voice. He had a bit of an accent, maybe Scottish. He pointed at me and Sam.

Uh, oh. Here it comes. I waited for him to tell us to shut up. Instead of scolding us, he smiled.

"You two have never been wrong! Miss, if you know about lilacs, go on and shout it out!" Mr. Burnside jerked his head toward Franklin. "He needs help up there."

"You think I should?"

Mr. Burnside and Sam both nodded. Mr. Burnside flitted his hands and mouthed the words "Go on! Go on!" I stood up slowly, hoping the radio listeners couldn't hear my knees knocking.

"Uh…Mr. Franklin? Over here!" My voice shook. I waved both arms over my head.

The sparse audience turned to stare at us. Much to my surprise, they smiled too. Maybe they were glad to see someone stand up to Franklin…or maybe they were hoping we would get kicked out for being such smart alecks all the time. Either way, the show was about to get a little more interesting.

Franklin placed his hand above his eyes like a visor. He squinted into the lights to see who called his name. "What the…Oh. Hello back there. It seems we have a young lady in the back row with something important to say. Something tells me we had better listen. Why don't you come down here and talk to us." Franklin smirked at his producer, who shrugged his shoulders.

A man from the studio motioned me toward an extra microphone the panel normally uses. I wound my way around the audience, stepping gingerly over wires that snaked all over the floor. For a minute, I was more nervous about tipping over the soundboard than I was about speaking over the radio. I made it to the stage area and took a seat on one of the stools.

"Hi there. And your name is?" Franklin asked.

"Hello, Mr. Franklin!" I bellowed into the microphone. It was my first time at a microphone; I made myself and the audience jump. "Oops…sorry," I whispered. I giggled nervously. "I'm Lilla. Um…Woodworth." I spoke at a normal level. I finally found my radio voice.

"Nice to meet you, Lilla."

At first, Franklin didn't seem as imposing as I imagined him to be in person. In fact, the way he leaned his chin on his hand made him appear bored. Maybe he was just tired. Maybe his generously applied aftershave made him woozy. He smelled like my grandfather, which was comforting. I started feeling guilty that I was there to contradict this old man on the air.

Franklin and his producer glanced at each other. Maybe it wasn't such a good idea for me to have gone up there. However, if I got up and went back to my seat right then, I'd feel pretty stupid. I decided to stay for one question before excusing myself to return to my seat.

"So, you like lilacs, do you?" Franklin finally asked.

"Oh! I adore them! They're my favorite!" I gushed. I couldn't believe I was actually talking on the radio. I wasn't nervous at all! No doubt, it was the subject matter. I could talk lilacs all day.

Slouching back in his seat, Franklin snickered. It wasn't a warm "Isn't she cute?" snicker. It sounded foreboding. I'm not sure how the live audience or the radio audience perceived it but I felt some bad vibes. I wished I hadn't gone up there. "Well, everyone, our new little friend Lilla is going to tell us all about lilacs."

Franklin nodded at me to continue. I looked at him with my mouth open. Aren't you going to help me? What should I say? I pleaded with my eyes.

He leaned back. I leaned forward, hoping for some sort of guidance. I looked over at the producer standing nearby. He looked as confused as I did. I spied Sam standing in the back of the aisle near Mr. Burnside. Both of them were lifting their arms up and out and mouthing, "Go on! Go on!"

"Well, Mr. Franklin…" I stammered. "I, uh…Actually, I wanted to say one thing about that man's lilacs, if I could?"

Mr. Franklin waved his hand loosely. I'll never know if it was to dismiss me or to encourage me. I chose to believe the latter.

Once I got my bearings, my speech picked up speed. I was nervous and excited about answering a caller's questions. I cleared my throat and dove in. "If he really wants happy lilacs," I began, "he should plant them out in the sun and away from those pine trees. His brother-in-law is right, the ground is too acidic…I mean, even if he adds stuff to the soil, it'll never be perfect."

Beyond Lilla

"That's fine, if…," Mr. Franklin tried to squeeze in a comment. Now he wanted to talk after hanging me out to dry! Take a hike, buddy!

"Oh! You know what would be great under those trees?" I interrupted him because I was nervous and excited. I looked at him sheepishly, but continued anyway, "Try rhododendrons! They'd love it under there. Then move the lilacs out in the yard, in the sun so everyone can see them. You'll have so many flowers your wife can fill vases all over the house. Oh, your house…will…smell…like…heaven."

My speech slowed down toward the end because Franklin distracted me with a great big yawn, which I'm sure was audible over the airwaves.

Immediately, the producer made a swift cut sign across his neck and mouthed "commercial!" to the person at the control board. An announcer in a side booth began his spiel about Clancy's Potting Soil. The studio had three minutes to put everything back to normal. It wasn't enough time.

From what Sam and I had seen during past shows, that director, Bob, literally ran this show. He lifted his whole arm to point at Franklin and said, "You're done. You were warned last week and the week before. Today you show up late and then treat everyone like you-know-what." Then Bob swung his arm toward the door to the street. "Get out. Now." Franklin leaned back further in his chair. He smirked at Bob. "I said get lost. Or do you need a hand from security?"

Franklin got up, threw his headset on the floor and stomped over to Bob. He clenched his jaw and spoke in a low tone right into Bob's face so the live audience couldn't hear. I should have been so lucky. They stood right in front of me. I felt trapped. If I ever get out of this seat, Sam and I are gonna run out the back door and never come back!

Sam quietly strolled from the back of the room and stood near the front of the audience. He must have read my mind. We raised our eyebrows at each other. I was biting the side of my lip to calm my nerves. We'd make a break for it as soon as the two men finished going at it.

"You son of a bitch! Who do you think you are? You can't kick me out," Franklin laid into Bob. "I still have two weeks left on my contract. You're not gonna swipe my last two paychecks out from under me. No sir!"

"You want your last paychecks?" Bob retorted. "Fine! They'll be in the mail on Monday! I want you out of here, Paul."

Bob jerked his head and eyes toward the door. He needn't have bothered. By the time he finished speaking, Franklin was halfway to the door, muttering obscenities the entire way. Franklin pushed the door open like a crazy man and flung it shut behind him, thus ensuring he went out with a bang.

Everyone in that silent studio sat there with our mouths hanging open. In exactly one commercial break the old regime had been ousted and a new one was about to be seated in its place. Albeit, after an incredibly awkward silence. Bob rattled orders to the production crew and pointed in all directions. He jumped over to the microphone just before the last commercial ended.

"Well, folks, this is Bob Anderson, in for Paul Franklin. It seems Paul has been called away from the studio. I apologize, but it looks like we won't be able to continue with today's show. We're going to broadcast one of Paul's previous shows for the remainder of the hour. Again, please accept our apologies. We'll be back next week with a brand new show."

He's not kidding, I chuckled to myself. I would hate to be in Bob's shoes. He has to come up with a completely new show in less than a week.

While Bob finished speaking, I silently slid off my stool. Sam waited for me just beyond the production area. I don't think Bob even knew I was still there. The audience murmured amongst themselves, trying to decide if they should leave or wait for somebody to dismiss them. As I gently laid my headset on my stool, someone yelled from the back of the audience.

"Miss! Miss! Could you answer a question for me about pruning my lilacs?"

I recognized Mr. Burnside's accent. He nodded in several directions to greet everyone in the studio. I had taken a step toward Sam when Bob put his hand on my arm to stop me. I looked at him with the same incredulous look I had given Sam when I thought he wanted to attack Franklin.

"Hey, Lilla. Whaddya think?" Bob asked. "Would you like to answer some questions today? See how it feels up here? We're already playing some old shows, so you won't be on the air. Everyone in the audience today came to hear about lilacs. We could at least have some sort of group discussion so their trip wouldn't be wasted. Do you want to lead a talk and maybe answer some questions?"

Fortunately, Sam had sidled up to the group. I held my hands out to him. They were shaking because I was so excited I could hardly contain myself. Sam held them still while we talked about the offer.

"Oh my goodness! Really?" I said to Bob. Then I looked up at Sam. "Wow, what do you think?"

Sam was as taken aback as I was at this offer. "Sure! Well, yeah, you should do this!" Sam said to me.

"Oh, no. I'm not staying up here alone. You're coming with me." I wrapped my arm around Sam and pulled him close to me. "This is Sam, my husband," I said to Bob. "Sam's been doing the landscaping for the new tracts over in Pittsford. He really knows a lot about lilacs – and tons of other plants. Can we do it together? Up here?" I motioned to the two empty stools.

"Sure! Sit down and make yourselves comfortable! You won't need the whole headset. We'll just set up microphones for both of you."

I was a little concerned the audience might think I ran Franklin out of town but everyone in the studio seemed so much more relaxed after he left. Bob's enthusiasm put Sam and me at ease. We settled onto the stools and answered question after question about lilacs, first from Mr. Burnside, then from Mrs. Goldenhat and then Madame Curlydoo. Our discussion lasted over two hours. We could have talked even longer if the station didn't need to set up the space for another show that evening.

It was almost 4:00 when Sam and I finally left the station. We thanked Bob for such a delightful opportunity. In turn, he thanked us for sticking around and said he was impressed with our knowledge. "This audience was the liveliest it's been in months! I don't know exactly what we'll air next week, but you're welcome to stop in to check it out."

Fortunately, for all of us, Bob didn't have to think too long or too hard about what would replace The Paul Franklin Show. By the following Wednesday, the station had received numerous calls asking if I would come back for another show. Some of the callers had been in the audience, but most of them had only heard the few sentences I managed to spill out before they yanked the show off the air.

None of the callers remembered my name so they'd say, "You know…that lilac lady." The station received many requests for "that lilac lady" to return for a show on lilacs since the past week's show had been cut short.

On the Thursday after that disastrous show, I received a phone call from Bob. He asked if Sam and I would consider doing a few shows beginning on Saturday…in two days. Real live radio shows that would be aired in full! Of course, we said yes.

Our first shows went well considering we were such novices. Lucky for us nobody stumped us with any difficult questions. We stuck with lilacs, a safe topic since we knew so much about them. During the weeks between shows, we'd study up on new topics for following weeks. Bob was impressed with how we assigned "homework" to ourselves.

After Paul Franklin's contract officially expired, the station offered a contract to Sam and me, which we happily accepted. The show was now ours! We could even name it ourselves. We considered at least fifty different names before settling on one of Sam's suggestions. Our new show was "Can You Dig It?" Again, I'll stress it was Sam's idea. I know, I know. It sounds corny as hell now, but it worked. The station hoped the earthy youth of the '60s and '70s would embrace the show. They did.

Listeners wrote to say the new hosts of the show were very refreshing. Everyone directed their comments to either Sam or the Lilac Lady.

Soon our friends and my coworkers at the garden store began calling me Lilac Lady as well. Once listeners discovered where I worked, they'd head to the store and ask for me. It didn't take long before I was the Lilac Lady around most of the garden folk. In a few years, I would become Rochester's Lilac Lady.

Chapter Eleven: Visiting Albert in New Hampshire

After my funeral stuff had calmed down and Marion had moved away, my thoughts turned to my brother. "You know, Amelia," I said one November day, "I've been thinking, I should go see my brother in New Hampshire. I told you he had that stroke, right? I wanted to go right after my funeral when I heard my nephew telling Helen about it, but I got sidetracked at Marion's house. I haven't traveled very far yet but I want to see how Albert's doing. What do you think? Should I go?"

"That would be nice, if you want to go," Amelia replied.

I was a bit disappointed when she spoke so nonchalantly. I was hoping for a more definite response. I wasn't sure if going to see my brother would be the right thing for me or for him. Would it upset him if he saw me? Would it cause any setbacks with his recovery? That thing with Marion was unplanned to say the least, a total accident. I didn't plan for her to see me but she did. I hoped she wasn't still talking about it to all of Helen's friends in Pennsylvania.

I thought Amelia might offer some insight about what happens when spirits visit their living relatives. Do we show ourselves to them? Do they want to see us or is it better to visit in secret and stay invisible? Amelia must have heard stories from other spirits who went to visit their families, but she remained evasive about offering any suggestions.

I'm sure it had something to do with her being buried somewhere else and never daring to go that far from Mount Hope. She'd never visited her real grave, much less any relatives who were still alive after she died. That was one area in which she didn't have any experience to share with me.

I was concerned about whether I should show myself. I was also nervous about traveling so far. As pathetic as it sounds, I had started to think of the cemetery as my home. It offered me a place of security and acceptance. I knew what to expect and who I'd see every day, whether it was Amelia and Harvey, or those two guys from down the street walking their dog every night.

There was the woman with the great jogging suits, who stretched at the front gate on Mondays and Fridays before jogging around the neighborhood. I'd grown accustomed to the familiar faces, both living and dead, inhabiting my small world of Mount Hope Cemetery and its nearby streets.

As for traveling any distances, I didn't know what to expect. Was it any different from popping over to the other side of Rochester and back? It sounded simple but I wanted some reassurance from Amelia. She wasn't much help. She allowed the cemetery fence to imprison her soul. I vowed not to become like her.

I tried a different approach. I told her, "I haven't even gone to see my own brother. What if he dies before I can see him? Most likely, he won't get stuck here like I am. He always had a better sense of direction. He'll probably end up in the right place, wherever that is. Then I'll never see him again." I thought Amelia might support someone who's seizing the last chance they might have to see someone they love. She still refused to share any wisdom.

"It's good to see the ones you know," was all she said. Did she mean the living people I know who are scattered throughout the country or my spirit friends right here inside these cemetery walls? She didn't emphatically agree with my idea to leave, but she didn't tell me that I shouldn't go, either. I needed help adjusting to being a free spirit without any restrictions of time and place.

Traveling after I died was an odd experience. Once I decided to go to my brother, I was free to leave, right then, that very second. No little tasks required my attention. I didn't have to tell anyone I was leaving. Nobody! Nor did I have to pack anything or stop at the gas station to fill up the car and get some spending money. It sounded great but I was still unsure if I should do this. Those last minute errands would have given me time to work out details for my trip or rethink it altogether.

I didn't know what might happen as I went further and further from my body. Maybe that's precisely what I needed, to get away from here and break this cycle. Yes, this might be my ticket to Sam. I just hadn't looked far enough! I made up my mind.

"Yeah, I think I'll go. My brother and his wife are the last ones from my generation still alive on my side, so it's important for me to share at least one last moment with them."

I started out of the cemetery hesitantly. I turned toward Amelia, and said, "I'll see you when I get back." Testing her the way a child tests his mother. Was she really letting me leave? I took a few baby steps and paused, glancing over my shoulder every few feet. I waited for her to put her foot down and give me several inarguable reasons why I should stay.

"Okay, you know where to find us. I hope all is well for your brother and his wife." Amelia bid me goodbye, I think. She resumed her daily roaming. Stuck in the same places, same times, and she said Harvey was set in his ways! I needed to leave. I wasn't about to let myself waste my eternity in a twenty-four hour loop.

Thus, I began my first long distance trip away from the cemetery grounds and my body that lay underneath them. Now, I needed to decide how to get to my destination. I could wish myself there and stand in front of my brother immediately, or I could go slowly, giving myself time to think along the way. I chose the latter. Of course, I still traveled more quickly than the traffic. Gliding gently over the buildings and trees, I sort of followed the roadways, though I cut straight across the nuisance curves that doubled back on themselves.

A weekend getaway does wonders for the soul. Gorgeous scenery flashed by. Traveling east, I watched the farms of upstate New York give way to the rolling foothills of the Adirondacks. Flying much more quickly than I realized, within an hour I found myself in the Green Mountains of Vermont. In the cemetery, most of the leaves had fallen from their trees, with the exception of a few weeping willow leaves clinging tenaciously to their branches. The November skies turned grayer and I guessed a little colder. The trees in Vermont were bare. Patches of snow already dotted the higher elevations. Oh, how I wished I could smell those pine trees!

I decided to travel closer to the ground, so I might get a better look at any wildlife, especially turkeys trotting through the fields. I don't know why, but the by wild turkeys strutting by the side of the road always amused me. Maybe it's because they were so real compared to the Thanksgiving turkeys, with breasts so large they could barely walk, much less fly. On this trip, I saw eight turkeys in one field alone. The only thing that would have made my trip better would have been if I had seen a moose.

Over the fifty years Sam and I traveled these roads to visit family, we never saw one moose. That was probably a blessing. The last thing anybody really wants to see is the front of their car going under the belly of a moose. That eight hundred pound body then falls on their car roof as they careen off the road. Not exactly the highlight of anybody's vacation.

This trip was so peaceful, with no real hurry to get to New Hampshire. If I wanted to move things along, I knew I could float over any hills. I wished I had visited my brother back in October when the fall colors were at their best most vibrant. I could have glided right over the buses full of leaf peepers as they chased peak colors all over New England. It was big business for the folks in those tiny towns. The inns were always booked. It was impossible to make good time driving behind lumbering buses constantly stopping for photo ops.

Despite the beautiful views of the New England countryside, Sam and I didn't do much sightseeing on our trips to visit my family in New Hampshire. Our work schedules were so hectic we wanted to get right to our destination so we would have more time to visit.

Determined to disprove the old New England adage "You can't get there from here!" we constantly searched for quicker routes to shorten the length of our drive. We found secret roads all around the little country towns. Some credit goes to our New York State license plate. Vermonters pulled off to let us pass. As far as they were concerned, the sooner we crazy New York drivers got out of their town, the better.

As I floated over the bare trees this November day, I still recognized some of our shortcuts. I drifted down toward the roadside, fading in and out of the tree line. I could have floated over everything but I wanted to see it as though I were sitting next to Sam in one of our old jalopies. Boy, if I had a dollar for every trip Sam and I made over this road… in all of our different cars. I'll never know how our first few rust heaps made it over these mountains. At least we had decent roads. I couldn't imagine traveling over the bumpy dirt roads in the "olden days."

I came upon the overgrown entrance to a narrow road that had been bypassed by new construction about eighty years ago. I used to glance at this road from the highway and wonder if anyone ever actually drove down this little lane. As Sam and I whizzed past on our way to New Hampshire, I'd savor how the dappled sunlight flickered over the quintessential New England dirt road with grass patches running down the middle. Now, heavy brush obscured the view from the main road. Saplings covered the entire road. I decided to explore it before the forest completely reclaimed it.

Why not? I didn't have to worry about getting lost or being late. The vanishing road took me back in time, even before my time, really. Sounds from the highway grew faint, although I was able to hear them from a much greater distance than if I still had a body with normal human ears. As the old road curved deeper into the woods, wintering birds treated me to a symphony of chirping.

The road snaked along gullies and behind boulders. I rounded one particularly sharp turn and tried to fathom how anybody could have ever maneuvered a vehicle on this road at all. Stopping at the edge of a steep embankment, I meditated to the trickle of a brook that paralleled the road for miles. Like many New England roads, this one probably started out as a horse trail, following the brook from one side of the mountain to the other. Later, it became wider to accommodate automobiles.

The roads that survived were paved, while roads like this reverted back to overgrown paths. That's why I was so surprised to see two figures moving about at the bottom of a gully.

As I looked closer, I realized they weren't hikers. They were spirits, like me. They looked busy, stooping repeatedly in the dense brush, picking things from the ground and trying to contain their collection in their ghostly cupped hands. I went down for a better look. I waited for them to acknowledge me, but apparently, they had no time for strangers. Two spirits, a man and a woman, appeared to be in their fifties. I estimated the style of their clothes was from the nineteen forties.

The man wore a suit and fedora, the woman, a slim fitted dress with matching hat. My mother and father had worn similar clothes. This couple certainly dressed nicely when they were alive. What could possibly possess them to traipse around these mountains?

181

I inched my way toward the woman spirit, so she wouldn't think I posed any danger. She didn't even glance at me. She bent down to the ground and gently pinched a very tiny speck of something between her thumb and forefinger. She delicately placed it into the palm of her other hand and bent down to collect another piece. Try as I might, I really couldn't see anything in her hands.

I moved in front of her and tilted my body and head toward her to gain her attention. "Excuse me," I called to the top of her head as she stared at the ground. "What are you doing, if you don't mind me asking?"

She stood upright, placed her hands on her backside, moaning and arching her back to stretch out those muscles after bending for so long. It seems she forgot two things. One, that she had supposedly been holding something in her hands, which probably slipped right through anyway, and two, she couldn't possibly be sore because we're ghosts. We don't have aching muscles. I know it's hard to let go of some of those little things that felt so good during one's lifetime, even if that lifetime was several lifetimes ago.

"What? Oh, hello!" She realized for the first time that someone was talking to her. "Oh, no, dearie, you needn't concern yourself with this. It's quite a job. I don't know if we'll ever finish."

"Finish what?" I asked. I looked around and still couldn't see anything going on.

"It's a long story..." She hesitated, giving me the chance to get away before subjecting myself to her longwinded tale.

"Believe me, I've got time," I joked. She nodded.

"Well, I'll try to make it much quicker and less painful for you than it was for us," she began. "We had this accident...no, wait." She fluttered her hand to dismiss her first few words. She put a hand on her chin, and decided to begin again. "Let's see...First we went to Albany for my mother-in-law. Well... for her ashes. The poor dear just couldn't hang on 'til Christmas." The woman clicked her tongue and swayed her head in sympathy.

"She always said when she passed away she wanted to be cremated and her ashes were to be brought back up north to Montpelier to be buried with my father-in-law, her husband. He died some years back. So my mother-in-law moved back to Albany, and so, we had to go to Albany to get her stuff and her ashes."

I wondered if the woman was Italian. Her hands flew all over as she told her story. I nodded sympathetically.

She sighed, and continued. "We had such a nice time with the family that last Christmas. We lived way up near Montpelier even farther north than Montpelier so we knew it would be a long time before we saw them again," she stopped and looked around. "We never thought it would be this long!

"There was a storm the day we drove home which was the day after Christmas. If only we waited one more day..." She sighed. "It wasn't the snow that got us, it was a stupid moose! Came out of nowhere! Right in the middle of the road, on that sharp corner up there. My husband tried his best to stop, but it was too slippery. The next thing we knew we were pitched down this hill."

I looked up the steep embankment. Oh, how horrible to be trapped inside a car rolling down a hill like that.

"Yes. It was very scary," She replied to my thoughts. "It happened so fast. The next thing we remember is waking up down here. Well, not waking up, but, well..." she shrugged.

"Yeah," I answered, "I know what you mean. I still haven't dared to say it myself."

"Well, at first we didn't realize we were...you know," she grimaced. "There was so much stuff all over the place we didn't see ourselves at first. You should've seen the mess! My word! All of our clothes up and down the hill. My brand new dresses. I never even wore them! Christmas presents flew all the way from this tree here to that big rock over there. All the food from the back seat was smeared inside the whole car.

"And then we saw the urn in this brook. It was completely empty! Ashes were everywhere! All over the snow. All over the car. All over our clothes. We ran around to scoop as much as we could back into the urn, but we couldn't catch any of it. We thought the snow made it slip out of our hands. When we tried to scoop it off the car we found our bodies. Our heads were...and then my arm...and...oh, it was just...I'll never forget it.

"We knew we were...you know, but we didn't know why we didn't go to heaven. After someone found our accident, they took our bodies away and all the stuff we had with us. Later in the spring, they came for the car.

"We figured when they took everything away we'd be free and clear to go to heaven, but no such luck. Where was everyone else? All of our dead relatives from then? And now, where are our other relatives who must have died since?"

"I don't know!" I cried. "I'm trying to figure out the same thing!" The lady looked alarmed. "Oh, sorry! Sorry," I said more quietly. "The same thing happened to me. I don't know what to do. I'm trying to figure out why I'm not with my husband. There must be some pathway I still need to find or something."

"Yes," the woman nodded. "That's what we think. The only thing we came up with is his mother's ashes. We still need to take them to his father's grave. We've been collecting them, but they're so tiny and they've flown so far we may just be here for eternity. We've been collecting those invisible suckers for nearly eighty years, now."

"Oh, gee. Good luck with that." I hoped I didn't sound sarcastic. I was sure most of the ashes had washed away in the stream within a week of the accident, and the rest of them had been absorbed into the ground over all these years. Yet, how can anyone, least of all me, fault them for trying to find any way out of this so they can move on?

"Wow, there must have been a million ashes to pick up." I said, as I scanned the forest floor. "I can try to help if you want. My name is Lilla, by the way. I'm heading to see my brother but I can stick around for a while."

"Nice to meet you, Lilla. Thank you for the offer but we'll be fine. Eh, it keeps us busy and out of trouble. The worst part is over." She shrugged. "I'm Eleanor Ashford and that's my husband, Harold."

Ashford? I stifled a smirk.

"It's okay to laugh, dear," Eleanor chuckled. "Believe me, if you only knew all the times I've sung about Mother Ashford's ashes. Singing helps pass the time."

Her husband, Harold, had worked his way toward us. He steadily picked at the ground, grasping at imaginary ashes. Harold stood and greeted me with a nod, then proceeded to share some lovely details about the crash, in case Eleanor's description wasn't graphic enough.

"How do you do, Lilla? Let me tell you, that damn moose took off with barely a scratch, with us just lying on the ground, dead as dead can be. Would you believe the son of a gun came back the next day? He ate our apple pie and licked up half my brains with it! It was two more days until they found us, or what was left after the critters got to us."

Gross. Thank goodness he stopped when he did. It must've been horrible for them to watch those animals chew on their flesh. I preferred Eleanor and Harold as they appeared now, so I shook off the image of their broken bodies and belongings scattered all over the hillside.

Instead, I chose to revel in the present of this crisp autumn day. Pine needles and golden leaves shone in the patchy sunshine of the November forest. Winter birds chirped from the branches. I wanted to enjoy more of it. If Harold and Eleanor didn't need me, I was ready to move on. "Well, if you don't need any help, I'm going to head for my brother's house. He lives over in New Hampshire, just over the border."

Harold stretched his ghostly arms as he scoped out the next place he would search for his mother's ashes. "Well, thanks for asking," he nodded. "We've got our work cut out for us but like Eleanor said, it keeps us out of trouble, all right. You go on. Have a good trip to your brother's place." He returned to his spot to pick for more ashes.

"Yes, dear. Have a safe trip," Eleanor said. Then she added, "Well, I guess there's not much that can hurt us anyway, right?"

"Yeah, I suppose you're right. Hopefully this won't take too much longer. It was nice meeting you! Bye!" I shouted over my shoulder as I moved deeper into the forest.

"Bye!" I heard Eleanor call. As the distance between us grew, I heard her singing ever so faintly, something about Mother Ashford's windblown ashes hiding in the trees.

After I left Harold and Eleanor, I wondered about all the times Sam and I drove past that old road. Harold and Eleanor had been there all this time, not that I would have seen them when I was alive. How much exists in this other world that the living never see? Well, maybe I'm just seeing it because I'm stuck here with nothing better to do. Can the other souls, the ones who have really crossed over, see any of this from where they are? I wondered. Do they come down to see and hear life's daily events, like watching soap operas? Perhaps. I held onto this belief in case Sam was one of them.

Meeting Harold and Eleanor made me realize how much I had never seen from the world of the living. Spirits coexisted in this secret parallel world, and they were all still dealing with their own situations. I was one of them, now. The living would no longer see me. They could walk right through me as the events of their lives unfolded around me.

****

When I returned to the main road, automobiles whizzed past my unseen form, confirming I had joined the ranks of Harold and Eleanor in their invisible world. No matter. I didn't come here to think about traffic. This trip was about my brother and the beautiful scenery that surrounded me as I flew to his home. It had been too long since I spent time in the New England countryside. My brother Albert and his wife Christine lived in a small town on the west side of New Hampshire. Nearby Hanover, a beautiful ivy-covered town, was home to Dartmouth College. My sister-in-law and brother had both taught English and literature classes there for many years.

They continued lecturing up until a few years ago. However, once they reached their seventies, it became difficult for them to maneuver those country roads for any distances, especially at night. Since my brother's stroke, I was sure they spent most of their time at home. I was afraid to see how feeble the stroke might have left my brother. I entertained the idea of going back to Rochester instead of into his house. I milled around the obstacle course in his front yard while mustering my courage.

My brother's yard was a hoot. For some reason, my brother, the English professor, fancied himself a gentleman farmer. He scattered his front yard with rustic Americana: a rusty tractor, a butter churn, a rain barrel planted with flowers, chairs woven from birch branches, and of course, his pride and joy was his tool shed that looked like an outhouse.

My brother was under the impression his historic collection constituted some sort of scaled down Colonial Williamsburg. Unfortunately, to everybody else's eyes it looked more like a hermit's land claim.

Passersby must have had a hard time believing the inside of this house had running water, much less original artwork and bookshelves lined with valuable first editions. Albert proudly obliged tourists who asked if they could photograph his property. I didn't have the heart to tell him it was likely they thought they had stumbled onto a hermit's lair.

Time had taken its toll on Albert's collection. What used to look fashionably rustic was now authentically distressed. It's amazing how old age sneaks up on us. As I looked around, I was glad I had sold my house when I did, before I couldn't keep everything manicured. I knew my brother would have a hard time leaving this all behind, despite its neglected appearance.

After I finished looking around the yard, it was time to commit to stay or go. I decided to stay, and entered slowly through the front wall of the house. Seeing Christine sitting on the couch, sorting laundry, watching an old movie on television, I thought the years had been good to her. She was petite but not frail by any means and managed to retain a somewhat fit appearance. It was about three years since I my last visit with her and Albert, when one of their sons brought them out to visit me. She must about seventy-five but could pass for sixty or sixty-five. That's not too shabby, at least from the perspective of a dead eighty-eight year old.

Back in high school, I worked in a small drugstore that offered discounts to seniors over sixty. I offered the discount to any customers who looked old enough, but first I double-checked their age. When I inquired in all seriousness if the little ladies were over sixty, they smiled. They'd stretch over the counter as far as they could reach and pat my hand. "You're so sweet," they would chuckle.

Of course, I gave them the discount. I didn't realize until years later that these women had to be at least eighty! To my sixteen-year-old eyes, sixty sounded like it would look really old. When I started receiving those discounts myself, I realized sixty wasn't nearly as ancient looking as my teenage mind had conjured.

Christine gathered neat stacks of socks and underwear into her arms. She walked slowly down the hallway, balancing her armload with her chin. I floated along behind her until she went into the bedroom.

I started getting nervous. No sign of Albert yet. Then I heard the refrigerator door close. My brother was in the kitchen, pouring himself a glass of milk. From the back, he looked like any old man you might see at a diner on Sunday morning: His demeanor slightly stooped, with thin gray hair, and his baggy plaid shirt which fit him better when it was new, probably about fifteen years ago. He took his glass over to the table and sat down to look out the window at his precious paradise.

On the wall near the table hung a picture of New Hampshire's Old Man of the Mountain, a rock formation that used to protrude directly out of the side of Franconia Notch up in the White Mountains. The Old Man was mostly a natural formation, but he had a few touch-ups over the years. Armed with a pair of binoculars, or a quarter for the viewing machines, tourists gazed up at the famous profile, which balanced precariously from the mountainside for many years. One night about twenty-five years ago, the Old Man came crashing down, his nose, mouth and chin disappearing into the thick of the forest, probably taking some pine trees down with them. Only his furrowed eyebrow remained to watch over the carnage.

If ten tons of granite hurtled down a mountain, and nobody was there to hear it, did it still make a sound? The answer was yes, if you counted the collective sighs of sadness echoed by the New Hampshire folks when they lost their famous icon. Oh, and what about all of the quarters, pencils, mugs, shirts, key chains, snow globes, place mats, pens, license plates and beer steins with the Old Man's picture? Were they rendered worthless or more valuable if manufactured B.C.: Before the Crash?

Alas, the Old Man's passing wasn't in vain, for his stony carcass was rescued from the mountainside and sold off as keepsake tokens, kind of like the Berlin Wall. If a child promised to be careful, his grandfather might let him fondle the precious remains while listening to stories of visits to see the Old Man of the Mountain.

My nephews belonged to the last generation that remembered seeing the Old Man when he still watched over the mountainside. My brother belonged to the last generation that actually cared. He kept the memory alive and well in that picture on his kitchen wall. It was poetic to see them in the kitchen together, The Old Man of the Mountain and the old man in the plaid shirt.

Albert didn't seem to have much of a problem getting around his kitchen. From my nephew's conversation about my brother's stroke, I didn't know what to expect. I was more than slightly relieved at his condition and was glad I came. My imagination conjured images of a drooling, paralyzed stranger. Either the stroke had been minor or the therapy had worked wonders.

Albert drank his juice and munched slowly on some cookies. It was hard to tell if he chewed so gingerly because of his dentures, the stroke, or old age in general. I couldn't detect anything unusually labored in his actions. Any unsteadiness in his hands could be just as much from old age as from a stroke.

I was glad to see Albert doing so well. It was hard to say what the future would hold. I didn't know if this might be the last time I would see him. For all I knew, he could die and see Sam long before I do. I moved around and down for a better look at his face. I hovered right in front of him, the kitchen table neatly slicing through the image of my body.

The tabletop concealed my lower half from Albert, while my head and shoulders appeared to rest on the top of the table, like the hairdressing doll I gave Helen one Christmas. I wanted Albert to know I was thinking of him. I hoped he would see me. He was the first person to whom I wanted to appear. Maybe someday he could let Sam know I'm still here.

Albert was absorbed with his cookies, taking little bites around the edges, saving the frosted parts until last. Yup, this was my brother all right. He always did have a sweet tooth. I wasn't sure if he could tear himself away from his snack long enough to notice me staring at him from the middle of the table.

Finally, the magic spell of the sugar rush was broken. As he lifted the last bit of cookie to his mouth he saw me. He jumped and dropped his cookie onto the floor. It's a rare occasion for my brother to fumble a cookie, and even more out of character to leave it on the floor. This time he didn't even look for it because he was so distracted by my apparition.

I smiled and reached up to touch his face. Naturally, that startled him all the more. He pulled his arms away when my hand came up through the table about a foot from where he saw my head and shoulders.

It never occurred to me how creepy it must look to have assorted parts of my body pop out of the table. I hoped he wouldn't run from me and hurt himself the way Cindy had. Instead, it was just the opposite: he sat glued to his chair. Slowly his expression changed from fright to confusion, then to sadness. It was a start, anyway.

I wished I could talk to him and tell him I was glad he was feeling better, but my voice couldn't cross back into his world. I would have to express myself as best I could with just facial expressions. I hoped he didn't think my presence was a sign he would die soon.

Whatever the case, he reached over to pass his trembling hand through my forehead. Of course, he couldn't feel anything. He convinced himself he must have been dreaming. He laughed quietly and closed his eyes for a second. I used this opportunity to grab my arms and disappear from his view. "Oh, Lilla, I really do wish you were still here with us. We never got to say any 'goodbyes'," he said when he finally opened his eyes.

When he had first seen me, his body stiffened with tension. Now that he took me for a daydream, he relaxed a little. His shoulders drooped and he sighed. I don't know if he was disappointed or relieved to think I wasn't really there. I guess it didn't matter. We both enjoyed one last chance to see each other, even if he thought it was only in his imagination.

"Hon, are you done with today's paper?" The sound of crinkling newspapers heralded Christine's approach to the kitchen. I thought it best to leave before Albert asked her if she could see me too. Let him have his little daydream. No need for any explanation other than he was thinking of his sister and felt like he could almost see me.

I moved out to the yard just as Christine entered the kitchen. I heard Albert say he had read the paper but still wanted to look at the sports page. First, he told her, he had to clean off his shoe because he had stepped on a cookie that he had dropped. Fortunately, he didn't say anything about me. I didn't want people thinking he was nuts, like poor Marion. As for me, I was happy to have had a quiet intentional visit among the living for once. I was getting comfortable with my ability to control when, where, and to whom I would be visible.

I weaved my way through the cluttered yard and headed up the road. I wanted to take in a little more of the local scenery before I went back to the cemetery. The blustery grayness of this dark November day conveyed a chill I could not feel. Heavy clouds rolled in and waited for their cue to release their snow. Pine trees waved goodbye to fall. Crisp leaves scratched down country roads but would soon be muffled by winter's blanket.

It was easy to see how the changing seasons of the area attracted more than just skiers and hikers. Artists and writers always had an affinity for this part of New Hampshire, too. Maxfield Parrish and Augustus Saint-Gaudens, two of the better-known old timers, had enjoyed the company of other local artists as well as their neighbors from the surrounding community.

For some reason, the newer talents preferred to keep a low profile, using the rural countryside to escape the public eye. Sometimes it worked so well you never knew about the famous people living in your midst until they died. Other times, as in the case of my brother's neighbor, the secret backfires.

Just down the road from my brother's house hung the sign for the Milford Art Institute. The institute had been built on the former estate of H.C. Milford, the reclusive author. He wrote several bestsellers in the 1950s and developed quite a following among college students. By using their own slang, he connected to their psyches and endeared himself to them. Soon he was barraged by hoards of students disrupting his privacy. They thought he had the answers to life's questions.

He tried hiding in the hills of New Hampshire, but this only challenged his fans. The locals remained tight lipped about the famous resident's whereabouts, but every so often some students' dumb luck led them straight to his doorstep. The poor old guy played into it every time. He'd come out, shake his fist and yell some indiscernible scholarly gibberish. Right about then, someone would snap a photo and slap it on the front page of a college paper, confirming the myths. We never really did find out what H.C. stood for but we joked it probably wasn't "Happy Camper."

The irony of the whole thing was that after H.C. died, his widow created the Milford Art Institute, one of the most famous artistic retreats in the country. The locals ate it up.

The secrecy they provided during H.C.'s lifetime was, they felt, an investment in their future. They were only too happy to accommodate "The Seekers," as they called the tourists.

Part of the legacy of H.C. Milford's secrecy was the challenge of the hunt. New attendees of the institute were given a vague map, using a scavenger hunt system through the town and local businesses, The Seekers would find the institute and the shop owners could cash in on the fun.

The Seekers would pile into a car and drive through the surrounding towns and back roads in search of all things Maxfield Parrish and H.C. Milford. My brother toyed with any Seekers who ended up on his doorstep by mistake. In their jubilation at thinking they'd found H.C. in the flesh, they failed to account for the fact that my brother was a good thirty years younger than H.C. Perhaps they mistook Albert for the personification of one of H.C.'s famous characters.

Albert would offer them coffee and tell them he was H.C., who had been dead for ten years. They almost always believed him; positive that H.C. must have started false rumors about his death so everyone would leave him alone. Albert usually confessed after about twenty minutes, when it became obvious he was fudging answers to pointed questions about H.C.'s work. Of course he knew the answers, but he was curious to find out if The Seekers knew as much as they professed. Surprisingly, The Seekers weren't angry. The hunt was fun and everybody was good natured about it, especially H.C.'s widow. She eventually sold the institute to investors and moved to Florida.

Albert and Christine both taught summer classes at the institute. The last I knew, they still attended lectures. They loved this artsy circle of acquaintances, sitting around the fireside, drinking port wine and discussing their latest endeavors.

Christine and Albert seemed in good shape. I didn't think they needed my help with anything, except maybe cleaning up their yard, but I was done with yard work forever. It was nice to check on them, and have a nostalgic chuckle about H.C.

I enjoyed my trip, but I was ready to return to my little world in the cemetery. This was a good jaunt, but I wasn't ready for any long distance trips for any length of time.

I did learn something on this trip, from Harold and Eleanor, picking up those ashes. Did I need to tend to some sort of task to earn my wings? Maybe I would figure out something when I returned to Mount Hope.

Tracy Fontaine

Chapter Twelve: Happy Holidays

Apparently, as my strength grew, so did my ability for immediate mobility. Even before I finished thinking about returning to Mount Hope, I found myself back in the cemetery. If I had planned a little better, I would have tried to land somewhere discreet, maybe behind the chapel. As it was, I popped up in the middle of a group of children's spirits, who were playing a game of tag. They all gasped when I suddenly appeared in their midst. It could have been worse; I could've materialized in the midst of some living children and frightened them to pieces. The spirit children at least knew who I was, but they were startled nonetheless. It wasn't like me to jump up from nowhere unless I was with Jodi.

I was a little befuddled myself. I had expected to take at least three smaller leaps to get back here. Landing on my exact target on the first try kind of threw me. The children and I stared at each other for a few seconds while I tried to figure out where I was.

I was still on high alert, ready to disappear if I accidentally ended up in a mall or something. Stupefied, I stood there trying to get my bearings. Finally, I recognized the Danforth crypt and some of the kids' faces. I relaxed a little, but the kids still gawked at me.

Thankfully, Jodi finally broke the awkward silence. I didn't notice her until she came from somewhere off to the side of the clearing. "You should see your faces!" she laughed and pointed at me and the children. "You numb nuts look like you've seen a goblin!"

Jodi, my goofy ambassador, dispelled the tension. It gave the twisted girl, who looked slightly goblin-like herself, a rare chance to comfort everyone instead of scaring them. For several minutes, we laughed at ourselves. Before I knew it, a tiny thing tapped me on the leg and yelled, "You're it!" Just like that, I leaped from my brother's decaying yard into a vibrant game of tag with dead children. I had a ball, tagging the kids, scooting out of reach as they tried to tag me back. It was great fun not having to "act my age."

Around your tenth birthday, everyone starts telling you to act your age, and it doesn't stop until you're dead. By the time you get the nerve to decide for yourself how to act, you're too damned old to keep up.

Well, I was keeping up now! That's for sure. Despite our ages at the time we died, the children and I were on equal footing now. We flew among the gravestones all night. Fatigue belonged to a world that grew more distant by the minute.

****

Blustery weather had finally found its way to Rochester. Snow-laden clouds filled the winter skies. Disciplined joggers still ran through the cemetery, but casual strollers became sparse. Faint tapping sounds resonated throughout the neighborhood. At first I thought somebody was chopping wood. The locals had been hammering a few nails here and there on the sides of their houses, too. I figured everyone was preparing their homes ready for winter. However, on one blustery night, Christmas lights illuminated the neighborhood, snaking around porches, railings and garages. Cheap plastic reindeer graced several rooftops. I swear people put out their decorations earlier every year.

"Harvey, have you seen the Christmas decorations on those houses?"

"I try not to," Harvey replied, expressing his usual distaste for the festively tacky.

"Oh, that's right. You're more the Metropolitan Home type."

"What? What's that?"

"Never mind," I sighed. Explaining a magazine that existed decades after Harvey would only make it worse, so I moved on.

"Isn't it early to hang those lights? It's not even Thanksgiving yet."

"Thanksgiving! That was last week, missy!"

"You're kidding!" I said. I looked at him in shock, yet I believed him. I never knew him to tease anybody - that was Jodi's job. I don't think he had any funny bones in his body. He smirked when he realized I was serious. I hadn't kept track of the passing days, but it made sense when I counted backward to Halloween.

Thanksgiving had come and gone right under my nose! Without that usual pre-Thanksgiving banter I shared when I was alive, I was really out of the loop. Even if the conversation was the same every year, it still added to the holiday anticipation. "Where will you go? What will you bring? Who will be there?"

And so on. Even at Winfield Acres we plastered cardboard turkeys on our doors on November first and started counting the days until the turkey dinner feeding frenzy. All the soft food we could ever want, served on one glorious tray!

Halloween was my favorite fake holiday, but Thanksgiving used to be my favorite real holiday. It wasn't only because I was with family and we ate from dusk 'til dawn. For me it kicked off the holiday season. It was time to start daydreaming about Christmas. Parties, shopping, baking…I loved it all! Piles of delicious food filled the house with mouth-watering aromas. I'd give anything to taste my mother's sausage stuffing or my own sweet potato casserole. Actually, I got that recipe from Sam's Aunt Sofie. I sighed longingly, realizing the best parts of Thanksgiving did me no good now. Since I couldn't smell the food or eat it, I wasn't upset about missing the actual Thanksgiving Day.

Maybe I even missed it on purpose. Truthfully, I wasn't feeling very thankful lately. I still wondered when I would get out of here and find Sam. After some more thought though, I realized it could have been worse. At least I didn't have a gruesome death. I made up my mind to be thankful I had such a peaceful death after a good long life. In dying, I had been "sprung" from The Acres. Now I could watch the Christmas season blink from rooftops anywhere I wanted to go!

Anyone would have been hard pressed to find any ghosts in the cemetery during those few weeks before Christmas. The children had been lured away by magical Christmas toyshop displays. Packs of little souls traveled through town, watching parents move toys from the shelves into their shopping carts. The young spirits from long ago marveled at the wonderful shiny new toys that practically moved by themselves. Playing with toys had gotten so easy over the years! You didn't even have to imagine your little train could make puffs of smoke or that your doll was crying. Somebody had seen to it that the toys could do all of those wonderful things and more! In this electronic age, my heart was warmed by any parents treating their children to "traditional" toys that didn't involve keyboards and screens.

The little spirits marveled at the many places children could visit Santa Claus to share their deepest wishes about what they would like to find under their tree on Christmas morning. Little Jimmy Danforth had seen Santa in fifty-three different places so far, which he thought must be a very lucky thing for all of those boys and girls. If they worried that Santa might forget their special Christmas request, they still had a second or maybe even a third chance to ask him in another place.

Sometimes the lot of us, children and adults, window-shopped at night after the revelers had gone home to hide their parcels. We usually waited until the shops had darkened for the night, because we could see but not be seen by the daytime shoppers.

Nothing compared to the Christmas display at the Bar None candy store, even if we weren't able to taste the luscious decadence of fine chocolates melting in our mouths. Like Wise Men drawn to the sparkling star of the display case, we worshiped row upon row of foil wrapped Santas. We basked in the glow of shelves of candy, every flavor and shape imaginable: chocolate, licorice, ribbon candy, the list goes on. Both young and old spirits fondly recollected a special candy from their time that made the world a better place.

As a kid, I was notorious for eating just the part of something that interested me, and leaving the spoils for someone else to clean up. One year I pulled all of the candy canes off Grampa George's Christmas tree. After I licked the red stripes off each candy cane, I piled their remains on Grampa's chair.

You should have seen Grampa trying to pull that white twisted mass of sugar off his recliner. He finally got it off, along with patches of the chair's well-worn seat. As I sat in the corner for the rest of that day, I learned that any little girl worth her sugar and spice does not mess with Grampa's chair.

Another time, at Great Aunt Greta's house, I ate the white tips off the candy corns. Then I put the remaining parts back in the candy dish. I don't think she found it until after my family went home. After that day, the candy dish was on top of the hutch when we visited, well out of my reach. I shared those stories with the kids. They were amused that someone so old was ever young enough to sneak into someone else's candy dish.

Jodi enjoyed the toy displays as much as any of the kids, even if she wouldn't admit it. One night I saw her rearranging the figurines in a manger display. She tucks in Baby Jesus for the night, and told the Holy Family and their guests she hoped they were all comfortable and well. It was so sweet! I chuckled as I watched discreetly from the next aisle so as not to disturb her. She caught me looking, though. She said she was just trying to tidy up after some other children had made a mess. "Those rug rats trashed this crèche! It's friggin' blasphemy!" she exclaimed.

She shifted her focus to the holiday dinnerware display in the house wares department, demonstrating an unnaturally intense interest in the napkin rings in case I was still watching, which I was. In the spirit world, she remained perched forever on the cusp of adulthood. So, even though I thought it might bore her, I made sure to include her when Amelia and I went to look at Christmas decorations in people's houses.

Jodi, Amelia, and I set off for some nearby homes, leaving the children to their own devices among the toy displays. Christmas voyeurism was the best kind. At first, I felt guilty for invading strangers' homes but then I justified it was all right during this time of year. The whole point of decorating was to show off the house for holiday company, right? Well, here we are! The three Christmas ghosts.

This was better than when Sam and I used to drive around to see Christmas decorations in people's yards. Try as I might, I could never get a good look inside their living rooms to see the rest of their decorations. As a ghost I could go wherever I wanted.

We traveled from house to house and snooped to our hearts' content. Candles, silver icicles, ornaments, and fancy candy dishes had been temporarily freed from their dusty storage bins. Swags of garland draped the foyers, and angels greeted us peacefully from their treetop perches. Every heirloom ornament told a story about a journey through different places and several generations.

Jodi, Amelia and I compared the decorations to those we each remembered from our own houses when we were alive. Jodi's and Amelia's lives had been so long ago and so different. They were still amazed how the volume of people's decorations had grown larger throughout the years.

Of the three of us, I was the only one whose home had even remotely resembled any of the ones we visited. After we marveled at twelve houses or so, the decorations all looked the same to me and Amelia. We'd had our fill of the hot items for that year. Jodi was bored to tears by then anyway, although she politely feigned interest. She was unaware of my increasing ability to read others' thoughts. Her desire to be elsewhere came across loud and clear.

"Well, how about it, ladies?" I asked. "Shall we continue this Holiday Tour another day?"

"Oh, yes! Let's!" Jodi answered too enthusiastically, then tempered it with, "It would be awesome to see more sometime!"

Just as we turned for the cemetery, I realized I almost forgot to visit my own former home. "Oh! Wait! Could we see just one more?" I pleaded meekly to both Jodi and Amelia. "I want to see my old house. You don't have to come if you don't want to. I thought it would be fun to see what it looks like now and how they decorated it for Christmas."

To my surprise, Jodi and Amelia both expressed sincere interest in joining me. I looked forward to showing them the home I shared with Sam and hoped it was decorated as nicely as when we lived there.

"Great! Come on! It's not far from here." I couldn't wait to see where the people in my old house had put the Christmas tree. In my opinion, there was only one place it should go: in front of the bay window overlooking the pond. On cold December nights, the Christmas lights reflected little spots of warmth onto the ice pond. Some of our Christmas trees were almost ten feet tall. To Sam's chagrin, I felt that a Christmas tree wasn't tall enough unless the angel's head touched the ceiling. Indeed, there used to be a permanent scuffmark on the ceiling where the treetop angel resided every year.

From the moment we turned toward my old neighborhood I babbled on and on. "I'm sure they painted over the spot on the ceiling. Who knows? They might not even put the tree in the same room. I can't wait to show you the fireplace! It's one of the main reasons we bought the house. It has black marble on the sides and it's huge. Really! It's almost five feet wide and nearly as tall!"

"It sounds like our fireplace back home," Jodi said.

"Yeah, mine, too," agreed Amelia. "My mother baked the most marvelous bread!"

I sighed, slightly disappointed my fabulous fireplace would be just another piece of the wall to them. "Yeah, I guess fireplaces like that were probably in every house back in your day. For us it was really elegant, though. I'd cover it with decorations for any special day: Halloween, Easter, you name it – I always had something set up there. For Christmas, I covered the mantel in gold fabric, and I put these really artsy ornaments all over it. Then I'd have a party just to show it off!"

Poor Jodi and Amelia. They must have tired of listening to my chatter. They probably couldn't wait until this was over so they could get back to the cemetery. I purposefully avoided reading their thoughts because I didn't want to sense they might not be as caught up in my nostalgia as I was. I rattled on and on, about dressing the house up for all of those holiday parties and stringing lights around all of the windows until we ran out of places to plug them in.

Sam and I loved all of our lights. Our guests loved them, too. But I think the electric company loved them most of all. We must have been their favorite customers, I thought as I hurried up our old lawn. It sparkled with a dusting of fresh snow. I would have to thank the man-in-the-moon for that tiny bit of nighttime glitter because the man in the house didn't hang any Christmas lights outside. Not one! Well, whoever lived there now wouldn't earn any brownie points with the electric company.

The lackluster appearance of the yard didn't dampen my Christmas spirit too much. Some people just aren't interested in decorating the outside of their homes. Hopefully, it meant they saved it all for the inside, which I couldn't wait to see. As I anticipated the holiday trappings I would surely find inside, I hurried through the south wall of the house to get to the living room as quickly as possible. Jodi and Amelia kept pace and were right behind me. We all entered the living room at the same time, stopping short to stare at the menorah on the mantel. Jodi and Amelia stood silently with me for a moment, then burst out laughing.

"Oooh!" I exclaimed, when I finally lifted my chin off the floor. "I can't believe it. I really wanted…"

I stopped because nobody was listening to me. They were still laughing. I scoped the room in vain for any minute piece of Christmas glitter. There was only a little yarmulke, resting on the arm of the couch. My exasperation only encouraged them. "Are you two done yet?" I snorted in displeasure.

Jodi answered first, trying to sound sincere through her twisted smile. "Yeah, I think so. It was just such a surprise after you told us about your bad-ass blowouts."

"Oh, Lilla. We're sorry they didn't decorate for you," Amelia said as she inspected the elegant menorah.

"It really is beautiful," I said. "Just not what I expected. It never dawned on me when I sold the house. I was so sad to leave my memories of Sam and our house I don't remember anything about the family who bought it."

Amelia passed her hand through the candles. "When I was a child my friend, Sarah, had one of these in her house. Her family lived on a farm near ours. Mother wouldn't let me go into their house because they weren't Christians. So, then, Sarah's mother said she couldn't come into my house. We were supposed to play in the barns or outside, but we snuck into each other's houses anyway.

"Sarah loved our Christmas tree. She wanted to have one, too. We imagined the only way she could have one of her own was if she was a Christian. Mother caught me emptying a bottle of rose water over Sarah's head to baptize her. Sarah and I both got a good scolding. We couldn't play together after that. She moved away a few months later and I never saw her again.

"It feels strange being here," Amelia continued. "It must be strange for you, too, Lilla. I think it amused me so because I imagined, 'What if Mother returned to our old house and found one of these in the parlor?' She would need the smelling salts!"

"Well, don't worry, I won't faint over it. It's actually nice to see what the house looks like without all of the other fancy stuff in the way." I shrugged. "Maybe it's better, actually. What if they did decorate for Christmas and the decorations were hideous? That might have been worse!"

I wondered if whoever lived in my old house had as much fun decorating each room as I did. I had always dreamt of living in a house like this.

I loved our Arts and Crafts style house with its leaded glass windows! I used to imagine the ghost of the original lady of the house sitting on my purple ottoman. She'd nod her head in approval as I arranged a new valance. I strove for an updated version of the original elegance she might have created herself when the house was first built in 1923.

I have to say I was disappointed in the present décor. I had used so many colors to bring life to these walls. Okay, maybe I went overboard with my bright orange living room back in 1972, but the current owners played it too safe for my taste.

Every room was off-white. I admit the furniture was pretty sleek, but I still thought the rooms were a little dull. Then again, perhaps the house's original owner would have liked this clean modern take more than my whimsical approach. Maybe she was glad when the new owners painted over my multihued walls. Wouldn't it be funny if she were still roaming around this house? If by chance we ran into her, I would have given her dibs on haunting rights. First come, first served.

Romantic charm still graced the neighborhood with which I had fallen in love years ago. This area, still replete with gardens and wrought iron fences, had been established in the 1920s. When Sam and I moved here in 1970, this was a great old house, a real fixer-upper with lots of potential. Amelia and Jodi laughed because this neighborhood was far from being developed when they were alive. They had watched this and countless other swathes of rural land give rise to homes of days gone by.

No doubt they had seen every style of furniture come and go over the years, so my reminiscing held no great impact. Jodi's and Amelia's possessions ended up in antique stores decades ago. It wouldn't be long before my stuff caught up with their stuff. "Modern" trinkets from my youth had already become kitschy collectibles in vintage stores. After a few more transactions, they'd end up in the antique store, too.

Sensing Jodi's renewed boredom, I quickened the pace of the tour. I took a quick swing through the master bedroom and…Whoa! An awkward interruption, thankfully only detected by Amelia, Jodi, and myself.

The writhing figures on the bed didn't know they had company, but we could see and hear them as plainly as day. The nude couple lay on top of the disheveled sheets, completely visible to us. For spirits there's no such thing as a blanket of darkness to provide privacy. We saw it all, whether we wanted to or not. Well, it was nice to see not everything had changed; those walls hadn't lost their magic touch from when young Sam and Lilla used to go at it.

After gasping, Amelia high-tailed it to the other end of the house. Jodi disguised her curiosity with a mask of disgust. While exclaiming "Oh, gross!" she tilted her head for a better view. I nudged her so she'd leave with me. I wondered briefly what her young mind must think of a scene like this.

Then I remembered the stuff I used to find in the chapel before they started locking it. This bedroom scene was tame compared to what Jodi may have witnessed over the years right in the cemetery. She left the bedroom with me, not necessarily because I had asked her too, but more likely because it was dull compared to teenage chapel sex.

We caught up with Amelia back in the living room. Jodi turned to me and said as casually as could be, "I've seen that old firkytoodling hundreds of times! It's still such a curiosity! I dunno. Everyone looks like they're having a hell of a time, but I don't get it." She shrugged and rolled her eyes, trying to figure out why grownups do what they do.

Well, so much for protecting the innocents. I thought I had to shield Jodi and Amelia from this big bad world because I was much older than they were when I died. But, let's face it. I was the new kid on the block. I was simultaneously the oldest and the youngest of the three of us. Jodi and Amelia had been around for so long, there wasn't much they hadn't seen.

After so many years, could Amelia really still panic at the sight of naked flesh, or was that how she'd been trained at Victorian charm school? It was a bit of a culture shock for me to realize how little I'd seen compared to the older souls from the cemetery. Well, we'd definitely seen enough that night. It was time to leave before Jodi decided to sneak back to the bedroom for a second look.

We passed through the back wall of the house so I could peek at the garden, even if it was covered in snow. Sam and I honed our gardening skills back there. Once we perfected a graft, we'd introduce it on our television show and photograph it for one of our books.

The garden came full circle during our time here. When Sam and I moved here, we'd look out the bedroom window and dream of what would be a beautiful garden someday. Then, when I had grown old and widowed, I would sit in the same window, looking out at overgrown weeds and brush, and remember what had been. How lush our garden was during the years in between, when we hosted all of those garden parties!

I was content with the little stop at our old house. I was glad to have shared it with Jodi and Amelia, even if it wasn't bursting with Christmas chintz. It was hard to believe Christmas was only a few days away. We spent our days in the cemetery, but at night we roamed the towns, basking in their holiday auras. On Christmas Eve and into Christmas Day a heavy snowfall blanketed the world around us. We danced through the snowflakes as they swirled through us. How strange it was not to feel the bitter cold of this stormy winter night. Not even to possess warm flesh for which snowflakes could land and melt into tiny wet droplets.

Christmas morning in the cemetery was incredibly quiet. Snow muffled the noise from plow trucks clearing the roads. Nobody else was on the streets yet. Even our cemetery "family" wasn't around. Everyone headed for houses that reminded each of them of Christmases they remembered. Although we were dead, we still enjoyed Christmas vicariously through the eyes of the living, especially the children. Even Jodi unabashedly joined a group of younger girls, hoping to watch some lucky child unwrap and play with a new dollhouse.

Amelia and I started toward the edge of the cemetery, trying to decide which street to go down first. "Hey, Harvey!" Amelia called out to one of the pillars at the front gate.

Harvey sauntered out from behind the fence. I didn't realize he'd been standing there. I sensed he wanted to join us but he would never leave the cemetery of his own volition. We would have to invite him. "Yeah? What d'ya want?" he asked Amelia.

"Lilla and I are going to spend Christmas out there. Would you like to go into some houses with us?"

"Might be tolerable. On one condition – none of them fake trees. I won't stay in no house with a plastic tree."

"Deal," I said. "You and I don't usually agree on things but I'm with you on that fake tree thing. Yuck!"

The three of us floated into the neighborhood as daylight shone on the new snow. Christmas energy filled every place we visited. First came the frenzied unwrapping of gifts, then deciding what gifts to use first, then everyone moved on to prepare festive dinners. Later, in the waning hours of Christmas Day, households settled down to nightcaps and one last round of leftovers.

Harvey behaved himself all day, which pleased me. I guess we entertained him enough that he forgot to grumble about anything. In only one house did I detect a hint of melancholy. He watched a toddler play with a little wooden train. Could the child have reminded him of his son after all these years? Amelia and I didn't speak during this visit, allowing Harvey to reflect on his memories.

Likewise, Harvey and I remained silent when we accompanied Amelia to visit her old house next to the cemetery. The festive flower shop on the first floor complimented the old Victorian home. I sensed Amelia entertained many memories as she floated through the ostentatious store.

Then we moved to the tiny upstairs apartments, which I think were rented by college students. In one apartment, there was a picture of a couple embracing in front of the library at the university. Other pictures on the walls featured towns surrounded by arid looking countryside. I wouldn't know these cities but they looked old. The other apartment had a tiny fake tree and a sink full of dishes. There wasn't much to see for me and Harvey but I was glad Amelia got to spend time in her old house.

She wasn't as talkative as I had been when I dragged her to my old house. I still wasn't strong enough to read her if she didn't want to share something, so I didn't know what went through her head that day. Even if her old house was different from what she expected for Christmas, I hoped she remembered her past Christmases there fondly.

At some point during that Christmas, everyone found something that reminded them of special memories from their lives. I made the most of my new existence this holiday season myself, exploring as I never had before. Being able to enter any dwelling and share pieces of so many lives was enchanting and exciting. How much longer, I wondered. If I'm still here in Mount Hope for years to come, would I continue to appreciate the holidays, or would I come to resent them as an annual reminder of my separation from Sam?

Tracy Fontaine

Chapter Thirteen: The Doctor Returns

After all of the holiday parties finally ended, strings of lights returned to their storage boxes and porches darkened once again. Christmas trees moved from living rooms to curbs. Strands of tinsel, fluttered in the January wind, waving goodbye as the population beyond the cemetery walls returned to work and school. Last month everyone had been dashing through the snow. Now they just trudged through the slush.

February snowstorms dumped a good three feet of dense snow on the ground. Gentle white tufts topped headstones. Some of the statues took on new identities. One saint sported a huge white Afro. One of my favorite statues became quite a fashion plate, with a pristine white stole draped over her Grecian robes.

Amelia's stone was the best, though - a woman on her knees praying to the heavens. The wind etched out the bottom of her snowcap until it resembled a chef's hat. I told Amelia it looked like her in her kitchen praying for her cake to come out right. Never one to miss a beat, Jodi declared it must be angel food cake.

The city only plowed the bare minimum of cemetery roads, so as not to damage the cobblestones in the older sections. Hardly anyone entered the cemetery, save for a few skiers. Since there were so few visitors, the cemetery became dramatically desolate. Daytime sunlight reflected gloriously off the icy pond. Snow blanketed ruts and tree roots, redefining the whole floor of the cemetery. Even better were the clear winter nights. Under starry skies, gravestone shadows sharply defined themselves against the sparkling moonlit snow.

Maybe because cold weather chills couldn't touch me anymore, my usual winter doldrums never came. Thank goodness, because this particularly long winter gripped the city well into April. It surely would have depressed the heck out of me if I was still alive. Eventually, however, the usual signs heralded spring's return. Tired birds flew back from their winter homes in the South and tiny buds popped out along the tree branches.

I swear this cemetery was always the last place in Rochester where the snow melted. The remaining patches of snow shrunk more every day until they were completely absorbed into the muddy earth of spring.

One foggy night I traveled down the quiet cemetery pathways alone, noting the crocuses popping up here and there. Boy was I happy to see those little guys! Within a week or two, their blooms would bring fresh cheer to these grounds. I looked downward as I moved along the trail of this heavily wooded area I had known so well during my lifetime. Apparently, I wasn't the only gardener who'd purposefully allowed this area to become overgrown. I'm sure casual passersby missed the narrow pathway altogether.

I guess it felt like we were preserving some of these oldest gravestones from vandalism and schoolchildren doing gravestone rubbings for art class. The names and prayers had worn away generations ago, but some sort of new intuition allowed me to read the faded words clearly. The names and dates were on file in the cemetery records office but some of the longer epitaphs had never been legible enough to transcribe completely. For the first time I could read the tributes to "My eternal love" or "my precious wife." They captured my attention anew until I had read them all.

After I finished the last one, I raised my head and noticed the spirit of a well-dressed man hovering down the path from me. Hmm, nobody I recognized. I supposed he could be a newcomer to the area. Judging from his clothing, he must have lived and died long before me, possibly even before Amelia. He wore a top hat and cloak over a well-tailored suit. I had never seen him before, yet something about him seemed familiar.

Then I remembered. Of course! The doctor! He had to be the doctor of whom Jodi and Amelia had spoken. He must be here to visit his wife's grave and tell the others about his most recent travels. This was exciting! I had wondered when I would finally meet him.

I figured I would introduce myself and get to know him before the others crowded around. I wasn't sure if he saw me, but as I approached quietly, almost meekly, he looked up and greeted me.

"Oh, hello, Ma'am. Lovely night, tonight!" He charmed me instantly.

"Yes, it's wonderful. Hi. I'm Lilla. Are you the doctor Jodi told me about?"

"Oh…yes. Yes! I don't believe we've met before. Are you new here?" he asked.

"Yeah. Well, by most of their standards." I nodded toward the expansive cemetery. "I've been here less than a year. I haven't been too far from here since I died, except to see my brother. I'm waiting to join my husband…" I looked down, trying to decide whether I should share my whole story. I decided there would be time for that later. I didn't want to bore him so I switched to a lighter topic. "Jodi tells me you travel all the time!"

"Yes, I do indeed. Did she tell you anything in particular about me…or the places I've been?"

"No, that's why I'm curious. I'd like to see so many places myself but I'm not sure I could get where I want to go. Or worse yet, what if I couldn't get back?" I laughed.

The doctor chuckled and replied, "Oh nonsense! It's all quite easy."

He resembled Sherlock Holmes in that cloak. I expected him to say, "it's elementary, my dear Lilla!"

He continued. "You and I have a lot of catching up to do before the others gather around. Those children always have so many questions! Would you like me to show you some of the things I've seen, maybe from the really old days?"

I nodded eagerly, happy to have the doctor to myself. Once it got out he was back in town the other spirits would start chatting him up and it would be impossible to get a word in edgewise. Besides, this might be a nice quiet time to show him my early years with Sam.

I held my hands out so he could take them in his and let me peer into his memories. I hoped he would focus on the light, exciting travels. I didn't really want to spend too much time in the part of his mind that still grieved the loss of his wife. Memories so close to my heart still bothered me. However, if he wanted me to see that part of his life so I could appreciate why he was so inspired to travel, then I would oblige him by letting him share those memories, too.

A touch of our hands, a tingle up my arms, admitted me freely into this man's past and him into mine. Like the other visions I'd watched, this one began with him as a child playing a long time ago, and in such formal clothing! Little knickers, like Little Lord Fauntleroy. He was born into comfort, for sure. I saw at least two maids and a nanny in his elegant childhood home. The image was fleeting.

Quickly, the child turned into a handsome young man wearing a dashing suit with long pants. Perhaps he didn't remember much from his childhood, or maybe he had so much to show me that he didn't want to exhaust me with trivial child's play. On the other hand, maybe my Little Lord Fauntleroy comparison annoyed him, and he decided to skip those years.

He walked arm in arm with a different woman at every event I saw in his memory. Dinners, dances, and finely dressed acquaintances populated his elegant past. I was thankful my ability to visit others' minds had gotten stronger over the past few months. At first, what I shared with Amelia and Harvey provided me with knowledge about them but it overwhelmed me and actually hurt my brain. Sharing thoughts was now effortless and much more enjoyable. My mind floated gaily through his social activities and parties. I felt relaxed, but something started to change. The images and the people in them turned sinister.

Well-adorned estates lit by chandeliers faded into dark streets in filthy neighborhoods. This same gentleman, still exquisitely dressed, escorted a young lady in a long blue cape down a narrow street. Without warning, a spray of red leapt out of her throat and seared my brain, just as surely as if acid had been thrown in my eyes. I screamed and pulled back but he tightened his grip until my arm burned as much as my mind. I didn't want to see any more of his thoughts but I was his prisoner. He showed me such terrible things I wished I were still alive so I could faint and tune them out.

My mind burned so badly I couldn't even see the nearest headstone. He blinded me to my physical surroundings, yet somehow forced detailed images into my thoughts. The woman in the blue cape lay on the ground, eyes and mouth open in a frozen expression of horror.

Her abdomen had been torn open, her blood and internal organs splayed halfway across the alley where she died. She was only the first. He slaughtered at least a dozen women, and he made me watch every one.

I struggled as hard as I could but my pathetic energy was no match for this most evil of spirits. I don't know how many women he killed, but he forced me to watch their eyes widen and listen to them scream as they died. Every time he plunged his knife, or whatever else was handy, into their bodies, another sea of red flooded my mind with unbearable pain. My arm burned as his hand tightened its grip.

His strength increased every time I screamed for mercy. I feigned exhaustion and went limp, hoping to fool him into relaxing his grip but he commanded my attention with endless images of murder. I couldn't turn them off no matter how hard I tried. He injected the pictures directly into my brain. Closing my eyes made it worse. At least if I kept my eyes open I could try to distract myself by looking at the headstones or trees.

Supposedly, Jack the Ripper is buried in Rochester. I wondered if this could be him. I think this man's body count dwarfed even Jack the Ripper's, if for no other reason than by his sheer longevity. In the relentless images, the man preying on these young victims was no longer a young chisel-faced ruffian but a pudgy middle-aged man. Then he turned into a stooped gray haired codger who could pass for anybody's sweet grandfather.

That's how the gentle old bastard lured his last victim. He pretended to have a heart attack and hid a knife under his shirt where his heart should have been. As for the end of his own story, he passed out after drinking too much one night and never woke up. There was no justice in such a painless death for someone like him. It was unfathomable this man could have killed so many and for so long.

I hoped witnessing the end of him also meant the end to this ordeal. He forced those grotesque images into my mind. His wicked memories would haunt me forever. If there was nothing else to show me, I prayed he would let me go. Instead, he had other plans. With his strong hands locked around my arms, he pulled me toward the edge of the path.

He gripped my left arm and lowered my hand until it pressed against a large stone on which I used to rest after tiring from gardening. I tried to fight him off, but he pushed my hand against the stone. Harder and harder he pressed, until, unbelievably, my fingertips started disappearing into the stone.

I would have stared in disbelief had it not been for the pain. The rock began to crush my very spirit. It hurt more than anything I ever experienced when I was alive. After I died, the only thing of which I had been sure was that I would never again feel physical pain. This couldn't be happening! I wailed so loudly I didn't recognize my own voice. I sounded like an animal caught in a trap.

"So what's next?" I thought. My body was gone. All I had left was my spirit and he was trying to kill that, too! He spent his life ravaging women's bodies. Is this how he planned to spend his eternity, finishing off their spirits, as well?

He continued pushing. My fingers had disappeared into the rock, and now the unyielding stone began to press into my hand. I grew weak. I clenched my left fist, hoping to make it bulkier and more difficult to push into the rock. I searched for strength from somewhere deep inside me.

As he pushed my hand further into the stone, I transported my mind back to the day Sam and I worked so hard in this soil. We planted that hedge of roses near the cemetery gates. My whole body was scratched by thorns that day but I barely felt it because of the enjoyment that Sam and I had accomplished so much together.

My brief respite was short lived. My attacker shook me back to the present and began to strangle me. Again, I forced my mind to retreat to the memories of my past. Instead of the reality of my attacker's determined hand around my throat, I imagined the soft strand of pearls Sam draped around my neck on our tenth wedding anniversary.

Oh, Sam! Even this isn't enough to bring you back to save me?

I prayed for more flashbacks – anything to disassociate my mind from what was happening. It was no good. The horror of the moment yanked me right back, my face inches away from my attacker's. Although he was a spirit like me, it seemed as if he was breathing fire onto my cheeks as he laughed.

Even that wasn't enough to distract me from the real danger of him pushing me into that rock.

Clenching my fist did slow him down, but it hurt even more as my hand, too, began disappearing into the rock. I wanted to reach over with my other hand and pull it out, but I was afraid he would push that arm in, too. Then I would surely be trapped. I'd never had to fight anything like this before. I tried to kick him and grab him. I tried to run and shove him away, but nothing worked. I screamed desperately into the night, for anybody, Jodi, Harvey, even souls that I didn't know, names I remembered from the gravestones. Didn't anyone hear me?

I fell to my knees and looked into his face for mercy that wasn't there. His eyes were cold. Now that I had fallen, he towered over me. My free hand went right through him as I flailed. My head swooned. Horrifyingly, that solid inanimate rock completely swallowed my hand. Just the fact that I couldn't see my hand anymore sent me into a panic.

I just wanted this to be over, even if it meant surrendering. He obviously was not accustomed to losing. If my one little hand ached now, what would it feel like when he crushed the rest of my spirit into the stony prison? If it weren't for the insane pain of just my hand being crushed and the fear of it intensifying as he crushed my whole being, I would have willingly just crawled into the rock myself and stayed there forever. Anything so he would leave me alone!

We both knew he would win. I accepted the fact I was about to disappear from earth for good when something hit me on my back. I thought he was about to beat me with yet another rock, but then I realized it wasn't him at all. Small objects bounced off my attacker and fell onto the ground next to us. Hail? No, that would drop through us, and besides, I'd never seen hailstones like that around here. Whatever it was, it distracted him enough to make him pause and glance over his shoulder.

Undeterred, he laughed and returned to finish me off. I couldn't see anything but his cape, though his movements became more determined, almost hurried. My hand was still stuck in the rock, but he wasn't pushing it any further. Some of his strength had waned into hasty bumbling.

I held my ground a little more firmly, but only because of those things flying around and bouncing off his head and his back.

It turns out they were rocks. I found out the hard way because another one bounced off my head and landed on the ground near my free hand. There was somebody else out there but whose side were they on? Finally, I realized more rocks were hitting him than me. Someone was trying to help me!

"Help me! Oh, help! Please!" I screamed to my unseen Good Samaritan. So many rocks thudded against my attacker that he actually raised his arms to shield himself. In doing so, he released his grip on my arm. Seizing my chance to escape, I tried to disappear as I had done so often but I couldn't move. I went nowhere. The rock imprisoned my hand, tethering me in place.

I couldn't pull my hand out so I wrapped my free arm around the bottom of the rock and lifted it a few inches off the ground, enough to drag it away. I shuffled with the weary determination of a dying woman carrying a forty-pound sack of potatoes to her starving children. Any step away from the soul killer was a step closer to freedom, so I dragged myself all of four feet away. By then I was lightheaded and could barely see if he was chasing me, but at that point he had his own problems.

From behind every bush and headstone, the other spirits converged upon him. Chaos erupted as rocks flew and voices cursed him to hell. From what I could tell, the children led the pack. They pitched rocks like fastballs into his face. They pulled on his cape like a pack of wild dogs.

I was almost frightened by the children's vengeance. They must know this man and showed him no mercy. He missed as he tried to grab the quick little ones. The pelting continued as the children remained just out of his reach. I don't know what he would have done with them had he caught them, but the children knew better than to get too close. Their tiny voices joined loudly, commanding him to leave us alone.

Joining the cavalry were Amelia and Harvey. What forces empowered them I could only imagine. The stones pelted by the children amounted to nothing more than nuisance ammunition, but Amelia and Harvey were super-warriors. They didn't throw rocks – they hoisted boulders.

They struck him repeatedly and ground the small boulders against his face and hands if he stopped moving for a fraction of a second. Imagine these beautiful free souls, advanced beyond the need of a body, duking it out with rocks like Neanderthals. If they were trying to encapsulate him into a rock, they would have to try harder than that. Having fed on generations of his victims' strength, he was much too strong.

His arms flailed as he tried to ward off my defenders, but the army of spirits relentlessly tore at him from every angle. Do you want to know the most frightening part? I don't think they damaged him in any way. He never faltered, never cried out for mercy as I had done. I think he tired of warding off this army of pests. I couldn't believe my eyes when he shook them off and started coming after me again. I thought I was safe but now it looked like he was really going to get me after all.

"No! Oh, God, no!" I cried as I shook my head and scooted backward along the ground. I used my right arm to lift and push me. My left hand, still inside the rock, dragged heavily, imprisoning me on the ground. Despite everyone's counterattack, he was back on top of me.

Suddenly, the biggest spirit I'd ever seen, a giant of a man, leapt out of the trees and knocked the soul killer completely to the other side of the clearing. The giant had actually used one of the tall obelisk monuments like a baseball bat and whacked the soul killer thirty feet into the air. The other spirits sensed it coming. They all leapt away before the first blow struck.

My attacker was by no means destroyed but he was done with us for the moment. When the giant started toward him again, the soul killer leaped up and cowered in the giant's shadow. As the giant raised the obelisk to strike again, the soul killer glared at me and snarled, "I haven't forgotten, Stefania."

Then he disappeared before the obelisk smashed the tree directly behind where he had been standing. The children ended up hitting each other with the last round of rocks they just launched across the now empty circle.

Except for my moaning, deafening silence replaced the intense commotion. I huddled over the rock, which had trapped me like a fossil.

Sympathetic spirits moved closer as I tried to free myself. I felt their sense of helplessness at my situation. The one thing I didn't expect to see was the tip of a boot and the edge of a man's coat. I looked up into the face of a well-dressed stranger. Fear filled my heart. He came back! Panicking I dragged my rock away from this man and the other spirits as I wondered about everyone's intentions.

Amelia came down to the ground and grabbed the rock to hold me in place. "No! Lilla! Wait – it's not what you think!" I don't remember if I didn't hear her or just didn't believe her, but I pushed her away so I could keep moving. She held on tightly. "Stop! It's not him!"

Soon Harvey was behind me to make sure I couldn't leave. He yelled more loudly than Amelia. "Whoa! Stop it, will ya?! Look at 'im! He ain't the bad guy. That's Doc! He's an okay fella. Calm down, now! Jeez Louise!"

If nobody around me was worried about this new stranger, I would listen to what they had to say. I stopped struggling but kept my guard up. I waited cautiously, while mulling over how I might escape with this rock still weighing me down. Then everyone started talking all at once.

"…sorry…sorry…should have taken care of this before!"

"Miss Lilla, we didn't know he was here…"

"…honest, we didn't… we should have gotten here earlier…"

"We hope you're all right! Sorry for the rocks – it's our only way to fight him!"

They apologized so profusely. At first I thought it was just for the rocks they bounced off my head. No, couldn't be that – we all knew it had to be done to get rid of him. So many of their apologies reached into my mind, I couldn't make heads or tails of the din. My friends meant well, but they gave me the creeps.

Their voices subsided as the new stranger, dressed a little too similar to my attacker for my comfort level, approached. He reached down and touched my right hand, still free and unharmed. I jerked it to my chest. I'd had enough hand-holding for one day, thank you very much. Wisely, he chose not to force the issue.

"There, there," he said gently as he backed down. "Miss Lilla," he spoke again, this time keeping his hands to himself. "I'm Dr. Klink, Graham Klink. I wish we could have met under better circumstances. Please believe me when I say I'm terribly sorry. I will accept the blame for everything that has just happened."

He sat on the ground next to me and spoke so sincerely. I finally gained the confidence to look directly at his face for the first time. No, he was definitely not the soul killer who had attacked me. Nothing but gentleness flowed from this spirit. His soft caring eyes were not to be confused with the cold charm with which the first stranger had duped me.

"Why are you blaming yourself?" I asked Dr. Klink. Before he had a chance to answer, I addressed the rest of the spirits. "All of you, everybody! You didn't cause this. I can't believe I was so stupid! I mean, just because you're all so wonderful, it never occurred to me I would meet anybody so dangerous." I futilely tried to pull my arm out of the rock, which didn't move. "God! I'm so stupid!" I repeated. "I thought I knew something, so I didn't even think before I opened myself right up to this! It's my own damn fault, and now look at me! I should've been more careful. I'm sure you all would have been more careful, even if you didn't know that man would come here and do those things." They exchanged silent glances but still nobody volunteered any response.

"But, you see, Lilla, we did know." Jodi's voice rose from the back of the crowd as she made her way toward me. The other spirits averted their eyes from her as she moved to the center of the clearing. Upon reaching the middle of the group, she lowered herself to the ground, facing me, and gently touched the rock. Its jagged surface reflected a strange opacity where it had gobbled up my hand.

"What do you mean you knew? You knew this man was coming for me and you didn't at least warn me? Now I'm stuck like this, and it hurts so much! Will I have to stay like this forever? Is this stony trap going to be my own personal hell?!"

"No!" Jodi grabbed and tugged at the rock so forcefully that she scared me into stunned silence. "Harvey – please get this off her!"

Her effort was useless, what with her childish hands and one of them lame at that. Come on, didn't they see how hard that man pushed my hand to get it in this far? Not to mention the agony I had suffered? My hand ached so badly now but it still didn't compare to the pain of when it entered into this solid piece of stone. I couldn't bear the thought of going through the worst part of it again, as my hand would have to pass back out of the stone the same way it went in. As the doctor and Harvey positioned their hands around the stone and wrapped their legs around the edge of Myrtle Gray's headstone, I told them not to bother. I would get used to lugging this thing around forever rather than go through that pain again.

"No, umm…No, really, it's okay. Please don't!" My whimpers weren't about to change their minds. Apparently, I had no say in the matter. They were going to yank on that rock, even if they pulled my hand off with it!

"No! Owwww!" My final plea was ignored as the two men pulled the rock toward them, lifting me nearly off the ground. I refused to let anyone torture me like that again, so I fought against them and begged for mercy at the same time.

"Please, just let me go! No! Don't do this to me!"

"Lilla! It's the only way!" Amelia shouted.

While Harvey and the doctor pulled on the rock, I pulled on my arm, hoping the rock would slip out of their hands so I could get away and avoid this altogether. Something terrible was happening; I knew it. As we continued this freaky tug of war with my arm, the pain began to shift, first from the bottom of my arm, then to my wrist, and eventually through my palm and fingertips.

It hurt like hell. With one last tug, mostly to escape from Harvey and Doc, I flew backward over thirty feet. Looking down, I expected to see the rock still encasing my hand, but it was gone. In its place was a gnarled mess that used to be my hand. Now it looked like a compressed, shriveled lump with several nubby protrusions that once were fingers.

"No! No!" I cried and shook violently to flick that vile thing off the end of my arm. I wished I had lost it with the rock, but it was there to stay. It was mine, forever scarring my beautiful free spirit.

The other spirits watched silently. Hesitantly, they offered condolences, which I ignored for the moment. I approached a silent Jodi, with her twisted face and grotesque arm and hand that looked eerily similar to mine. I swear I saw tears in her eyes when she looked at my hand and then into my face. She raised her hand toward mine as a gesture of comfort, then questioned her judgment and backed down. We stood with our arms at our sides. I couldn't look at either one of us. Now I understood.

"Lilla," Jodi's very serious and sincere thoughts floated to me from her youthful old soul. "Please believe me when I tell you we were looking for you to warn you. I'm sorry we didn't get here in time."

Whereas I had difficulty looking at Jodi a minute ago, I now couldn't take my eyes off her misshapen face and entire arm. If my young spirit friends hadn't come along when they did…I shuddered to finish the thought. I looked away when I thought about the pain Jodi endured, much greater than I had to bear.

"You poor thing! You've suffered so much more than me!" I multiplied the continuing dull ache in my hand by ten, trying to imagine what it must have been like for Jodi.

"It's okay, really. It doesn't hurt any more. Yours won't either, soon. But, you can see it will always be there." Jodi spoke softly and nodded toward the lame side of her body.

"Does everybody here know that man? How come I've never seen him?" I asked the crowd.

Most of the other spirits had drifted away. Those who remained avoided my question. their eyes affixed to the ground. Doctor Klink finally spoke, "You might not believe this, but I've been chasing him for over a hundred years. His name was Massimo Sabati. He was pure evil, even in life. I think you have a good idea what I mean, Miss Lilla."

I nodded silently as he continued. "Besides those poor women whose names we'll never know, I believe he took the life of my dear sister, Serina, God rest her soul. Nobody could prove it, not even me, though I watched and waited. I figured he'd get nervous and make a stupid mistake somewhere along the way and I would lead the law to him. But you know, he always stayed two steps ahead of me, and more women met their untimely fate at his hands.

"Then my wife Mary became ill. I tended to her needs until she passed away. I missed her so much, and I was just too old to keep hunting for Massimo. My one comfort until I died? I figured what I couldn't get around to, God would finish. Massimo would rue his deeds when he had to answer to Him." Dr. Klink shook his head and laughed at the failure of his faith.

"I don't know if it was one of God's mysterious ways, but do you know we died not more than a month apart, Massimo and me? Yes, ma'am. After I died, I waited for Mary to come for me, but as you may have guessed, it never happened. I was getting used to the idea that I was to remain here instead of joining my Mary. Then he showed up, as shocked as I was. He left, and I hoped it was for good, but he only went on an adventure, of sorts. He picked up a few not so nice parlor tricks along the way, including the one he shared with you…and Miss Jodi."

Jodi and I realized that with Doctor Klink's last words, all eyes rested on us. We stared at the ground until he continued. "The next time he came around," Dr. Klink motioned to Jodi, "he cornered her up near the stone wall over on the north side. It was almost too late before we knew he was here."

Dr. Klink touched Jodi's shoulder as he finished his story. "After that horrible night I vowed to protect everybody I could from him. Now I try to stay ahead of him. When I can, I warn others to stay clear, and not to be fooled by his charm. What the others say is true – I do travel and I do come back with quite a few tales, but most of them involve my attempts to catch him. He came here tonight, I had just arrived myself to warn the others…but I was too late."

"Why didn't anybody tell me about this before?!" I demanded, furious that nobody had even mentioned any of this.

Amelia accounted for everyone's twenty-twenty hindsight. "We didn't want to scare you. It's been so many years since anybody's seen that man, we didn't think he would ever come back. When we saw him, we looked for you, to warn you…" Her voice trailed off into a mumbled apology. After thinking on it a bit longer, she justified their silence. "Besides, would you have believed a story like that? We do tell some crazy stories around here."

I smiled at my friends. I wanted to hold a grudge, but I couldn't stay angry with them. Their actions thus far had been nothing short of genuine caring. We each had our quirks. That's for sure. I know they would have warned me if they had any inkling at all about Massimo returning.

"You know, you're right," I sighed heavily. "I don't know if I would have believed you, especially if Jodi tried to convince me she wasn't fibbing!"

Chuckles rippled through the spirited group. Jodi, Amelia, Harvey, and the doctor laughed heartily at the doubtful possibility of me believing a story like that coming from Jodi. The older children, close to Jodi's age, whirled around the trees, their youthful energy charging the night air. Our somber frightened mood dissipated rapidly now that we were safe.

Dr. Klink left shortly after. He didn't want to lose Massimo's trail and I didn't want him to either if it meant he could save someone from sharing my and Jodi's fates. With apologies still tumbling out of his mouth, Dr. Klink disappeared from our sight.

It was the children's spirits, however, who truly saved my future well-being that day. Led by my friend John, who'd watched the excavator drop the dirt into my grave, several of the youngest spirits enclosed me within a circle. I remained seated on the ground, letting them pat my cheek, to express messages that I was okay. They couldn't wait for me to play with them again, when I felt up to it of course.

Feeling almost back to my old self, I reached out to hug John. We wrapped our arms around each other, but when I looked over his shoulder and saw that one of my hands was now a disfigured claw, I pulled it away and tried to hide it.

I could not bear to look at it, or to have others gawk in morbid curiosity, much less touch it. I felt like I could never again share with any other spirits. Like Jodi, my past would remain a guarded mystery to others. The older spirits who stood nearby accepted the decision I'd made, however rash.

Time may or may not heal all wounds. That was for me to decide when I was ready. Fortunately, the children gave me a little nudge of badly needed encouragement.

I kept my deformed hand out of sight, but John, my brave little friend, laid his hand on my good arm. His child's touch was gentle, almost healing compared to the unyielding stone that had imprisoned my other hand.

John wanted to let me look into the world he remembered when he was alive. Not five minutes before I had vowed never to share anything with anyone ever again, the first of the children came forth to share his world with me. The innocence of his touch encouraged me to let this happen. I was a little nervous. Recalling Jodi's words about frightening the children with adult situations, I paced my memories to match my age with John's. While my life unfolded chronologically, beginning with toddlerhood, his images flowed in the same manner with which children tell stories, a little disjointed and very animated.

What he remembered were happy things that should be part of every child's life: catching frogs, singing with his parents while his mother played the piano, eating his grandmother's cookies, wrestling with his brother. His first and only ride in a car threw him into a fit of crying because it went so much faster than his family's horse-drawn wagon. He was quite a character until he acquired a fever. It must have taken his life mercifully fast, for he didn't remember it as a lengthy frightening ordeal, just only as something that happened before he entered this world.

When the pictures of his life ended, so did our sharing session. I eased my arm away from his hand. He was able to glimpse as much as he needed to see of my life, a childhood surprisingly similar to his in many ways, with the exception of different clothing and far more automobiles. He was tickled that I used to dress my cat in doll clothes and make the poor thing ride in my doll carriage. It's not something a little boy might do but he sure found it funny.

John stepped aside to make way for Jimmy and Cathy Danforth. They argued over who would go first, which amused me. There was no hurry – we had all the time in the world and then some, but try telling them that. Cathy won and proceeded to show me the dolls, cakes, and parents that filled her brief world until she drowned in the pond near her house. Her mother, weak and sickly after delivering newborn Jimmy, hadn't seen her slip out of the house.

Jimmy started his story at that point, and he showed me his boyhood: climbing trees, fishing, playing with the boys next door. His childhood ended shortly after he collapsed in school from a terrible pain somewhere in his side. He doesn't remember what happened after they took him to the doctor, except that he came here and found his sister who had died when he was a baby. That explained why so often I'd heard Cathy demand Jimmy's obedience because she was older. Theoretically, she was right, but it was hard to accept based on appearances alone because they both appeared as the ages at which they had died.

A couple of the older boys around Jodi's age approached me as well. They'd been especially brave today, fighting off Massimo. Apparently one of them, Richard, died in a farm accident back in 1941. He was helping his uncle while his cousins were off at war. Eventually, both cousins returned safely from the war but Richard died in a farm accident when he was fifteen. The other boy, Trent, died in 2000, from rhabdomyosarcoma. It was strange to hear him rattle off such a complicated word.

Kids from the distant past spoke of mysterious fevers or just "sickness." They faced primitive treatments and hasty deaths. Newer souls like Trent, armed with modern medicine, knew the scientific names of their illnesses. These children described in painstaking details the attempts to cure their cancers – surgery, radiation, chemotherapy, and then the death that released them from all that.

Several more children shared their lives with me, remembering childhood play or helping with family chores, each of their lives cut short. Illness claimed the most lives, but two children had died in a house fire, and another from an infected cut on his arm. Several children died in the terrible orphanage fire of 1901. I was grateful they shared their memories with me. Sharing life stories with adults was so different than sharing with children.

Events of adulthood linger more heavily on one's soul. I didn't realize it when I exchanged life stories with Amelia and Harvey, probably because my own adult experiences lent me equal footing. Emotions from the children's pasts were very light. Their memories caused barely a ripple in my thoughts, but left me with a sense of well-being. It hardly seemed appropriate.

After all, I just watched the passing of ten children, yet their souls thrived and they seemed happy. The children showed me I could still share if I wanted to, despite my shriveled hand and injured trust.

As everyone left the clearing, they filed past me to tell me they were relieved I was okay. The children headed up the rear, before flying off into the trees. Lastly, was the real hero of the night, Horatio, the mighty giant. He sat on a large stone beside me. Even with his large legs folded as small as he could, his knees still grazed the bottom of his chin.

"Are you okay, Lima?" he asked very animatedly.

"Oh, yes! Thank you so much! I know I can never repay you, but I'm eternally grateful…literally. Oh, and it's Lilla. That's so weird! Two people in one day called me by the wrong name. First, that horrible Massimo called me Stefania. Then you call me Lima. You must have talked to Althea. She's the only one who calls me Lima."

"I am Althea," the giant replied. "Well, I mean, I'm her, too."

"I swear, doesn't anyone around here stop joking for a minute?" I snickered and shook my head. Did he expect me to think he was a little girl? He smiled so wryly it almost forced me to believe him. As gullible as I was, I wouldn't let myself fall for this one.

"Oh, come on," I laughed again. I swatted his arm with my good hand. "Thanks for the story anyway. God knows I need a laugh today."

"No, really." He smiled, but his voice became serious. "Sometimes I am Althea, but she wouldn't have been very helpful tonight, so I came like this."

"Come to think of it," I wondered aloud to the giant, "when I was talking with the other kids earlier, I didn't see Althea. You're starting to scare me, Now I don't know who I'm talking to. And now I'm worried about Althea." My voice shaking, I called out, "Althea! Althea, if you can hear me, please come out! This isn't funny today!"

"I'm fine…I mean, she's fine." The giant answered. He chuckled a little.

"I know it's confusing. Right now I'm Horatio. I don't come around here much, at least not in this form. When I'm Horatio, I spend my time out West, on the plains. I used to work on the railroad."

I rose slowly and backed away so I could escape. Whoever this spirit was, he was nuts, and he was big. I wanted to get as far away from him as I could.

"Oh, hey! Don't fly the coop yet! I'm leavin' soon, too. I have lots of places I want to see myself."

Darn him for reading my thoughts! I felt guilty he knew I thought he was crazy. I sat down but I was still ready to take off if I needed to.

I was glad I stayed because Horatio told me how he was not only Horatio and Althea, but had been a host of other persons as well, though he could only take one shape at a time. I started to believe him. It brought back memories of Spooky Marcy and her friends talking about past lives. Some of the things Spooky Marcie told me were pretty nutty, but I listened for the entertainment value. In my heart though, I always thought it might be possible to die and come back in another life.

Horatio seemed so sincere. My gut told me I should believe that he and Althea shared a soul and somehow occupied different bodies at different times in history. Horatio said his soul must really like it here on earth because he remembered at least five different lifetimes. He felt like there were as many as three more he hadn't discovered yet. His lives went far back in history.

The oldest one he remembered was from sometime in the 1200s. He was a twelve-year-old-boy in Japan. He drowned when he and his father were bringing in a load of fish for their village. After that, he worked as a Chinese tracker on the Yangtze River. The back-breaking labor of pulling tons of cargo up the river drove him to an early grave as well. The most recent and miserable past life he recalled was someone named Margaret in the 1980's. She overdosed one night after shooting someone and stealing his drugs. His life as Horatio lasted the longest from what he remembered. Horatio worked hard on the railroad in the late 1800s and lived well into his seventies.

Today I sat with Horatio. Tomorrow he would be somewhere else, and possibly someone else. Maybe Althea, maybe not. Like picking out clothes, he changed souls every day. He might even return as a newborn baby someday, ready to experience yet another completely new life.

Horatio liked the surprises of each different life. I gave him lots of credit to take a chance on a life with no guarantees. I don't know if I could do it – my life with Sam was blissful. I think I'll stick with memories of a good life and hopefully not have to ever jump into another one.

Before Horatio left, I thanked him for letting Horatio come into Althea's world to save me. Giant Horatio nodded and excused himself in a very genteel westerly way. "Always glad to help. You take care of yourself, Lima." He tipped an invisible hat brim and disappeared. As I wondered where he vanished to, dawn broke and the sun came up to dissolve the shadows of that very long night.

Chapter Fourteen: The Lilac Festival

Thanks to my run-in with Massimo Sabati in that desolate corner of the cemetery, my outlook had taken a nosedive. The peaceful solitude I savored at the beginning of winter had worn as thin as the patch of dirty ice on the pond. I enjoyed it for a while, but now it was quiet and creepy.

Mount Hope's shadowy hillsides clung to their snow long after the surrounding neighborhoods had thawed. Still wary of being alone in the deep parts of the cemetery, I stayed near the outskirts, waiting for the living to come back. I wanted to see people, and lots of them. I should have been careful with what I asked for. It wouldn't be long before I rued my wish.

I rarely visited my own grave, which didn't go unnoticed by Amelia, Jodi, and Harvey. I wouldn't blame them if they abandoned me because I was so neurotic. They were really understanding, especially Jodi. In between her own wanderings, she'd come over to see how I was getting along. I felt like a reverse shut in, more like a shutout, convincing myself bad things would happen if I ventured into the surroundings I had just begun to think of as home.

I stole glimpses of the inside while hugging the surrounding walls. Whenever temptation called me to venture farther into any of the pathways, all I had to do was look down at my gnarled hand. It didn't hurt, but its grotesque appearance made me shudder and retreat back out to the edge of the cemetery.

The best days were when Jodi, Amelia and I left the cemetery altogether to visit the most bustling places we could find. We went to grocery stores, museums, movie theaters. Sometimes we went to people's houses, especially during parties. I could see why it was one of Jodi's favorite pastimes. I, too, relished that the living couldn't see my horrible hand as they went about their business all around my invisible form.

Finally, finally! At the end of April, the cemetery thawed and visitors started returning! Things had gotten lonelier than I realized. I couldn't believe I was even happy to see the dog from down the street chasing squirrels through the petunia bed.

"Have a ball, you mutt!" I shouted, but the smelly bugger couldn't hear me. The cool spring mornings resembled the cool fall mornings from around the time I first arrived. Joggers, their visible puffs of breath leading their way, wound through the old twisting roads in the very back of the cemetery. Even though the living couldn't have prevented an attack from another spirit, I still found comfort in their presence. This safety in numbers afforded me the courage to go back there myself, although a heightened wariness accompanied me constantly.

Keeping my guard up, I scoped my surroundings. I wanted to know who was near me and what they were doing. I knew I was really looking for Massimo. I don't think I was being overly foolish or cautious. He was frightening but I vowed to get over him. If I let his memory haunt me for as long as I roam the earth, he will have succeeded in destroying me as surely as if he had made me disappear into that rock. I wouldn't let him win.

Eventually, I convinced myself he would be a rare visitor, if he even returned at all. I wouldn't let the memory of that attack mar the rest of my existence. Maybe it was a case of mistaken identity anyway as he thought my name was Stefania. I feared for the real Stefania if he ever caught up with her.

Besides, with so much going on all over the place, I didn't have time to entertain my fear for long. Parades of daily visitors marched through my small world. It went like this: morning joggers, grounds keepers, stroller brigades, dog walkers, evening joggers, pretty much in that order. Each group segued from one to the next, as each day progressed from morning, to afternoon, into evening. As I followed people's tracks and listened to their conversations, I grew fondly familiar with their daily lives.

It was my way to keep in touch with their world. As long as I was sentenced to remain on earth among them, I didn't want to sever those ties. If they neared an exit while telling an interesting story, I'd follow them right out the gate and down the street so I wouldn't be left wondering how it came out in the end.

There was the day two women jogged by, wrapped up in juicy conversation. I recognized one woman who always wore the great sweat suits back in the fall. She had sharp clothes and a sharper tongue to match. She was easy to find and worth following.

That day she bent her friend's ear about how she and her almost-ex-husband met for coffee to sign their divorce paperwork and ended up sleeping together after she had just started seeing someone new.

"Oh, shit, Maggie!" her friend exclaimed with what little breath she could muster while jogging.

"Yeah, I know. It gets worse," Maggie panted.

"Don't tell me you're seeing him now, and still seeing Aaron, too?"

"No way! It was only once, but that's all it takes," Maggie chuckled between pants. "I didn't get my period. Let me tell you, I ran to my doctor so fast! Guess what?"

Her friend gasped and stopped running. Maggie kept going making her friend catch up. "Maggie! Seriously, you're not…"

At that point, the women jogged out the gate, with me right behind them.

Maggie, still jogging, released a few words at a time, between breaths. "Oh, God! No! It's even worse than that. I'm in menopause! I can't believe it! I'm not pregnant. I'm old!"

That's all? I followed them for two blocks to find out Miss Fashion Plate is going through menopause? The two women stopped to stretch in one of their yards. The saga had run its course, so I went back to the cemetery to wait for the next interesting tidbits to come along.

Amelia met me at the gate. She and Harvey had been admiring the tulip bed, although in Harvey's case that might be too strong of a word. She nodded toward the street from where I had returned. "My, aren't you always the curious one? Did you hear anything good?" She laughed.

"Nah, not really," I chuckled. "Just the usual mid-life-crisis, stuff. How about you? I saw you follow one couple right into their house the other day!" I teased her back. In our close-knit group, very little went unseen. She'd tailed a man and a woman out the gate, up their walkway and right through the door.

"Oh, well, they're doctors!" She explained the difference so I could understand what justified her pursuit more than mine.

"They talk about interesting diseases and sick people. I don't know what they're saying most of the time, but I know it's serious. I watch their eyes when they use those long medical words. Sometimes I think how glad I am that I'm not a living person, left so sickly, like those poor people they talk about. I wonder if the really sick patients might pass away and join us here."

"Well, they can visit, but they can't stay. Remember? I got the last parking space," I quipped.

Amelia chuckled. "Oh, yeah," she replied.

My enjoyment at eavesdropping on the living was my coping mechanism to mask how much it bothered me that I didn't belong wholly anywhere. If I remained here on earth in this state, I was sentenced to lurk in the shadows of the daily routines of the living as an outside observer. They would never know I existed. In reverse, I couldn't allow myself to become attached to any of living people by adopting them as my surrogate family. I wasn't ready to concede that I might never move on. I needed to be ready to leave if I ever got the call to do so.

I relished the freedom to choose whichever people I found the most interesting that day, and spend as much or as little time with them as I wanted. I liked the proximity of others but I didn't need them staring at me, praying for my soul. Sam and I had a comfortable following, but we weren't rock stars or anything. We certainly weren't well known enough to merit vigils by our graves. A few extra people would stop by for a year or two, but that would pass eventually. I'm not one of the famous people buried here. In a few years they'll ask "Lilla who?" and I'll probably be dropped from the tours altogether.

For the time being, though, I did see more people pass by my grave then I remembered from the year before, probably because I died in the fall. The year hadn't gone full circle yet. I didn't know what to expect when spring arrived. It was nice to see a few extra people stop and take note of Sam's grave and mine.

On days I didn't feel like eavesdropping on walkers, I turned my attention to the spring blooms. Tiny buds on the lilac bushes told me it must be somewhere near the beginning of May.

I was giddy thinking about the Lilac Festival that year. True, my days as Grand Marshall of the parade were over for good, but truthfully, the last few times had worn me out.

When I was getting on in years, the festival organizers wanted to show their affection as much as they could before it was too late. Out of all of the times I was the Grand Marshall, three of them were after I turned eighty years old! Not that I wasn't flattered, by any means. It just meant a long day for me.

First, the parade, followed by a luncheon, then a jolting drive up Lilac Hill in a rattling golf cart driven by a good-hearted volunteer. My large hat and giant corsage garnered lots of nodding, smiling and hand-shakes along the way.

This year I couldn't wait for the festival. I had it all planned out. The parade and festival were in Highland Park, about a block from the cemetery. I could see the whole parade, not like the days of when I was the Grand Marshall when all I could see was the car in which I was riding. After that, I could go to the park to see the flowers and festival booths all day, every day. Sadly, I remembered I would be unable to smell the lilacs. Maybe if I remembered the fragrance vividly enough, I could fool my nose into believing I really smelled those heavenly flowers.

Anticipation of the festivities started creeping into the neighborhood as well. Lilac Festival banners fluttered gaily from lampposts, over boldly lettered signs declaring "DO NOT BLOCK DRIVEWAY." Traffic increased, and rental companies erected tents in the park and along Highland Avenue. The Co-op building buzzed with activity as festival organizers instructed volunteers on their duties.

More than a few extra cars cruised through the cemetery too, probably hunting for parking spaces. More than likely, they were looking for a place to turn around so they could go back down Highland Avenue without getting lost down a side street. At least that's what I thought at the beginning, but I changed my mind when not one, but three cars stopped in front of Sam's grave and mine. Out popped a dozen or so people, none of whom I recognized, mostly adults with a few small children.

The children managed to squirm their way out of their parents' arms and down to the ground, where they chased a frog under the bench. This left the adults free to talk and me free to listen. I hung back, near the chapel, arms carefully wrapped around each other, my shield up. I had become lax about that until "my accident," as I came to call my run in with Massimo. I learned to keep my emotions in check and hadn't felt as emotionally volatile as when I first appeared after my death. After the accident, I wanted to be sure others didn't see my hideous hand. I was frightening enough as a regular ghost.

"Oh, this is so pretty here!" exclaimed one woman as she cupped her hand around the first of the lilac blooms and inhaled its sweet aroma. One of the men, her husband I guess, walked over to her and took a camera from her other hand. He stepped back and took a picture of her, framed by the lilacs and our graves. Charming. That would look nice over a mantel. Then he took quite a few more photos of the whole area, including the graves around the Sisters of Mary Chapel and even behind the lilac bushes. I don't know why but something told me to stay out of the path of his camera.

While he busied himself with his photo shoot, the rest of the group fanned out. A couple of women walked around the chapel, trying to identify the saints pictured on each window. When they came around, they knelt in front of our graves to read the dates and inscriptions. The man handed the camera back to his wife, then took it back, proclaiming, "Just one more," as he clicked a shot of the chapel roof. He returned to his wife again, who tucked it into her purse.

"Well, do you think you've got anything good enough for the tabloids?" she teased him.

"Hey you never know. She could be here right now, laughing at us," he responded. "We'll find out when we enlarge the pictures and play with the light. It's too hard to see on that little screen."

He was right on one count, I was there but I wasn't laughing. He called out "Hey, Rick! Did you see anything? You know, before you looked through the camera?"

Did he just call that guy "Rick"?

"Oh my God," I thought. It was the cameraman from the news truck who had brought sightseers. I needed to keep a low profile. I should have blinded him permanently when I had the chance!

Rick laughed. "No way, man. I didn't even know what was going on! It was just being in the right place at the right time. Shit, I was halfway blind! I didn't even know what I was looking at until we went over everything at the station.

"We didn't believe it when we replayed it," Rick continued. "Lots of people still don't believe it but some say they saw a ghost or something around here. We don't know if it's real or if it's even her." He nodded toward my grave.

While the rest of the group bantered about whether my ghost or any other ghosts existed in general, Rick and the other guy stepped away from the group to grab a smoke. While they puffed their cigarettes, I saw Harvey weaving through this quirky little gathering, making the darnedest face. I didn't care what he was thinking, because I was too busy praying they wouldn't see him. That's all I needed, a two for one special on spooks.

"Don't be silly, they won't see me," Harvey sent me his word. Strangely enough, he had his hands clasped in front of him, the first time I'd seen that. He'd been dead for so long, it was probably unnecessary and only for my benefit. I sent him my gratitude secretly across the group.

I never thought I'd say it but thank God for restless children! After the tykes chased the frog away, they started pulling grass and throwing it at the adults.

"Hey! Hey!" one of the women said to the giggling kids. She picked one of them up off the ground and wiped the dirty grass from his hands. She sighed. "I think it's time to go. It's almost somebody's n-a-p time."

"Yeah," agreed Rick. "It was good while it lasted. We'll come back another time. She'll still be here."

Blessedly, this field trip came to an abrupt end. Everybody sorted themselves back into their vehicles.

"Hey, thanks for taking us here," one of the other women said to Rick as she headed for her car. "This place is so huge I never would have found this little grave on my own!"

"Yeah, it's cool," her husband agreed as he strapped one of the children into a car seat. "My sister loves ghosts! She's into this. She's been dying to come here. Now I can tell her where to look."

"Maybe I should sell tickets!" Harvey said jovially, as the cars maneuvered their way toward the cemetery gate.

"Oh, Harvey! Don't even joke about that!" I loudly responded, not at all amused. "Can you believe that? Do you think that camera guy really got pictures of me? Remember when I told you I thought I saw you when I used to garden here? Did anyone else? Did they get your picture or anything?"

"Nope. I made folks leave real fast a couple of times, but they didn't come back to take my picture or nothin'. Must've figured it was better to leave the ghosties alone. Not like now. Why, you could be famous! The Mount Hope Ghost!"

"Hey. That's the 'Lilac Lady' to you, mister, but you're not helping, Harvey. What if they come back with more people? What if someone sees me? It could get much worse. I don't want hordes of people chasing me for pictures. Oh God, I'm turning into a recluse side show, just like H.C. Milford!"

"Well, that's up to you. You say you don't want them crowdin' around, but you stand right there and take it, like you're waitin' for 'em to find you. Just go somewhere else! Like this!" With that, Harvey was gone. However, he didn't go too far away. He was just hiding out somewhere else in the cemetery, as I knew I should have done. I tried to keep my distance, I really did, but everyone knows how hard it is to stay clear of a gathering crowd. It's like a train wreck. I had to look, or at least listen!

****

When the vendors set up shop and Security took their places, I knew the Lilac Festival had arrived. Shuttle buses unloaded tourists who lined up along Highland Avenue, making it official. Let the parade begin!

I wish I could have watched it with the same carefree anticipation I felt only two days before. I wanted to march with all of the bands and swirl through the floats with reckless abandon! Instead I lurked in the branches of a pine tree, with my arms securely wrapped around each other.

As self-conscious as I was, however, I still reveled in the whole celebration. Sixty years of nostalgia flooded my face with the broadest smile I'd ever worn. How precious to see the twirling dancers and hear the crisp music from local bands whose names I'd almost forgotten!

"This is for you, Sam," I waxed lovingly.

I wondered if he could see the crowds celebrating. He could never have imagined the interest he sparked in these gardens would resurrect the largest festival in Rochester! I waited to see the Grand Marshall waving from a convertible, winding up the end of the parade. It was some middle-aged man this year, nobody I recognized, probably a politician or something like that. Whoever he was, he looked like he enjoyed the hubbub. I hoped he enjoyed shaking hands.

As the last car made its way down Highland Avenue, parade goers spilled into the street and descended voraciously on the attractions. As the beginning mayhem subsided, they worked themselves out of the bottleneck at the edge of the park and into the makeshift village.

Booths lined the path that curved through the park's small hills. Vendors readied for the onslaught of frenzied consumers indulging in delicious consumption and impulse buying. Just like in my glory days, there was a perpetual line for kettle corn.

The Lilac Pavilion loomed over the children's activities. Some parents skillfully avoided that area while they shopped, saving it until their kids had become intolerably bored. Other parents unleashed their kids immediately into the games to get it out of their systems. I don't know which strategy proved more effective, but someone usually left crying.

Truthfully, the vendors and sales pitches at the festival weren't my cup of tea. It was a little too commercial for my taste, but I loved seeing so many people enjoying themselves in the park. My true passion was always the flowers themselves, but if someone selling handmade jewelry brought a few more people into the park, that was all right by me. Eventually people rambled out of the gauntlet of booths toward the flowered hillside, the real star of the show.

This was what the Lilac Festival was all about. Over a hundred lilac bushes of every variety blanketed the hill. The serenity was, perhaps, more greatly appreciated after the frenzy of the vending areas. Nothing made the world disappear like those warm spring days, sitting in the middle of the beautiful lilacs, absorbing their aroma.

At the risk of being seen, I flitted carefully through the festival. How could I not after all it had meant to me? If I hid in the cemetery with the festival less than a block away, my memories of the past and curiosity of the present would gnaw at me the entire time. I took precautions, for what they were worth, so as not to be seen. I folded my hands around my arms, and kept to the shadows. Unfortunately for me there weren't many shadows, which was great for the festival.

Gray Rochester skies gave way to brilliant sunshine, which probably helped account for the largest crowd I could remember. Locals did not take this nice weather for granted. On more than one occasion, driving rains closed the whole festival down for days. Not that day, though. It must have been a record-breaking scorcher. Sweat poured off people as they waited in line for lemonade. If that heat lasted for the entire festival week, my poor lilac bushes would wither in days!

It killed me that I couldn't smell anything, especially my beloved lilacs. I thought I could force my memories to create an illusion of lilac scents, so I immersed myself into one of the larger bushes laden with humongous blooms of the darkest purple. Inhaling deeply I waited for them to infuse my senses with their perfume. Nothing. "Forget it," I told myself. If lilacs couldn't revive my sense of smell, it was hopeless.

Well, they were still pretty to look at, anyway. Maybe Jodi, Amelia, and I could come back that night to wander freely around the park. I considered staying right in that bush until an unsuspecting victim leaned into it for a big sniff and got an eyeful of me instead.

No, I wouldn't really do that. I was just testy because I couldn't smell the flowers. I shouldn't scare someone for fun. They would run off and start more rumors I would regret later. That was one fire which didn't need any fueling. I suspected it was out of control already.

"Where's Lilla?" wasn't the game I wanted to play. It had been a nice afternoon. I would quit while I was ahead and lie low in the cemetery until after dark.

I ended up lying much lower than I expected because a tiny mob had gathered right where I wanted to be. They milled around my grave and the chapel. Some of them sat on the grass and on nearby headstones. Festival goers often strayed into the cemetery for a peek around, but this was more than the usual overflow. Their voices buzzed with small talk about keeping their eyes open for any Lilla sightings. One group sitting in a circle not too far from Sam's grave caught my eye: Spooky Marcie and her ultra-spooky friends, all of whom probably saw me at my funeral.

I steered clear of that bunch, for sure. I wished they would leave. That was my special place, dammit, and I should be able to stay without being harassed! Maybe they wouldn't see me, but I didn't want to risk even a tiny glimpse. The cemetery gates couldn't close soon enough that night as far as I was concerned.

I pulled back from the crowd and tried to figure out what time it was and how much longer I needed to wait until the authorities kicked them out. You can guess who pulled up. My buddies from Channel Six. Cameraman Rick, who I'm sure played a large part in this circus, hopped out of the truck. As he fumbled with his equipment, I mused how I might blind him in one eye, no, both eyes, and still not be seen by anyone else. Realizing I could never pull it off, I tucked myself into a pine tree behind the chapel so I could hear everything.

The reporter wasn't the same woman from my funeral, though. Rick was probably still mad at the other one for laughing at his blind eye and giving him the finger. This reporter was a very tall black woman who wore a nicely tailored orange linen pantsuit. While Rick readied his camera, she checked her hair and makeup in the news truck mirror. She moved in between the camera and the crowd and began her spiel.

"This is Rebecca Dean. I'm standing here in Mount Hope Cemetery, where there have been reported sightings of a mysterious figure."

"Nobody is certain who or what they've seen…or even if it's real, but many locals believe it to be the ghost of the woman who was buried here last fall." The crowd parted as the camera panned in for a close-up of my grave.

She continued as the camera refocused on her. "Lilla Woodworth was a local gardening expert. Rochester knew her as the Lilac Lady, and indeed, that is what the locals have dubbed this apparition. As you can see behind me, some believers are waiting to catch a glimpse of the Lilac Lady. Expectations are especially high during this week of the Lilac Festival."

People behind Rebecca cheered and waved. She turned sideways as the camera panned the crowd, stopping for a close-up of one of Marcie's friend's t-shirt. Air-brushed across the front was an angelic long-haired blond beauty, a heavenly creature wearing a long flowing dress. The caption read: "Lilac Lady, 1940-2028?" I think it was supposed to be me on that shirt. Never mind the fact that I lived in the twentieth and twenty-first centuries, and never wore a dress like that in my life. Not to mention the fact that I had been a brunette, not a blond, and never came as close to being one tenth as gorgeous as the picture on the t-shirt.

Apparently even the psychic types felt the need to romanticize the whole ghost thing. I guess we must all dress like the Victorian era, whether we were there or not. Well, fine, if that's what everybody was looking for, maybe they could chase Amelia or Jodi instead of me. However, my friends, noticeably absent, would never forgive me if I turned the crowd on them.

What's next after t-shirts? Mugs? Key chains? Just like the Old Man of the Mountain. My memory would be another Lilac Festival booth full of trinkets. I'd be worth more dead than alive. The whole prospect sickened me as my thoughts ran rampant. I hoped it wouldn't become that big of a phenomenon, especially if I didn't let it. I had to hide from these people where they wouldn't see me, and I didn't see them.

When I looked at the groups looking for me, my imagination went haywire. I was more afraid of the living than the dead, at that point. I had to shield myself from them, if only to clear my head for a bit. I knew if I didn't get out of there soon, my emotional state would get the best of me.

I was afraid I might let my guard down enough for them to see me. This was different that the attention I enjoyed when I was The Lilac Lady. It's much more pleasant being followed than chased.

As much as I dreaded it, my only option would be to go underground as I had done that one time with Jodi. I remembered how much I hated being underground and how I vowed never to do that again. I debated whether to dip one toe in at a time or take the plunge. I opted for the plunge because I needed that force to break through the surface of the solid earth. Moreover, I knew if I didn't go all at once, I wouldn't go at all. With my eyes closed, fearing the impact, I plummeted head first through the tree branches and entered the dense earth once again.

My airy soul turned into molasses, slowly folding itself around the pieces of dirt, each grain so tiny but as unyielding as the walls of the chapel. I was suffocating again, even more than that first time because of the prospect of remaining there for an indefinite amount of time. If I worked my way underground toward the crowd, could I hear what they said? Probably not, and worse yet, what would happen if I was overcome by a panic attack and leaped out of the ground, gasping like the last time? They'd definitely see me if I carried on like that. I definitely wouldn't be as pretty as the picture on that t-shirt, especially with my freaky hand.

I couldn't let them see me with that horrible crushed mess at the end of my arm. Was it my vanity or my privacy I sought to protect? My privacy came first, but if they saw my creepy hand, I wouldn't just be "the ghost of the Lilac Lady." I would be "the ghost with the claw." Even more fun to capture on film.

I couldn't stay underground any longer. It had only been a very short while, but it felt like forever already. I managed to maneuver myself away from the crowd before I exploded out of the ground. I restrained myself from gasping and sputtering. I was relieved to be back on the surface, moving freely through air instead of laboring through dirt.

The eager crowd held me at bay in the treetops while they talked to the departing news team. It seemed they all had a different angle. They either saw something, or knew someone who knew someone that practically talked to the Lilac Lady.

They were convinced they would see her too, either that day, or the next, or sometime that week during the festival.

The news truck drove out of the gate, weaving through more sightseers. Shaking once again, I found myself backing away in the opposite direction. I wound up in the very back of the cemetery, where I first saw Jodi. The crowd near my grave was not visible from here and their voices were barely audible.

Annoyed, I sat on a gravestone. Amelia sidled over. "What are you doing over here? Your audience is waiting for you!" She joked, but she stopped smiling when she noticed my frustration.

"Amelia, I don't like this. I don't want to be a freak. What should I do?" I asked her.

"I told you what you should do!" Harvey snapped as he passed by. Then he disappeared, off to who knows where.

I explained to Amelia. "He said I should leave but I don't want to. Where would I go? I just want to be invisible long enough so they'll forget about me."

"I know. It happened to almost all of us when we first came here. We must have some sort of presence they sense. Usually, it was only couple of relatives who claimed they saw us. Right after we died, they would look for us. Sometimes they saw us, but more often than not, they only imagined they did. You just had a few more people in the right place at the right time that saw you."

"Yeah, and now I can't shake them off. I'll wait until tomorrow to see if fewer people come around but God only knows what's going to happen if they show it on the news."

"I'm sure tomorrow will tell what's in store for you. Well, there's some good news for now." Amelia pointed to a police car driving slowly from the back of the cemetery to the front. A cemetery employee herded people toward the gate. Hallelujah, it was closing time!

"So long everyone, don't let the gate hit you on your way out!" I sang.

Finally, dark serenity returned to my place of rest. I celebrated by doing nothing except leaning against the side of the chapel without worrying about being seen. Maybe this would work out okay, after all.

I weighed my choices and decided I would stay inside the chapel at night and go elsewhere during the day, to avoid the thrill seekers. I could live with that.

Unfortunately, I soon realized the thrill seekers were one jump ahead of me. They showed up that very night. Long before they came anywhere near me, I heard a small group, a couple of girls and four boys, rustling the bushes and shushing each other. By the time they arrived at my grave with their cameras and phones I had risen to the top of the chapel roof to watch them. They got high and talked for at least a couple of hours, watching for ghosts.

So, that was how it was going to be, was it? Jeez, that really stunk. No more peace at night than I had during the day. On the off chance, if someone captured my image on film again, I could forget ever having this place to myself to share my quiet time with Sam's memory. I weighed my options. I thought about staying nearby and checking in once in a while. I realized if I let my guard down for one second or if something frightened me unexpectedly, I would jump. That was all it would take for someone to see my flash or something even more solid. Then I could forget about ever finding peace and quiet in this spot.

Leaving temporarily became the only option, for the time being. Over time, if nobody saw me, I would fade into an urban legend. People might talk about it but they wouldn't believe it enough to hop in the car and search for me.

I hadn't done myself any favors in the past few months by hiding out as I did. In my desperation for Sam to find me, I had shackled myself to our final resting spot and turned myself into a prisoner. My God, here I was free from money, time, and age. What was I doing lurking in the shadows of a graveyard? The only thing that found me was a crowd of sightseers. I couldn't wait here like this anymore. I had to go out and look for something or someone to help me move on.

Somewhere else I might find spirits, more gifted and more powerful than I was, who could help me. If the living hadn't backed me into this corner, I might not have realized how helpless I had become. I guess my pursuers liberated me by scaring me out of the gate for my own good.

As I left the cemetery, I saw Harvey near the big fountain. "I'm leaving," I said, "but I'm coming back – just not for a while."

"I know," he replied, not surprised. "I'll be here. See you when you get back."

"I'm sure you will," I laughed. Of course, Harvey would be there. He was as much a part of that cemetery as the front gate. Actually, I think he'd been there longer than the front gate.

I didn't say good-bye to anybody else. That sounded too long term. I wrapped my hands around each other and hesitantly started out. My plans, unformed. My destination, away.

Chapter Fifteen: Breaking Away

Hovering above the treetops, I left my home in Mount Hope Cemetery and headed away from Rochester. I didn't know, or care, where I was going. I would travel on whims and larks to places I'd never been. I looked forward to seeing new people and places. Should I go up north or out west? I had been to California once but I'd never seen the Grand Canyon or the heartlands in the Midwest.

Now that I could move so quickly, I didn't have to lollygag past anything I didn't want to. If I wanted to be somewhere in particular, I only had to think it, and I was there as soon as I finished my thought. The hardest part was deciding where to go first.

Whizzing over the countryside, I imagined I would arrive in Oklahoma any second. As I flew farther and farther south past the hills of Pennsylvania, Virginia, and Tennessee, toward North Carolina, it became clear I wasn't heading west at all. Nor did I intend to. Not quite yet. "Jesus, what am I doing here?" I asked myself. Something inside drew me to revisit the place where Sam and I first met.

"Goodness, Woman!" I chided myself as I neared my destination. "Break out of this mindset and quit pining for Sam. He's not here anymore than he's back in Rochester. You have the whole world to see, dammit! All right, a quick stop here for a few minutes. Let Sam know you're thinking of him and then go."

I needed to stop here in case Sam was searching for me. These little stops were my trail of breadcrumbs. Footprints of my soul, touching down here and there…in case anyone needed to find me.

The minute I left Mount Hope I knew I'd come here. When the gawkers from the Lilac Festival forced me away from my own grave, I knew I had to leave but I was so panic-stricken I couldn't decide where to go. After ditching the crowds, I could think in peace about going to other places that meant so much to Sam and me.

Once I admitted that to myself, serenity washed over me. I didn't have to mask my intentions by stumbling there "accidentally." When I closed my eyes and concentrated, I found myself in a place dear to my heart. I stood in front of a tiny house just outside of Clinton, North Carolina. I became weepy looking at the house where I spent three of the best years of my life.

When I saw how much smaller it was than I remembered, a new wave of gratitude swept over me. Sam's Aunt Sofie and Uncle Buell lived there and opened their home to me when I needed it most. They let me live with them in their tiny three bedroom house during my last three years of college. At the time, Sam's older cousin, Charles, had recently married and moved to Raleigh.

Sam, whose family back in Rochester was barely getting by, came down to Clinton for college. To save money, Sam stayed in Charles' room for his entire four years of college. After Sam and I started dating, I moved into his younger cousin Caroline's room with her. If it hadn't been for Sam and his extended family's hospitality, I never would have finished my education at Watkins University or any other college. Not under the circumstances I faced at the time.

My first college year was destined for disaster from the word "go." I wanted to attend college so I could run my own greenhouse someday. Mr. And Mrs. Fulton, close friends of my parents, owned a garden supply store and flower shop. From the minute they hired me to work during school vacations I knew that's what I wanted to do for a living, too.

How I loved tending the seedlings! I relished the feel of the cool damp dirt as I carefully potted tender plants for customers. Mr. Fulton wanted to nurture my newfound passion. He told me he heard about a good program at Watkins University down in North Carolina. He even met some of the instructors at a symposium.

My family's financial situation, however, made it unlikely I would ever attend college. I sent out a few applications anyway, hopeful that funds might magically appear. Watkins University came through for me in ways I couldn't have imagined. Not only did they accept me into their horticultural and land management program, but they also gave me a full scholarship, including room and board.

My parents worried terribly about sending their daughter all the way to North Carolina for college but I tearfully convinced them that this opportunity of a lifetime was too incredible to refuse. A little intervention on Mr. and Mrs. Fulton's part didn't hurt, either. Reluctantly, my parents drove me, and my belongings, from our little town in northern New Hampshire to a train station in Massachusetts.

They cried for an hour until I boarded the train. When the train began moving, my parents remained on the platform waving goodbye, my father drying my mother's tears. I held mine back until the station was well out of sight. Then it was my turn to cry for three hours.

Eventually, dusk enveloped the scenic countryside. The train clicked into a soothing rhythm that calmed my nerves and lulled me to sleep. I was finally able to dream of new adventures at my lovely college.

Watkins University had once been one of the largest plantations in North Carolina, owned by Jebediah and Mary Watkins. According to the stories, they not only surpassed other local growers for cotton production, they were also rumored to have old money from jewel mines somewhere. Somehow they survived the Civil War with their property and their lives fairly intact.

Unfortunately, looters heard from the servants that the family had hidden jewels, and the master and mistress were constantly sneaking off to count their riches. The looters threatened the couple and killed Jebediah.

When they were about to burn down the house, Mary Watkins, hoping to be spared, repeatedly screamed about rubies in the cellar. The would-be thieves searched the cellar and the rest of the house, looking for rubies or other jewels, but found nothing. Then they killed Mary, too, for lying to them.

The looters ignited the house, but rode off before the flames really took. Some of the remaining house servants quickly extinguished the fire. They saved that beautiful house, even if its namesakes had perished. The property changed hands several times after the war, until the government purchased it and established a university around 1900. They restored the buildings as well as the original Watkins name.

Pictures I had seen of the house and surrounding ivy-covered buildings oozed southern charm. It was breathtaking! I couldn't believe I had the good fortune to attend school in a place like that. Scenes from Gone with the Wind fueled my fantasies of becoming a beautiful southern belle, wrapped in delicate dresses. Surely I would be courted by debonair gentlemen smoking their pipes. Maybe I would learn to ride a horse, sidesaddle, of course.

I don't know how I let my expectations become so outlandish. It didn't take long for me to realize I was just another poor kid from The North.

I'll never forget my first day in North Carolina, or at Watkins. In 1958, my little hometown in New Hampshire might as well have been on a different planet. When the train doors opened at my destination, a hot southern breeze blasted me into a whole new world of culture and lifestyles. Specifically, it was my first encounter with black people.

My little town way up north was as white-bred as you can imagine. Everyone I knew was as pale as I was. There just weren't any black folks in my town. Up until I was about ten, I had only seen them in movies and newspapers. During my teen years, I did see a few black people when traveling to different parts of the state or down to Massachusetts, but it wasn't the same as walking shoulder to shoulder and speaking to one another.

The bustling maze of people at this steamy train platform rendered me dumbstruck. I wandered through the multicolored crowd in a stupor. Somehow, I retrieved my suitcases and trunk from the baggage area.

A black porter approached me and asked me a question. I couldn't stop staring, more out of a sense of wonderment than anything else. His skin was darker than his brown uniform. "That's neat!" I thought.

He spoke again, but because he had such a heavy southern accent I couldn't understand him. After two tries, I finally figured out he wanted to help carry my bags to a nearby cab. I probably intrigued him as well with my heavy New England accent when I accepted his offer and told him how far I had traveled. To a casual observer, the whole exchange might have been comical.

I thanked him with a nod when he finished loading my belongings into the cab. He held out his dark hand. I stared at it for a few seconds. Finally, I mustered the courage to gingerly shake it. After another nod and a mumbled thank you, I slipped into the back seat of the cab, too nervous to realize I had just cheated him out of a tip.

My cab ride from the train station to the college turned out to be more pleasant than expected, thanks to the talkative driver. He was middle aged, balding and a little pudgy. His grandfatherly mannerisms put me at ease.

After pegging me as a nervous newcomer, he doubled as a tour guide, pointing out tidbits about the town and college. I struggled to understand his southern drawl, but I got the gist of what he said. I appreciated the chance to acclimate myself to the dialect before entering the campus. During my difficult days ahead, I would relish his generosity.

As we entered Watkins' campus, I told him I needed to go to Plummer Hall, where I would live during my school years there. He drove slowly through the rows of three and four-story brick buildings, searching for the right dormitory. As we passed one particularly drab building, I saw the sign for Plummer Hall.

"Oh, there it is!" I exclaimed. "Right there!" The cab continued creeping forward as my cab driver looked ahead. "Stop!" I yelled. The cab stopped so abruptly I nearly fell off my seat.

"Where is it, did you say?" the cabbie asked.

"Right back there," I pointed behind us.

"What's the name of the place, again?"

"Let me check," I replied as I reread the acceptance letter for the thousandth time. I had known the name of Plummer Hall by heart for months, but now I was so nervous I doubted myself. "Plummer Hall. Yes, it's definitely Plummer Hall."

"Oh, you must be mistaken, miss," he shook his head. "I bet you mean Palmer Hall. People are always gettin' them mixed up. Don't you fret, darlin'. I'll get you to the right place." He chuckled as he prepared to continue forward.

"No. I'm sure. The sign is right on the lawn, and it's the same as the name in my letter. Can you go back there to make sure?" He paused before attempting to turn the car around. I couldn't understand his reluctance.

"Well, okay, we'll look and see." He doubled back to the building, which was indeed labeled Plummer Hall. I was finally there! He turned to look at me in the back seat. His confused face peered over the seat at my nervous smiling face.

"Miss, are you sure you got the right place? You're s'posed to live here?"

"I'm pretty sure. It's right here in the letter I got. Why?"

"Well, this here's where the colored girls live. I think you must be mistaken, miss. Lemme see your letter."

"Colored girls?" I asked, as segregation leapt out of the lore of "other places" and into my daily life.

"Yes'm. The white kids live in the buildings at the other end of this road."

With shaking hands, I fumbled through the small satchel I had kept in the back seat with me and produced my scholarship and acceptance letters. After more rifling, I found my housing assignment letter. It clearly stated that as the recipient of the Emma Johnson scholarship, I was to live in Plummer Hall, free of charge, for the duration of my schooling at Watkins University. Tears welled in my eyes as I wondered what was to become of me. There must have been a mistake in my housing assignment. I hoped they could find a new place for me to live.

The driver parked the cab in the shade of a tree. He told me to wait in the car while he spoke to the dormitory staff. With my papers tucked under his arm, he knocked on the front door and a nicely dressed black woman escorted him into the building. I remained in the hot car but rolled the windows down to capture what breeze I could. Twenty minutes passed. Then another car arrived. A white man stepped out, bent down to glance at me, and then entered Plummer Hall.

The curtains in the Plummer Hall windows took on a life of their own, rapidly opening and closing, as everybody inside had to see the action themselves. Voyeurs on all floors discreetly pulled the curtains back on the sides and centers, and then quickly closed them when my gaze approached their windows.

I prayed somebody would come out to get me soon. The smell of smoke emanating from the car seats was making me nauseous. The prospect of leaping out of the cab and puking my brains out in front of all those prying eyes horrified me.

Finally, after an hour of deliberating, the powers that be decided the scholarship would be honored and I would live in Plummer Hall. My benevolent cab driver and the other man, the Dean of Housing, carried my belongings past a sea of silent, dark faces, up to my room on the second floor.

A group of white students had gathered, disbelieving that I was going to live in the colored dorm. Little did I know someday I would marry that tall blond boy standing in the back. The thing Sam remembered most about that day was how amused he was when he heard me speak, something about getting my sweatah out of the cah.

I thanked my cab driver profusely for all he had done and apologized that I couldn't afford a larger tip, and that even included the tip I should have given to my porter. I wanted to hug that kindly gentleman, but intimidated by the gathering crowd, I settled for a gentle handshake. He took that opportunity to discreetly return my fare money and tip. I clutched it in my sweaty hand and turned to enter Plummer Hall, making history as its first white resident.

As she guided me through the foyer, the housemother, Miss Turner, introduced me to the black female students who would be my new dorm mates.

"This is Gloria, and Jolene, and Martha."

I didn't hear anything after the first three names. "Hello, hello," I mumbled to the group as we passed. I was so tired and confused I wasn't able to put together any names and faces at that point.

Their replies were a polite murmur.

"Good Evening."

"Afternoon."

"Hi."

I couldn't tell who said what.

After exchanging formal greetings with students who were as bewildered as I was, I followed Miss Turner to my room to unpack, settle in, and hide. Miss Turner was very kind, and understandably nervous about my presence.

I couldn't stop staring at the floor. Miss Turner leaned over and tilted her head to get my attention.

"You must be hungry after such a long trip," she spoke hesitantly. The little quiver in her voice contrasted with her large broad build. "The rest of the girls ate a couple of hours ago, but I can bring a tray up for you, if you'd like. Would'ja like that?"

I nodded. I mouthed the words, "Yes, thank you," but no sound emerged from my lips. Despite my lame response, I was extremely grateful for her offer. As hungry as I was, I still wouldn't have had the nerve to ask for anything to eat, and certainly wouldn't have ventured down to the kitchen to get it myself.

I opened my trunk and took some hangers out of the closet. Miss Turner returned with a plate of mashed potatoes and a roasted chicken breast. I sat at my desk and devoured the delicious food in ravenous silence. Sensing how lonely I must be, she stayed while I ate at the desk. It gave her the chance to share helpful insights about getting along at Watkins University.

Miss Turner sat on a bed and cleared her throat. "Well, ya see," her gentle voice belied the difficult words she spoke to her only white charge whom had ever lived in Plummer Hall, "the college here? It's been integrated quite a while now. Well...sorta. Some classes are mixed, but the houses aren't. That's why we were all surprised when you came to us today."

"I'm so sorry!" I blurted out as I swallowed the last of my food. "I didn't know that. I don't want to get anyone in trouble. I'll see if they can move me to the right place. Or maybe..." My voice faded as I whispered the last part, "Maybe I should go back home."

"Oh, no, child!" Miss Turner said. She patted the bed, gesturing me to sit next to her. I dabbed around my mouth with my napkin. Feeling teary, I gripped my napkin as I sat on the bed.

"No, no. I'm sure you worked as hard to get here as any of the other girls. What's done is done. No one's gonna make you leave. But, the dorms are full this year and the other dorms are even more crowded than this one. So, you see, you'll be living here with us for a while. And we're happy to have you.

"This room is yours. It's a nice room. You can see Watkins Hall from your window. Bathroom is the next door down on the left. Here at Watkins the students don't just sleep in their dormitories."

"We eat our meals together in our own dining rooms, too. It's more like family that way. And just like family, we all pitch in to keep our home up.

"Everyone does a little somethin' to help out, no matter what dorm they live in. Little things like dustin', washin' the linens, or helping out in the kitchen. Things like that. Later this week you and I can find a little job for you, once you're more comfortable with, uh…dorm life." Miss Turner spoke gingerly while searching for the right words. She gave my hand a squeeze, reassuring me that she'd find a way for me to help that was comfortable for all of us.

I felt badly for poor Miss Turner. She took a deep breath before explaining the social climate here on this southern campus. Her hand, still resting on top of mine, comforted me. It was big, and soft, and safe, like my mom's.

"College can sure be different than where everyone grew up. You'll make all sorts of new friends here, and in your classes. Oh, and on weekends, the Student Forum has mixers in Graham Hall. There's music and dancing. The boys and girls always have so much fun!"

She cleared her throat again, and continued, "Friday nights are for the colored kids. Saturday nights for the white kids." Mixers? They called them mixers, but the black and white students attended on separate nights?

"Oh," was all I could think of to say. I felt my eyes widen a little. If Miss Turner noticed, she didn't let on. She knew I was trying to digest the information about this new place. She looked me in the eyes to make sure I understood.

"Most of the girls here in Plummer Hall, they like to go to them Friday night Mixers. But Mr. Johnson…He's in charge of housing and all that. He thinks it would be more comfortable for you to go to the Saturday Mixers. There, you'll make lots of friends to go to the football games with, and to the soda shop in town!"

So there it was. I was living with the colored students but I was expected to partake in the activities with the white students.

My heart went out to this poor woman assigned to lay down the law for this ignorant white girl who just fell from The North into her lap. This was turning out more like The Wizard of Oz than Gone with the Wind. She was my Glenda and I was her Dorothy.

I appreciated her candor, for no doubt she would be held responsible for any of my breeches of conduct. She went on to tell me that, as with all students, I would need to notify her of any comings and goings outside of class time. Gentlemen callers, to be entertained in the green sitting room, were only allowed on Saturdays and Sundays, from 1 p.m. to 6 p.m. Curfew was at 8 p.m., unless I was at the library, or had received permission for a later return.

All off campus dates must be chaperoned by a senior student or resident assistant. If I should need such a chaperone, Miss Turner would contact the dormitories housing the white students. It would be more appropriate for one of them to chaperone me, lest someone mistake Miss Turner for my maid. I thought, once she sees my well-worn clothes, she could rest assured that nobody in their right mind would believe I came from a household that could afford a maid.

She thought I should know one more thing, so I would understand something very important about my scholarship. My scholarship was designated for a colored student, and up until today, everyone here was under the impression that it had been awarded as such. Emma Johnson, the namesake of my scholarship, had been a house servant at the Watkins Plantation.

Her relationship with Jebediah Watkins became common knowledge when she became pregnant with his child. This so infuriated his barren wife, Mary, as soon as the light-skinned baby girl was born, mother and child were sent away from Watkins' Plantation. Nobody knew what happened to the baby, but it was rumored that Mary Watkins sold the baby up North, and shipped Emma off to the Deep South.

During Emma's journey, she escaped to the North, where she worked in a textile mill. Through some fortunate circumstances, and her talent with a sewing needle, she became a couturier to the wealthy. She established a successful business, but never had any more children. By living meagerly and investing wisely, she accumulated a large bank account.

During Emma's later years, Watkins University was established and ahead of its time as an integrated college, perhaps to make amends for its tragic past. Emma never knew what happened to her daughter. Did Mary and Jebediah raise her as their own?

Did they keep the child on as a house servant or a field slave? Or was the baby sold to another slave owner? She always wondered if her daughter might be alive and had children of her own. She established a scholarship fund for a deserving black student on the off chance it might someday benefit a descendant of hers or any other former slave from the Watkins Plantation. It was her dream to offer a future to generations of black students yet to come.

Miss Turner fell silent for a little bit as I mulled over her words. I realized there was not a mistake in the Emma Johnson scholarship itself, nor in the housing assignment at Plummer Hall. The mistake was me. When I applied for that scholarship, I didn't recall seeing anything about a specific race. The scholarship committee must have assumed I was black, and I certainly was needy. Voila, one messed up situation, and one fretful student.

I was confused and tired. I missed my parents and my room. I hated to admit it but I even missed my brother, Albert. I held up amazingly well throughout that entire day, but that last bit of news threw me over the edge. I cried on Miss Turner's shoulder. "I'm sorry!" I blubbered. "They'll think I stole the scholarship…and…and they'll kick me out. I didn't take it on purpose!" I cried and cried. There's nothing like teenage angst to break the color barrier.

Miss Turner wrapped her strong, brown hands around my little white ones. "There, now," she said softly. "That is not going to happen. Don't you worry about anything as big as that. Uh huh, things might get tough, that's true. And folks'll surely talk about things that are none of their business. But nobody's gonna kick you out, you hear me?"

I lifted my head and nodded silently. Miss Turner handed me a handkerchief to dry my tears.

"You just pay attention to your studies. That's why you're here," she told me. "The best way to be strong is to get a good night's sleep, starting now. Good night, sweetie. I'll see you in the morning."

Miss Turner closed my door on her way out and took my empty plate back to the kitchen. It was time to look around at my new home. My room, with two dressers and two beds, was clearly meant to house two students, but I appeared to be its sole occupant.

I found a shoe on the floor near one of the dressers. My intended roommate probably dropped it when she moved out after catching sight of me in the cab. I held the shoe hostage for a while, hoping its owner would come and talk to me, but she never did. When I set the shoe in the hallway two days later, it was gone in less than fifteen minutes.

After a grueling two days of travelling and my nervous perspiration in the southern heat, I wanted nothing more than to take a bath. However, I wasn't ready to leave my room. I hid in my room until the wee hours of the night, to spare myself and my dorm mates the embarrassment of exposing too much of my pasty skin among their dark complexions. While biding my time, I had fallen asleep on top of my bedspread, fully clothed. Around two in the morning, I tiptoed to the bathroom. After checking to make sure the door was locked, I drew the deepest, hottest bath I ever took.

Just as I peeled off my sweaty dress, Miss Turner knocked on the door and asked who was up so late. Her sleepy voice grumbled it was too late for primping. I stuttered back that it was only me, trying to take a quick bath when it wasn't so crowded.

"Well, okay," she replied more gently. "Be quick about it and then get to bed."

There was a moment of silence. Even though I didn't hear any footsteps I thought Miss Turner had left. Then she whispered gently, "You know, it can get pretty hectic around here in the mornings. All my girls running crazy getting their things ready for classes and such. Tomorrow's just Orientation Day, but that doesn't matter. They can't find their hair ribbons. Their shoelaces break. Or they miss their folks and they don't want to leave their room."

That last one had me written all over it. I wasn't looking forward to going down to breakfast and meeting everyone all at once, but Miss Turner offered me a way around that. She continued whispering from the other side of the bathroom door. "You know, since you're so...new to the school, why don't you come down early with me to the kitchen tomorrow and help out with breakfast? Things get so loud up here with all those girls getting themselves ready. It's much quieter downstairs. It'll just be you, me, and Gloria. She's my other breakfast helper, such a nice girl."

"So nice! You'll really like her. We'll start cooking breakfast at six. I'll stop by your room to get you on my way down to the kitchen in the morning. How's that sound?"

"Yes! I'll be ready." I answered quickly and a little more loudly than I intended. My voice echoed in the tiled bathroom. I hoped our conversation didn't wake anybody.

"All righty. I'll see you at six o'clock. You get to bed soon, now."

"I will. Thank you, Miss Turner. I'll be ready at six."

From the start, Miss Turner and I communicated very well, listening to what went unsaid as much as the words we did say. We spoke volumes between the lines, trying to make the best of the situation.

With the dimly lit bathroom all to myself, I finally washed away some of my stress. I was in college, a lucky unexpected break for me, despite the strange circumstances. What was done was done and I was going to learn all I could, just like Miss Turner said.

Tracy Fontaine

Chapter Sixteen: Blending In

Miss Turner was so kind to me; I wanted to do all I could to help her. She asked me to be ready by six o'clock in the morning to help with breakfast. I was more than ready. I was dressed and sitting on the edge of my bed by 5:45 so I didn't miss being escorted to the kitchen by Miss Turner. Sure enough, she gently knocked on my door a minute before six o'clock. I flung open the door before she had a chance to ask if I was up yet.

"Well, you are an early bird!" she whispered. "C'mon, let's get some breakfast on the tables. These girls'll be hungry! I just can't sleep these first few days. I've been up since five! Before I came to get you I started getting things ready in the kitchen."

Miss Turner led the way downstairs. The stairway had large solid square banisters made of darkly stained wood. There was a landing in the middle where the stairs turned and led into the dining room. The room wasn't large, but somehow they managed to squeeze five tables of four into a neat little arrangement. I guessed there must be twenty of us girls living in this house. I tried to picture eating here with the other girls. I was sure everyone already had her favorite dining companions. Who would want to eat with me?

Miss Turner patted me gently on my back with her right hand as we passed the tables. The kitchen door was on the left of the wall close to the bottom of the stairs. Miss Turner had no sooner pressed her other hand on the kitchen door to swing it open, when one of the girls bounded down the stairs. She had one braid on the right side of her head. The rest of her hair hung in a wet cluster against her left cheek.

"Miss Turner! Miss Turner!" the girl said as she caught up to us. Miss Turner turned and moved her hand from my back to the girl's arm.

"Jolene, you be careful on those stairs, child. We don't need any busted ankles on the first day. Jolene, this is Lilla. Lilla, Jolene."

Jolene looked at me and said quietly, "Hi. Nice to meet you."

To which I meekly responded, "You, too."

Jolene glanced back and forth between me and Miss Turner. I could tell she would have preferred to speak to Miss Turner alone but Miss Turner stayed next to me and finally asked. "Sweetie, what's wrong to make you run down the stairs like that?"

"Um. The lady's here to see Gloria."

"What lady?" Miss Turner turned around and started walking around the stairway toward the living room.

"No!" Jolene protested. She tugged on Miss Turner's arm. She glanced at me out of the corner of her eye and addressed Miss Turner directly in the face. She tilted her head and over- enunciated her words. "You know. The...la...deeee!"

"What...Oh!! Oh, goodness! Yes, yes," Miss Turner replied and relaxed her shoulders when she understood. "Good Lord. Is that all? It's not her first, right?"

"No, Ma'am," Jolene said. She looked at me out of the corner of her eye as she cupped her hand to Miss Turner's ear. I heard her whisper that Gloria got blood on her dress and couldn't get it out.

Miss Turner sighed. "Mercy." She turned to Jolene. "You go tell Gloria I'm comin'. And tell her not to rub it too much until I bring the cleaning powder!" Jolene nodded and ran back upstairs.

"See. I told you, if it's not one thing, it's another. Somethin' new every day." Miss Turner rolled her eyes and smiled. She enjoyed the mayhem of taking care of all of these girls. She began walking back through the dining room, speaking over her shoulder. "Lilla, you follow me," she said as she pushed open the kitchen door.

She didn't have to say it twice, as I was right on her heels. We entered a long, bright yellow kitchen with tall white cupboards that soared to a ten-foot ceiling. On the long wall to our right was a large window that looked out onto a lush yard with several giant oak trees and a little pond way in back. Beneath the window was a deep basin sink that nested in a countertop of shiny white tiles. The countertop was nearly as high as my chest. A worn wooden stepstool leaned against the bottom cupboard. The stool was large and sturdy. I suppose it needed to be if Miss Turner had to get something from the top shelf.

On the opposite long wall to our left was a mammoth black gas stove with six industrial burners. Past that, there were more countertops, and a refrigerator twice as wide as me. Next to which, stood a large chest freezer. On the short wall opposite the wall where we entered was an open doorway leading to a small pantry.

A sturdy long butcher-block table dominated the center of the room. Miss Turner walked to the pantry in the back. She bent down to grab a bottle of cleanser to clean the blood off Gloria's dress. I had followed her so closely, when she stood up and turned around she almost bowled me over.

"Whoa!" she cried. We grabbed each other's arms so we wouldn't fall down. She looked skyward and clutched her heart. "Goodness, child. Don't sneak up on me in the kitchen, 'specially if I got a knife in my hand! I might be large, but I move fast down here in the kitchen!"

"Oops. I'm sorry," I replied. I backed away so she could get out of the pantry.

"I gotta get this upstairs before that stain sets in Gloria's dress. You're just in time to turn that bacon and start the grits. The water's ready on the stove and there's the bowl of grits. Just dump 'em into the pots and keep stirrin'. They'll be ready by the time the stampede starts." Then she swung open the kitchen door and left me alone to make breakfast for twenty people!

I hadn't noticed the two pans of bacon on the stove until Miss Turner said something, but the bacon was starting to smoke and I needed to turn it right away. I found a fork with a long handle, but even with that long fork, it was scary. I arched my arm to dodge the grease spatters as I flipped the bacon over. Thankfully, I had gotten there before anything burned.

Everything seemed so large. I felt like a kid in Grammy's kitchen again. How I wished I could pull up a seat on that stool and idly watch my grandmother bake her molasses cookies…maybe sneak a piece of cookie dough when she wasn't looking… Memories were great, but they wouldn't get breakfast on the table. This was no time to daydream. I snapped myself back to the all-to-real task at hand.

I needed to tend to the large pots on the other front two burners. I stood on my toes to peer down into the simmering water. A film of butter floated on top. This must be for the grits Miss Turner mentioned. I had never seen grits, much less cooked them. I thought they must be like oatmeal or something. There was a big bowl of dry grainy stuff behind me on the table. I figured those were the grits Miss Turner mentioned, so I poured them into the pots. I divided half of them into each pot and stirred them with a long wooden spoon. The pots were still like water. That doesn't look right…I was probably supposed to put a bowlful into each pot.

Scanning the room, I noticed a sack leaning against the table leg. "Harper Mills Grits. Good for your family!" That must be the stuff.

Reaching under the table I tried to pull out the sack but it was too heavy to budge. I knelt down next to the table and reached into the opening of the sack. I used my empty bowl to scoop some out and divide it between the two pots again. Quickly I stirred the new grits into the first batch I had added. The ingredients in the pots looked better, for a minute. Then things started to thicken, and thicken, and thicken, until my spoon hardly budged.

"Oh no! Oh!" I said aloud. I had added too many grits! I knew if I didn't do something soon I'd have two pots of cement on my hands. I ran around the big table over to the sink and started running the water so it could get hot. I flung open several cupboard doors until I found a small pot. I filled the pot with lukewarm water and ran back around that big table as quickly as I could to dump the water into the pots. They were almost full as it was so I couldn't add as much water as I would have liked.

The water lay on top of the sticky mass. I reached down into the water and poked at the grits until they started to break up and float into the new water. As much as I tried, they wouldn't blend in. Clumps floated around my spoon as I switched back and forth between the two pots trying to scrape more of the grits from the bottoms of the pots. My spoon kept getting stuck in the mess, and when it broke free I flicked grits and water down the sides of the pots and all over the stove and wall. There was too much water in the top of the pots. I could stir them so much better if they weren't so full.

I used the little pot I had found earlier to scoop out some water and clumps from the first pot. Then I ran around the table to dump my first batch down the sink. In my hurry, my aim was off and half of the water and clumps flew onto the countertop and splattered the window. "Oh, darn!" I exclaimed but there was no time to clean anything yet. I had to get back to the stove. I gave a quick stir to the first pot, which hadn't improved much. It was still a clump underneath cloudy water. I began to scoop water from the other batch but I leaned onto the pot and burned my arm.

When I felt the shock of that heat, I jerked my arm. The small pot in my hand hit the side of the large pot. The small pot clanged to the floor and rolled under the table leaving a mess of water and clumps of grits all over the stove and floor. I reached under the table to grab the pot, and accidentally leaned on the bag of grits, knocking it over and sending it spilling into the watery mess I had created.

"Oh, no!" I groaned. I stood in the middle of the mess with the sticky pot dangling in my hand, my shoulders limp with defeat.

While still grieving the loss of the grits, I became aware of the smoke from the bacon. The bacon! I dropped the little pot and it clattered to the floor as I swooped over to the frying pans. I grabbed the fork to flip the bacon but it was too late. My grandfather liked his bacon incredibly crispy, but even he wouldn't have eaten those charred nuggets. I lifted it onto a platter, just to get it out of the pans before it started a fire. I placed the plate of bacon on the table so Miss Turner could tell me where to dispose of it. I turned off the burners, but I didn't know what to do with the hot greasy pans so I left them on the stove.

What would Miss Turner say to this? She was so nice, but even she must have her limits. Breakfast was ruined, and the kitchen looked like a war zone. Clumps of grits stuck to the stove, the sink, the floor, and even the window! It was hard to believe there was any left in the pots, but there was, and it would probably take two days to chip it out.

Hurricane Lilla had destroyed breakfast in less than fifteen minutes. I only hoped I could clean most of it up before Miss Turner returned and had to find something to feed those poor girls!

As I started walking toward the pantry to look for cleaning supplies, I heard Jolene's voice. She spoke as she opened the kitchen door, "Miss Turner sent me down here to see if you need any…" She stopped, with the swinging door open halfway. "Lord!" she exclaimed when she saw the kitchen. Then her eyes widened as she gasped inward.

Another girl spoke from behind Jolene. "Is that her?" she asked as she stood on tippy toe to peer over Jolene's shoulder. She leaned on Jolene, causing both girls to take an awkward step into the kitchen. They stood up quickly. The door closed behind them, exposing the disaster on the stove. After a moment of silence, they started laughing so hard they had to lean against each other for support. Together they pushed the door to leave, but something blocked the door so they couldn't get out. It was Miss Turner trying to get in. She must have backed away, because suddenly the door swung out and the two girls staggered out, still in stitches, into the dining room.

"Girls! Girls! Calm yourselves!" Miss Turner said as the door swung shut.

I was alone while they spoke on the other side of the door. I heard several voices out there, but I only caught some of what was being said. I heard the key words, though: "No breakfast, not even grits…what're we gonna eat, now?" Soon more girls made their way downstairs. New voices chimed in concerns about not having anything to eat before they had to leave for orientation. The louder it became out there, the more nervous I felt. I thought I might be sick. The grit splatters on the floor looked pretty gross. I could probably throw up right in the middle of that mess and nobody would even notice.

"Hush, everybody! Hush yourselves! Jolene! That is enough!" Miss Turner actually raised her voice, and those girls listened. I didn't hear another word as Miss Turner cracked the door just wide enough for her to squeeze into the kitchen. She gave a serious look back through the doorway at the hungry girls. "Give me a minute. You'll have your breakfast."

Miss Turner didn't even flinch at the disaster as she flew to the back pantry. Before I could muster my first words of apology, she had begun slicing two big loaves of bread.

She generously smeared butter and jam all over the slices. She wrapped each slice in a large napkin. Then she went to the door and opened it wide enough to hand out one slice at a time.

"You girls take this and get on over to orientation. Remember, you'll have lunch there today, and then you'll come back here for dinner later when that stuff is all over."

"But, Miss Turn…"

"Hush, Martha. You girls better get going or you'll be late."

So off they went. Those poor girls had to eat bread and jam out on the sidewalk on their first day of college. I was prepared not to eat at all. My self-imposed penance for the mess I made was to clean Miss Turner's kitchen. While Miss Turner was handing the bread slices out to the girls, I filled a bucket with water. I figured I better start with the floor so we didn't track grits through the rest of the house.

I started to mop under the table when I heard the front door close. The girls had left for their orientation. Miss Turner came over to me. I stared down at the gooey mess I was pushing around with my mop. I didn't want her to see the tears in my eyes. She reached over and gently took the mop from my hand. I had no choice but to look into her eyes.

"Child, what are you still doing here?" she asked me ever so quietly.

Somehow, I managed to speak without crying. "I have to clean this up."

"No, ma'am. Uh-uh. You better get yourself to orientation, too. You don't want to be a delinquent on your first day, do you?" Miss Turner smiled. She even chuckled. I don't know if she really felt it or if it was just to get me through this, but it did comfort me.

"I can't leave this mess for you to clean up."

"Look here," she nodded toward the table. "There's one more piece of bread and jam left. Someone has to eat it. Might as well be you. You take that bread and get on down to The Commons with everyone else. I'll have this place clean in twenty minutes. I told you I move fast down here." She handed me the bread and patted me on the shoulder to herd me out the kitchen door.

Sure enough, when we returned to Plummer Hall later that afternoon, the kitchen was spotless. It was lucky for all of us that orientation was an all-day affair. Miss Turner didn't have to worry about serving lunch to anybody that day.

Thankfully, when we returned to our dorm that afternoon I didn't hear anybody talking about that morning's breakfast disaster. Actually, I didn't hear them talk about much of anything. My first few days at Plummer Hall were quiet. Really quiet. My black dorm mates and I weren't sure where to start the dialogue. I'm sure I was mostly to blame. I'm afraid I was still in awe of their dark skin and hair. I still struggled with their southern accents, too. My dumbfounded silence cast a pall over every room I entered, swiftly killing any conversations.

I continued to use the bathroom at odd hours, when I knew I would be alone. Miss Turner assigned me to assist in making breakfast in the mornings, which allowed me to avoid eating in the dining room. I ate my breakfast in the kitchen while I finished my work. I did that more for the other girls than for myself. There was no reason they should have to eat in nervous silence. They chatted much more comfortably about their classes than when I plopped myself down in their midst.

My first conversation with one of my dorm mates occurred over a pot of grits. Gloria, the other student on breakfast duty, gave me a crash course in grits and helped me get the measurements correct. As we stirred our steaming pots, we would converse about our families and how we ended up at Watkins. Over our morning stirring sessions, she became my closest friend at Watkins, though we only socialized this freely within the isolation of the kitchen until the other girls got to know me, too.

She and Miss Turner bridged the chasm between me and the other girls at Plummer Hall by telling us a little about each other. Gloria told them how my uncle taught me to play the piano, which earned some points with Sara. Her aunt had taught her the piano as well. Miss Turner made special introductions between me, Charlene and Mary. We all had little brothers at home. We shared stories about how they drove us crazy.

By the end of the first week, the silence dissipated into genteel conversations about schoolwork. I finally ate meals at Gloria's table with some of the other girls. Gloria coaxed me out of my room in the evenings to join them in the parlor as well.

Even though I finally mastered the art of grits, I think some of the girls still harbored resentment toward me because they had to eat cold bread and jam their first day. Since then, I tried complimenting the food, to show my appreciation for girls who prepared the other meals. Besides, I didn't know what else to say to most of them.

"Oh, this chicken is so good!" I exclaimed at one of my first dinners out at Gloria's table. "My mother never makes chicken because my father likes steak so much."

"Never makes chicken?" a girl exclaimed from a nearby table. "Never?"

"Uh-uh. We usually have steaks or roasts and stuff like that. But I really like chicken, like this."

She and a couple other girls raised their eyebrows. Another girl shrugged. It was a strange reaction, but at least we were talking. During each meal, I tried to contribute a little to the conversations. Eventually we shared a few laughs at our table.

Not everyone rejoiced at my increased comfort level. Understandably, more than a few girls considered my presence nothing less than the theft of a black student's education. When I was studying, I could hear their voices echo from the bathroom. I think I heard Carla say her cousin couldn't get into Watkins, and maybe she could have if I didn't take the scholarship. Someone else agreed it wasn't fair I stayed after the university learned about the mistake.

I couldn't believe the next part, but I guess I brought it on myself.

"And did you hear her say they eat steak every night at her house? Come on!"

"Yeah, who here on a scholarship eats steak every night!? They've gotta be hiding some money somewhere so she could get that scholarship!"

I was flabbergasted! They had no idea my uncle had a beef farm. My father helped him run the place. That's why we ate so much steak! It was cheaper to pay my father in beef than money.

How could I blame them for thinking any of those things? I respectfully kept a cool distance from them, and built friendships with those who would have me.

Unbeknownst to me, my reputation preceded me even before I started classes. Black and white students alike eyed me as I went to and from Plummer Hall. Among my mostly white classmates, I remained an outsider and always would be. That was even before I opened my mouth to release my coarse New Hampshire accent into the midst of their sugary southern voices. I was in awe of the grace of the southern girls, both in the dorm and in my classes.

The few northern campuses I had visited teamed with casual students wearing oxfords and turtlenecks. Whereas, these southern coeds wore dresses and heels to class every day, and their hair was always coiffed ever so nicely. The girls in my dormitory never even appeared in the dining areas without proper outfits.

My field of study didn't open many social doorways either. Most of my dorm mates studied teaching or office skills, always smartly dressed and professional. I, however, returned from potting classes with dirt under my fingernails and in my clothes, and from pruning classes with scratches on my arms.

Most of the girls in my classes were white, but I found myself as socially awkward around them as I was with my dorm mates, as they were all so poised. Several classmates were tiara-certified beauty queens, preferring their hard-won pageant monikers to their real names. In four years of college, I never did find out Miss Anston County's real name. She let us call her "Annie" for short.

Although I never discussed my scholarship with my classmates, they knew I received serious financial aid of some sort. They politely avoided pressing me for details. I painstakingly assembled outfits from my closet full of hand-me-downs, but I still looked much more casual than the other girls did.

Mrs. Fulton, from the flower shop, had given me something special for my college wardrobe, though. "Here, Dear. Here's something I made for you to take to school," she said when I stopped into her house to say goodbye before leaving for school. "I know your school is way down south, but it gets chilly there, too." She handed me the most gorgeous cable knit sweater, new, and just for me.

When one of the girls from my classes invited me to join her and some other girls at a football game, I excitedly accepted, and I knew just what to wear. I threw on my favorite dungarees, tennis shoes, and my precious sweater. I offered to meet the girl outside the library, halfway between our dorms.

I skipped along, feeling sporty and fun. My glee lasted about five minutes, until I turned the corner to greet my friends. They all wore lined pantsuits with low-heeled dress shoes. This was as casual as they dressed. I was impressed their conversation didn't stall when they saw me.

"Hey there, Lilla," chirped Audrey. "Ready for some real football, southern style?"

"Yes, this will be my first college game," I answered politely. Since I didn't possess the harmonious southern accent of my coeds, I compensated by using the most polite grammar I could muster.

"Come on, y'all," said Mae. She bounced off toward the athletic field in her gorgeous pink outfit. Her long blond curls swirled in the breeze. "Let's hurry! Bruce is in the starting lineup!" she announced over her shoulder.

When we caught up with her I noticed how impeccably clean her hands and nails were. If I didn't know it, I would never have guessed she was in the same horticulture classes as me. I scrubbed my hands raw that morning, and still had traces of dirt under my nails.

"How do you think you did on Mr. Macy's test yesterday?" I asked her. "The written part was not too bad, but it was difficult for me to prune that rose bush. The thorns poked right through my gloves!" I showed her the thorn mark on my thumb.

Mae stopped for a minute and looked at me while the other girls caught up to us. "Lilla, I tell you, I refuse to stick my hands in that dirty stuff! I'll read the books and take the tests, but I can't have scratches running all up and down my hands! Could you imagine me going to a social with broken nails? Mother would have a fit!"

"Won't you get in trouble if you don't work with the plants? I mean, are we not supposed to learn how to plant these things ourselves?" I asked her.

"Daddy wants me to learn about this stuff, but after Bruce and I get married, we'll run Daddy's business from the top. I only need to learn the books."

Mae came from a different world than me. She was a tourist skimming through the scenery of college life. She was going to marry her rich boyfriend and manage Daddy's company. She would never soil her hands during her lifetime. My future depended on total immersion in my classes, no matter how dirty.

I was trying to imagine what it would be like to live in Mae's world, when the other girls caught up to us. The talk turned to everyone complimenting each other on their dresses and pantsuits. Nobody noticed or cared that I was dressed like a fisherman, so off we went to the football game on a beautiful October day. Except that we were in North Carolina and it was eighty degrees.

The morning had been cool. It hadn't occurred to me how warm it would get later in the day. Up North, it was a no brainer. This is what everyone wore to football games! I hadn't acclimated to the southern life yet. I roasted at the game, but dared not remove my sweltering sweater. Exposing my tattered t-shirt underneath would have looked even worse among the neatly pressed pantsuits that surrounded me.

One good thing resulted from my dressing like a Northerner: I caught Sam's eye. Although we shared many classes, we hadn't spoken, save for a few quick hellos. Sam had been leaning against the railing for twenty minutes watching the game. I was sitting on the edge of the bleacher in the third row when he finally approached me. Later we'd find out both of us were thinking about the other more than that silly game.

"Uh, hi! How ya doin?" Sam mustered up the nerve to speak first.

I had admired him for weeks and grew flustered, as if I wasn't sweating enough already in that chunky sweater. "Hi. I'm fine, thank you, and yourself?"

"Good. Good. I'm Sam by the way. Hey, how 'bout that Mr. Isham? His tests are the hardest!"

"Oh, he's the worst! I studied all night for that test last week and I still got a B! My name is Lilla." Wow! That cute boy was talking to me! His accent was the closest voice to home I'd heard since I came to school. He told me later he was thinking the same thing. When I showed up at the game in that cable knit sweater he knew I had to be from the North somewhere.

"It's nice to meet you Lilla. You don't sound like you're from around here," he said.

"I'm from New Hampshire, close to Canada."

"Wow! I'm from Rochester, New York. It's at the top of New York. We have Lake Ontario there, but across the lake is Canada," he smiled as he spoke.

"I have to ask. Do you ever have a hard time understanding some of the people around here or is it just me?"

"Not too much," he answered. "But I have family down here. Boy, if I didn't have my cousins translate for me I'd be in serious trouble."

He quickly charmed me with his refreshing Rochester accent. We started talking about being Northerners in this southern town. Our conversation moved effortlessly to our classes and our families. We talked until the game ended, and for two more hours after that. He told me about his hometown and that he came to Watkins University so he could live with his aunt and uncle while he attended college. He wanted the experience of going away to college, but he couldn't afford to live in the dormitories. He would get his education and his aunt and uncle would get to spend time with their nephew. In addition, his parents didn't have to take a second mortgage to pay the bills. Everyone was happy.

That's how two poor kids from the North found each other. From that day on, we were inseparable and college life became bearable. Not terrific, but at least I had a confidant who could relate to feeling like a fish out of water. With my parents' letter of permission, Sam's Aunt Sofie and Uncle Buell signed me out of my dormitory to have dinner at their house on Saturday nights before Sam and I went to the mixers. Thanks to Gloria and a few other friends I had found, life at Plummer Hall was okay, but certainly not paradise. I couldn't help feeling some continuing resentment from my dorm mates about my scholarship.

I didn't find solace in the campus either. The white students in my classes weren't comfortable with me in their midst. They considered me black by association. I tagged along at some of the social events but none of the white girls really reached out to form a close friendship with me. Surviving my first year didn't mean I could live through three more.

After spring break, I started getting nervous as everyone selected their housing for the following year. I confided in Sam as we walked to the greenhouses one day. My mind was so preoccupied with my housing problem I didn't hear Sam ask me about our final project we were working on. I just stared ahead.

"Hey, Li, what's wrong?" Sam asked.

"Nothing," I lied.

"C'mon. Tell me." Sam put his arm around me and I started to cry. "Oh, Baby, what's the matter? School's going okay. Your grades are good. Aren't you glad summer break is almost here?"

"It's my dorm. I can't go back next year. It doesn't feel right, but I can't stay in school if I don't keep my scholarship, and I can't move to another dorm. Oh Sam, I just don't know what to do!" I turned into his arms. He hugged me as I sobbed. "And the worst part about leaving school is I might have to leave you!"

"Don't worry. I'll find you no matter where you go. But I think you'll come back here next year."

I backed away from Sam and shook my head, "No, you don't understand what it's like. If I didn't have you and Aunt Sofie and Uncle Buell I don't know what I would have done. I mean, Becky and Gloria are so nice. Becky's the one who let me wear one of her dresses for our social last week. Remember? And the other day I heard Mary and Marjorie talking in the bathroom about how I helped them with their flower arrangements for their social last month. They said I was really nice and they didn't mind that I'm white."

"Oh, that is great! See? You have friends here. You just had to get to know each other."

"Yeah, but a few weeks ago Jolene's family came to visit and I heard them saying stuff about it not being right that I was still using the scholarship and living in that dorm."

"Jolene's little sister even stuck her tongue out at me when nobody was looking! I feel like they might be right about the whole thing. I mean, how would I feel if someone came out of nowhere and took my scholarship?

"When school ends in three weeks I don't want to see all of the parents when they come to pick up the other girls from my dorm. Sam?" I paused and chewed on my bottom lip as I did when I was uncomfortable. "Can I ask you a huge favor? I was thinking about moving my stuff out of my room the day before everyone else's parents come to bring them home. Could you ask Aunt Sofie and Uncle Buell if I could move my things into their house for a couple nights? And maybe I could stay at their house my last night? It would only be until my train leaves the next day. No, wait!" I grabbed Sam's arm when I changed my mind. "Don't ask them. My stuff would be in their way…Aunt Sofie would feel like she has to make a special dinner. Never mind. I'll be okay."

Sam pulled me back into his arms and started laughing. "Oh, you poor thing. You are a mess. Don't worry, Li. Everything'll be fine," he said. He chuckled a bit and stroked my hair. "I have an even better idea. How about if you move your stuff into their house for the next three years?" he asked.

"Oh, Sam, really? Really?" I smiled through my tears. Backing up to look into his eyes, I knew it was true.

"Yeah, they love you! They know you feel out of place sometimes. They want to make sure you're happy at school. You're practically family to them. They said they'd even call your parents to make sure it's okay."

"That is so great!" I cried for joy and hugged Sam so hard I thought his eyes would pop out of his head.

The next day we set out to ask everyone's permission for me to move in with Sam's aunt and uncle. To my surprise, the scholarship committee unanimously agreed to continue my full academic scholarship, and with my parents' permission, they allowed me to live off campus. The committee was greatly relieved by my suggestion as they had met several times to discuss this situation. Parents of some of my dorm mates justifiably wondered why their black daughters couldn't live in the white dormitory, while a white girl held a private room in the black dormitory.

I moved into this tiny house for my remaining three years of school to live with Sam and his generous family. Aunt Sofie and Uncle Buell were practically insulted when my parents tried to send them rent money.

"No, no!" Uncle Buell told my parents over the phone. "Don't you know your northern money's no good here in the South? That little girl eats like a bird! And we love having her around. You might need to send some earplugs," he'd joke. "You should hear the girls chatter all night!"

Aunt Sofie and Uncle Buell suggested the school could funnel the housing allotment of my scholarship to a black student who could use it. My parents were very grateful, too. They worried long distance about my happiness during my first year, and initially they suggested I return to New Hampshire.

Thankfully, Watkins University was far enough to be too costly for them to visit me. As strange as my situation was to me, it would have been bizarre for my parents to walk through that front door into the same crowd of silent dark faces that   greeted me on my first day. They wouldn't have believed I made peace with the living arrangements and was getting along just fine.

If the same living situation loomed ahead for the next fall, there was a chance they might not have allowed me to return. There were days I seriously considered leaving school, but I knew if I did I would end up working for Mr. and Mrs. Fulton in the flower shop. Then, when they retire, I'd work for the next owner, never able to run my own business without the proper education.

I did my best to earn my keep at Aunt Sofie's and Uncle Buell's house. I spent many mealtimes standing over the old porcelain oven, cooking breakfast every day and helping with dinner. Aunt Sofie was amazed at the gusto with which I cooked and ate grits, the first Northerner she'd seen enjoy them so much. She taught me how to cook greens as if I was born and raised on them. My mother was a little disconcerted when I returned home one summer and grabbed the beet greens she was about to discard, cooked them and ate them with the same relish I usually reserved for her famous pineapple upside-down cake.

I need to take my hat off to Sam's cousin Caroline, too. Although she was only fourteen when I moved into her room with her, she had already become a little lady. The two of us agreed it was nice to have a "sister" around instead of brothers all the time. She coached me in the poise I'd envied in my southern classmates. She spent hours taming my frizzy hair into a structured bob.

I wasn't thrilled about spending so much time on my hair but I played along. After the notoriety of my first year, I welcomed the opportunity to blend into the crowds at school. Better to be the anonymous student than "that poor Yankee girl." As hard as I strove to remain invisible on campus, it was hard to believe that less than four years after college, I embraced recognition when Sam and I began hosting gardening shows.

Without the housing difficulties and misfit status that plagued my first year, I concentrated better on my studies. Sam and I graduated with an excellent education and fond memories of Watkins University.

Of course, some of my favorite memories were coming home with Sam every night after classes to this little house. I noticed the outside of Aunt Sofie's and Uncle Buell's little house was sided and someone had added a larger porch, but the inside of the house hadn't changed much. As I wandered through the tiny rooms, I was amazed at how they still looked familiar. The chipped appliances in the kitchen were probably the same ones I'd used back in 1960. I enjoyed the memory of the people I loved in the kitchen I remembered.

"My God! This rickety house is over a hundred years old!" I thought to myself. I shook my head in awe at how quickly time passed.

Tracy Fontaine

Tracy Fontaine

Chapter Seventeen: Rubies in the Cellar

Before leaving the place that I would forever know as Aunt Sofie's and Uncle Buell's house, I ran my hand around the entire length of the porch railing. Happy memories warmed my soul. I hoped a little bit of my energy flowed back into the house so other spirits might know I had been there. It was hard to leave, but this was to be a quick stop. My search for Sam must continue. If I didn't find any pathway to him in one place, I would move on to the next place. This search could take years, God forbid, so I needed to keep moving to cover as much ground as I could. I still wanted to see my old campus once more, too.

Housing assignments at Watkins University became integrated three years after Sam and I graduated. Those first couple of years must have been real doozies, especially in the bathrooms. I'm sure a semester or two passed before everybody recovered from their separate but equal pasts to fashion a livable comfort level with each other.

Empty for summer break, the sleeping campus remained undisturbed as I wafted silently through its buildings. Annual group photos of dormitory residents lined the foyer of Plummer Hall. I waxed nostalgic at the changing clothes and hairstyles over the years. Of course, the faces themselves changed the most. There was the photo from the school year 1958-1959, my one year as a dormitory resident. If you look closely, you can just make out a thin white line that was the edge of my arm. Self-conscious about being the only white subject in the photo, I cleverly concealed myself behind the widest girl in Plummer Hall.

As I glided past the row of photos of Plummer Hall residents, years of a completely black student body became sprinkled with increasing numbers of white faces. Similar photos must line the hallways of the formerly white dormitories, only in reverse colors, sort of like negatives of each other. It struck me as funny, how the negatives turned into positives. In the darkness of my empty dorm, I reflected on the good times I had at Watkins.

My memory preserved it as a great school with excellent professors. And in reality, although I was self-conscious about living in Plummer Hall, a couple of girls from my dorm kept in touch with me for many years, as did Miss Turner, until she passed away in 1974.

Spiriting into the night, I left Plummer Hall even more invisibly than I did the first time. Blessedly unnoticed by anybody, I felt relieved my short-lived notoriety was long since over. I moved across campus unseen, but I was not alone. Someone was searching for something. Emotions burdened the air, similar to the presence of the spirits inhabiting my Mount Hope surroundings. Soon after sensing the emotions, I found the source. A spirit so tiny I nearly missed her, drifted out of the shadows and onto the porch of Watkins Hall. She carried a rock and set it on the steps of The Big House, as everyone called it, for it was the original manor of Jebediah and Mary Watkins. Administrative offices occupied it ever since I could remember. While studying the Watkins brochures, I foolishly thought I was going to live in that beautiful mansion. My spacious room would overlook the ivy-covered veranda. Life is funny, so full of reality checks.

The little spirit drifted through the closed front door into Watkins Hall. Of course, I had to follow her. At this rate, if I followed every spiritual tangent that crossed my path, it would take forever to get to any future destinations. Then again, forever is the one thing of which I had plenty, so what the heck. It would be fun to ask her about this place.

Who knows in what time period she lived. I was sure she had interesting stories to share about her life in these parts so distant from my New Hampshire childhood. I wanted to know all she'd seen in the years after her death, too. Did I walk through her spirit on my way to classes seventy years ago? Perhaps I stood near her right here in Watkins Hall, although I had only been in this building twice as a student, and even then only in the Housing Office on the first floor.

If she lived here at some point, maybe she could show me the rest of the building and tell me about its history before it was a college. People used to say this building was haunted, but don't they say that about all old buildings with colorful pasts?

If you believe the campus folklore, Mary Watkins' ghost ran around this place doing strange things. Certainly, the childlike spirit I saw couldn't have been Mary.

Quickening my pace so I wouldn't lose track of the little one, I hurried through the front door of Watkins Hall. While I didn't recall the details of the offices themselves, I remembered I was always impressed by the age of this building. The feeling returned, as I imagined society ladies of long ago, descending the grand staircase into the parlor with their billowing skirts trailing behind them.

Even though these romantic fantasies never came true for me, perhaps that little girl had seen these places in their heyday. The spirit dashed down a back hallway and if I didn't keep up, I'd never get to compare her reality with my daydreams. She slipped through a corridor I never noticed, past a kitchen and through another doorway which led to a rickety stairway.

She descended the stairs to the cellar, seemingly unaware I had followed her. When I entered, she stood on the far side of the room facing the crude stone wall. Living people wouldn't have been able to see their hands in front of their faces down here, but our spirits moved effortlessly through the dark underground room. As I neared a pile of rocks on the dirt floor, I announced my presence by making a noise as if I was clearing my throat.

She pivoted to face me and that delicate little creature turned into a snarling monster. Her wild eyes looked both terrified and evil. I grinned in disbelief, waiting for her to start laughing. This had to be a joke, but it wasn't. Arms flailing, she flew toward me. I retreated backward, but realized I was trapped between her and that pile of rocks. A quick glance from the rocks to my deformed hand told me I must fight like I never had before. No way would I let this creature destroy me by pushing me into those rocks.

She was even more dangerous than my first attacker because a sweet, innocent package masked her vicious demeanor. I severely underestimated her strength. She grabbed me and I fell backward. My back arched over the rocks, as my hand reached for any way to defend myself. It happened so quickly I didn't have time to burrow into the dirt floor. I would have moved too slowly through the ground anyway. The protection it offered me from my tiny nimble attacker was questionable at best.

She clawed at my arm with dangerous intent. I tried to grab a rock to throw at her but I missed and my hand went into the floor. The ground underneath me felt different, it lacked resistance, more like air rather than solid earth. I hoped I could make myself tiny enough to slip into that space and wait until she left. Then perhaps I could work my way underground to safety. It was my only hope at the moment.

Swiftly I slipped my body off the edge of the rock pile and onto the floor. The crazed child jumped on top of me, screaming and grabbing at my arms, trying to push me into the stones. I dodged to the side and down quickly, until I was under the floor and the rock pile. I entered an open space larger than I had imagined. In fact, it was another small room, about six feet square and barely high enough for a grown person to stand erect.

A ladder stood near the wall under the rock pile. It led to a trap door that wasn't visible from the level above. What was left of rough-hewn planks lining the walls and ceiling probably dated back to the original plantation days of almost two hundred years ago. A rusty kerosene lantern hung from a hook by ladder. Not even a speck of light could penetrate this hole. Whoever visited this place would have relied heavily on that lantern.

Several inches of muddy water covered the floor in that subterranean room. I didn't mind that my nose didn't work. I could smell the rotten walls and furniture well enough with my eyes.

Someone had furnished this hole in the ground. Who would ever want to live down here? The small decaying bed in the corner must have been elegant in its day. Beautifully carved animals paraded across the headboard. What was left of the rotten bedspread lay across the bottom of the mattress. Rats had chewed on fragments of lace along the edge of the bedspread. Their droppings were everywhere. I hoped I scared them away before they came to scare me. Just because I was dead didn't mean I enjoyed the company of all God's creatures, and certainly not rats.

The legs of a tiny table and chair were nearly decayed, causing them to lean precariously against the wall. A tea set and a small Bible rested on the table. The day would soon come when the table and its contents would collapse onto the floor in a heap and dissolve in the mud.

Several pegs protruded from the wall about three feet from the floor hanging from them were two small dresses. So delicate! So old! I was sure they would turn to dust if touched, even by my ghostly hand. I noticed the absence of any bonnets or shawls.

Something felt very tragic about this room. It resembled a cage. I glanced overhead and thought of that child's spirit, so full of hatred, and I began to guess why. I passed my hand over the deteriorated bedspread and across the little chair. Why would anyone imprison this child? Maybe she had been born crazy or perhaps disfigured. I tried to think of a different way out where I wouldn't have to face her again. As much as I didn't like it, I could burrow through the earth. It would not be a problem as long as there were no huge boulders that I couldn't go around.

As I took one last look at the dresses hanging on the pegs, I made a horrible discovery between the bed and the wall. I thought one of the dresses had disintegrated into a heap on the floor, but I realized the little girl's skeleton was still inside that dress. I gasped and knew if I possessed a human body that could cry, I would have wept for the sad cold ending to her life. No child could have done anything to deserve this. I had to see her again. First I would provide her with a shred of dignity. I just couldn't leave her bones lying in a pile on the floor.

I wrapped my hands around the ends of my arms to form a circle and pushed through the soggy ground to come up from underneath the pile of bones. I formed a solid ring of energy that raised the fragile pieces. If I had tried to move each bone from the floor to the bed individually, I would never have been able to reconnect them correctly. I would have ended up with a jumble of parts.

Slowly I lifted, my energy focused as intently as if I was lifting a tractor-trailer, not two pounds of soggy bones. Her remains rose off the ground, blessedly intact, and high enough for me to lay her on the bed. Some of her bones bore tooth marks. How gruesome! I hoped that after she died, her spirit left this room before she witnessed the rats chewing off her flesh.

I straightened her bones and her brittle dress. I set the remains of a China doll's head, whose body had also been eaten, on the bed as well. The tattered blanket evaporated into pieces of dust when I tried to move it. I covered the skeleton as best I could, and tucked her in one last time.

Returned to the room above, I prepared to face whatever I might find. It couldn't be worse than this. I went back through the same part of the cellar floor where I had entered this room, carefully avoiding the pile of rocks so I wouldn't get stuck in them. If the banshee child pursued me, I would squeeze through the maze of crevasses between the rocks. That was my back-up plan if desperation set in. I slowly reappeared through the floor. There was no sign of the little girl.

I left the safety of the underground room for the unknown of the main cellar. The child reappeared and rushed at me faster than I believed possible. Caught between her and the pile of rocks, I braced myself for another fight. Standing as firmly as I could, I waited for impact as her spirit rushed into mine. Arms spread, she slammed into me with incredible strength. Instead of trying to destroy me though, she hugged me around the middle of my legs. In a gush of unexpected kindness, she embraced me and pulled me away from the rocks and the hidden trap door underneath.

She wouldn't release me. I feared she might be trying to drain my energy and absorb it into herself. She loosened her grip from around my legs but grasped my hand firmly so I wouldn't leave. The little girl wouldn't take her eyes off the floor where the hidden door lay under the rocks. Then she pointed to it and looked up at me. "No, no," she repeated, reinforcing the idea she didn't want me to go there. I assured her it was okay and I wouldn't go back. Clearly, this poor child had lived and died in that horrible room.

I knelt down and ran my hand gently down the side of her face. "You poor thing," I said to her. "What happened to you?" I needed to know who had done this to her. I remembered what Jodi said about children being frightened by what they see when they visit the mind of an adult. I didn't see how anything from my gentle life could frighten anybody who had been forced to live underground with rats. Heck, she didn't even care that one of my hands was all twisted.

We sat together on the bottom step of the narrow stairway that led to the kitchen. I didn't know if she had ever entered into the mind of another, so I took her hands carefully into mine and asked if she would like to show me how she got down there and if she would like to see pictures of me at her age. She nodded and let me hold her left hand and wrap my right hand around her arm.

I felt the delicate energy of her childhood but it was different from the other children with whom I'd shared memories back in the cemetery. Her spirit was much heavier, more burdened by a sadness usually possessed by adult spirits who've lived longer and dealt with many more concerns. As the images of her short life formed, she conveyed to me she thought she was four-years-old, and her name was Ruby, though nobody had called her name for many years.

"Ruby. Ruby," I repeated to myself. Why does that sound familiar to me? "Oh, my God!" I cried. It hit me like a truck. I yanked my arms from Ruby's, releasing such strong energy we both flew to the floor, which frightened both of us. It took me a couple of minutes to coax the trembling Ruby out of the corner. I looked down at the child as her story became dreadfully clear. She didn't need to show me anymore because I pieced together the rest of her tale based on the stories I heard years ago in college.

When the looters set fire to the plantation, Mary Watkins ranted about her precious rubies in the cellar. Meanwhile her husband lay dead from a gunshot wound. Her legendary last words weren't "rubies in the cellar," but "Ruby's in the cellar!" The thieves shot her because they couldn't find any ruby jewels. The real Ruby was never discovered by anybody.

Everybody knew Mary Watkins couldn't have children. Her bitterness about her barren state, common knowledge at that time, fueled stories about her cursed family. The way Mary and Jebediah died was the final curse to their family. Nobody ever mentioned a child. Outside of Mary and Jebediah I don't think anybody knew about this little girl until now.

How did Mary get this child who carried such a shameful secret that she was left to rot in a room that wasn't even a cellar? I wanted to see how Ruby ended up down here, so we rejoined our hands. The children's stories I shared back in Rochester didn't take much time to share, but Ruby's story was especially short.

She only had a narrow lifetime of memories, confined to that tiny room. When Jebediah and Mary Watkins died, so did their secret. Their quick deaths at the barrel of a rifle couldn't compare to the lingering death of this child left to waste away.

Ruby's memory conveyed images of Jebediah and Mary Watkins' comings and goings. Mary spent her days here, singing and playing with Ruby like this was the most normal thing in the world, the woman-child coming down to play with her child-doll. Ruby showed me as much of her life as she could, but I still wished I could see how she came to live in that wretched hole. Such an event precluded her conscious memory. She let me hold her hands once more and concentrate very hard on trying to see what hid beyond her memory.

I watched her as a toddler and tried to reverse the clock of the vision even further. I had no idea what I was doing. If it didn't work, the mystery would remain as such. A dark room came into focus, but not the room under the cellar. A black woman gave birth by candlelight. There were other voices in the room, but their faces remained in the shadows. I could only make out the space between her legs where the baby's head crowned.

When Ruby was born, a second black woman gently cleaned her and wrapped her in a blanket. Somber faces greeted the child. The birth mother remained on the table, arms outstretched to receive her baby, but the other black woman handed the baby to delicate white hands reaching out from the shadows.

The mother on the table wept helplessly. "Please, please! It's my baby. Just let me hold my baby! Please just once!" she cried as the pale hands moved the baby from her reach.

A harsh man's voice bellowed from the shadows. "Shut up! Get yourself cleaned up! Then clean up the filthy mess you left all over the place!"

The other black woman helped her wipe off the blood and get down from the table. Both black women wiped what blood they could from the table. The little cloth they were using was quickly saturated and left a thick burgundy smear across the table's surface.

Barely able to stand, the new mother looked toward her baby in the arms of another woman. She took one painful step toward her baby, but was stopped by a riding crop pushed squarely across her chest.

The man holding it reached back with his other hand and knocked on the door behind him. He opened it a few inches and herded the new mother toward it. When she saw the burly men with the wagon outside, she shook her head and stopped in her tracks. The man near the door stepped toward her and raised the riding crop over her head as a warning. Crying and pleading for mercy, she lifted her arms to shield herself and cowered against the doorway as she left.

The other black woman yelled out, "Emma! No!" then pleaded on Emma's behalf. "Please! You can't send her away from her baby!"

The man with the riding crop laughed. With a deep voice he replied, "Well, you ain't got to worry 'bout missin' her none. You goin', too. Now get your behind out there with 'er before I beat the both of you!"

Large hands reached in from the darkness outside and pulled both of the hysterical women out to the wagon.

The door closed and the cart rattled off into the night, separating mother and child forever. The secret remained in the cabin with her new parents, Mary and Jebediah. People get goose bumps when they see famous ghosts. Can ghosts get goose bumps when they see legendary people? I think I did when I realized Ruby's mother was the Emma Johnson! The same Emma Johnson whose scholarship made it possible for me to come here as a student. Ruby was her illegitimate child with Jebediah.

The stories were true, except the part about the baby being sold to the North. That baby didn't go anywhere except straight into that cellar in the cloak of darkness. No descendant of Emma Johnson ever shared in the wealth of the Watkins family, nor in any money Emma had bestowed on Watkins University.

Ruby and I released our hands from each other, much more gently than the first time. I had seen all she could show me and beyond. Had she witnessed herself taken from her birth mother? Did her child's mind understand? I don't think she was able to access that part of her memory herself.

Apparently, she couldn't remember her birth and infancy. I know I couldn't remember mine any better after I had died than when I was alive. For all I knew, she probably saw my birth just now and knew more about it than I did.

She didn't seem any different than a few minutes ago. Her focus was on preventing others from accessing the awful room from which death was the only escape. She had built the pile of rocks, hiding the door to prevent others from becoming trapped and forgotten as she had been.

"Oh, my! What happened to your hand?" She caught me off guard even though I expected the question sooner or later.

"Oh that happened…another time." I sheepishly stole Jodi's words for lack of a better reply. Should I say more? I knew Jodi wanted to spare me from her frightening tale for as long as possible, but she and the others should have given me some sort of warning about the evils of this world. It was the least I could do for others that asked, although I watered it down for Ruby. She shouldn't have to watch the attack through my memory any more that I wanted to relive it in the telling.

Looking her in the eyes I told her, "A bad man did this to hurt me but my friends back in the cemetery saved me. Be careful of others like us. Not everyone is friendly. Some are not to be trusted."

"Yes," she replied, "do be careful! Some people are just dreadful! I liked Thomas, and Julia, and Bernard." She paused to think. "I don't remember all their names…but Melinda was wicked! She was hateful and I hope she never comes back!"

Again, I remembered how deceiving looks could be. Here I thought I was the grownup teaching this little girl a thing or two, but once again I failed to appreciate that some young-appearing spirits had been around much longer than me. How naïve to believe I was the first spirit she had met during her two hundred years. She's held her own for this long. I guessed she could take care of herself.

Ruby and I went upstairs and out of Watkins Hall to the university gates. It appeared that Ruby decided to leave with me. The thought hadn't crossed my mind to invite her to come with me. I felt guilty about not asking her in the first place, but if she wanted to join me, I would have been all too happy to liberate her from this property.

I flattered myself with delusions of saving souls. It turned out she wasn't planning to accompany me. She was escorting me off the property to make sure I stayed away from her underground prison. No emotional attachment ebbed from the little girl's spirit, which was just as well. My original intent had been to pass through. She could hold me to it by ushering me out of the gate. Her world was here, alone, except for occasional passersby like me.

She was one of those spirits caught in a continuous loop. Her memories she shared with me revealed that each day of her last two hundred years had been devoted to hiding the trap door from others and waiting for her parents to return. She put rocks on the trap door, went to the gate to look for her parents, then back to check the door. Her routine would continue as long as Watkins Hall stood, or in the unlikely event her tiny body is discovered.

We exchanged goodbyes at the gate. Mine sounded more like a question, in case she changed her mind to leave with me, but she made sure I kept moving, alone. Before she turned back into the university, she looked back and forth to see if her parents were on their way back, which, of course they weren't. She shrugged her shoulders with a child's exasperated huff, picked up a tiny stone from the ground and returned to Watkins Hall.

I have to say, that reunion was the creepiest one I had ever attended at Watkins. As Ruby's glow faded into the background, I thought of our strange connection through Emma, the woman who'd given her life and me a chance at life. If not for my scholarship in Emma's name, I never would have come here and met Sam, gotten my education, and achieved my dreams. I couldn't wait to share Ruby's story with Amelia, at least to give Ruby some sort of legacy and ensure she was not a Forgotten.

I wondered if it was mean of me to leave Ruby behind like that, but she practically pushed me out the gate and didn't looked back. Moving tentatively down the road, I peeked over my shoulder until trees obscured the front gate. No one in sight. Pretty much what I expected.

****

As I turned to exit, I ran smack dab into Santa Claus. Well, okay, it wasn't really Santa Claus, but it was the ghost of a burly teddy bear of a man.

No telling what color his fuzzy head of hair and beard had been during his lifetime, but they were shockingly white now. It didn't matter that he looked like Santa. All I knew was he appeared so suddenly he scared the daylights out of me. I flew into a rhododendron bush and waited to see if he was friend or foe. The next thing I knew, he was bending over the bush apologizing up and down for scaring me.

"I'm sorry! I'm sorry!" he exclaimed as he rubbed his fist in circles around his chest. "I'm afraid I come up too quickly and scare people. I don't mean to! I always think I should make more noise to let them know I'm coming!" He laughed heartily. His affable manner coaxed me into the open.

The entire time he spoke, his hands moved rapidly, using sign language. Thank God I could read his thoughts because I sure as heck couldn't understand his signing. Thousands of deaf people in Rochester and I still never got the sign language thing. It wasn't for lack of trying either, because I took two sign language classes. And, at the risk of being accused of eavesdropping, I watched people signing whenever I could, for practice.

I could hold my own in French and knew a few German phrases, but sign language was a lost cause. Deaf people thanked me for grabbing a pen and paper rather than making them endure the tortuously slow, and often incorrect, motions of my hands. Let them try understanding my signs with this claw I'm sporting now. I snickered to myself as I hid my deformed hand behind me.

Unbridled excitement tumbled from this stranger as he said, "I've seen and heard the most amazing things! Yes, heard! When I died, I could hear for the first time ever, so I listen to everything I can!"

I imagined the feast of sounds he must find around every corner. When my body died, my sense of smell and touch died too, but my sight and hearing became incredibly strong. After nine months, I continued to remark at the clarity of distant and minute sounds. But to hear it all for the first time at this level, all at once…no wonder he was so excited. He continued signing so quickly with his ghostly fingers that his hands became a blur in front of him. Not that it would have done me any good if I could have followed them anyway.

He paused and looked around, up at the trees and vines. "Isn't this great? Listen. Can you hear that?"

"Yes, it's really loud," I agreed, speaking to him for the first time. A cacophony of critters livened up the still night with their chatter. "Too many bugs for me but I guess it doesn't matter now that they can't sting me or fly into my ear anymore."

"Yes, they just sing in our ears!" he replied. "Next, I might go to South America to hear the sounds of their forests. I bet it's even louder than this. Or I might go back to England…ooor…maybe China. I haven't been there yet!" He laughed so warmly I took an instant liking to him.

When I told him I wanted to go west, to the ocean, he became so excited I believe if he had any skin he would have jumped out of it. He told me, "Go! Go! Don't wait! Why, it's so remarkable! I lived in British Columbia. When I died, I followed the coast all the way to Chile. I was obsessed with the sea. Now I know what people meant when they talked about waves crashing. I never knew water could be so loud! Well, I'm off so see the next sights! Be well and safe travels!"

And just like that, he disappeared, off to his next destination. He cracked me up. He was a bundle of energy. After hearing his enthusiasm, I looked forward to reaching the west coast myself. It didn't matter that I didn't learn his name or anything else from his past. That was fine with me.

Normally I would have wanted to connect my hands with him to see his life, but Ruby's story wiped me out for a while. Knowing how much adventure this guy put into every place he went was enough to give me the travel bug. Now I wanted to get to the west coast. Sam and I always talked about it, but we never got around to taking that trip. I didn't find any traces of Sam at this place where we had spent so much time together. Maybe his spirit was out there visiting places we missed when we were alive. It was a long shot, but it was all I had. Crossing my fingers that I would be closer to finding Sam, I closed my eyes and thought about California.

Tracy Fontaine

Chapter Eighteen: Chloe and Natasha

It turns out I wasn't the orienteering expert I thought I was. Instead of landing near a crashing sea of west-coast waves, I ended up in a desert in the middle of nowhere. I really missed my mark. Vast expanses of sand surrounded me. I watched the sunrise that morning in North Carolina, and I got to see the same exact sunrise all over again, which astounded me. It was even better this second time.

Crimson gashes cut a fiery swath between the earth and sky. Shadows appeared around rocks and plants as the sun rose to reign over this arid kingdom. My second sunrise of the day started me thinking how fun it would be to outrun daybreak across the country or even around the world.

Imagine picking a spot that has just felt the tips of the earliest rays of the morning sun and traveling ahead of full daybreak. What if a spirit kept outrunning the sun and got so far ahead of it that she ended up in the next day? Someday I would have to try that.

My "to do" list grew longer each day, which both entertained and concerned me. As time passed, was I unwittingly accepting the possibility I might remain here on earth? How long did it take for Jodi's, Harvey's, and Amelia's denials to wane into grudging acceptance? What about the other spirits I met along the way? Had they made peace with their existence? Maybe they were in denial about their denial. Given more time, I supposed I would understand. Whoa! Did I really just think that? God help me. I wasn't ready to give up yet. At what point will I stop searching and accept I'm stuck here? Five years? Ten years? A hundred?

Morning shadows stretched westward across the desert floor, pointing me to the ocean. One more, small leap of my thoughts should get me there. If I did it soon I could watch my third sunrise that day. Although, I never meant to end up in the desert, it pulsated with incredible energy. Visible waves of heat, light, and red, glowing rock formations called me to bask in the intense daylight for a short while longer. I also felt another tug, one that wasn't part of the desert itself.

Something drew me to look more closely at my surroundings. I felt a blur of grouped thoughts, similar to the air surrounding Mount Hope Cemetery, where many spirits hovered in close quarters.

There must be someone else like me around here. I moved in the direction of a faintly pulsing energy. Sure enough, about a mile from where I landed, a dozen or so spirits hovered in a tight group, facing a set of railroad tracks. Hundreds of miles of uninterrupted tracks in each direction, yet these spirits practically stood inside of each other. It didn't make sense. All of their energy must have pooled together and pulled my spirit off course into the desert on my way by.

I don't think they called me on purpose. They didn't seem to need my help or anything. As I approached, they remained aloof. I know they saw me, but apparently they had more pressing issues at hand than greeting a stranger. This punctual crowd checked and rechecked invisible watches that were as dead as they were. They alternated between shifting their feet, rolling their eyes, and scouring the horizons for approaching trains. I had no idea if trains still traveled these endless tracks, or from which direction. Still nobody spoke to me, but if they had, I would have told them rush hour ended a long time ago.

Men and women wore business attire, suits, dresses, but no hats. I'd say they might have lived during the 1980s or later. One woman wearing jeans and sneakers was accompanied by a similarly clad boy who looked about ten. He pulled on his mother's arm incessantly. His poor mother repeatedly hushed him as she'd probably been doing for years.

The closer I got to the group, the more intently they checked their watches and scanned the sky. What were they looking for? Rain? Maybe the last time they stood on a train platform it was in a rainy city, but I doubt there were frequent showers out in that desert. I knew they saw me standing next to them, but they worked harder to ignore me.

I caught the kid staring at me so I said hi. He quietly said hi back, before his mother jerked his arm to face him forward. She looked at me while scolding him, so I spoke right into her face before she stared at the empty train tracks again and pretended not to see me.

"Hi. I'm Lilla. I just was passing through and I noticed your group here. Are you all waiting for something?"

"We're going home!" the kid cheerfully volunteered as he looked from his mother to me.

"Peter, that's enough!" His mother's words wiped the smile from his face. He must have known he was in trouble. I didn't care. As long as he was answering, I was asking.

"Oh, that's nice! Where's that?" I addressed him directly.

But Peter obeyed his mother's orders and remained silent. Other spirits began staring at us. Peter's mother warned him with her eyes while she spoke to me, hoping I would go stand by somebody else. "Uh, we were on our way home. Well...we still are. It's hard to explain. His father's been waiting and we're finally leaving. I'm not sure when. Someone's on their way to get us."

Was she as confused as she sounded, or was she afraid to say too much? Her sheepish glance back toward the group assured me it was the latter. My interest was too aroused to stop now, though.

"Oh, really? Who's coming to get you? Where are they taking you?" I asked the mother.

"There was the accident and we were separated. But they're coming back to bring us where we were supposed to go in the first place." Every time she spoke, she looked around for some help from the others but they ignored us. They still watched for that train.

"You mean you died in the accident and you stayed here?" I hoped my wording was okay and they knew they were already dead. "You're leaving this place soon?"

"You better believe it, and we're never coming back. We're not supposed to be here," She answered in the most definite and determined voice yet.

I tempered my growing excitement of what this might mean for me. "How will you get to the next place? Do you know where it is?"

"We're not sure how we'll get there, but everybody's waiting for us, so they'll help us with the right directions. So far, all they've said is to wait here so that's what we're doing."

Here I am, too. Why had their energy sidelined me on my way to the coast? Destiny must have led me here to begin my passage to the afterlife. Screw the ocean! I'm getting outta here!

Victoriously, I threw up my fists despite the unnerved expressions of the other passengers. Then I quietly put my arms down by my sides. My thoughts leapt from my head before I could contain them.

Oops…too much? Too bad!

Now the others noticed me. They stared at me hard, maybe hoping to intimidate me to where I would leave. "So that's what it takes to get your attention!" I joked with the stone-faced group. "Oh, come on! I wasn't that out of line. Hey, I don't belong here either. My husband is somewhere that I'm not, and I can't take it anymore, all right? Something must have brought me to you. I can't explain it but I can feel it. If you guys are getting out of here, I'm coming, too!"

Defiantly, I took my place behind the cold shoulders of the insular group. They nudged each other and whispered to each other. Finally, they elected one unlucky spokesman to weave his way out of the group and set me straight.

"Ma'am?" the young man addressed me. He was a little heavy, but nicely dressed in a buttoned shirt and dress slacks. He touched my arm to get my full attention. When we made contact, I saw and heard his last living moments. Screeching train wheels, broken glass, passengers and belongings flying through the air. The train cars buckled and crashed into smoldering heaps on the desert floor. Ear-curdling cries for help permeated this vision, which was as horrific as it was brief. Unprepared for the sudden flash of mass death, I jerked my arm from his touch and gasped. He appeared puzzled while he waited for me to regain my composure. Maybe he didn't realize how jarring of an image he had just flung into my head.

"I'm sorry I jumped," I apologized, even though I didn't think I was guilty of anything. I said it to be polite. "It's just that when you touched my arm, I saw the whole wreck. It must have been horrible. When did it happen?" I asked the spokesman.

"'93. Most of us were on our way home from work."

"And you've all been here ever since?"

"Yeah, more or less. A few people took off to be with the rest of their families."

"Their families down here?" I motioned toward some unseen towns in the distance. "Or…up there?" I raised my eyes and face skyward.

The man chuckled. "I don't know. Some of each, I guess."

"But you guys are waiting for someone to come and get you, right? Maybe to take you to a doorway or something? Some way to move on?"

"Yeah, that's pretty much it. You, too?"

"Oh God, yes! It's not fair! Ever since I died last fall, I've been trying to get to wherever my husband is. I almost gave up, until that one woman told me you're all leaving soon. However it happens, I want to go with you."

"Well, that's just it," he said.

Great, here comes the letdown.

"We can't take anybody extra. When they come, they're only gonna be looking for us." He pointed at himself and then the rest of the crowd.

"What about the people who left already? Can't I just take one of their spots?" I argued with the man. As my voice rose the others stared harder, but I didn't care.

"Well, no. I don't think it works that way. You weren't originally part of this group. I'd guess you could say these tickets are non-transferable."

I clicked my tongue and heaved an exasperated sigh. "Tough beans. I'm going to wait anyway. Maybe they'll let me through, too. If I can't, then maybe I can at least get a message to my husband."

"Ma'am, Lilly is it? I don't think that'll work. You should move along."

"Lilla. And I'm going to wait right here. I'd never forgive myself if I didn't at least try to get through whenever I have a chance. You can't stop me from trying!"

He sighed. He turned to the others, who scolded him for giving up. "She can't stay here! Are you crazy?" Those were the only things they expressed loudly enough for me to hear. The rest of their thoughts were silent and very mean. I'll spare you the words that seeped from their angry minds.

The spokesman threw his hands up and shrugged his shoulders. "Hey, what else do you want me to do?" he shot back at them.

"Know what? If you want to get rid of her so much, do it yourselves," he muttered as he pushed back through the group to his original place up front. Then he looked at his watch and at the tracks leading to the horizon.

Everybody else turned back to face the tracks as well. Fine with me if they didn't speak to me, but I wasn't going to miss my chance to at least glimpse the other side. I went to a large rock about twenty feet from the group, and sat my tenacious little self down on a big rock to wait. And wait. And wait. Many trains traveled back and forth but none of them stopped. Did any of those live passengers glimpse the pale faces that whisked by their windows?

As many trains passed so did the days, until it had been two weeks since my arrival. The group waited and checked their watches. Nobody spoke to each other and I dared not ask, "How soon is soon?" I had been under the impression their salvation train was supposed to arrive any second. This was getting ridiculous. Maybe they signaled them to hold off until I got bored enough to leave.

The only other person as antsy as me was the kid. Every so often, he broke free of his mother's hand and drifted away from the crowd. I think he wanted to join me on my nice comfy rock, but before he sidled within ten feet of me, his mother reeled him in.

"Peter!" she'd yell, and he'd return to her clutches.

Loneliness and boredom still hadn't grown enough to chase me away. I could stick it out for much longer than they could imagine. Things were about to get a little more interesting, anyway. Through the brush and around the rocks, two new ladies spirited across the desert, arm in arm. "If they had been victims from the train wreck, there goes my seat," I thought.

Upon closer observation, I realized they couldn't have been in that wreck. From their bonnets and laced shoes, to their long dresses and shawls, they were from long ago, pre-Amelia even, from way back in the early 1800s. Nice old-fashioned country ladies. Even though they appeared only to have been in their thirties, I imagined them to possess that comforting grandmotherly essence of lavender and apple pie. As they came closer, I couldn't help overhearing the thoughts they quietly shared between themselves.

"Huh. They're still here," said the taller of the two women.

"Of course. You expected any different?" answered the other.

"But why – oh wait. There's one sitting on that rock. She wasn't there before. She's new, isn't she? That's odd." The two women cut a wide swath around the group over to where the rock and I had been keeping each other company.

"Hi. Are you here to get picked up with them, too?" I asked the newcomers.

"Picked up? For what?" the shorter one asked me.

"Well, I'm not really sure," I shrugged. "I guess to go to the next place, wherever we're supposed to go when we die."

The two women glanced at each other. The taller one asked. "Is that why you're here?"

"Yeah, I didn't come here on purpose. I was on my way to the ocean and found them all waiting to 'move on.' I guess that's what people call it. So I'm waiting too. I really want to find a way to my husband, Sam," I said. Whispering, I added, "They're so rude, though. They told me I couldn't go with them. But if a passageway or something opens up, I'm gonna try to go through anyway."

The two women exchanged glances. They obviously knew more about the situation than I did. The taller one, the more talkative of the two, whispered back, "Oh honey, they're not going anywhere. You think you've waited a long time? They've been here for over thirty years."

"But they said it would happen soon." I shrugged. "I've been here for two weeks, so even if I have to wait three months, that's still not too bad."

"But you see, nobody's coming for them. They don't understand. They're stuck in the day they died. They're trying to get back on the same train that dropped their souls here so many years ago."

"Well then, why are you here?" I asked.

"Oh, we're just checking up on them," the taller woman continued. "We saw the train crash. Well, we heard it. We were in Victorville, about eighty miles from here. When the train crashed, we heard the most dreadful screams coming from this direction. I'll never forget the sound! All those souls ripped from their bodies all at once…like thunder across the desert."

"Awful, just awful! The ones who died that day stayed to watch the rescue and the clean-up. It took weeks. We watched, too. It was a horrible sight.

"After about three days, two more souls who died in the hospital came back, too. Then, that woman with the short jacket…she came along about two years later. They've all been here ever since, just waiting. We tried to tell them this isn't how they'll find their way to their next life but they won't listen. Sometimes we look in on them to see if they're all still here. I think the last time was about ten years ago. Wouldn't you say, Natasha?"

"Mmm hmm," the shorter one replied. "And they're all in the same exact place. Take my advice dear. Don't fritter away your days waiting here with them. You won't find your husband out here. It's not the right place for you or them either. Chloe and I tried telling them but they won't listen to us. Now we just hold our tongues."

"How do you know so much? Do you have any proof?" I asked skeptically. I wasn't about to abandon this spot based on rumors.

Natasha looked up at Chloe, who finished breaking the bad news to me. "I'm sure you can tell, we've been here for a long time. We've met so many others like us. Some, such as you, are forever searching for their heaven. Others just stay here and exist as though nothing happened. Like them." She nodded toward the train passengers. "Time stopped for them on the day they died and there they'll stay, maybe forever. They won't be able to take you through any doorways."

"Great." Disappointment clouded my face. "I've seen the same thing in the cemetery where I'm buried. In my heart, I hoped things might be different here. I guess I should have known better."

Natasha offered me some words she knew I wanted to hear. "Oh, don't worry. Forever is a long time. Maybe you will get the chance to find your husband. Others have, you know…" She stopped short. Without turning her head, she peeked out of the corner of her eye to see Chloe's stare.

I caught their little exchange, which made me want to know more. I wanted as much information as they would share, to help me decide whether I should stay here or not. "What? What's going on?" I asked. I glanced back and forth to see if either of these two could answer my questions better than the train-wreck victims.

After a period of silence, Chloe managed to pick up the conversation, but it sounded like she was making it up as she went along. "Well," she started with a forced chuckle, "we know these souls are here to stay, but we've seen other ones leave all of a sudden. Here one minute, gone the next. We know…well, we can feel… they're no longer on the earth the way you and we are now. It's almost impossible to know how or when you'll find your opportunity to finish your journey. But I'm pretty certain you won't find it here. Go wherever you want. You might stumble onto the right pathway when the time is right."

After Chloe's vague babbling, her and Natasha's stares melted into relaxed smiles. They stood arm in arm. Natasha patted Chloe's hand and said, "Well, we should go. How about Boston next?" she turned to Chloe. "You know how I love those little shops in town."

"That would be wonderful! And then, maybe to Panama?"

"Okay!"

It was impressive they'd seen so many places and traveled with such confidence. I wouldn't have expected that since they looked so old fashioned. Maybe they would be able to tell me when I might be getting close to Sam.

"Excuse me. Natasha and Chloe? Um…Could I come with you? Just for a while. You could tell me what I'm supposed to be looking for. I wouldn't know it if it bit me. I might have missed the right sign four times already. You've met so many souls! You could tell me who seems to be on the right track…or the wrong track." I rolled my eyes toward the train wreck crowd, who checked their watches for the millionth time. Deep down, I knew Natasha and Chloe were right about this being the train to nowhere. I wasn't sure if they wanted any company so I was relieved when they let me tag along.

After Chloe glanced down at Natasha, she gushed, "Oh, yes, do come with us. We'll have fun! We never tire of new towns, and we've developed quite a list of favorite places."

Natasha nodded rapidly. "Wait until you see the bakery we're going to today - my favorite one in Boston. That's where I really wish I had a body so I could try everything." She sighed. "But, we have to settle for tasting the goodies with our eyes now. To Boston?"

"Most certainly," replied Chloe.

"Oh by the way my name's Lilla."

"Nice to meet you, Lilla!"

Chloe reached for my arm. I extended my good one and she touched my elbow. The next thing I knew, the three of us stood in one of the most scrumptious bakeries I'd ever seen. We ogled the dessert case, imagining their delicious tastes and aromas. After we teased ourselves with the delicacies we could never eat, we slipped out the window to a sidewalk in a bustling city neighborhood. Busy people passed through us, oblivious to the invisible newcomers in their midst. Chloe and Natasha beamed at the sight of this little row of quaint, weathered, shops surrounded by modern high-rises.

Heads held high, they meandered down the street, nodding and greeting strangers along the way, regardless that nobody saw them. I could barely keep up as they flitted from shop to shop, chatting incessantly. Kitschy bargain stores and antique shops shared this funky neighborhood. Chloe and Natasha relished the chance to tell my young soul how they used many of these items every day.

Before I realized how quickly time passed, the shops closed for the night. Now the street belonged to us and we were free to play with shelves full of gadgets. In the stillness of the dark shops, our invisible hands turned cranks, rattled spoons, clanged pots, and rearranged furniture. I can't believe nobody came to check for burglars. I found an old hand mixer, so I stuck it into my abdomen and gave it a whirl. Hysterically amusing myself, I told Chloe and Natasha I was making scrambled eggs.

I did a similar thing about thirty years ago when a friend of mine and I were rummaging through a junk store. My friend said I was disgusting but at least she laughed. Natasha and Chloe weren't disgusted, nor were they amused. In fact, they weren't anything. Their faces were completely blank. I might as well have said grapes have eyes. It was just nonsensical to them. Then again, when they were alive, eggs came from chickens, not women. They nodded politely and moved on to the next aisle. They knew I thought I had made a joke. About what, they had no idea.

They were really in tune with each other, reminiscing about their good old days and the people who inhabited them. They obviously had so much fun together. I couldn't help but wish for a companion I had known during my lifetime.

With my luck, Spooky Marcy's friends will find me someday when they die. Hopefully, I'll have moved on by then.

"You are so lucky to have someone like Natasha here with you. Were you sisters or cousins or something, when you were alive?" I asked Chloe as she removed a pot she'd been wearing on her head. She had me and Natasha laughing so hard, my cheeks would have been sore if I were alive. She laughed, too, for a bit. When we all calmed down, Natasha moved next to Chloe, and rested her hand on Chloe's arm.

"We were never related, not like you think," said Chloe. Both of them looked to the floor, raised their sheepish gazes toward each other and then toward me. Natasha slipped her arm around Chloe's waist and rested her head on Chloe's shoulder. Both of them glowed. The connection between their souls positively electrified the air around us.

"Oh! I'm sorry, I didn't realize," I stammered and rolled my eyes at my own naiveté. "I'm pretty thick sometimes. I'm the one who needs a hit on the head with that pot to knock some sense into me! I just didn't see it. I wouldn't have expected…I mean…" My faltering apology deteriorated.

Natasha touched my arm ever so slightly. "It's okay dear, really. You're not the first one to be surprised, even in these modern days. Try to imagine how things were in our lifetimes. It wasn't until death that we could travel through these streets together, as a couple."

"Yes, and we hold our heads ever so high now, as we see the world together," Chloe added. She kissed Natasha on her forehead.

"When I saw your clothes and spoke to you, I guessed you might have lived in the 1800s. Being like that was something I never thought of from way back then. People didn't even talk about it during much of my life. I can't even imagine what it was like for you."

"Lonely. Pretty much just very lonely, for most of my life anyway," Natasha sighed.

Well, since they were being so open, I wanted to ask them many more questions about what their situation was like in those days. Of course, by the latter part of my life, couples like Chloe and Natasha would have been able marry each other and live the lives they had only dreamt about.

Sam and I had acquaintances, both men and women who did marry someone of the same sex. But I imagined such a relationship would have been difficult to carry on a hundred and fifty years ago. I figured I'd keep firing questions at Chloe and Natasha until they told me to shut up and mind my own business. "Did anybody else know? Did you get to live together?"

"Oh, heavens no! We lived separately for most of our lives," Chloe answered and then surprised me yet again when she said, "I was married and had children, you know."

This was weird to me, but then I thought about how strongly tradition dictates so much of what we do. That probably happened to many people, trying to live the same life everyone else had lived for generations. People got married and had kids because that's just what people did, just like their parents, sisters, cousins, etc.

"Did you know you loved each other even when you were married to your husband? What were your lives like since you couldn't be together? If I'm being too nosy tell me to shut up any time."

"Oh, not at all, dear! If you want, we can show you all there is to know from our lives," Natasha kindly offered.

She held out her hand, which I embraced with my good hand. Warily I lifted my gnarled hand, ready to withdraw it if Natasha showed any reservations about touching it. Instead, Chloe gently took hold of it and then held Natasha's other hand in hers. This was different. I thought I would learn about Natasha's life first, and then see Chloe's and put the pieces together afterward. They explained that to know one was to know the other. This is how in the quiet darkness of a little shop, the three of us held hands and watched each other's lives.

Chloe, born in 1840, had just celebrated her twentieth birthday when 15-year old Natasha arrived in town to live with her aunt and uncle. They were neighbors and quickly became friends. Only they felt something more, something deeper than friendship. They couldn't understand these feelings. They could neither deny them nor act on them. Physical contact was limited to sisterly gestures like a pat on the hand or the brushing of each other's hair.

Natasha was especially wary of any overt affection. She wouldn't let me see any farther into her past, but I later learned the reason her parents sent her to live with relatives three states away had something to do with an indiscretion between her and a schoolgirl chum.

Just when Chloe's parents feared their twenty-one-year-old daughter would never marry, Frank Piffard, a local farmer, asked for her hand and she agreed. After all, marriage and children were the proper course for every young woman's life, weren't they? Any woman would have been honored to marry such a good man. While Chloe could never feel the same love for Frank as she did for Natasha, she did love his kindness. He treated her wonderfully and over the years, she bore him five children, three of whom survived into adulthood.

As for Natasha, she never married. She inherited her aunt and uncle's boarding house when they died, and there she cooked and cleaned for strangers passing through town. She pined for Chloe and the days they spent together before Chloe's marriage. Still, they were able to steal away occasionally for a picnic while the children attended school. They talked about their days, and how much more wonderful each day would be if they could be together.

Hidden in the privacy of the tall field grass they shared small delicate kisses with each other. Then the grass swayed in the wind and blocked my view of them lying in each other's arms. I could hear soft moans among the rustle of their skirts amid the prairie grasses. I'm sure that was intentional, similar to how Amelia cloaked some of her thoughts from me. Chloe and Natasha didn't want to show me everything, for which I was grateful. Before they departed their cuddling spot, they would share one tiny kiss that would have to hold them over for the next week or two.

Winters were especially long and trying, for they were limited to a gentle squeeze of the hand during afternoon tea. Frank was so generous about the time Chloe spent with her lonely spinster friend that Chloe and Natasha's secret love endured throughout Chloe's thirty-six year marriage. Chloe's children and their families lived in distant towns by the time Frank died in 1897.

She did miss him so. She grieved the loss of her husband and friend. It pained her to sell the family farm with all of its memories, but she could no longer manage the upkeep alone. She moved into Natasha's boarding house as a long-term resident. Natasha "retired" and closed the boarding house to future guests, ensuring privacy for herself and Chloe.

The next few years were the happiest times of their lives for Chloe and Natasha. Living under the same roof at last, they maintained the outward appearance of two elderly women sharing living expenses and housework. However, within the privacy of their first home together, they finally experienced the relationship they thought they could never share.

Initially, it was hard for me to understand how Chloe could have this kind of love after having had a husband, but the look on Chloe's face when she rolled over to give Natasha her first good morning kiss after thirty-six years of loving her from a distance, was so pure and sincere, I couldn't help but feel happy for them. And every day after that got better and better, until Natasha died in 1905.

Chloe maintained the most incredible composure at her soul mate's funeral, donning the mask of close friend for one last time. Two years later, Chloe passed away. When her body released her spirit on that bitter winter day, a soothing wave of warm light washed over her soul. Frank and the two children who died at birth called her to join them in the beautiful comfort of eternity.

"Mother!"

"My Dearest!" Frank called. "It's so wonderful you can be with us, now!"

Chloe reached toward the light. She could almost and feel the touch of their hands. Her babies! So close again at last! She felt happy, and healthy, and free. But a sweet, melodious voice beckoned her from the earthly world of winter storms and sweltering summers.

Natasha, whose ghostly voice went unheard for three years, called to Chloe from the living room of their home, next to the sofa where Chloe's lifeless body lay. "Chloe, my sweet! Come here, stay with me. I've been waiting for you, right here the whole time!"

Chloe stopped and lowered her hands mere seconds before entering eternal paradise. She turned and cupped her hands to her mouth at the sight of Natasha's outstretched arms. "Oh, Lovely, I've missed you so!" she cried as she rushed into Natasha's embrace. She tugged on Natasha's arm, rushing both of them toward the warm glow on the other side of the room. "Come on! Let's go together!"

Natasha stopped and pulled back. "I can't. I need to stay here…with you. I can't go further. Nobody from my family is calling me from there now. I'm afraid they won't have a place for me, and I won't be any happier with them up there than I was when they were all living down here. No, I cannot go. You're the only person I've ever loved this much. I want us to be together. Here. Will you stay with me? Please, oh please, Chloe, I love you so much!"

Chloe squeezed Natasha's hand and hesitated in the middle of their living room. This was a very tall request, even for a lifetime companion. Natasha's pleading face in the living room and the voices of Chloe's family calling from that brilliant place vied for Chloe's soul. As Chloe paused for several intense moments to decide her eternal fate, Natasha continued begging for her continued companionship.

"Please, Chloe! We don't have to hide in this house anymore! Sweetheart, think about it – we can go anywhere we want. Together, finally together! You were a good wife and mother…Your family had you for so many years while I waited alone. You and I were together for such a short time. Even then we had to live in secret. Please, stay with me. See the world with me. The days, the nights, the cities and mountains…They're all waiting for us! All our lives we had to live a lie or live alone but now we're free!"

Natasha's powerful words reeled Chloe straight back into her arms. They kissed each other's faces all over. Still embracing each other, Chloe and Natasha looked over their shoulders at the glowing portal to the afterlife. Then they floated in the opposite direction, through the living room wall and out to a brand new life on earth. As that chapter of their story ended, the walls of Chloe's old living room faded into the walls of the little shop where we now stood.

Tracy Fontaine

<u>Chapter Nineteen: Chloe's Other Secret</u>

I released Chloe's and Natasha's hands. "Phew!" I sighed. My mind was exhausted after that emotional two-for-one special.

Chloe lifted Natasha's hand to her lips, kissed it, and held it gently against her neck. They both looked shyly at me for my reaction to their story. I'm sure they sensed that at the beginning, the whole thing was a little unusual for me to process. However, by the end of their story, I was okay with it. I was all too familiar with the desire to spend eternity with that special someone so dear to one's heart. How could I not be happy for them?

"Wow, you waited so long! I can't imagine how hard it must have been not to be with each other. What would people back then have thought of your relationship? They probably wouldn't have believed such a thing existed. Was there even a name for it?"

Natasha chortled. "Most folks would have called us Lesbos but the name my mother used for it was 'the devil's work.' They saw me kissing a girl from school. It was the only time we kissed, but my parents were so ashamed they sent me to live with my aunt and uncle before the town busy bodies started wagging their tongues. Of course they never told my aunt and uncle why then sent me here. They told them it was because they thought it would be good for me to learn how to work at a business like the rooming house."

"Chloe, your husband, he never knew, right? He couldn't have known."

"Goodness no! He was such a good man. I truly loved him. He provided everything for me and the children. Although sometimes I felt guilty because I loved him more as my provider and my children's protector than as a husband."

"Forgive me for asking, but do you ever regret not joining him and your children? I mean, you were so close. The light in your living room – it was absolutely dazzling. That's what I thought was supposed to happen for me, that Sam would call me to that same place. I'm trying to figure out why it hasn't happened for me yet. Why does it work for other people?"

Chloe and Natasha's faces clouded over. I guess I was too hasty in exposing my personal agenda. Apparently, I veered too quickly from the point of Chloe and Natasha's forbidden-love-found-love story. I realized I should have reveled in their happiness a little longer. They conferred on what to tell me next.

Chloe spoke slowly and deliberately. "Well…actually I have been to see my family. I've shared their company on several occasions."

"How!?" I gasped. "How did you do that?" I cut her words short and grabbed her arm. She was the closest link yet to my gateway to Sam. I was going to grill her for everything she was worth. Chloe and Natasha stared silently back at me, insulted at my disregard for the beauty of their love story. I sensed I had been too aggressive.

When Chloe recovered her voice, it was terse and a little shaky, as she tried to maintain her coolness. "I guess I should have known better than to tell you about seeing my family. I only told you because I didn't want you to think I was cold enough to turn my back on them while they called me from heaven.

"My husband Frank always was and still is a special soul. In death, he learned the sacrifice I made to share his life and raise our children. His love for me has grown so much. There's room in his heart for my time here on earth with Natasha. He and the children welcome my visits. They treat me like a queen, but they also accept my needs here on earth. Needs that were denied us our whole lives. For me, having both worlds is my heaven. We shared our story with you, hoping you would understand and be happy for us, too."

"Hey! I understand better than you think," I replied defensively. "Don't you see? I'm suffering like you were, only in reverse. I was lucky to spend my years on earth with the love of my life, but we've been apart for over fifteen years. I'm trying to find him so we can have what you have now. Actually, what you've had for over a hundred years now. Eternity is a hell of a long time. What if I never find him?"

"It's not as simple as you think." Chloe chided. "I can't even tell you how to start looking because the times I leave earth are just by chance. At certain times, the line between here and there lifts and my family escorts me into their world. But I always return to Natasha and our world here."

The pitch of Chloe's voice rose. Trying to maintain her composure, she continued, her voice quavering, "This is where I'm happiest. I would hope you could be happy for us, too."

"Won't you at least give me an idea where to start?" I pleaded.

Chloe and Natasha stood arm-in-arm, stone–faced, exasperated by my tenacity. Party time in the gadget department was over. We left the small store in silence as dawn broke over the surrounding buildings. My brief kinship with these two adventurous spirits evaporated as quickly as the morning dew on the city streets. Granted, they weren't as close to me as Amelia and Jodi, but even as far as our new friendship went, things were different between us after that.

They weren't as friendly as before. They tolerated me in hopes that I would leave them alone. I became the little sister they couldn't shake, always seven paces behind them. I lingered far enough where they could converse in secret, but close enough to spy on their every move. I watched for any signs of Chloe's family and the doorway full of light from the other side.

I trailed them as if they were on invisible leashes. We meandered around Boston and then north into some quaint towns in Massachusetts. Similar to back home, the number of spirits still inhabiting their lifetime destinations never ceased to amaze me. Dead shopkeepers greeted oblivious living customers as they entered the stores. A concession vendor still poised in front of a ballpark shouted outdated prices for hot dogs. A nanny sat in the park. The children she once guarded had long since grown and died as well. For them, and so many others we passed, life as they knew it still existed, just like the train wreck victims waiting in the desert.

Then there was the fireman who stood by a riverside park in an old mill district. Arms outstretched and eyes searching upward, his intense concentration couldn't be broken, despite the many questions we asked him about why he stood there and what happened. Chloe, Natasha, and I gathered around him. We raised our eyes to share his vision but we saw nothing. I'm sure we looked pretty silly, the four of us staring into the air, only one of us knowing why. Finally, Natasha looked down and found a plaque next to one of the benches. Back in 1893, a fire raced through the mills, killing fourteen factory workers and two firemen.

The building was razed and this park was dedicated to those victims of the fire. In the mind of that fireman, the fire raged on to this day. What did he see? Smoke pluming out of broken factory windows? Streams of water pouring from the horse drawn carts? Was he waiting for victims to leap into the safety of his arms?

I suppose I could have laid my hand on his coat to view the details of that last day of his life, but the plaque told me enough. It didn't seem right to bother him. Besides, I didn't want to watch doomed victims leaping from smoky windows to their deaths. Chloe and Natasha must have felt the same, for none of us questioned him again after we read the plaque.

We lingered for a while, wondering about the tragedy of that day, and if that fireman rescued anybody before losing his own life. Eventually we ran out of scenarios and moved on in search of something less somber. I didn't know where we were, somewhere not far from Boston, I think. I wasn't involved in the decision-making as far as destinations went. I pretty much just clung to Chloe's and Natasha's skirt tails. They whispered between themselves and checked over their shoulders to see if I had trailed them. I knew I was no longer wanted but my chance to find Sam might happen at any moment. I hoped Chloe would take pity on me and help me seize my opportunity.

After one particularly lengthy whispering session between Chloe and Natasha, they led the way to a very exclusive neighborhood of opulent mansions like none I'd ever seen. This was off limits to mere mortals, but we simply glided in. The area radiated old money from the gilded age. The houses were something, all right…but the gardens. Oh, the gardens! All bloomed with show-stopping reds and golds of early fall. Immersing myself in the nooks of one of the lushest gardens I'd ever seen was sheer delight, the greatest therapy for my frustrated soul.

Chloe and Natasha strolled through a water garden. Thoroughly smitten with each other, they gazed into each other's eyes and shared gentle kisses. It was sweet, and I held back to give them time alone. I wondered if Chloe shared moments like this with her husband when she visited him in heaven?

God knows I'd been hounding Chloe and Natasha for weeks now, so I guess I owed them a little privacy. I backed away from the clearing and entered a small garden near the terrace of the huge home that overlooked this estate. These mammoth gardens made the gardens at my old house look like bonsai plants.

After I had seen all of the best parts of the gardens, I went to find Chloe and Natasha. I had granted them a healthy dose of privacy but it was time to check in so I didn't lose track of them.

Not to worry, Natasha was right where I'd left them. I didn't see Chloe, but even spirits had to get some air after such intimacy. Natasha looked at me silently as I entered the clearing. I stood opposite her, on the other side of a little stream that fed the water lily pond. She seemed pensive, perhaps a little melancholy. We kept each other company without exchanging any words. The gurgling of the brook prevented our silence from becoming awkward.

As much as I enjoyed the respite from the outside world, I reached a point where I started to wonder where Chloe was. She had been gone longer than it had taken me to make my way through the rest of the gardens in the entire estate. Natasha began to fidget, which prompted me to break the silence.

"Natasha, where is Chloe? I thought she might be somewhere around here, but I haven't seen her. Have you?"

The look on Natasha's face and her halting effort to answer me, confirmed she'd been dreading that very question. "She…uh, She'll be back soon."

"That's not what I asked," I said flatly, as I crossed over to her side of the stream. "I want to know where she is. Now."

"I don't think she said exactly where she was going." Natasha's voice quavered as she backed away from me.

"But you know, don't you?" I inquired threateningly. To make sure she didn't disappear on me, I reached out and took hold of her arm up near her shoulder so she couldn't wriggle away. When the energy from my hand electrified her soul to mine, she became my captive. She stared at her arm and then back at me, unable to believe I possessed such power. Actually, I was surprised at my own strength but I didn't want her to know that. So I continued playing tough.

"Is Chloe with her family, on one of her visits?" I demanded. I clutched her arm tightly.

Natasha gasped and tried to twist free of my grip. "Please, she told me not to say anything."

"So she is there then? You know she is. Tell me how she does it."

"I don't know! Please, you're hurting me!" Natasha begged for mercy, but I wasn't ready to relent until she revealed Chloe's secret.

I gripped her arm so tightly my head throbbed with my own angry energy. "C'mon! I know you know! Tell me everything you see and hear when Chloe goes to see her family. You know how much it means to me!" I screamed into Natasha's face and twisted her arm to let her know I wasn't fooling around. After following them for weeks, I was insane; I had lost control of myself.

I witnessed the terror in Natasha's face as she begged for mercy. I hadn't seen a look like that before, yet it seemed familiar. Then the realization of what I was doing wrenched my gut. I hadn't actually seen that look before. I had worn it myself, when Massimo Sabati attacked me. Now, here I was, imprisoning Natasha in the same ironclad grip with which Massimo tried to destroy me. I was inflicting that same evil onto someone else! Sam would not want his Lilla to act so cruelly, even if it meant we would never see each other again. I must let go.

Just as I was about to release Natasha, a ball of fire barreled between us, breaking our connection. Natasha and I flew to the ground in opposite directions. It was Chloe. After she landed near us, she reeled around and grabbed my good arm. She yanked it so hard I faltered and almost lost my footing.

"You want to see Sam!? You really want to see him? Let's go! Right now!" With that, Chloe yanked me off the ground and into another dimension. She pulled me faster than I had ever flown on my own.

Oh my God! I'm going to see Sam! I can't believe this is finally happening! I knew someone would help me if I waited long enough!

Chloe glanced back at me with eyes full of rage. I held onto her hand for dear life in case she was planning to throw me somewhere just to get rid of me, but she held onto my hand as tightly as I had gripped Natasha. Chloe wasn't going to cut me loose even if I asked her to.

In mere seconds, I saw it. The light! I saw it and I felt it! Peace washed over me. I wanted to cry for joy. The light grew brighter and warmer as we got closer. After another second, I had to shield my eyes from its brilliance. It was getting too warm. Actually, it was downright hot. I didn't know how it could be, but I was getting uncomfortable with this whole thing.

Suddenly Chloe yanked on my arm and tossed me even closer to the light. She let go and I tumbled out of control into the blinding heat.

Oh, God! This must be what Amelia warned me about! I asked too many questions and Chloe had dragged me to hell!

I came to rest in the middle of nowhere. There was no earth around me, no clouds…just bright light. I couldn't hear anything or see anything beyond my own body. I pantomimed my hands in front of me to look for a portal of some sort like I did when I first died. This must be the last hurdle to make it to the other side. Chloe was gone but I felt other presences around me. They weren't well defined. I couldn't even tell if they were men or women… or human.

"Sam! Sam! Can you hear me? Help me! I can't make it by myself!" I waited for what seemed like an eternity. For all I knew it could have been.

"Lilla. Oh, my Lilla. I can't believe you're here!

"Sam!" I screeched. "Sam! Grab me! Pull me through! The light is burning me! I can't see anything!" I squinched my eyes completely shut. Moving forward with my arms, I grasped the air in front of me.

"No Lilla, I can't!" Sam's voice cried back to me.

"What? Why not? I'm so close. I'm here. I've made it this far. I'm in the light but I can't see you. Can you see me? Just reach out and grab my hand!" The heat was intense. I didn't know how much longer I could wait until Sam helped me cross over.

"Oh, baby, you don't know how much I want to," Sam's voice was everywhere and nowhere. "I've been waiting for you, too. But it's not your time. You're not supposed to be here."

"What do you mean? I've been dead for almost a year! It's past time for me to be here. I couldn't find my way on my own. Chloe helped me get this far. I need you to help me come through the rest of the way. Please, Sam! I love you so much. I can't stay in this heat. I need to come over to where you are."

"Lilla, I love you more than anything and I want us to be together as much as you do, but it's not up to me. There are other reasons you can't stay here. I can't explain. But, I know you can't stay where you are right now. Chloe shouldn't have brought you there. It's not safe."

"It's not her fault. I wouldn't rest until she showed me the way. I don't understand why I can't come to you. I've been trying to find you for a year!"

"I know. I saw you, baby. I was everywhere you went. I wished I could have let you know. But it's not me you should be looking for. It's you."

"Me?" I asked Sam.

"Yes. There are still things you need to understand before you can make it through."

I was burning up in that heat. I knew I had to leave soon. I was going to be forced back to the regular world where I had been wandering for the past year.

"Sam, I can feel myself burning up. Whatever happens, I need to know you're okay. Are you okay, honey?"

"Oh, sweetie! It's more perfect that you ever imagined. There are no worries. It's perfect peace. We will be here together someday, I promise. I'm sorry but you must go back. I'm so sorry. You won't be able to survive much longer if you stay there. Li, I love you so much."

"Oh, Sam! I love you, too! Wait for me..." My voice became a whisper. I felt Sam's presence fading from me.

I knew I had to leave but since I hadn't brought myself to that spot I didn't know how to get back to the other world. Thankfully, someone pulled me in the right direction. It was Chloe again.

"Had enough?" she asked as she pulled me back through space. She was as angry as ever but at least she brought me back to my familiar world.

We landed in the same spot from where she grabbed me. There stood Natasha, rubbing her arm I had gripped so violently only a few minutes ago.

"Oh my God!" I cried. From what I could see, it didn't look like I left any visible scars on Jodi's arm like the ones Jodi and I bore. But I knew what I had just done went beyond physical trauma. Neither of us would ever forget it. I raised my hands to my mouth in shock. I never would have believed I could act so violently toward anybody in my desperation.

"Oh my God!" I said again. "Natasha! What have I done? I'm so sorry!" I extended my hand to apologize, but she retreated to the other side of the pond. Who could blame her? I remained where I was, granting her a safe distance from me.

"I don't know what's wrong with me," I said. My eyes darted between Chloe and Natasha. "I can't believe I went so crazy. You know I've just been waiting for my chance to see into the next world, even for just a second." Even then, I somehow managed to twist my apology into an excuse, none of it believable any more, even to me.

Natasha found her voice, and lots of it. Her angry words tumbled across the pond. "Of course we know why you followed us, but Chloe doesn't know how to help you. She would if she could, but things are different for everyone. She only knows how to reach her family. That's it! And that's why she had to go without telling you."

Chloe rushed over to Natasha's side. She wrapped her arms around her and hugged her tightly. "Okay. It's okay," she whispered to the top of Natasha's head. Then she looked over at me. "Now do you see why I didn't take you with me in the first place? I wasn't trying to keep you from finding your husband. It's just not your time."

I sighed. "I believe you," I said to Chloe. "But what does it mean that it's not my time? Sam said the same thing. How can everybody know this except for me?"

"I can't tell you anything specific. Your husband couldn't tell you, either. It's something we can only see from being on the other side and looking back. That's why Natasha couldn't help you down here."

Natasha nodded in agreement with Chloe. "She's right. I don't understand why it's not time for you to move on. I've never been on the other side so I can't see the things that Chloe can."

"Lilla, look at me," Chloe commanded. Our eyes locked as she continued. "After all this time, you do realize it's possible you may never move on. I swear to God, I hope you do someday, but you've got to face the possibility the rest of your future may be right here on earth."

"I know." My lips quivered as I whispered my response. When my voice returned in full, I turned to Natasha and continued. "I'm so sorry for acting the way I did, Natasha. For what I did to you, and for not believing you and Chloe. I hope you can forgive me for how I acted. I am so ashamed and sorry." My voice trembled with emotion. "I'll leave you both alone, now." I looked at Chloe. "Thank you for bringing me as close to Sam as you could and letting me hear his voice. It means the world to me to know he sees me down here. I'll keep hoping for myself that I'm given the same chance as you to cross over and be with my husband someday. You're so lucky. Goodbye. I hope you have a many good years together."

Natasha nodded and smiled through tightly pursed lips as I turned to go. She respectfully shared Chloe with her family in death, just as she had in life. Possessing neither the desire nor the ability to find her own family, she shouldn't be forced to help me find mine.

Chloe nodded too, but her smile was gentler. Yes, she did have her Natasha here on earth with her but she understood my longing to join my husband.

****

These past few months, I had gone so far from my home in Rochester. I came close to finding my eternal home with Sam, but not close enough. It was wonderful to hear his voice again but it was all too brief. It pained me to not be able to see him. I had searched for him all this time only to discover I was searching for the wrong thing. What unfinished business could I possibly have down here?

I had been obsessed with finding Sam for my own happiness. It crushed me I wasn't able to join him, but I was so thankful he was safe and happy. With the likelihood I might be stuck here for good, I had to admit that, even though I'm not where I'd like to be, I am safe and surrounded by caring souls.

I returned to my own niche in Mount Hope, and headed straight to Sam's grave. Someone, Marion and Helen perhaps, left flowers between our graves, a bittersweet welcome back to the old neighborhood. I sat quietly for several hours, pondering my life, and if I was destined to remain on earth in death as well.

After my death, I hadn't spoken to Sam at length because my world was confined within the cemetery walls. I used to imagine he saw the little things that happened to me so close to his own grave. Now I know he watched me the whole time, no matter where I went. He saw me calling his name from here all the way down to Watkins University.

"Oh, honey," I said to Sam. This time I smiled because I knew he heard me. "I was so close! I wish I could have at least felt your touch. I know you can see me. Send me any kind of help you can so I can stay with you next time. If you keep trying from your end, I'll keep trying from mine."

That's how I struck a deal with the memory of my dead husband, hoping he would hear my pleas. Maybe he could send me some sort of sign about what business I needed to finish so I could join him for good. If it's not my time now, when will it be? Months from now? Years from now? I might be stuck here on earth for decades that stretch into centuries. I'd have to prepare myself to deal with that possibility. I plucked a flower from the arrangement that lay on our graves and kissed it. Then I laid it on top of Sam's grave. "I love you, sweetheart," I said as I rubbed my hand across the grass. Peace washed over me because this time, I knew he heard me.

Tracy Fontaine

About the Author

A native of Claremont, New Hampshire, Tracy Fontaine graduated from SUNY Cobleskill and also Rochester Institute of Technology, where she studied technical writing and health care sciences. She is a laboratory technician at the University of Rochester Medical Center in Rochester, New York. She lives in Rochester with her husband. This is her first book.

Tracy Fontaine

OUR VISION

Our goal is to help you get your story into print. It really is that simple.

As authors ourselves, we understand the frustration of repeated rejections from the big publishing companies and the elitist agents. It becomes a Catch-22 when you have to be a big name in order to get published and become a big name. We're here to eliminate that step and the potential heartbreak that accompanies it and put the power back in your hands.

We are not a "vanity publisher" who charges you as much as $8,000 to receive a handful of substandard paperbacks, just so you can hand them out to the relatives at Christmas and never sell another copy. We get you published and marketed both in paperback and e-book format on Amazon.com and other major online retailers. We also don't charge to get you published, we only charge a small fee for preparing your book.

You earn up to a 60% royalty rate with us, instead of the typical 10% that the traditional publishing houses pay. Why should you do all the work and allow them to keep 90% of your profit? And the best part is, you retain 100% of the rights to your work!

THE FUTURE IS NOW!

Gone are the days when an author would sit in front of an old manual typewriter, rubbing holes in the paper or filling their office garbage cans with unsalvageable scrap. The publishing industry is evolving. The old publishing houses are becoming dinosaurs. E-books are everywhere. They are cheaper than old-fashioned books, use less paper and ink, faster to produce, take up less space and can be read on any computer, e-reader or Smartphone.

Success comes to those who make opportunities happen, not those who wait for opportunities to happen. You can be successful too, you just have to try...

A recent poll suggested that nearly 85% of parents would encourage their child to read a book on an e-reader. More than 1 in 5 of us owns an e-reading device and the number is climbing rapidly. For every 100 hardcover books that Amazon sells, it sells 143 e-books. They also never go out of print!

Hundreds of thousands of independent authors, just like you, are selling their profitable work as you read this. E-book sales have grown over 200% in the past year and account for more than $1 billion in annual sales.

Chances are, you don't even know the difference between a PDF, mobi, ePub, doc, azw, or the fifteen other competing formats struggling to coexist on the sixteen types of e-reader devices such as the Kindle or the Nook. Even if you are able to keep up with all the devices and their formats, do you want to spend the money for expensive software to convert your files, or the many hours it will take to figure out how it works? Will you be able to create an interactive table of contents?

Our editors are professionals with experience in computer science, graphic design and publishing. We can do the work or you, creating a top-notch book that you will be proud of. Of course, you still have to write it, but that's the fun part...

BE A PART OF OUR COMMUNITY

Reach your intended audience in the worldwide marketplace by distributing your work on Amazon, Barnes and Noble and other major online booksellers. Earn royalties, get feedback, Join the discussions in the forum and meet other people in our community who share the same interests you do.

We will publish your fiction or non-fiction books about just about anything, including poetry, education, gardening, health, history, humor, law, medicine, pets, philosophy, political science, psychology, music, science, self-help travel, science-fiction, fantasy, mystery, thriller, children and young adult, etc....

http://www.starrynightpublishing.com

Made in the USA
Columbia, SC
08 August 2018